TO TEMPT A ROGUE

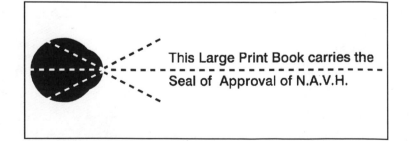

This Large Print Book carries the
Seal of Approval of N.A.V.H.

TO TEMPT A ROGUE

CONNIE MASON

WHEELER PUBLISHING
An imprint of Thomson Gale, a part of The Thomson Corporation

Detroit • New York • San Francisco • New Haven, Conn. • Waterville, Maine • London

LIBRARY OF CONGRESS CATALOGING-IN-PUBLICATION DATA

Mason, Connie.
    To tempt a rogue / by Connie Mason.
      p. cm. — (Wheeler Publishing large print romance)
    ISBN-13: 978-1-59722-519-9 (alk. paper)
    ISBN-10: 1-59722-519-3 (alk. paper)
    1. Arizona — Fiction. 2. Large type books. I. Title.
PS3563.A78786T63 2007
813'.54—dc22   2007002365

Published in 2007 by arrangement with Leisure Books,
a division of Dorchester Publishing Co., Inc.

Printed in the United States of America on permanent paper
10 9 8 7 6 5 4 3 2 1

To Lee, Bev, Angie, Pat, Mary and Teri,
my cardplaying buddies
in Buchanan, MI.

PROLOGUE

Tucson, Arizona
1884

The man in the bed was dying. Ryan Delaney knew it wouldn't be long before he breathed his last.

"You're my last hope, Ryan," Bert Lowry rasped. "I have no sons, no male relatives to turn to. That's why I wrote to your father, my best friend, asking for help. I'm sorry I didn't know your father was dead. We didn't write regularly. But I sincerely thank you for coming, Ryan. If you can find my missing daughter for me, you'll make a dying man happy."

Bert's head fell back on the pillow, his frail body all but drained of energy. Ryan suddenly realized he truly *did* want to help Bert find his daughter. What had started out as a lark, an adventure different from the mundane existence of ranch life, had quickly changed into a mission of mercy.

"I'll do my best," Ryan promised, "but I'll have to know more than I do now. Are you up to telling me about your daughter and where she might be found?"

Suddenly the door to the bedroom was flung open, and a stunning, dark-haired beauty entered. "Papa Bert! Mrs. Dewey told me you had a visitor. Are you sure you're up to entertaining company?"

Her sweeping gaze traveled the length of Ryan and back, then she gave him a brilliant smile, obviously liking what she saw. "I'm Teresa Cowling, Bert's stepdaughter. I don't think we've met."

"This is Ryan Delaney, Teresa. He's here at my behest," Bert explained. "You know how long I've been trying to find my daughter. Well, Ryan is going to help me. He's the son of my oldest friend."

Teresa sent Bert a disgruntled look. "You're wasting Mr. Delaney's time, Papa Bert. Have you mentioned all the money you've spent trying to find a girl who's probably dead by now? I'm all the daughter you need, even though I don't carry your blood."

"Now, Teresa," Bert soothed, "we've been through all this before. As long as hope exists, I won't give up on finding Kathryn."

Rogue Ryan's appreciative gaze settled on

8

Teresa. Because of his thorough knowledge of the fairer sex, he immediately took note of her sensual nature. The signals she was sending him were more than just casual interest. He was well aware of her exotic beauty, of her curvaceous body, and of the invitation in her blue eyes. He knew she was assessing his interest in her just as he was evaluating hers in him. He didn't think he was reading her wrong and wondered what it would take to get her into bed. He decided this adventure was going to prove more enjoyable than he had anticipated.

Reining in his wayward thoughts, Ryan belatedly realized that Bert was speaking to him again, and he pulled his attention away from the tantalizing cleavage visible above the square neckline of Teresa's dress.

"Don't mind Teresa, Ryan," Bert said. "She's a mite jealous. She's had my sole attention all these years and hasn't yet accepted the fact that I have a blood daughter. I couldn't believe it myself when I learned about Kathryn six years ago."

Ryan's attention sharpened. "You first learned of Kathryn six years ago?"

"That's when I received a letter from Rena Johnson, a woman from my past. She told me we had a daughter together." He looked off into space, his stark features softening. "I fell in love with Rena almost twenty years ago. We had a brief but passionate affair. I would have married her if it hadn't been necessary to marry a widow with money. My taxes were in arrears and I was on the verge of losing my ranch."

"Papa Bert!" Teresa cried, aghast. "Are you saying you married my mother for her money?"

"That's the gist of it, Teresa, though I grew quite fond of Leona after we married. And when you arrived here as a grown woman I treated you like my own."

"Please continue," Ryan said, noting Bert's pallor. He couldn't promise he'd actually find Bert's missing daughter, but there was something about the thwarted love story that intrigued him.

"Rena's letter stated that she was dying, and that she wanted me to raise our daughter after she was gone. She'd married a man named Deke Johnson, who she described as a drunk and a womanizer, and she didn't want him raising Kathryn after she was gone.

"At first I thought it was a hoax and did nothing about it. But the longer I thought about it, the more I began to believe I really did have a daughter by Rena. Leona's lingering illness and death during this time delayed my investigation. A whole year passed from the time I received Rena's letter to the day I hired a private investigator. The delay cost me dearly."

"Did Rena tell you where to find Kathryn?"

"Rena and Kathryn were living in Tombstone with Deke Johnson when she posted the letter. Both Rena and Deke were dead and buried by the time the detective I hired arrived in Tombstone. He learned that Rena did indeed have a daughter named Kathryn. But the girl disappeared after Deke's death. I hired Pinkertons to track her down, but they found no trace of the girl. They did locate the house Rena and Kathryn shared with Johnson, though. It's situated at the south edge of Tombstone, and to my knowledge still stands empty. They also learned one other pertinent fact. Johnson had a son named Lex who left town years earlier and is reportedly riding with the Barton gang. Perhaps locating Lex would be a good place to start."

"How did Deke Johnson die?" Ryan asked.

"A month or so after Rena's death, he was caught cheating in a poker game and was shot to death."

Ryan's brilliant green eyes narrowed thoughtfully. "That's not much to go on."

"It's . . . all . . . I have," Bert said, his voice noticeably weaker now.

"Papa Bert needs to rest," Teresa said as she grasped Ryan's arm and guided him toward the door. "You can talk to him later."

Ryan left without protest, silently agreeing with Teresa. He closed the door quietly behind him and accompanied her down the stairs to the comfortable parlor. He plopped into an overstuffed sofa and stretched out his long legs.

"You must be tired," Teresa said, sitting down beside him.

She leaned close, and he caught a whiff of violets. He always was partial to violets. "A little. It's a long way from Dry Gulch, Montana."

"Tucson is a long way from anywhere," Teresa returned shortly. "Sometimes I wish . . ." Her sentence ended abruptly, and she smiled beguilingly at Ryan. "Are you married, Ryan?"

"Married? Me? Ha! That day will never come," he said with conviction. "My brothers might have succumbed, but marriage is not for me. There are too many women out there for me to settle on just one."

"I'll bet you've kissed a lot of girls," Teresa said coyly.

A roguish smile lit up Ryan's green eyes.

"That's one bet you'd win, Miss Cowling."

"Call me Teresa and I'll call you Ryan. I'll bet you never met the right woman, that's why you're against marriage."

"The right woman doesn't exist," Ryan quipped.

He stared at her lips. Full and lush and red, they were parted slightly, as if in invitation. He smiled inwardly. All his instincts told him that Teresa was ripe for a mild flirtation. If she was so eager, who was he to resist? He didn't intend to leave until he'd learned everything Bert knew about his daughter Kathryn, and in the meantime, a little dalliance with Teresa would keep boredom at bay. By the time he'd leave, Teresa would know exactly how Rogue Ryan had earned his name.

CHAPTER 1

Tombstone, Arizona
1884

"Do you have to leave, Ryan?" Terri pouted as she stretched languidly on top of him. "The next one is for free if you'll stay a little longer."

Rogue Ryan gave her a cocky grin. "That's mighty tempting, darlin', but I've already dallied longer than I should have. I came here for information, not to get laid," he quipped.

"No harm in getting both," Terri said saucily, brushing her ample breasts against his naked chest. "Besides, handsome, green-eyed men like you don't come my way often. Angie always takes the young ones for herself. If she hadn't been occupied when you arrived she would have grabbed you for sure."

"I never could resist a beautiful woman," Ryan said as he parted her legs and thrust

15

upward into her heat.

Terri squealed in delight and gave herself up to Ryan's expert lovemaking. He was the only man who didn't treat her like a whore just because she was one.

Ryan finished dressing and let himself out of Terri's garishly decorated room, assimilating the information he'd learned since arriving in Tombstone yesterday.

Terri had told him that Lex Johnson wasn't unknown in Tombstone, although she knew nothing about his family. The Barton gang were also frequent visitors, although they hadn't been seen in town recently. Ryan knew that the best source of information usually could be found at the local bawdy house — that's why he had visited The Bird Cage first. He hadn't intended to get involved with any of the girls, but Ryan couldn't resist doing what Ryan did best. He fully intended to return one day and sample Pat, Bev, and Lee. In his opinion, The Bird Cage sported the best whores in Arizona territory. Mother Mary, as the madam was fondly called, ran a damn decent house.

The sun was just starting to set when Ryan left The Bird Cage and headed over to the bank to withdraw funds on the letter of credit he had brought with him from home. As there were two customers ahead of him when he entered the bank, he paused to study the wanted posters pasted on a blank wall. After a brief glance he turned away, then whipped around for a double take. His second look revealed the picture of a man who looked strangely familiar.

The drawing was crude, but the resemblance was unmistakable, even down to the beard Ryan had grown these past weeks. The man in the wanted poster looked uncannily like him. He took a closer look, unaware that the bank clerk was watching him. The poster identified the man as an outlaw wanted for bank robberies in Tucson and Yuma. He bore several aliases. Ryan rubbed his bearded chin, wondering if, without the facial hair, he'd still resemble the outlaw.

Ryan turned away, saw that the other patrons had finished their business, and approached the window. The clerk continued to stare at him, his gaze shifting between Ryan and the wanted poster. When Ryan reached into his leather vest for his letter of credit, the frightened clerk flung his hands up and began to shake violently.

Not knowing what to make of it, Ryan

said, "I want . . ." His sentence ended abruptly when the clerk began pulling money out of the drawer and piling it on the counter.

"Don't shoot, mister," the clerk begged. "Just take the money and go."

Stunned, Ryan said, "You don't understand. I want . . ."

"T-T-There's more in the safe," the clerk stuttered, pushing the money toward him.

Thoroughly exasperated, Ryan shook his head as comprehension finally dawned. Wouldn't Pierce and Chad get a kick out of him being mistaken for a bank robber? He chuckled over the outlandish notion. No matter how humorous the situation, though, Ryan knew he had to put a stop to it before it went any further.

"Listen, I'm not . . ."

Suddenly the bank door flew open and four men entered. Their hats were pulled low to partially cover their faces, and their guns were drawn and cocked.

"Don't nobody make a move," one of the men growled. He motioned to the bank clerk with his gun. "Pile the money on the counter and be quick about it."

He must have realized belatedly that money was already stacked on the counter, for he shoved the brim of his hat up with the barrel of his gun and said, "What the hell!"

"He's got the money all ready for us, Billy," the man standing beside Billy said.

"Shut up, Lex. Let me figure this out," Billy growled.

When Ryan heard Billy call his companion Lex, he realized he had gotten himself smack dab in the middle of an honest-to-God bank robbery by the Barton gang. And the man Ryan had been searching for was standing just a few feet away. He stared at Lex Johnson, wondering how in the hell he was supposed to ask Lex about Kathryn while looking down the barrel of a gun.

Billy Barton's shifty gaze moved from the clerk to Ryan, then at the money piled neatly on the counter. Ryan could tell the exact moment comprehension dawned, for the outlaw's eyes narrowed on him in surprise.

"Now ain't this somethin'," Billy cackled. "Looks like this here gent had the same idea we did."

"There's only one of him and four of us, Billy," Lex said. "Let's grab the money and hightail it outta here. It ain't healthy to stick around."

Ryan thought of the dying Bert and knew he couldn't let Lex escape so easily. He might never find Lex again. He cast about for an answer to his dilemma and found it. Throwing caution to the wind, he said, "There's enough money here for all of us. I only want my fair share. I'll ride with you, and we can divide it later."

"Why should you get a share?" Billy snarled.

"Because I was here first," Ryan said evenly. "And because I'll follow you to hell and back if you don't."

"You got balls, mister," Billy said after some thought. "You'll get your share if you make it outta town alive." He motioned to his men to begin scooping money into the saddlebags they had brought in with them. "Clean out the safe, too," he ordered. Lex moved with alacrity to obey.

Minutes later Ryan made a hasty exit with the Bartons, adrenaline pumping through his veins as he leaped upon his prancing horse. Never in his wildest dreams had he imagined this scenario. From the corner of his eye he noticed a young boy dressed in baggy clothing waiting with the Bartons' horses. Then he heard a shot, and he looked back toward the bank.

Having found his courage, the bank clerk stood in the doorway, waving a gun and shouting, "It's the Bartons! They robbed the bank!"

The gang members had mounted up and were preparing to ride hell for leather when the clerk got off a lucky shot. Ryan saw Lex fall from his horse and sprawl still as death in the middle of the dusty road. With a start Ryan realized that the Bartons had no intention of turning back for their fallen comrade. They were hightailing it down the road as if the devil were nipping at their heels. Ryan was momentarily stunned, then two things happened at once.

Marshal Wyatt Earp rushed toward the fallen outlaw, as the youngster in baggy clothing, who had remained outside the bank as lookout, slid off his horse and knelt beside Lex. Since Ryan had more or less sealed his fate when he had gone along with the Bartons, he had no choice but to flee with the gang. Yet the sight of the lad on his knees beside his wounded comrade gave him pause. Obviously the lad had no idea of the danger he was placing himself in by remaining behind.

Driven by concern for the youngster, and acting from pure instinct that Pierce would have called plumb foolish, Ryan wheeled his horse toward the boy. Time was running out. The law was nearly upon them, and curious townspeople were pouring out of

21

stores and homes. Determined to reach the lad first, Ryan spurred his horse forward, then reached down to sweep the boy up before him on the first pass. Bullets whizzed by him as he bent low over the boy and let the animal have his head.

"Keep down!" Ryan shouted when he felt the lad stirring against him.

"Bastard! Put me down!" the boy cried, struggling against the restraint of Ryan's arms. "I can't leave Lex."

"Ungrateful urchin. I didn't risk my life to see you hang," Ryan growled. "There's the Bartons up ahead. Looks like they're heading for the border. Once we're on the other side I don't care what you do with your life."

That shut him up, for he settled down after that. It wasn't long before they caught up with the rest of the gang and crossed the border into Mexico. They stopped to camp beside a stream when it became too dark to continue. The lad slid to the ground and disappeared, while Ryan took care of his horse. Ryan saw him later, sitting away from the others beside the campfire, chewing on a piece of jerky. Something about the boy didn't set right with Ryan, but he couldn't for the life of him decide what it was.

Ryan was still thinking about the kid when Billy Barton joined him. "If Lex was here he'd thank you for takin' care of Kit. Lex hooked up with the kid before he joined us. They was both runnin' from the law. Kit was young, but I had no objection to lettin' him join us as long as he pulled his weight."

"How old is Kit?" Ryan asked.

Billy scratched his wild thatch of matted hair. "Don't rightly know. Sixteen or seventeen, I reckon. He was just a tad when Lex brought him here. They been ridin' with us four or five years now. Kit has grown some since then, but not much. He's gonna miss Johnson."

"Kit must know Johnson well," Ryan said thoughtfully.

Billy shrugged. "About as well as anyone here. Why?"

"No reason. I feel kind of responsible for the kid. I'll keep an eye on him for you if you want." If Kit was as close to Lex as Billy suggested, then he might know something about Kathryn, Ryan reflected.

Billy sent Ryan a calculating look. "Is that your way of askin' if you can join the gang?"

Ryan grinned. "I was hoping you'd ask me."

"I don't even know your name."

"It's Ryan."

"Ryan what?"

"Does it matter?"

"Don't reckon it does. Is the Tombstone bank the first job you pulled?"

"Neither the first nor the last," Ryan lied. "I usually work alone but I wouldn't mind joining up with you. How about it?"

Here was the excitement Ryan had longed for when he'd left home! The exhilaration of what he was about to do, the thrill of danger, sent adrenaline charging through him. Ranching couldn't compare with this kind of adventure. Right now he didn't have time to think about the consequences of his folly.

"With Lex outta commission I reckon we can use another gun," Billy said. "Poor bastard will hang if he ain't already dead. Kit ain't good during robberies so we can't depend on him. We keep him around because he's a passable cook and good with the horses. The Tombstone job was only the third time he rode with us. He usually acts as lookout while we're inside the bank."

"You won't regret it," Ryan said, elated.

"I better not," Billy warned. "Hey boys," he called out, capturing the attention of the other gang members. "This here is Ryan. He's joinin' us on a trial basis. The ugly brute with the crooked nose sitting across from us is Clank," Billy said by way of introduction. "The half-breed is Durango.

24

You already know Kit."

Ryan nodded to each man in turn and was rewarded with answering grunts. From all but Kit, who ignored him.

"We better hit the sack if we want to get an early start tomorrow," Billy said, yawning. "We'll have to lay low for a while so don't expect no action until the heat dies down."

"I can use the rest," Ryan said as Billy and the others hoisted themselves to their feet and found their bedrolls.

The forced inactivity suited Ryan perfectly. He intended to hang around only long enough to find out what Kit knew, if anything, about Lex Johnson and his stepsister, Kathryn.

Ryan watched through slitted eyes as Kit moved away from the campfire, away from the rest of the men, and lay down on his bedroll. His movements were almost too graceful for a boy, and he seemed frail for his age. It looked as if his shoulders were shaking, and Ryan wondered if he was crying. Obviously Lex had been like a brother to Kit, and leaving Lex behind to an uncertain fate must have been traumatic for the lad.

Feeling charitable — and something else he couldn't name — Ryan made his way through the sleeping men to where Kit lay wrapped in his bedroll. Ryan knelt down and touched his shoulder.

Kit bolted upright. "Keep your filthy hands off me!" he hissed. "Haul your ass back to your bedroll and leave me alone."

Ryan sat back on his heels, stunned by the undeserved diatribe. "I just wanted to make sure you're all right."

"Ain't nothin' wrong with me," the boy said sullenly as he lay back down. "I take that back," he added grimly. "I could use a shot of whiskey."

"Sorry, no whiskey. I know you and Lex were friends. I thought you might be lonesome."

"You thought wrong, mister. I ain't no puking baby."

Ryan stared at the lad, his gaze settling on the tangle of blond hair cropped short, then moving down over ridiculously long golden lashes, a straight nose, and full lips. Something stirred inside him. Compassion? Pity? It was difficult to describe until he knew the kid better. One thing he did know. The kid was a filthy, foulmouthed juvenile who belonged in school, not riding with a gang of outlaws. His hands and face were so dirty that Ryan could barely see his smooth jaw beneath all the grime.

Ryan rose abruptly. "Pardon me for trying to be friendly. I don't need a foulmouthed little urchin cussing me out. Good night, brat."

After a short walk behind a tree to relieve himself, Ryan settled down for the night. But sleep eluded him. He lay awake a long time thinking about the unexpected turn his life had taken. If Pierce and Chad knew what he'd done they'd kill him. That was the trouble with having two older brothers. Both tried to tell him how to run his life. That was the main reason he'd left Dry Gulch. That and the sickening marital bliss both his brothers seemed to have found. Love and marriage. It might work for his brothers, but it certainly wasn't a state he aspired to.

No sir, he thought, grinning to himself. Rogue Ryan liked a variety of women, almost as much as women liked him. If there was one subject Ryan knew well, it was women. Not that he didn't relish a good fight when the occasion warranted. He and his brothers weren't known as hell-raisers for nothing. But now that Pierce and Chad had wives and families, it was left to him to uphold the reputation earned by the Delaney brothers.

Ryan's last thought before sleep claimed

him was that perhaps this time he'd bitten off more than he could chew. Being on the wrong side of the law was a new experience. Hopefully he wouldn't live to regret his rashness.

Ryan awoke to the mouthwatering aroma of coffee and bacon. He opened his eyes and saw the outlaws beginning to stir. With dawn just breaking, an eerie grayness had settled over the mesquite-covered ground. Ryan gathered his gear and walked to the stream to wash and shave off the beard he'd grown. He was kneeling at the water's edge to rinse the shaving soap from his face when he heard footsteps behind him. He whirled, his hand going for his gun. He saw Kit standing behind him and relaxed.

Kit's surly expression gave Ryan the impression that the boy wasn't thrilled to see him.

"What are you doing here?" Kit asked.

"Same thing you are, I reckon. Only you need it more than I do. Don't you ever wash? And look at your hair. You hiding rats in there?"

"Go to hell," Kit said petulantly. "You ain't my keeper."

Ryan stared at the boy, his eyes narrowing thoughtfully. This was the first really good look he'd had of the lad in full daylight, and he knew immediately what had been bothering him. Was he the only one aware of something that should have been obvious to everyone? If there was one thing that Rogue Ryan knew well, it was women. He was familiar with their bodies, their voices, their mannerisms, their femininity. It took no great skill for Ryan to see through Kit's disguise, despite the baggy clothing and dirty face. Her sky blue eyes and long burnished lashes were too feminine, her features too delicate. Ryan had to hand it to Lex. His taste in doxies was impeccable.

Kit was a woman, not some downy-faced lad. He'd bet the ranch on it. And she was probably older than she looked.

"What are you staring at?" Kit challenged.

Ryan shrugged. "Just wondering how you stand the dirt. The water's not too cold, why don't you strip and have a good wash?"

"Why don't you mind your own damn business?"

Truth to tell, washing was exactly what Kit had intended to do before she'd found Ryan at the stream. She knew none of the Bartons would think of washing or shaving, and she had expected to find a secluded spot for her own morning ablutions. Of course she'd have to dirty her face and hands again to maintain her disguise, but at least her body would be clean. Without Lex here to protect her privacy, finding time for herself was going to be difficult.

"You sure are a cocky kid," Ryan said. He looked amused at something, and Kit wondered what she had said to entertain him.

This outlaw wasn't like the others. She'd been with the Bartons a long time and had learned a great deal, more than she wanted, about outlaws, and Ryan didn't fit the mold. Who was he and what did he want? He was a handsome devil whoever he was. His tall, muscular frame possessed not one ounce of fat, and if she were one to succumb to charm, the man's smile alone would reel her in like a fish on a line. She stared at him, intrigued by his eyes. They were the clear, cool green of grass after a spring rain. Thank God she was too smart to fall for the handsome face and impressive body of the dark-haired rogue. Men like Ryan thought themselves God's gift to women.

Outlaws were the scum of the earth, Kit maintained. They were cruel, hard, and had no respect for human life, male or female. Kit had learned volumes about outlaws in the five years since Lex had taken her under his wing to "protect" her. She'd been thirteen at the time, and she'd had no choice but to accompany him since her mother was dead and Deke had been killed over a card game, leaving her to fend for herself. The first year or two they had lived on their own, from hand to mouth, barely existing between robberies. Then Lex had met and joined up with the Bartons, and life had become a little easier with big money from bank robberies and such to split.

It soon occurred to Kit that Lex, though his intentions may have been good, had thrust her into a dangerous existence. It hadn't been all bad when she was young, but as she'd grown older and matured, the situation had become downright sticky. Now, without Lex to protect her, the whole charade could explode in her face.

"I gotta go," Kit said, turning abruptly. Ryan made her uncomfortable. He looked at her as if he could see through her disguise, though she knew she'd done nothing to rouse his suspicion. "Billy won't like it if the bacon burns." She turned and fled, unwilling to answer the unasked questions visible in Ryan's brilliant green gaze.

Ryan stared at the elegant line of her departing back, his mind awhirl with questions. He understood why Lex kept his doxy's identity a secret. He wouldn't want to share her either. He speculated about her age. She couldn't have been very old when Lex joined the Bartons, for she didn't look a day over twenty or twenty-one. He certainly couldn't tell from her body, for she kept it well covered.

There wasn't a hint of breasts beneath her baggy jacket, but he'd be willing to bet they were ample. Lex wouldn't have kept her with him if she hadn't pleased him. Ryan grinned. It might amuse him to play Kit's game for a while. Besides, he was here for one purpose. To find Kathryn. Lex wasn't around to answer his questions but his doxy was. If she'd been with Lex five or more years, she probably would know about Lex's family.

Still smiling, Ryan returned to the campsite. The men had already eaten, and he poured himself a cup of coffee and ate what bacon remained, gobbling it down as he saddled his horse.

"Where you been?" Billy questioned.

"Taking a leak," Ryan said tersely. "I'll be ready to leave when you are."

"There's been a change in plans," Billy said. "We're stoppin' in town first. There ain't a drop of whiskey among us, and the boys' throats are parched somethin' fierce. The rotgut tequila the cantina sells is better than nothin'. And there's a couple of black-eyed *senoritas* there always willin' to earn a couple of pesos."

"You'll like Carmen," Durango said. "She's got the purtiest tits this side of the Rio Grande."

"I prefer Lolita," Clank argued. "She's got a set of muscles between her legs that can squeeze a man dry."

Ryan glanced at Kit, wondering what she thought of all this bawdy talk. He supposed she was used to it by now, for she didn't bat an eyelash. She was a cool one, he'd give her that.

"Which woman does Kit prefer?" Ryan asked, earning a startled glance from Kit.

Billy gave a loud guffaw. "Kit? That wet-behind-the-ears kid ain't never had a woman to my knowledge. Won't be long, though. He's at an age where he's probably hornier than a billy goat. Ain't that right, Kit?"

Kit chose not to answer, and Ryan was sorry he'd asked when Clank and Durango offered Kit some raunchy advice that must have burned her ears.

"Let's get going," Ryan said in an effort to change the subject. "I can almost taste that tequila."

"Kit can ride with Ryan," Billy said, mounting up.

Ryan mounted and held out his hand for Kit. Ignoring the offer, she leaped up behind him.

"If you're going to ride pillion, you'd better put your arms around my waist. I don't want you to fall off."

"I like this way better," Kit rasped, grasping his belt instead.

"Are you always so disagreeable?" Ryan taunted.

"Always. Especially when nosy polecats like you ask too many questions."

Ryan bit back his smart retort. It wouldn't do to make an enemy of Kit when she might hold the key to Kathryn's whereabouts.

"I'm sorry if I rubbed you the wrong way," Ryan said. "I'm too new here to make enemies. How about a truce? I can be a good friend should you need one."

Kit mulled over Ryan's offer. Lord knows she needed a friend. Especially with Lex gone. As far as brothers went, Lex left much to be desired, but he'd been all she had. She worried excessively about him. Was he dead? In jail awaiting trial? Or had a lynching mob already gotten hold of him?

A friend. Kit wished she had the luxury of having a friend, but it was too dangerous. Friends demanded a certain sharing of thoughts that she couldn't afford. Should the Bartons learn she was a woman, they would find an unpleasant use for her, and that she couldn't bear. No, she decided. Becoming friends with Ryan was unthinkable.

"A truce then," Kit agreed. "But I don't need no friends. Me and Lex kept to ourselves, we didn't need anyone else."

"I'll bet," Ryan said. An undertone of sarcasm laced his voice as he imagined the intimate relationship between Lex and Kit.

Conversation came to a halt as Ryan concentrated on guiding his horse over mesquite and cactus dotted ground and around washes, gullies, and ruts that could prove fatal to both horse and rider. The town rose stark against the blue sky and brown earth. It consisted of a cluster of flat-roofed adobe houses, wooden huts, a church situated in an open plaza, a general store, and a cantina. Chickens, goats, and children scattered as they rode into the plaza. Women stood in open doorways while old men chatted in groups around the plaza. The younger men could be seen working in the communal fields behind the church.

Everything seemed to come to a standstill as the Bartons rode into town. If the town had a name it wasn't posted anywhere within sight. The outlaws reined in before

35

the cantina and dismounted. Ryan followed suit, trailing them inside. All five of them lined up at the scarred bar and ordered tequila. He watched with admiration as Kit knocked back her drink and smacked her lips. He wondered if she was a lush but decided she wasn't when she declined a refill and strolled outside to wait for the others.

Almost immediately the men were joined by two sloe-eyed *senoritas,* who, while not young, were still fresh enough to satisfy men who weren't too choosy. Clank and Durango disappeared with them behind a grubby curtain, and before long Ryan heard sounds of sexual activity taking place.

"Better get in line, Ryan," Billy advised. "Later on the whores will be busy with their regular customers, and you don't want them after they opened their legs for every man in town. That's why we always come for the women early in the day."

"I think I'll pass this time," Ryan said. "I had a woman in Tombstone." More than one if the truth be told. "Think I'll go outside and keep young Kit company."

"Suit yourself," Billy said. "I'm waitin' on Carmen."

Ryan went outside, squinting against the blast of sunlight after the dimness of the cantina. He saw Kit sitting under a scrawny tree and went to join her.

"Are you finished already?" she asked, sending him a disgusted look. "You're a fast one, ain't you?"

"I passed on the women," Ryan said. "The teq wasn't bad, though." He took off his hat and wiped the sweat from his brow.

Kit looked at him with renewed interest. "You passed on the women? I'll be damned. What's with you? Are you partial to boys?" She scooted away from him. "If that's your preference, just keep your distance, mister."

Ryan erupted into raucous laughter. Kit's remark was the first time anyone had ever accused him of not liking women. "I like women just fine so you don't have to worry. Besides, you're a little too dirty for my tastes. It just so happens I don't need a woman right now. What about you? Boys your age are usually randy as goats. If you need some pointers, I'll be happy to tell you how to go about it."

"No, thanks," Kit returned shortly. "I know what to do with a woman. I just ain't ready yet."

Ryan's dark brows cocked upward. He had to give Kit credit. She had an answer for everything. "Are you hungry? I can go back inside and get us a plate of beans and tortillas while we're waiting for the others."

"I reckon I can eat something," Kit allowed.

"Be right back."

"If you change your mind about the women, I don't mind waiting," she called after him.

Ryan chuckled all the way to the cantina.

CHAPTER 2

"How long have you known Lex?" Ryan asked as he shoveled beans in his mouth with his tortilla.

"Long enough," Kit said warily. "What's it to you?"

"Just curious. Billy said you and Lex have been with the gang four or five years, so you two must have been together at least that long. Where did you meet?"

"Around." Kit regarded him through slitted eyes. Ryan was far too inquisitive for her liking. Why was the outlaw so interested in Lex? Throughout the years she'd learned to keep her thoughts to herself and to communicate as little as possible with the other gang members. Just because Ryan seemed different from the others didn't mean she should let her guard down. The strange attraction she felt for the handsome outlaw meant she had to be more vigilant than ever.

"You don't talk much, do you?" Ryan said

in an effort to draw her out.

"I talk when I've got something to say," Kit shot back. "If you're so anxious to spill your guts, why don't you tell me about yourself? How long have you been running from the law?"

"Long enough," Ryan returned, obviously no more anxious to reveal his past than she was. "I wonder how long before the others are done with the women?" he said, nodding toward the cantina.

"I reckon they'll be done soon. They're never here more than a couple of hours. Towns ain't healthy. Not even Mexican towns. The Bartons aren't popular with the law south of the border, either. By the time I buy a horse they'll be ready to ride." She rose and walked to an enclosure where several horses were kept. A man came over, and they began dickering on a price for the horse Kit favored.

Ryan walked over to join her. "Can you afford that animal?"

"I've got money," Kit replied. "I always pay my own way."

By the time Kit had settled on a price and paid for her horse, Billy, Clank, and Durango had finished with the women.

"Let's ride," Billy growled when he saw Kit and Ryan standing beside the newly purchased horse.

Kit was preparing to vault atop her mount when she felt Ryan's hands on her waist. Before she could protest, he tossed her onto the horse's back.

Kit fumed in silent rage. She neither needed nor wanted Ryan's help. The arrogant outlaw was becoming a problem. Who did he think he was, anyway? He was an outlaw, no better than Billy and the others when it came right down to it. He might be handsome and well-spoken, but he was as likely to end up swinging from a rope as any other outlaw.

Kit didn't want that for herself. As soon as she learned Lex's fate, she would leave the gang, turn respectable, and find an honest man to love. If there *was* such a man in this world. She wasn't very knowledgeable about men, at least not the respectable kind. Sending a hooded glance at Ryan, she imagined a man worthy of her love. He'd be handsome and strong, yet tender and giving. She wouldn't mind at all if he looked like Ryan.

Ryan watched Kitty with a sideways glance and stifled a groan. The foul-mouthed little scamp didn't know he had seen through her disguise and probably had no idea what she was doing to him. He vividly recalled how tiny and supple her waist had felt when he'd lifted her onto her horse. His manhood stirred, and he tried unsuccessfully to think of anything but Kit and the treasures that lay hidden beneath her baggy clothes. Instinctively he knew her breasts would be soft and full, her legs long and shapely. He shifted uncomfortably, wondering how long it would take him to charm her out of her clothing.

It was almost a relief when they reached the hideout a short time later. Ryan wasn't sure he could take much more of watching Kit's taut little rump bouncing against her saddle. Ryan couldn't decide whether to let her know he'd seen through her disguise and offer his protection or continue the charade until he'd gained the information he sought. Whatever he decided, he knew for a certainty he wasn't about to leave until he'd bedded Lex's doxy.

Instinct told Ryan that Kit wasn't a whore in the broadest sense of the word. He even suspected that she'd known no other man than Lex and was completely out of her element without her protector. Ryan knew what would happen to her once the Bartons learned her secret, and he didn't wish such a fate on any woman.

The decision to protect Kit without her knowledge came easily to Ryan. All the Delaneys were compassionate to a fault, though they would be the first to deny it.

Located in a tangle of mesquite and tall cactus, the outlaw camp was situated snugly against a butte. It wasn't much, consisting of two thatched huts and a lean-to for the horses, but they did have access to a stream that provided fresh water. It was crude at best, but at least the huts gave them a roof over their heads in inclement weather and a place to stay while hiding from the law.

"The smaller hut belongs to Lex and Kit," Billy said to Ryan as they led their horses to the lean-to. "You and Kit can share it now. Clank and I bed down in the larger hut, and Durango usually sleeps outside. Injuns don't much care for walls."

"I'll sleep outside," Kit said, slanting a panicky look at Ryan.

"I don't eat filthy brats," Ryan said, stifling a smile. "What are you afraid of, Kit?"

"Certainly not you," Kit said, storming toward the hut.

"Where are you goin'?" Billy growled. "Fix us some grub. We didn't have time to fill our bellies in town."

There was just enough daylight left for

Ryan to see the disgusted look Kit sent Billy. "You should have spent more time eating and less time screwing."

"If you'd a done a little screwin' yourself you wouldn't be so disagreeable," Billy tossed back.

"Maybe I'll just light out of here and go my own way," Kit threatened.

Billy gave her a menacing scowl. "You ain't goin' nowhere, kid. You ain't smart enough to dodge the law and you'll break under pressure if you're caught. Sure as shootin' you'll bring the law down on us and we'll all end up like Lex."

"Fine, I ain't going nowhere," Kit said as she slammed pots around. "Someone start a fire."

"I will," Ryan volunteered, reaching for a pile of wood stacked next to the firepit.

"Call me when the grub's ready," Billy said, heading for his hut.

"A fat rabbit or two will taste good with the beans," Durango said, taking up his bow and arrows.

Clank followed Billy inside the hut, leaving Ryan to tend the fire while Kit put beans on to cook.

"Did you mean what you said about leaving the gang?" Ryan asked once they were alone.

"You heard what Billy said. I ain't going nowhere. I was only joshing. Besides, I can't make plans until I know what happened to Lex."

"You and Lex were pretty close, weren't you?" Ryan asked with casual interest.

"Yeah, we were as close as . . . brothers. He took care of me when I had no one else."

Ryan laid another log on the fire. "What about your family?"

Kit went still. "They're all dead."

"Did Lex have a family?"

"I . . . why are you so interested in Lex?"

Ryan shrugged. "Just making conversation."

"You talk too much," Kit grumbled, turning away.

Ryan fell silent. A short time later Durango returned with four skinned and gutted rabbits. He spitted them on sticks, set them before the fire, and went down to the creek to wash the blood from his hands.

"Durango's not much of a talker, is he?" Ryan said.

"A man learns not to blab in this business," Kit said with a wisdom born of experience. "One's survival depends upon it. I'm surprised you haven't learned that yet."

Ryan had nothing to add to that, so he

concentrated on keeping the fire going. When the meal was done, Kit called the others, and Ryan had no further opportunity for private conversation. After the meal had been devoured, the outlaws sought their beds, leaving the mess for Kit to clean. Ryan watched as she gathered up the dirty plates and made her way by hazy moonlight to the stream that ran behind the huts at the base of the butte. Ryan offered to help but Kit objected, so he stretched and said he was going to bed.

Ryan waited a few minutes before following Kit down to the stream. He told himself he only wanted to protect her against wild animals and such, but he knew he was only fooling himself. He didn't know what he expected to learn, except that he wanted to discover the real Kit, or whatever her name happened to be.

Ryan moved stealthily down the path, crouching low so as not to be seen should Kit happen to glance over her shoulder. He saw her kneeling at the edge of the narrow stream, a pile of clean plates and utensils sitting beside her. He sought refuge behind a mesquite tree when she stood and glanced nervously over her shoulder.

Ryan watched with avid interest as Kit, apparently satisfied that she was alone, peeled off her coat. He nearly lost his breath when she shed her vest and shirt. For a brief but memorable moment he was given a breathtaking view of a pair of full breasts balanced above a slim waist. When she turned away from him and dropped her baggy trousers, his heart slammed against his chest.

She wore cotton drawers, but it took little imagination for Ryan to visualize her sweetly curved thighs and the perfect mounds of her buttocks concealed beneath the thin material. What really fired his blood was the thought of that soft, hot place between her legs. After a brief glimpse of the womanly form beneath the baggy clothing, Ryan didn't know how much longer he could wait to possess her.

Mesmerized, he watched her wade into the shallow stream, sit down, and spash herself with water. She didn't wash her hair, and Ryan wondered what it would look like once those shorn locks grew out and received regular washing. She finished quickly, but Ryan's body had already turned to stone. He couldn't ever recall getting so hard so quickly with so little stimulation. Yet all it took was one look at Kit's breasts to turn mild desire to gnawing hunger. Perhaps he should have taken advantage of

Carmen or Lolita in town.

He remained hidden as Kit dressed, and he was more than a little surprised when he saw her smear fresh dirt on her face before gathering up the clean plates and starting back toward the camp. He waited until she'd had sufficient time to reach the hut and settle down in her bedroll before following.

Nebulous moonlight filtered through the grimy window as Ryan let himself into the hut with his bedroll. He saw her lying on a cot in the corner, rolled up in her blanket, nothing but her tousled curls and elfin face visible, but he could tell by her breathing that she wasn't asleep. He spread his bedroll atop the second cot and sat down to take off his boots.

Kit stared at Ryan with suspicion and couldn't help asking, "Where have you been? I thought you had gone to bed but you weren't in the hut when I returned." She wanted to ask if he had followed her but feared his answer.

"I took care of my horse and smoked a cigar."

Kit let out a sigh of relief. No one must know she was anything other than what she claimed to be. Trusting a man was new to her, and she didn't know enough about

Ryan to tell him the truth. It didn't take experience to know the handsome outlaw was different from the men she knew.

Ryan stood abruptly, his powerful form bathed in moonlight as he shrugged out of his shirt, removed his gunbelt, and unbuttoned the flap on his pants. The breath caught in Kit's throat. She wanted to look away but couldn't as he peeled his denims down his legs and stepped out of them. She was almost disappointed when she saw that he wore long johns, but at the same time, she was enormously relieved. As he turned to settle down on the cot, Kit saw a telltale protrusion tenting out the front of his long johns. She shut her eyes and turned her head. Then she heard him chuckle and wondered what he found so amusing.

"Good night, brat," Ryan said with amazing good humor.

Did he know she'd been watching him?

"Go to hell," Kit shot back, turning toward the wall.

The following days were a test of endurance for Kit. Ryan made her life a living hell. She had only to turn around and he was behind her. He dogged her steps, constantly plaguing her to wash, to comb her hair, and strangely, to stay away from the Bartons.

Ryan had gone hunting with Durango early this morning, and she couldn't believe that she actually missed him. When she looked up from the campfire now and saw him riding into camp, her heart stirred with excitement.

The feeling made her nervous. She was powerfully attracted to Ryan and had to constantly fight the feeling for fear she'd say or do something to alert him to her charade. Her problem as she saw it was that she could easily picture him in a respectable setting, becoming the kind of man with whom she could spend the rest of her life. She started violently when Ryan strolled up beside her and placed his hand on her shoulder. The heat of his touch seemed to sear her clear through.

"I hope you and Durango brought back something besides rabbit," she said tartly. "I'm getting bored with the same fare."

"How about venison tonight?" Ryan said. "Durango is cleaning and skinning a buck right now." He opened his fist and showed her a sliver of soap resting in his palm. "I'm going down to the stream to wash. Want to join me?"

"I ain't dirty."

"You could have fooled me, brat. Come on, don't be shy."

Without giving her a chance to protest, he grabbed her about the waist, threw her over his shoulder, and started toward the stream.

"Put me down, you musclebound jack-ass!" Kit wailed. "Damn your stinking hide. I said I ain't dirty."

Ryan grinned, making her even madder. "I don't know what your aversion is to water. Maybe Lex liked his wo . . . er . . . friends dirty, but I don't."

He had reached the stream, and Kit clung to him as he paused briefly at the edge before wading out to the middle. The water barely came to his knees. She squawked in surprise when he tossed her into the water. She came up sputtering and cursing, using words normally heard only in saloons, and she heard Ryan chuckling in response.

Arms and legs flailing wildly, Kit lit into him, enraged when his laughter turned into loud guffaws. "Damn you! What's so funny?"

"You, if you think you can hurt me," Ryan said, choking on his own laughter. "Do you want the soap?"

"I don't want anything you've got," she said, stomping out of the water. Her clothes were dripping, and she suddenly realized she was in danger of being exposed. Hunching her shoulders so her coat wouldn't cling to her breasts, she hastened back to camp and into the hut before the others noticed.

Ryan watched her go, still chuckling to himself. This charade of hers was more fun than he had anticipated. Such a gullible little witch, he thought as he admired the sway of her shapely hips as she walked away. Didn't she realize he was on to her? Dimly he wondered if Lex's doxy would consider having sex with him. Kit gave him an itch that definitely needed scratching. He felt his loins stiffen as he recalled her naked body poised at the edge of the stream, shimmering like pale ivory in the moonlight. He'd wanted her then, and he wanted her now.

He envisioned himself possessing the little wildcat as he quickly stripped and washed. Then he donned his denims and carried his soiled clothing back to the hut. Kit, who had already changed into dry clothing by the time he entered, was sitting on her cot, drying her boots. Ryan tossed his dirty shirt and long johns at her.

"Wash these when you wash your own clothing, will you?"

She tossed them back. "Wash them yourself, I got better things to do."

"Like what? Lex isn't here. You're at loose ends and have nothing better to do. Why are you so damn stubborn?"

He sat down beside her, placing his arm around her in a gesture of camaraderie. He felt her stiffen and try to duck beneath his arm, but he held her fast.

"Why did you let Lex talk you into leading a life of crime?" Ryan asked, hoping to gain her confidence. "You couldn't have been more than a youngster at the time."

Her chin lifted fractionally. "Lex was the only one who cared about me. This life hasn't been so bad," she lied.

"You and Lex must have grown close over the years," Ryan probed.

"What's it to you?" she asked defensively. "Why are you so damn curious about Lex?"

Ryan shrugged. "Just trying to make friendly conversation."

"I ain't in the mood for talking."

"I kind of like talking, myself. Tell me about Lex. Did he tell you anything about his family? Did he have a sister?"

Kit's eyes narrowed, and Ryan thought he saw a hint of fear in those blue orbs. "I don't know a thing about Lex's family," Kit claimed. "You know the code of the West. Ask no questions and you'll hear no lies. You're the one who seems out of place here. You don't act like no outlaw to me. You don't even own a last name."

"Looks can be deceiving," Ryan said.

"And my last name is Delaney." He rose abruptly, before Kit's curiosity blew his cover. "Reckon I'll go help Durango with that deer. You might want to start the fire and put some beans on to cook. How about some biscuits? You know how to make biscuits?"

Kit gave him a sullen look. "Ain't nobody complained about my cooking yet."

Ryan made a hasty exit. Being around Kit was becoming damn uncomfortable. Now that he knew what lay beneath her baggy clothing he couldn't control his body's reaction to her. How could anyone in possession of their right mind not know that Kit was a woman?

Kit grew more and more obsessed with Ryan each passing day. She didn't know what was wrong with her. She'd lived with men so long that she'd begun to act like one — until Ryan Delaney had come along, with his infectious grin, handsome face, and hard body, and changed everything. Suddenly, for the first time in her recent memory, she had begun to think like a female. Whenever Ryan came near her, her body reacted in puzzling ways. Her nerve endings tingled, a vibrating began in her lower regions, and she found it difficult to breathe. It was becoming increasingly difficult even to think coherently when Ryan questioned her about Lex.

That was another mystifying aspect about Ryan. She could think of no earthly reason for Ryan's interest in Lex's family. Her mother and Deke were dead, and so might Lex be, for all she knew. That just left herself, and she couldn't imagine why anyone would be interested in her. She didn't even know who her real father was. Rena had started to tell Kit the day before she died, but time had run out for the poor woman before her father's name had left her lips. Kit supposed it didn't matter. No matter who her father was, she'd still hate him for abandoning her pregnant mother and leaving her to fend for herself. Because her mother carried an illegitimate child she had been forced to marry a drunken, wife-beating bastard like Deke Johnson.

It was becoming increasingly difficult for Kit to sleep in the same room with Ryan. She waited now in dread for him to come to bed. She had retired early, as was her habit, preferring solitude to sitting around listening to the men's vulgar talk. She heard Ryan's footsteps approach the hut, and she closed her eyes, pretending sleep. But some perverse imp inside her made her watch as he undressed.

During her years with the gang she'd been exposed to various parts of men's bodies without being affected by the sight. Mostly she'd been disgusted, but there was nothing disgusting about Ryan's body. For one thing it was clean. Rippling muscles and bulging biceps made it evident that Ryan Delaney was not the kind of outlaw who sat around between robberies guzzling whiskey and growing soft. He looked like a man who didn't fear physical labor.

A beam of moonlight filtering through the dirty window revealed more of Ryan than Kit wanted to see, but she couldn't close her eyes. When Ryan shrugged out of his pants, she was shocked to see that he was naked. She'd expected to see him in long johns, but obviously the heat had convinced him to discard them. In the brief moment before he climbed into his bedroll, he paused and stretched. Her breath caught in her chest when she saw the hard mounds of his buttocks and sculpted length of his powerful thighs. As if aware of her scrutiny, Ryan turned slightly, giving her a full view of his lean stomach and that dark place between his thighs where his male appendage hung full and heavy from a thick nest of black hair.

She bit her tongue to keep from gasping aloud. She didn't know if he realized she was watching him, but it no longer mattered, for Ryan had crawled into his bedroll and turned away from her. She knew Billy and the others slept fully clothed and realized that Ryan was an enigma. Nothing he said or did placed him in the same category as the Bartons.

Kit lay awake a long time, fantasizing about making a life with Ryan. But living outside the law wasn't the kind of life she intended for herself. Even knowing that Ryan was an outlaw didn't stop her from imagining what it would be like having him permanently in her life. Of course it would mean discarding her disguise and exposing herself as a woman, but she'd contemplated doing just that for a long time. She was old enough and independent enough now to make a life for herself. She didn't need Lex to protect her. Thinking about Lex presented another problem. She needed to find out soon what had become of him.

Before she fell asleep she decided that no matter how attracted she was to Ryan, he was an outlaw and definitely not the kind of man with whom she wanted to spend a lifetime.

"We're runnin' outta tequila," Billy complained the following day after a breakfast of cold biscuits and leftover venison.

"We could ride over the border and get some real whiskey," Clank suggested.

"It's too dangerous," Billy argued. "I wouldn't be surprised if the posse is still searchin' for us. We're gonna have to quench our thirst with the rotgut from town."

"Suits me," Durango grunted. "I've been hankerin' for a woman again."

"What about you, Ryan? You game for a trip into town? You passed on the women last time. You oughta be ripe now."

"Sure, I'm game," Ryan said. "How about you, Kit? I'll show you the ropes if you're shy."

Kit sent him a malevolent look. "No, thanks. I ain't anxious to get the clap."

"The women are clean," Billy claimed. "Mount up, boys, I aim to be the first in line."

"Come on, Kit," Ryan said, yanking her up by the collar. He didn't know what devil made him do it, but he wanted to see how Kit would react under duress. Of course he would intervene before she was actually exposed as a female, but he couldn't resist having a little fun with Kit.

"You're going," he said, dragging her to her horse and tossing her into the saddle. Keeping her reins in his hands, he mounted his own horse and joined the others as they rode out of camp. He gave Kit no chance to protest as he kept a tight hold on her horse's reins.

"I ain't going in there," Kit muttered when they dismounted before the cantina a short time later.

Ryan had intended to let her off the hook once they reached town, but he hadn't counted on Billy's interference.

"It's time you had a woman," Billy insisted. "You're a grown man . . . almost," he added, eyeing her smooth chin. "I had my first woman at thirteen. I know you're older than that. Haul your ass inside and pick out a woman."

Ryan could tell that Kit was beginning to panic. Her blue eyes were rolling wildly, as if she were searching for a place to hide. Her face was white, and she looked as if she wanted to vomit.

Deliberately he went to Kit and placed an arm around her shoulders. He felt her quaking and wished he'd kept his mouth shut back at camp and left Kit to her own devices. He'd never been consciously cruel to a woman, and he didn't intend to start now.

"Tell you what," he said, thinking fast. "I'll go last and take young Kit here inside with me. Kind of show the boy the ropes."

Billy shrugged. "Suits me, as long as Kit gets initiated proper like." He turned to Kit. "Don't look so scared, kid. Once you've had it you'll be wantin' it regular like. Lex should have seen to your education a long time ago."

"Bastard!" Kit hissed when the men entered the cantina, leaving her alone with Ryan.

"Don't worry," Ryan said. "It won't be as bad as you think. Trust me."

"Trust you!" Kit spat. "If you only knew . . ." Her mouth clamped tightly shut, refusing to say more.

Ryan could add nothing to that. They sat in silence until Billy came out of the cantina, carrying several bottles of tequila. He stuffed them in his saddlebags and walked over to join them.

"As soon as Durango's finished, Lolita will be free. Unless you'd rather have Carmen."

"Lolita will do just fine," Ryan said. He pulled Kit to her feet. "Come on, brat.

Watch carefully, you're bound to learn something. You and the boys can go back to the camp," Ryan said to Billy. "Don't know how long we'll be."

"We'll wait," Billy said, smirking. "I wanna see the kid's face when Lolita gets through with him."

Ryan nodded and dragged Kit off with him just as Durango strutted out the cantina door and walked toward them. Lolita was waiting inside for them. She motioned them toward the curtained alcove, smiling beguilingly at Kit.

"Does the little *hombre* want to go first?" Lolita asked in halting English.

Clank came out from behind the second curtain, winking at them. "Good luck, kid," he said. "Lolita will treat you right."

Ryan thought Kit looked green around the gills, so he quickly hauled her behind the curtain and shoved her into the only chair in the squalid room.

"I can't," Kit gasped, looking away as Lolita began removing her camisa and skirt.

"That's enough, Lolita," Ryan said, placing a hand on the whore's arm to stop her. "We've changed our minds."

Lolita looked from Ryan to Kit, her dark brows raised. "You do not want Lolita? Billy said to show the young *hombre* a good time.

That it's his first time."

Ryan dug in his vest pocket and produced a five dollar gold piece. Lolita's eyes sparkled when he flashed it before her. "This is more money than you can earn in half a year, Lolita," Ryan said. "It's yours if you do as I say."

Lolita eyed him warily, then dropped to her knees before him, her hands on the buttons of his fly. "Is this what you want, *senor?*"

Kit reddened and looked away as Ryan hoisted Lolita none too gently to her feet. "No, it's *not* what I want. The coin is to buy your cooperation and your silence. If Billy or the others ask, you're to tell them you showed us both a good time. Is that clear?"

"You don't want Lolita?" the woman repeated, pouting.

"Another time. Kit isn't feeling well. But I want the others to think we both enjoyed you. Do you understand?"

"*Si, senor,* I understand. You are very generous. When your *compadre* is feeling better, I will show you both the very best time. And I will tell no one what has passed between us."

Ryan tossed the coin at Lolita. She caught it handily and slipped it into her pocket. "Much obliged, Lolita," Ryan said, tipping his hat. "You can go through the back door if you'd like. Kit and I will sit here a while longer before joining the boys."

Lolita did not argue as she slipped through the curtained alcove and out the back door.

"Why?" Kit asked, looking stunned.

"I don't believe in making someone do something they don't want to do," Ryan said. "You're just a kid. There's plenty of time to do this."

"But . . . you didn't . . . didn't Lolita appeal to you?"

"Let's just say I wasn't in the mood," Ryan said. "This was a bad idea. I don't like anyone watching when I take a woman."

"Can we go now?" Kit asked, obviously uncomfortable with her surroundings.

"I reckon it's time." He stopped before her, hands on hips. "Just remember," he said by way of warning, "I don't plan on sticking around long. What if Lex doesn't come back? Who is going to protect you?"

Kit's chin shot upward. "I can take care of myself." She glanced at the rumpled bed and grimaced in distaste. "Let's get the hell out of here."

"How did it go?" Billy asked, grinning at Kit. "Did Ryan show you how it's done?"

"He probably still don't know. I bet his

little pecker shriveled up the minute Lolita spread her legs," Durango guffawed.

That remark produced a round of laughter that increased as Kit's face reddened.

"Knock it off," Ryan barked. "Kit did just fine for his first time."

The tittering continued as they mounted up and rode off.

CHAPTER 3

The situation was becoming desperate. Kit felt as if her world was disintegrating. She placed the blame for her distress squarely on Ryan Delaney's shoulders. The man was simply too attractive, too big, too male for her physical well-being. He disturbed her in ways she never thought possible. He made her aware of her femininity and put ideas in her head that she'd never before entertained, let alone imagined.

Ryan had only to give her one of his beguiling smiles and turn his sexy green-eyed gaze on her, and she all but melted into her boots. Kit knew how dangerous it was to remain with the Bartons. Fear of being unmasked rode her mercilessly. Without Lex to protect her, she risked being exposed as a woman, and that didn't bear thinking about. Even more worrisome was the peril Ryan presented to her very existence. Her attraction to him could become her undoing.

Kit soon realized it was imperative that she leave the Bartons. Nevertheless, she couldn't bring herself to leave until she learned what happened to Lex. She surprised the gang one day by announcing that she was going to Tombstone to inquire about Lex's fate.

"It's too dangerous," Billy said, dismissing her words with a careless wave of his hand.

"I need to know," Kit insisted. "No one paid much attention to me during the robbery. I can sneak in and out of town without anyone the wiser."

"No," Billy said firmly.

"I'll go with Kit," Ryan offered.

"I don't know," Billy contended. "Your face is as well known as ours."

"Not without the beard," Ryan claimed.

"I'm going no matter what you say," Kit said, firming her jaw. "Lex and I were together a long time. I need to know what's become of him."

"Clank will go," Billy decided. "He's the least likely to be recognized. What do you say, Clank?"

"Sure, boss. I'll leave as soon as I get my gear together. Two days to Tombstone, two days to return, and another to find out what happened to Lex. Look for me in five days. Anything you want while I'm in Tomb-stone?"

"Yeah," Durango growled. "Some decent whiskey."

"Chewin' tobaccy," Billy added. "Wouldn't mind a few tins of peaches, either. Buy them, Clank, don't steal them. Don't want no more trouble in Tombstone."

Clank grinned. "Don't worry, boss, I sure as hell don't want to end up like Lex."

Kit watched with trepidation as Clank packed supplies in his saddlebags and left camp. She had a bad feeling about Lex, and each day without word from him only added to her worries. Lex wasn't the best of brothers, but he was all she had.

Ryan felt a pang of pity for Kit. She looked so woebegone when Clank left that he wanted to put his arms around her and comfort her. But he knew where that would lead. Despite her rough speech and masculine clothing there was a fragile vulnerability about Kit that made him want to protect her. He admired her courage; it took an extraordinary woman to carry off a charade as long as Kit had. He'd never known a woman with Kit's remarkable fortitude. Not for the first time he wondered about her background, and he made a silent vow to find out where Kit had come from and exactly what she was to Lex Johnson.

"I wouldn't get my hopes up about Lex," Ryan said, placing an arm around Kit's shoulders. She stiffened and removed his arm.

"You think he's dead, don't you?" Kit asked.

"He was seriously wounded. Even if he recovers he's bound to be tried and convicted. I know Lex means a lot to you but I think you should expect the worst."

"I can take it," Kit said, swallowing the lump in her throat.

"Will you stay with the Bartons if Lex . . . doesn't make it back?"

"I hadn't thought that far into the future," Kit hedged.

"You're just a kid. You've got your whole life ahead of you. Get out while you can," Ryan advised. "You don't belong with hardened criminals."

"And you do?" Kit taunted.

"More than you." He wanted to say more but was wary. If he let on that he knew Kit was a woman, he might draw Billy's attention to her and that was too dangerous. It could lead to more trouble than he could handle by himself. The longer the Bartons thought Kit was a boy, the safer she'd be.

The following days passed slowly. Kit kept herself busy planning for her eventual departure. She intended to leave the camp disguised as a boy and arrive at her destination dressed as a woman. Lex had purchased women's clothing for her on one of his trips across the border, and she'd kept the articles hidden in a wooden crate beneath her boy's togs.

Kit felt confident that none of the Bartons would recognize her dressed as a woman. Confident enough to return to Tombstone as Kathryn O'Shay. Kitty, for short. Her mother's name had been O'Shay before she'd married Deke Johnson, and the few people that mattered had known she wasn't Deke's daughter. She reckoned few people in Tombstone would remember Deke, Rena, or Kitty after all this time.

Clank returned to camp five days after he'd ridden off. Billy spoke with him privately, away from the others. Kit was on pins and needles as she watched them converse in low tones. She was about to barge in on the conversation when Billy called her to join them. From the corner of her eye she saw Ryan fall into step behind her.

"The news ain't good, kid," Billy warned.

"I didn't expect it would be," Kit returned. Her gaze shifted to Clank. "Lex is dead, isn't he?"

"Sorry, kid. He died there in the street. Talked to the undertaker myself. Lex was shot through the heart and was probably dead before he hit the ground. He didn't suffer none, in case you're wonderin'."

Kit ducked her head and nodded. It wouldn't do to let the Bartons see her trembling lower lip. Men didn't cry.

"Much obliged, Clank," she said raggedly as she turned away. "Reckon I'll go on down to the stream and fetch some water."

"I'll come with you," Ryan offered.

"No! I want to be alone," she added more reasonably.

"Let the kid be," Billy said. "Him and Lex were best buddies. I reckon he ain't learned yet that it never pays to get too close to anyone in this business."

Kit could feel Ryan's gaze on her as she headed down to the stream. She didn't want him to follow. She didn't want anyone to see how frightened she was without Lex to protect her. From the time she was thirteen she'd had no one but Lex to rely upon. For six years Lex had kept her safe and seen that her belly was full when she was hungry.

70

Well, Kit acknowledged, as safe as Lex could make it given the reckless life they led. She had literally grown up in his careless custody. He had taught her to ride and shoot and cuss like a man. He had disguised her as a boy and taught her to survive in hostile territory when they joined up with the Bartons.

Kit reached the stream and sat down on a rock to contemplate her uncertain future. Lex was gone, and her entire life was suddenly without direction. She didn't want to cry over a scoundrel like Lex, but she couldn't help it. She realized that remaining with the Bartons now was tantamount to sitting on a powder keg in the middle of a forest fire. She knew instinctively that it was time to leave. She'd lay her plans, bide her time, and sneak away when the time was right. There were so many things to consider and so little time to do it. Her head spun with ideas, some quickly discarded as unworkable. If only she could trust Ryan. But she couldn't. He was an outlaw. He was no more trustworthy than the Bartons. Drying her eyes, Kit returned to camp, determined to leave her life of crime behind.

Ryan felt a curious relief when he saw Kit returning to camp. He wondered if she loved Lex Johnson and realized she must have. Few women would remain so long with a man they didn't love. Kit couldn't have been more than a child when she took up with Lex, he speculated. Dimly he wondered what would make a girl leave home and take up with an outlaw. It just didn't make sense. Unless . . .

Could it be? His senses reeled with sudden comprehension. Had the woman he sought been under his nose the whole time? That notion gave Ryan an entirely new perspective on the situation. One that bore investigating.

That night Ryan decided to question Kit more thoroughly about Lex and Kathryn. He waited until supper was over and she sought her bed before following her into the hut. He was determined to solve this mystery.

Ryan entered the hut and struck a match to the lantern. "Do you feel like talking?" he asked as he stood over her cot.

"No. I feel like sleeping."

He pulled the blanket off of her, grimacing in disgust when he saw she'd gone to bed in the same dirty clothes she'd worn all week. He'd meant to ask subtle questions, but her surly attitude sent his good intentions fleeing as he blurted out, "Your lover is dead. What are you going to do now?"

She jerked upright, her face a study of fear and anger. "What in the hell are you suggesting? Lex wasn't *that* kind of man. Neither am I."

"That's right, Kit, or whatever the hell your name is. You're not a man at all, are you? You're Lex's doxy."

Kit shot to her feet. Doubling her fists, she drew back her arm and aimed a blow at Ryan's stomach. To Ryan's surprise the blow connected, knocking him back on his heels. He doubled over and scowled up at her. "What in the hell was that for?"

Kit faced him pugnaciously. "I don't like what you just said."

"Why not, it's true, isn't it?"

"You must be pretty hard up to think I'm a woman."

"You must be pretty stupid to think I wouldn't know. Billy and the others are blind not to have noticed what's so obvious to me. I doubt they ever took a good look at you."

"You're wrong," Kit bluffed. "Go away and leave me alone." She turned back to the cot.

Ryan straightened, grasped her by the collar, and hauled her against him. "Wrong, am I? Would I do this if I was wrong?"

Holding both her wrists behind her with one hand and tilting her chin with the other, he crushed his mouth firmly against hers. Her lips were closed so tightly that he had to use his tongue to force them apart. His kiss was not gentle. It was meant to dominate, to prove that he recognized a woman when he saw one. And for the first few moments, it was precisely that kind of a kiss. But the moment Ryan felt her lips soften and part beneath his probing tongue and tasted the sweetness of her mouth, his own mouth gentled, becoming coaxing, almost teasing.

He drew upon her lips with an expertise that had earned him the name of Rogue Ryan. Then he felt her legs start to crumble beneath her, and his powerful arms tightened around her. Her angry gasp finally brought him back to his senses, and he released her mouth while he continued to hold her.

"Would I kiss you like that if you were a lad?" Ryan asked bluntly, watching the color slowly drain from her face.

She backed away from him, wiping her mouth on her grubby sleeve. "Maybe you're one of those men with perverted tastes," she said sullenly.

"Do you still insist you're a man?"

"It's the truth."

Ryan had tolerated all he was going to. If he had to strip her naked in order to get her to admit the truth, then so be it. Grasping her lapels, he peeled the jacket from her shoulders, then tore off her vest. Kit protested wildly but hadn't the strength to stop him. When he ripped away her shirt, sending buttons scattering, Kit seemed to deflate before his eyes.

The perfect twin mounds of her breasts popped free, their coral peaks stiffening in the cool night air. Her skin was creamy white, without a blemish of any kind. Her bones appeared almost fragile without the protection of her baggy clothing. Her arms were well-toned and rounded, her waist slim and seductively indented. Liquid heat surged through him as he stared at her breasts.

"Bastard!" Kit hissed.

Ryan's mouth felt like a desert. Never had he wanted to touch someone as badly as he wanted to touch Kit. Throwing caution to the wind, he reached out to caress a warm breast.

Kit wanted to melt on the spot. She had no muscles at all. His kiss had been sweet bliss, all hard pressure and heat, and more devastating than anything she'd ever experienced before. It had been her first kiss ever, and her lips still burned from the torrid heat of his mouth. His hard, callused fingers upon her bare flesh felt nothing like she imagined a man's touch would be. His caress was actually gentle, almost reverent, a far cry from what she knew of the way the Bartons treated women.

Kit knew Ryan was taking unspeakable liberties with her body but couldn't muster the energy to stop him. For the first time in her life she felt the surging power of raw desire, and it frightened her. When Ryan took both her breasts in his hands and flicked the nipples with his thumbs, Kit made a strangled sound deep in her throat and pushed his hands aside. This couldn't be happening. How could Ryan Delaney have seen through her disguise so quickly when the Bartons hadn't suspected after all these years? According to Ryan, he had known from the very beginning.

That thought frightened her. What had given her away? If what Ryan said was true, then obviously the Bartons had never really looked at her. Or did Ryan's intimate knowledge of women let him see what the Bartons so obviously missed?

Finally finding the willpower to put distance between herself and Ryan, Kit moved away, grabbed her shirt, and held it protectively in front of her. "Don't touch me!"

"Why? I know you like it. Lex has been gone a long time, you're probably aching for it about now. I want you, Kit. I'll keep your secret, if that's what's worrying you."

"You think I'm Lex's . . . Lex's . . ." She couldn't even say the word.

Ryan's dark brows angled upward. "Aren't you? You've been with Lex a long time, what am I to think? Give me another explanation if there is one."

Leery of Ryan's interest in Lex and Kathryn, Kit feared telling him the truth. Until she knew why he was asking personal questions, she didn't dare give him her real name.

"Assume what you want," Kit said, shrugging. "You will, anyway. But no matter what you think about me, that still doesn't excuse your despicable behavior. I can't count the times you have undressed in front of me, or embarrassed me in front of the Bartons. If you knew I was a woman you could have spared my feelings." Her voice rose to a shrill hiss. "You dragged me along to the cantina and insisted I be with a woman. Have you no shame, no compassion?"

Ryan had the decency to look embarrassed. "The Delaney brothers aren't known for their virtues. If I have compassion I keep it well hidden. I thought your charade damn amusing. It seemed improbable that the Bartons could remain ignorant of your sex when I saw through your disguise that first day."

"You thought I was Lex's doxy!" Kit charged.

"Prove that you're not," Ryan countered. "Tell me who you really are."

"I don't have to prove anything to you." She turned her back on him and slipped her arms into the shirt. "What are you going to do now?" she challenged, spinning around. "Are you going to tell the Bartons?"

Ryan gave her a slow grin. "Now why would I do that? I have no intention of sharing you with the others. I want you all to myself. Was Lex your only lover? Did you love him?"

The rage that had been building inside Kit exploded. "Go to hell!" she cried, flying at him with flailing arms. It really hurt to know that Ryan thought so little of her. How dare he imply that she would . . . would allow him liberties. It had been so easy to imagine Ryan as a respectable citizen, making her forget what and who he really was. She must have been crazy, or under some kind of spell to imagine herself half in love with an outlaw.

"Leave off, Kit," Ryan said, holding Kit at bay. "You can't hurt me."

"I sure as hell can try. You're a heartless bastard, Ryan Delaney! I might not know much about being a lady, but I do know you're no gentleman."

Not one to accept an insult gracefully, Ryan said, "Ha! You wouldn't know a gentleman if one came up and tipped his hat to you."

Kit had heard more than enough. Grabbing her jacket, she fled out the door and into the night. She ran toward the stream, losing herself amid the mesquite and tall cactus. She feared Ryan might try to follow, but a quick glance over her shoulder convinced her that he'd given up on her.

Tears were flowing freely down her cheeks when she finally ran out of breath and stopped to rest beside a boulder. She slid to the ground and rested her head against the rock, staring at the star-studded sky as she contemplated all the unhappiness she'd encountered in her short life. If Kit had ever been truly happy, she had no memory of it. Images of days spent with her mother came close, but living with Deke Johnson had taken all the pleasure from her life.

Her mother had married Deke shortly

after Kitty's birth, and Kitty had known no other father. But Deke had never acted like a father to her, or a loving husband to Rena. He'd been strict, demanding, and brutal, thinking nothing of beating both Rena and Kitty during his drunken rages. If Deke hadn't been killed so soon after Rena's death, Kitty knew she would have had to flee. Deke had made it clear that he expected Kitty to take her mother's place in his bed.

Though Lex was an outlaw, he'd always treated her like he would a sister, and for that she'd be forever grateful. Kitty didn't know what would have become of her had Lex not shown up after Deke's death. Not that she'd led such a great life with Lex, but at least he had protected her in his own clumsy fashion.

Kit gasped and looked up when a shadow fell over her. She hadn't heard Ryan approach and wondered how such a big man could move so stealthily. But there was a great deal she didn't know about Ryan Delaney.

"I'm sorry," Ryan said, easing down beside her. "I had no business accusing you of anything. I don't care what you and Lex were to one another, and furthermore it's none of my business. I have no right to criticize. My own reputation is far from pristine."

Kit stiffened when his arm came around her, but she made no protest when he pulled her against him. It had been a long time since anyone offered comfort. "I wanted to be alone."

"And I wanted to make sure you were all right. Have you thought about your future? How long do you intend to remain with the Bartons now that Lex isn't here to protect you?"

"I haven't decided yet. Perhaps I'll stay indefinitely," she hedged. "The boys don't expect too much from me, and I can be useful here."

"How?" Ryan scoffed. "Have you no regard for your own safety? One day the law will catch up to the gang and you'll be right in the middle. But the greater danger lies in having your disguise blown. Do you have any idea what will happen to you when the Bartons discover you're a woman? It *will* happen, you know."

Kit nodded. Indeed she did know, and had given it considerable thought. "I'm careful. Billy and the others are just too dumb to suspect anything. I've been a boy to them so long they can't see me as anything else. I've got some money saved, but not enough.

A couple more bank robberies, and I should be in a better position to leave."

"I've got some money. Let me help you."

Kit bristled with indignation. Accepting money from Ryan would put her in his debt. "No. I don't want your money."

She felt Ryan's arm tighten around her and wanted desperately to give in to the urgent need to seek the comfort of his big body, but she deliberately held herself aloof. Once she left the gang, and she knew she would, she wanted nothing more to do with outlaws. When she shed the trappings of Kit, she intended to leave her old life behind and never look back. And that meant forgetting Ryan Delaney.

"Look at me, Kit," Ryan said, tilting her chin upward. "I don't want to see you hurt by the Bartons."

She stared at him, mesmerized by the way his green eyes sparkled in the moonlight. Almost like jewels, so clear and bright, yet mysterious and seductive. There was more to Ryan Delaney than met the eye. More than he wanted her to know. When his mouth hovered close to hers, she was surprised to find herself leaning toward him, craving his kisses. At the last moment, before their lips touched, she tried to pull away, but Ryan wouldn't allow it.

She closed her eyes as he dragged her against him, holding her steady as he plundered her mouth. She couldn't withhold the sigh of pleasure that escaped her throat, nor the tiny shudder that slid down her spine. The kiss he'd given her inside the hut had only whetted her appetite for more. She knew instinctively that Ryan Delaney was very good at this, even though she had no guidelines to use for comparison. She started violently when she felt his hands on her body, beneath her shirt, caressing her breasts with his rough palms, and all thought of right or wrong deserted her.

She raised her arms to the hard curve of his shoulders as the heat of desire throbbed through her, settling low in her belly. She moaned in protest when his mouth left hers, then she felt his mouth on her breasts, laving her nipples with the rough pad of his tongue. He held her so close that she could feel the hard ridge of his sex pressing against the soft place between her thighs. She tensed, suddenly aware of what was going to happen next. If she let Ryan have her, she'd become the doxy he'd accused her of being, making her no better than Lolita or Carmen.

She pushed him away. "No, I can't do this."

She felt Ryan sag in disappointment. She was more than a little surprised when she realized he wasn't going to force her. The kind of men she knew wouldn't hesitate to take her against her will.

"It's your decision, Kit," Ryan said in a voice made hoarse with frustration. "I've never had to force a woman, and I don't intend to start now." He rose and held out his hand. "Come on. It's late. We both need to get some sleep."

Fearing his touch because of the way it made her feel, Kit rose without help and started back to the hut. Ryan fell into step beside her. She struggled to ignore him, wondering how in the hell she was going to be able to resist him. For the first time in her life she knew what it was to want a man. Ryan made her aware of her sexuality, of the inner urges of her body, of her need to be held and loved. But it wasn't just any man she wanted.

She wanted Ryan Delaney, a man she couldn't have if she intended to make a new life for herself. Once she left the Bartons she could never look back. Ryan was part of the life she wanted to forget.

A tiny voice inside her told her it wasn't going to be easy to forget Ryan Delaney.

■ ■ ■ ■

Ryan could tell Kit was disturbed, but he didn't know how to help her. If only Kit would confide in him. He was already half convinced that Kit was actually Kathryn, but he had no solid proof to carry back to Bert.

Out of concern for Kit, Ryan was delaying his own departure. Something about the little wildcat captivated and seduced him in the most elemental way. He wanted her. He'd wanted her from the first moment he'd known the grubby lad was a full-grown woman. He hated to think what it would do to Bert should Kathryn turn out to be Kit, a woman who'd lived and ridden with outlaws.

Ryan was sound asleep when Kit left the hut carrying the saddlebags she'd packed earlier. He thought nothing of her absence the following morning when he awakened and saw that her cot was empty. Kit often arose early and went down to the stream to wash before the others awakened. But when she didn't return in a reasonable time, Ryan knew something was amiss. Even Billy remarked on her absence as the day waned.

By late afternoon all four men spread out to find her. By nightfall the general consensus was that Kit had left for good.

"Good riddance," Clank said, pouring himself a cup of coffee. "The little bugger wasn't worth much, anyway."

"He might lead the law to our hideout," Durango contended.

"Not if he values his life," Billy growled menacingly.

Ryan said nothing. He was worried about Kit, and his concern surprised him. It wasn't his nature to become involved with a woman. Love them and leave them was his motto. He feared Kit couldn't manage on her own, that she'd get into trouble. Without money to sustain her, there was only one place a woman could go for work. He'd heard the story from more than one woman. Left on their own they usually ended up in a bawdy house, selling themselves to randy customers.

Kit's failure to return after several days made the Bartons jumpy and anxious. They kept looking over their shoulders, as if expecting the law to swoop down on them.

"I ain't gonna sit around and wonder if Kit set the law on us," Billy announced a few days after Kit had left. "We've sat on our butts worryin' about it long enough.

What say we ride to Nogales and hit the bank there?"

Clank and Durango gave enthusiastic agreement.

"Get your gear together, boys, we're ridin' out at dawn."

Billy's announcement gave Ryan the impetus he needed to set his own plan into motion. He was worried about Kit and realized he wouldn't rest easy until he found her. He hadn't followed immediately because he wanted to be on hand should she decide to return. But too much time had passed since her departure. He knew now she wasn't coming back, and it was time for him to move on. There was no way in hell he was going to help the Bartons rob a bank. If the law didn't kill him, his brothers would.

The night was hot and humid, and the tequila bottle was being passed freely around the campfire. The men drank until the bottle was empty, then one by one they staggered off to bed, filled with tequila and thoughts of their next job. Ryan waited in the hut until he was sure the outlaws were asleep, then he gathered his things and slipped out the door.

Hugging the ground, he worked his way to the lean-to, where his horse was stabled.

Working stealthily, he saddled his mount and tied on his bedroll. Then he threw the saddlebags over his horse's withers and led the animal away from camp. When no outcry was raised, he mounted and rode hell for leather toward the border.

CHAPTER 4

Kit found a desolate spot outside Tombstone where she felt it safe to make the transformation from Kit to Kitty O'Shay. She'd been riding for two days and felt reasonably certain that she hadn't been followed. Kitty couldn't decide if she was disappointed that Ryan hadn't cared enough to follow or relieved to be rid of him and his infernal questions. A little of both, she suspected.

Kitty washed thoroughly in a stream of water splashing down from between two rocks, scrubbing her riot of short curls until the blond locks glistened like gold in the sunlight. Then she quickly donned the chemise, petticoat, and dress that Lex had given her months ago. The clothing felt strange, so unlike the trousers she'd worn for so many years.

Kitty knew her hair was unfashionably short, but there wasn't much she could do about it until it grew out. Meanwhile, she covered her shorn locks with a bonnet and tied the ribbons beneath her chin. When she mounted and rode off she no longer resembled the lad known as Kit.

Kitty had thought long and hard about where she should settle. Tombstone, being the only town she knew, seemed the logical place to go. Of course she'd been in countless towns in Arizona, and even some in Texas with Lex and the Bartons. But most had been fast trips in and out, usually just one step ahead of the law. What made Tombstone attractive as a destination was the promise of a roof over her head. Lex had told her just recently that the small house Deke Johnson had owned was still unoccupied, that Lex hadn't sold or rented it. It probably was even more ramshackle than she remembered, but it was better than sleeping under the stars or paying money she could ill afford for lodgings.

The sun was setting on the sparse collection of buildings when Kitty turned her mount down Tombstone's main street. She headed to Mrs. Dooley's boardinghouse, hoping to buy a decent meal, her first in three days. She'd stopped in a small town just over the border two days ago and bought jerky and beans and hardtack. She hadn't built a fire, fearing human predators in this untamed territory, so she'd not even had coffee.

The boardinghouse was just as she remembered — maybe a little more run down and in need of a coat of paint, but still welcoming. She dismounted and knocked on the door. A small, round woman wearing spectacles answered on the second knock.

"Are you still serving meals, Mrs. Dooley?" Kitty asked. The delicious aroma of roasting meat wafted through the hallway, making her mouth water.

Mrs. Dooley looked at Kitty over the rim of her spectacles. "Do I know you, dear?"

"I'm Kitty O'Shay, Rena Johnson's daughter. I left Tombstone six years ago to live with . . . relatives. I was hoping you'd remember me."

The woman's brow cleared. "Of course I remember you. You disappeared quite suddenly after your stepfather's death. Come in, come in. What are you doing back in Tombstone, dear? Are you married?" She glanced through the open door. "Is your man with you?"

Kitty stepped into the foyer. "I ain't . . . I mean I'm not married, ma'am. My circumstances changed recently, and I returned to Tombstone to pick up my life. I was hoping

I could buy a meal. If my stepfather's house is still unoccupied, I plan to move in and look for work."

"Work? Oh, dear," Mrs. Dooley said, shaking her head and clucking her tongue. "Tombstone hasn't changed all that much since you left. Decent work is difficult to find for a woman. You should have stayed with your relatives until you found a husband."

"It wasn't possible," Kitty hedged. "I'll find something."

"I'm sure you will," Mrs. Dooley said doubtfully. "I was just setting the table. Dinner tonight is roast beef. I usually charge seventy-five cents."

Kitty knew the widow had a crippled son to support and needed every penny she could get. "I can pay," she said, digging in her pocket for the correct change.

"I wouldn't let you go away hungry even if you couldn't pay," Mrs. Dooley said, giving her a motherly pat. "Perhaps you'd like to eat in the kitchen before the others arrive. You can keep me company while I make dessert."

"I'd like that," Kitty said.

A few minutes later she was digging into roast beef, boiled potatoes, peas, and biscuits that melted in her mouth. She couldn't recall when she'd had such a delicious meal. Not since Rena was alive, surely. Her own cooking skills, consisting mainly of fixing beans, biscuits, and wild game, left much to be desired.

"Do you intend to live alone in Deke Johnson's house?" Mrs. Dooley asked as she put the finishing touches on the chocolate cake she'd just taken out of the oven.

"Do you know if it's still unoccupied?"

"Haven't heard any differently. Let's see, how many years has it been?"

"Six," Kitty said as she dipped a piece of bread into a drop of gravy remaining on her plate and popped it into her mouth.

"I passed by a month or so ago and noticed all the windows had been shot out. The house is in desperate need of attention. I fear it will be too much for you, dear. I have an empty room you could rent. Five dollars a week including breakfast and dinner."

Kitty considered the offer but decided against it. "I could save money by living in Deke's house," she said. "I'm sure it will be just fine with a little fixing up. This meal is delicious, Mrs. Dooley. I remember how much I enjoyed the food you sent over when Mama was sick."

"Your mother was a fine woman, dear,"

Mrs. Dooley said as she served Kitty a generous slice of cake. "Too good for the likes of Deke Johnson. The world is well rid of that one. I was relieved when your relatives came and took you away."

"I reckon I'd better get going," Kitty said after finishing the last bite of cake. "I'd like to inspect the house before dark."

"Let me know if I can help," Mrs. Dooley said as she dished the food up into serving bowls to place before her boarders.

There was still plenty of light left when Kitty turned her mount toward the little clapboard house in which she'd once lived. It sat forlorn and neglected at the end of a dusty street at the edge of town. Kitty hitched the horse's reins around the porch railing and cautiously mounted the rotting steps.

Except for having no windowpanes and being in dire need of a coat of paint, not much had changed about the dwelling. The front door stood ajar, and she pushed it inward. The hinges squeaked eerily in the pre-dusk silence. Something brushed against her leg, and she jumped in alarm. Her heartbeat returned to normal when she saw it was only a squirrel. She stepped inside and was immediately carried back to the past.

In her mind's eye she saw her mother, coughing her life away while her stepfather loomed menacingly over her. She saw herself cowering in a corner as Deke raised his fist and knocked her mother off her chair. Deke was drunk as usual. She recalled his bleary gaze on her, and she felt the pain of his blow as if it were actually happening. She shook her head to clear it of terrifying memories and searched the room for a lamp. She saw one, still filled with oil, sitting on the kitchen table, and she left the house to retrieve matches from her saddlebags.

She lugged the saddlebags inside, closed the door, and set them on the floor while she rummaged inside for matches. She found them easily, and within minutes the lamp's glow was dispelling the unfriendly shadows. What she found when she inspected the interior of the house was not comforting. Thick cobwebs were draped from the corners and hung from the ceiling. Broken glass from the windows littered the floor, and what furniture remained showed signs of vandalism.

The rusty iron cookstove still remained intact, however, and Kitty was thankful for that much. The scarred kitchen table and two unbroken chairs looked pitifully inadequate. The rocking chair her mother had sat in was relatively undamaged except for a broken slat or two. The cupboards were bare, and the curtains her mother had so lovingly made had long since rotted. Grass, dirt, animal nests, and tumbleweeds littered the floor.

Disheartened by the mess, Kitty walked into the bedroom and was somewhat cheered to see the bed intact and still covered with the quilt her mother had made long ago. A chest of drawers and a nightstand were also essentially undamaged, though thick with dust.

Before tackling the mess inside, Kitty returned outside and led her horse around to the back. She tethered the tan gelding to a tree, where he could forage on the patchy grass until she could buy him some feed. Then she unsaddled him and robbed him down with his blanket. After that chore was finished, she returned to the house and contemplated the chaos.

Exhaustion rode her, making her want to run and leave all this behind. Perhaps she was foolish to think she could restore a house that should have been torn down years ago. She was too tired to begin tonight, so she took her bedroll outside behind the house and curled up in her blanket. As she sought sleep, Kitty's thoughts wandered over dangerous territory.

Ryan.

His name produced an ache deep inside her. She recalled every minute detail of his handsome countenance and rugged body. His shiny dark hair and laughing green eyes were a study in contrasts. His features weren't classical, leaning more toward rugged and masculine. She recalled the bold slash of his brows and firm jaw. There was coiled strength in his powerful body, and supple grace in the long muscles of his thighs and legs.

With a pang of regret, Kitty wished she had let him make love to her. But the voice of reason deep inside her reminded her that sharing that special intimacy with Ryan would ultimately have led to disaster. She knew that once she made love with him, she'd never want to leave him.

Kitty wanted nothing more to do with outlaws, even handsome outlaws like Ryan Delaney. She knew she'd done the right thing by refusing him, but it had been the most difficult thing she'd ever done. Ryan had made her feel like a woman for the first time in her memory. He'd made her aware of her own sexuality and produced a wanting in her that went far beyond simple lust. She had never imagined herself feeling that way about any man. When sleep finally came, Kitty's dreams produced a restlessness in her she knew only Ryan could assuage.

Kitty attacked the house early the following morning after a visit to the store for cleaning supplies, a large apron, and enough food to last a week. The storekeeper had recently purchased the business from a previous owner and therefore didn't recognize her; he just asked if she was new in town. Before returning home to tackle the dirt and grime, she ate a hearty breakfast at the cafe.

Four days later the house was as clean as Kitty could make it, and the broken window glass had been replaced. She'd paid a handyman recommended by Mrs. Dooley to fix the windows and repair the furniture. The stove had been scoured and renewed with stove black until it gleamed. All this had taken a toll on her small hoard of money, and Kitty knew that she would have to look for a job before she ran out of cash.

Using more of her precious savings, Kitty purchased several changes of ready-made clothing and underwear, choosing serviceable materials with simple lines. Satisfied that she'd done all she could to make her home comfortable, Kitty set out early one morning to look for work.

She soon learned there was a dearth of job opportunities for women in Tombstone. The town was still an untamed outpost on the edge of a desert just a short distance north of the Mexican border. Its reputation for lawlessness was legendary, despite having a marshal to uphold law and order. Among the few businesses that lined the dust-clogged main street were a general store, bank, livery, hardware store, feed store, dress shop, drug emporium, blacksmith shop, cafe, combination barbershop and bath house, Chinese laundry, a doctor's office above the drug emporium, and Mrs. Dooley's boardinghouse and restaurant. Of course that didn't include the undertaker, five saloons, two more than when she'd lived in Tombstone, and three bawdy houses.

The storekeeper, Mr. Edmonds, had all the help he could use with his wife and two daughters. The dress shop was barely surviving in a town like Tombstone, where few women cared about fashion. The bank, hardware store, and feed store hired only male clerks. Doctor Harper's wife acted as his nurse, and the drug emporium didn't need any help.

Kitty even tried the Chinese laundry, but Lin Hue had a slew of relatives working for him. The blacksmith and livery and undertaker were out, and so were the bawdy houses. Kitty was promised work at the cafe when an opening became available, but that wasn't helping her out now.

That left the saloons. Kitty walked past each of the five saloons, trying to find the courage to go inside one of them. Disguised as a lad, she wouldn't hesitate, but everything had changed when she'd put on a dress. The Lucky Wheel was new and unfamiliar to her. It advertised home cooking in addition to strong drink and gambling. Kitty stood before the swinging doors, peering over the top. The saloon was empty but for the bartender, who was standing behind the bar polishing glasses for the evening trade. It was now or never, Kitty thought as she swung the doors wide and stepped inside.

The bartender looked up, frowning when he saw a woman standing uncertainly just inside the door. "Can I help you?"

"Are you the owner?"

"I'm Griff, the bartender. Chet Marlow owns the Lucky Wheel."

"Is Mr. Marlow in?"

"Is he expectin' you?"

"No. I'm looking for a job. Do you know if he's hiring?"

He regarded her from beneath bushy black brows. "You'll have to ask the boss. I don't do nothin' but pour drinks and evict rowdy customers. You'll find him in his office. That's it behind the bar. Knock on the door first."

Summoning her courage, Kitty marched up to the door Griff indicated and gave a sharp rap.

"Come in." The voice behind the door was muffled, but the command was distinct enough for Kitty to hear. She took a deep breath, opened the door, and stepped inside.

The man seated behind the desk was drinking coffee and pouring over a raft of papers. He let Kitty stand there a full minute before looking up. Then he did a double take, his gaze drifting appreciatively over her slim figure.

"What can I do for you, miss?"

Chet Marlow looked to be around forty years old. He had brown hair, brown eyes, and was dressed somewhat flamboyantly in a dark suit, white ruffled shirt, and red satin vest draped with a gold watchfob. He was clean shaven but wore long sideburns reaching nearly to his chin. Kitty shifted uncomfortably beneath his assessing glance.

"My name is Kitty O'Shay and I need work," Kitty said. "No one seems to be hiring, so I thought I would inquire here."

Marlow rubbed his chin, his expression thoughtful. "What can you do?"

His question startled Kitty. "I . . . I'm a hard worker."

"Can you dance?" Appalled by the suggestion, Kitty shook her head in vigorous denial. "What about singing? Do you sing?"

"N-no, I don't sing or dance, but I can wait tables and scrub floors, if nothing else is available."

"I have a Mexican kid who comes in and cleans up every morning. I hate to turn a looker like you down, though. I can use another hostess. Take off your bonnet."

"What?"

"Take off your bonnet. My customers prefer blonds, and I can't see the color of your hair with it covered like that."

Kitty hesitated, then she did as she was told. He'd have to see it sooner or later, she decided. She wasn't prepared for Marlow's startled look when her mop of blond, earlobe-length curls tumbled from beneath her bonnet.

"What in the hell have you done to your hair?"

Kitty's jaw jutted out pugnaciously. "I cut it. What difference does it make?"

Marlow regarded her through narrowed eyes, and Kitty thought he was going to tell her he'd changed his mind. She was more than a little surprised when he said, "It's just different enough to intrigue my customers. Well, will the job of hostess suit you?"

Kitty had no idea what the job entailed and didn't particularly like the sound of it. Her jaw firm, she said, "I ain't no whore."

"I don't hire whores," Marlow retorted, startled by her coarse speech. "I hire hostesses. What the girls do in their spare time is their business. I don't engage in upstairs trade, if you get my meaning. There are sufficient sporting houses in town to satisfy the male population of Tombstone. My hostesses wait tables, coax the customers into buying drinks, and serve them. Some sing and dance. I deal strictly in gambling, drinking, and musical entertainment. And I run a fine restaurant for my male customers."

"In that case I'll take the job, Mr. Marlow," Kitty said.

"Don't you want to know what the job pays?"

Kitty flushed. "Of course. I assume you pay fair wages."

"The wages are fair but not generous. But

the tips more than make up for it. Your hours will be from six in the evening until two in the morning with your evening meal provided. How does five dollars a week sound?"

"Sounds fair," Kitty said, thinking of all the money the Bartons took in a single bank robbery and wasted in places like this.

She'd never gotten the same share of the loot as the others because she'd never actually participated in the robberies, but she'd always gotten something. Lex had spent his money on liquor, gambling, and women, but she'd managed to hang on to most of hers. Unfortunately it wouldn't last long if she didn't have a steady income coming in.

"When do you want me to start?"

"Molly quit last week to get married, so I'm short a hostess. Can you start tonight? Do you need a place to stay? Some of the girls rent rooms above stairs."

"No," Kitty said. "I'm living in a small house my stepfather owned. I'll be here at six o'clock, Mr. Marlow. You won't be sorry you hired me."

Kitty left Marlow's office, sailing past Griff, who was polishing the bar. "Did you get the job, miss?"

"Yes, thank you, Mr. Griff. I start tonight."

"Folks around here call me Griff."

"I'm Kitty O'Shay. Please call me Kitty. See you tonight, Griff."

Kitty had just reached the door when Marlow came out of the office and hailed her. "Oh, Kitty, I forgot to tell you, the dress you're wearing will never do. I keep a variety of gowns on hand for my hostesses. Come a little early and pick out something that fits. Ask one of the other girls to show you where to find them."

As she walked home, Kitty wondered what hostesses were expected to wear. If it was one of those skimpy costumes she'd sccn girls wear in some of the saloons she'd visited with Lex, she didn't think she could do it.

Kitty stared at herself in the mirror. A buxom blond named Nellie had introduced herself and taken her to a small dressing room upon her arrival at the saloon that evening. When shown the gowns available to her, Kitty felt immediate relief. Though most gowns were in vibrant shades of red, green, scarlet, and blue, with rather immodest necklines, they at least covered her ankles. She'd chosen a gown in red satin that didn't appear too provocative, but when she donned it and looked at herself in the mirror, she was astounded by the sexuality of the woman staring back at her. She knew without a doubt that should any of the Bartons come into the saloon they'd never recognize her.

She wasn't sure about Ryan Delaney, though. A man who had seen through her disguise at first glance surely would know her dressed in woman's garb.

"Are you ready?" Nellie asked, popping her head through the door.

"All ready. How do I look?" Kitty asked, spinning around for Nellie's benefit.

"Like that dress was made for you," Nellie said. "You'll be a big hit with the customers. Just remember to smile and keep your backside protected. Turn your back on a customer and before long your bruises will wear bruises."

"I'll remember," Kitty promised. She took a deep breath and nearly popped out of her bodice. "And I won't do that again, either," she said in dismay as she pulled the bodice up to a decent level. "Let's go."

That first night was an eye-opener for Kitty. She'd seen how the Bartons had behaved in saloons, but she'd never imagined she'd be the recipient of so many coarse jokes or unwelcome groping. By the time she went off duty at two the next morning, she'd learned that the men who frequented saloons had little respect for women. She'd done her best to fend off unwanted advances but hadn't been able to keep from being mauled a time or two when her hands were occupied. She imagined she'd learn to do better as time went by.

The next evening a drunken customer put his hand down the front of Kitty's dress, and she hauled off and smacked him. He fell backward, upsetting a table, surprise written all over his face. Then she shocked both the customers and her coworkers by placing her hands on her hips and spitting out a string of shocking cuss words. She ended by saying, "Piss off, you drunken polecat. Touch me again and I'll kick you in the balls so hard you'll never bother a woman again." She lifted her gaze to include every male customer in the room. "And that goes for the rest of you damn buggers."

Silence fell over the room like a blanket of smoke, so thick it could be cut with a knife. Someone in the back of the saloon tittered nervously. Then little by little the noise level was restored as the men turned back to their drinking and gambling.

"Weren't you being a little rough, honey?" Nellie asked, sidling up beside her. "The boss wants to see you in his office. He heard you, and he doesn't look too pleased."

Kitty glanced toward the office and saw Marlow beckoning to her. She could tell that spouting off like she had didn't endear her to the boss, but what was she supposed to do? Let the man maul her? She knew she was in for a tongue lashing when Marlow's expression turned as dark as a thunder-cloud.

"What in the hell was that all about, Kitty?" he asked the moment she was inside the office.

"The man insulted me," Kitty said with a calmness she was far from feeling.

"Cussing him out was bad enough. Did you have to hit him, too? You should have told me or Griff and let us take care of it."

"I'm sorry, I'm used to taking care of myself."

"Where did you learn to use that kind of language?"

Kitty flushed. She was so accustomed to expressing herself in the language used by the outlaws that it was difficult to remember to monitor her speech. When she was angry the coarse words flowed naturally. Kitty despaired of ever becoming an honest to God lady.

"I reckon I listened to my brothers when I wasn't supposed to," she lied.

"The customers like women who at least

pretend they're ladies," Marlow said. "Try to contain your anger from now on, Kitty. The next time a customer bothers you, come to me with your problem. If I hear another outburst like that I'll have to let you go. It's bad enough having to contend with rowdy men. You'll soon learn that being pawed comes with the territory around here. All the girls put up with a certain amount of it. Some even like it."

Kitty's fists clenched at her sides. Defending herself had always been second nature with her. If she'd acted like a sissy with the Bartons they would have become suspicious. But getting pawed was something she'd never get used to or enjoy. "I'll try to remember, Mr. Marlow," she said tersely.

"Good girl. Now go back out there and smile."

Ryan rode across the border into Arizona two days after he'd left the Bartons and at least ten days behind Kit. He'd tried to put himself in Kit's position while pondering the places she might have gone. She could have even ridden into Texas or New Mexico if she really wanted to lose herself, he considered. But the more he thought about it, the more convinced he became that she would go to a place she knew well, like

Tombstone. He figured she had some money or she wouldn't have left in the first place. But how much did she have? Surely not enough to support herself for long.

Purple shadows hovered over the dusty streets and collection of adobe and wooden buildings as Ryan rode into Tombstone. With his beard shaved off he hoped he wouldn't be identified as one of the men riding with the Bartons the day the bank was robbed. He was counting on it, in fact.

Ryan's first stop was the Penny Ante Saloon. His throat was parched, and he needed a beer to quench his thirst. The room was crowded with noisy, rowdy customers, and Ryan finished his beer quickly, then headed over to the barbershop and bathhouse for a desperately needed bath, shave, and haircut. An hour later he walked out feeling like a new man, freshly barbered and shaved and wearing clean clothing. He dropped off his dirty clothing at the Chinese laundry and went in search of a meal.

The cafe was crowded and didn't look like much to Ryan, who was accustomed to Cookie's superior cooking back home in Dry Gulch. He spotted the Lucky Wheel saloon across the street and saw that they advertised home cooked meals along with their usual fare of gambling and drinking.

He crossed the road and entered through the swinging doors. He spied an empty table and quickly claimed it.

A plump blond came over, and he asked for a menu. She produced one, and after perusing it, he ordered beefsteak rare, mashed potatoes, a plate of beans on the side, and beer. While he waited for his meal to arrive he sipped on the beer and gazed idly around him. His first desultory sweep of the room provided nothing to pique his interest so he sat back, pulled his hat over his face, and dozed while he waited for his meal to arrive.

Kitty was serving a customer across the room when Nellie came up to her and handed her a tray. "Take this to the customer sitting at the corner table, will you, Kitty?" she asked. "I have another order that needs to be served right away."

Kitty accepted the tray from Nellie. "Sure is busy tonight."

"Yeah, I'll be glad to get off my feet. Haven't had a chance to sit down a minute since I came in at six. I'm glad I decided to go to bed alone tonight," she said, poking Kitty in the ribs, "if you catch my meaning."

Kitty knew exactly what Nellie meant. She knew for a fact that she was the only hostess who didn't earn extra money by sleeping with customers. Lord knows she'd had plenty of chances in the several days she'd worked at the Lucky Wheel.

Kitty balanced the tray in front of her as she approached the table, her mind drifting aimlessly as she thought about her growing aversion to working at the Lucky Wheel and what she was going to do about it. So far no alternative had presented itself.

She reached the table and set the tray down. She spared the customer a fleeting glance, noting that his hat was pulled down over his eyes and he appeared to be sleeping. She cleared her throat and said, "Your food is here, sir."

Ryan recognized her voice before he opened his eyes and saw her. He lifted his head and pushed his hat back from his forehead. His mouth dropped open, shocked to the core at the sight of the strikingly beautiful woman with a shape to die for who stood before him. She was nicely rounded and enticingly arrayed in red satin. Her riot of short curls was tied back with a ribbon, which didn't quite succeed in keeping the unruly tresses from curling around her elfin face. As often as he'd thought about Kit in the past few weeks, he'd never visualized her like this. She was alluringly lovely. A seductive vision to haunt a man's dream. And she worked in a saloon!

"My God, it's *you!*" Ryan said when he finally found his tongue. "What in the hell are you doing in a place like this?"

Kit looked as if she wanted to faint. Her face drained of all color as his name trembled from her bloodless lips. "Ryan. I . . . I . . . what are *you* doing here?"

"Looking for you. But this is the last place I expected to find you. Were you working in a saloon when you hooked up with Lex?"

Kitty's mouth turned downward. "Think what you want," she hissed. "I never expected to see you again. When I left the Bartons I cut all ties with the likes of men like you. Go away, Ryan." She turned away.

He grasped her wrist. "Oh, no, you don't. We need to talk. What time do you get off work?"

"I have nothing to say to you." She tried to pull free, but she was too firmly in his grip. "Dammit, Ryan, let me go!"

"Is this man bothering you, Miss Kitty?"

Ryan glared at the dapper man addressing him. "Who in the hell are you?"

"The owner of this establishment. I suggest you let Miss Kitty go. No rough stuff is allowed in the Lucky Wheel. You can finish your meal if you behave yourself. The entertainment you seek can be found at any of the bawdy houses in town."

Reluctantly Ryan released Kitty. "Miss . . . Kitty and I are old acquaintances. I wouldn't hurt her for the world."

Marlow stared at him. "You'd better not." Then he turned on his heel and walked off. Kitty started to follow.

"I meant what I said, Kitty," Ryan called. "We need to talk. I'll wait for you."

"You'll wait forever," Kitty said, flouncing off. "I don't consort with outlaws."

CHAPTER 5

Ryan hung around the saloon until he could no longer stand the sight of strange men panting after Kit . . . no, Kitty. She called herself Kitty now. He'd have to remember that. Regardless of what she called herself, Ryan found it difficult to watch Kitty dodging every drunken man who attempted to pinch and prod her despite her best efforts to elude their groping hands.

Did she enjoy being groped? He didn't like to think so. The thought of men using her like a whore sent rage seething through him. He had almost disabused himself of the notion that Kitty had been Lex's doxy. It seemed logical to him now that Kitty was actually Kathryn, Lex's stepsister, the very woman he'd been searching for. The idea that Lex had taken young Kathryn with him after Deke Johnson's death made sense. But unless Kitty confirmed her identity, he was no better off than he had been when he began his search.

In some ways he was worse off. The "lad" Kit had tempted and seduced him from the moment he'd seen through her disguise. He couldn't look at her without wanting her. He'd seen how beautiful she was beneath the dirt and grime, but he had no idea how alluring she'd look dressed in skirt and petticoats. Her skin was creamy and flawless, and her hair, shiny clean now, put the sun to shame. Even short, her hair was lovely; a perfect frame for her unblemished features.

Ryan tried to keep from staring at Kitty's full breasts, but each time she bent to serve a mug of beer to a customer they nearly spilled out of her dress. How could he not look? He wasn't the only man in the room staring at her rounded breasts, and it took all the strength he possessed to keep from flinging her over his shoulder and carrying her away before she made more of a spectacle of herself. But who was he to dictate to the feisty little outlaw? Perhaps he was all wrong about Kitty being Kathryn and she actually enjoyed this kind of life.

The little spitfire was just begging for trouble, Ryan decided, and he was just the man to give it to her. He couldn't help himself. Bedding Kitty suddenly became Rogue Ryan's mission in life. Kit, Kitty,

Kathryn. Doxy or innocent. It made no difference. Ryan couldn't recall when he'd wanted a woman as badly as he did Kitty. Nor could he remember when a woman had gotten under his skin so quickly. Sitting back and watching Kitty was driving Ryan crazy, so he paid his bill and left. He'd learned the location of Deke Johnson's old house from his investigation during his previous visit to Tombstone and rode off in that direction. Even in the dark Ryan could tell that the house had undergone a slight transformation, and he supposed Kitty was responsible. It still needed a lot of work, but he saw immediately that the windows had been repaired since he'd last seen the house.

A single lamp shone through a front window, a beacon in the darkness to welcome Kitty home, he supposed. Ryan led his horse around to the back and hobbled him beside Kitty's mount, within easy reach of a pile of tender hay. Then he turned his attention to the house. He tried the back door and found it locked. He didn't bother attempting to enter by the front door, for he knew it would be locked, too. When he found the back windows latched, he walked around to the side. Luck was with him. He discovered that the bedroom window was closed but not properly locked because of a broken latch that hadn't been repaired correctly. He eased the window open and climbed inside.

Kitty was exhausted when she left the saloon. Marshal Earp was making his rounds and offered to walk her home. Kitty eagerly accepted, for she fully expected Ryan to be waiting outside the saloon for her and hoped he would go away when he saw the marshal. Truth to tell, she hoped he was smart enough to maintain a low profile in Tombstone. Lawmen had long memories, and she knew they would remember both the bank robbery and the Bartons. She nearly collapsed in relief when Ryan was nowhere in sight.

Kitty tried to convince herself she didn't care what happened to the outlaw, that her life would be less complicated without him and his kind, but her heart refused to listen. Something about Ryan Delaney spoke to her on a profound emotional level she wasn't prepared to deal with. Maybe she would never be.

Kitty thanked Marshal Earp for his escort when they reached her house. He tipped his hat politely and left her standing at her door. Kitty removed the key from her pocket, unlocked the door, and stepped inside, thankful that she'd had the foresight to light a lamp before leaving for the evening. She picked up the lamp and stood in the middle of the room, trying to determine what was amiss. A prickling sensation nipped at the back of her neck, a shiver ran down her spine, and all her senses tingled with awareness.

Her gaze probed the darkness beyond the circle of light provided by the lamp, but she saw nothing, heard nothing. Yet she couldn't shake the feeling that she wasn't alone. Dismissing her unwarranted fears, she walked into the bedroom and set the lamp down on the nightstand. Then she poured water from the pitcher into the bowl so she could wash. After another quick look around, she removed her shoes, stockings, dress, petticoats, and chemise, and splashed water on her face, neck, and arms. She would have continued with her ablutions, but the prickling along her spine became more pronounced.

She heard a noise somewhere in the dark shadows of the room and whirled away from the washstand, clutching the towel to her chest. She heard a strangled sound, the kind someone in pain might make. She reached for the loaded gun she kept in the nightstand drawer and was stunned to find it missing. She spit out a curse.

"Are you looking for this?"

Ryan stepped from the shadows into the halo of light, so close she could smell his special scent of leather and musk. Her gun was resting in the palm of his hand. He offered it to her, and she snatched it away.

"I thought you might shoot first and ask questions later, so I took the liberty of unloading it," Ryan said. He opened his other hand, revealing six bullets from the empty chambers. He tossed them carelessly on the floor.

"Damn you!" Kitty hissed. "How dare you break into my home. I told you we have nothing to talk about. I want to forget I ever consorted with outlaws like you and the Bartons. I've had enough of outlaws to last a lifetime."

Ryan's gaze traveled down the length of her naked body, and he felt an uncomfortable tightness in his groin. He stared at her legs. Long, slim, and shapely, he couldn't think beyond that soft place at the juncture of those enticing limbs. His mouth went dry, and he swallowed convulsively. He cleared his throat and lifted his gaze to her face, trying to concentrate on anything except his throbbing erection.

"I have this gut feeling you're hiding

something from me, Kitty. What is it?"

"If you insist on having this conversation, turn around so I can make myself decent," Kitty said.

"There's no need, I've already seen you."

Kitty paled. "Liar!"

"I followed you down to the stream one night. You thought I'd gone to bed. I watched you shed your clothes. You have a lovely body, Kitty."

"What in the hell kind of man are you, sneaking around and spying on a woman like that?"

"A curious one," Ryan said without remorse. "I knew you were no lad and wanted to see for myself what lay beneath those filthy rags you wore. You're far too beautiful to be masquerading as a boy."

"I don't care what you saw then," Kitty sputtered. "Turn your head."

He gave her a beguiling smile. "Very well. Make yourself decent, though I can't deny I prefer you this way."

"You would," Kitty spat as she reached for her nightgown. When Ryan turned around, she quickly pulled the voluminous white gown over her head. It settled comfortably around her bare toes.

"You can look now."

Ryan turned and burst out laughing.

"How prim and proper, Kitty." He ambled over to the bed and sat down. "You may as well join me, this may take a while."

Kitty gave him a wary look and perched as far away from him as possible in the limited space. "Say what you've come to say and get out."

"It's not that easy. I'm not sure where to start."

"The beginning would be a good place. Make it quick. I'm exhausted. I've been on my feet since six last evening. It's now past two in the morning."

"Kit . . . Kitty, I think the best place to start is by telling you I'm not an outlaw. I've never been an outlaw. I'm a rancher from Montana. I have two brothers who will kill me when they learn what I've been up to."

"You must think me a gullible nitwit, Ryan Delaney. Have you forgotten that bank robbery you participated in? In my books that makes you an outlaw."

"Contrary to what you believe, I wasn't in Tombstone that day to rob a bank," Ryan explained. "The bank clerk mistook me for an outlaw whose picture hung on the bank wall. I'll admit there was a vague resemblance, but I repeat, I'm not an outlaw. I was in the bank that day to withdraw money from my account."

"That doesn't make sense," Kitty charged. "Why did you ask to join the Bartons if you were an innocent bystander?"

"Because of Lex Johnson."

"Lex? What has Lex got to do with anything? I never did understand why you were so damn interested in Lex and his family."

"Your language, Kitty, is appalling. But we'll talk about that later. Just tell me why you were so close-mouthed about your lover."

Kitty leaped to her feet. "You don't know a damn thing about me! I'm not a whore. Lex was my . . ."

"Your what?" Ryan prodded. One way or another he was going to get the truth from her.

"Why do you care?"

"I don't give a damn about Lex Johnson, but I've spent months looking for his stepsister. I'd hoped Lex could tell me where to find Kathryn. She disappeared six years ago. I heard that Lex rode with the Bartons, and when they robbed the bank I happened to walk into, it seemed as if fate had given me the opportunity I was looking for. Unfortunately, I hadn't counted on Lex getting killed. When I learned that Kit and Lex were as close as brothers, I hoped Kit could tell

123

me what I wanted to know. I knew I was courting danger when I asked to join the gang, but I couldn't let a dying man down."

Kitty's face was a mask of confusion. "A dying man? You're talking in riddles. What do you want with Kathryn?"

"Are *you* Kathryn?" Ryan asked bluntly. "I've suspected it for some time now. There's no use denying it. Either you're Lex's stepsister or his doxy. There are no other explanations for disguising yourself as a lad and traveling with Lex and the gang. I can understand his wanting to protect you if you're his kin, but I can also accept his reason for wanting to keep you for himself if you were his doxy."

"Why are you looking for Kathryn?" Kitty asked warily.

Ryan tried to concentrate on her question, but her full lips kept distracting him. They were pursed in thought, and he remembered how sweet they had tasted when he'd kissed them. He wondered what she would do if he pulled her into his arms and kissed her until her mouth softened and opened to him. He wanted to feel her breasts pressed against his chest, wanted to settle himself in the cradle of her soft white thighs. Wanted to thrust his aching sex into that hot moist place between her legs.

"Ryan, I asked you a question."

Ryan forced his mind away from that thought and tried to concentrate on the conversation at hand. It took a moment to recall her question and another before he felt focused enough to answer.

"I'm simply doing a dying man a favor," he explained. "Kathryn's biological father is looking for her. Bert Lowry has been actively searching for Kathryn since receiving a letter from a woman named Rena. Rena's written confession was the first he knew he'd had a daughter with Rena from a long ago relationship. Rena said she hadn't long to live and asked Bert to come and get his daughter. She didn't trust Deke Johnson to raise the girl after she was gone. When Bert sent someone to Tombstone to find Kathryn she was gone, and no one seemed to know where."

Kitty's mouth fell open, and her eyes widened with dismay. "You're lying."

"Why would I lie? Are you ready to admit that you're Kathryn Lowry?"

Kitty's chin rose stubbornly. "I'm Kitty O'Shay."

"O'Shay," Ryan repeated. "Rena's was O'Shay. She was your mother, wasn't she?"

"Damn you! Who gave you permission to pry into my life?"

"So you *are* Kathryn Lowry."

"I don't know if I am or not," Kitty responded. "Mama never told me my father's name. I just knew it wasn't Deke Johnson. She tried to tell me a few days before she died but by then she was too far gone."

"Weren't you even curious before that?" Ryan questioned.

"No!" she said vehemently, surprising Ryan. "I wanted nothing to do with the man who got my mother pregnant and then left her to fend for herself. She married Deke because she had no one to turn to after her aunt turned her out. It was the worst mistake of her life. She would have had a better life scrubbing floors for a living.

"Deke drank and gambled away every cent he earned at the livery where he worked whenever he was sober. Mama took in laundry to keep food on the table. Deke beat my mother during his drunken rages, then he turned his heavy hand on me." She flushed and looked away. "After Mama died he wanted more from me than I was willing to give. He said I was full grown enough to take my mother's place in his bed. I was glad when Deke was killed!" she cried. "Even if it meant having to survive on my own. I'll never forgive my real father for putting Mama and me through years of hell."

Ryan's heart went out to Kitty when she began to sob into her hands, as if the memories were more than she could bear.

"Don't cry," Ryan urged. He lifted her chin and brushed away her tears with his thumbs. The innocent gesture led to something more intimate as he caressed her smooth cheek with his knuckles.

"Tell me about Lex," Ryan probed. "What was he to you? You weren't blood kin, your relationship could have been . . . of an intimate nature."

Kitty bristled angrily. "I wasn't his doxy, if that's what you're getting at. Lex always treated me like his little sister. I didn't know him all that well because he left home when I was a small child. He took me away when he found me alone after Deke died. He wasn't the best of brothers but he protected me like he was blood kin."

"I wouldn't exactly call bringing you to live with outlaws protecting you. I shudder to think what could have happened had any of the Bartons discovered you were a woman. Do you think Lex would have been able to protect you against so many?"

Kitty shrugged. "I tried not to think about it. Besides, Lex and I were going to leave just as soon as he saved enough money. He was going to take me back home, fix up Deke's house, and settle me in Tombstone until I found a husband. Unfortunately Lex wasn't very good at saving money. I hoarded what little I had, that's how I was able to leave when I did. Were the Bartons angry at my sudden disappearance?"

"You might say that. They're probably livid now. I left much in the same way you did. I waited several days for you to return, and when you didn't I decided to follow."

"How did you know to look for me in Tombstone?"

"Just a hunch. Where else would you go? I'm offering you the opportunity to put this life and all the hardships behind you, Kitty. I'm taking you to Tucson to meet your father. Bert is anxious to see his only daughter before he dies."

Kitty stared at him in consternation. He looked dark, dangerous, and more outlaw than rancher.

"I ain't going any place with you, Ryan Delaney. Bert Lowry can go to hell for all I care," she said irreverently. "I've never cared to know who my father was, and I'll always hate him for what he did to my mother. I don't want to know him. Besides, I don't believe half of what you've told me. Especially that part about being mistaken for an outlaw at the bank the Bartons robbed. It's just too much of a coincidence."

Kitty saw a glint in his eye as he gave her a bemused grin . . . a slash of white against his dark skin. "I don't believe you're strong enough to defy me," Ryan challenged. "I'm not returning to Tucson without you, even if I have to use force to get you there."

"Don't threaten me, Ryan. I don't frighten easily," Kitty said with asperity. "I think you'd better leave now. I've got another hard day ahead of me tomorrow. Some of us have to work for a living."

"Kitty, listen to reason," Ryan cajoled. "What is it going to hurt to see your father? The man is dying. Grant him his last wish. He had no children with his wife, only a stepdaughter he's fond of. How can you be so heartless?"

"I learned life's lesson well," Kitty said bluntly.

"So did I," Ryan admitted. "But I can still feel compassion for a dying old man."

Kitty gave a snort of disgust. "If you're a wealthy rancher like you said, you know nothing about hardship, or hunger, or disillusionment. You probably have a wife and several children waiting for you at home."

Ryan's face hardened, erasing all traces of the laughing, carefree man she'd thought him to be. She sensed something deep and disturbing in his past, something dark lurking beneath his roguish smile.

"I have no wife," he said in a voice that left no room for doubt. "Marriage isn't for me. Women have their uses. I like them excessively and enjoy their company. But I don't trust them. Pierce and Chad found two good women and seem to be managing fine, but it wasn't easy for them. They went through hell. I don't intend to make that mistake."

Kitty wondered what woman had soured Ryan on marriage. He couldn't be thirty yet, too young to be so bitter.

"Were you disappointed in love?" Kitty ventured.

"No. It's more of a family thing. Pierce almost lost his life because of a woman's lies. Chad left home because he couldn't live with the mistaken notion that he had caused the death of several people. A woman's lies drove him from his home. It's a wonder either of my brothers found love at all, considering their aversion to marriage. Our own mother left us for another man when we were still young enough to need a mother. I'm made of stronger stuff than my brothers. I don't need a wife. The world is full of beautiful, available women."

"And I won't make the mistake of accepting a father I've learned to hate."

"You don't even know him," Ryan argued.

"I don't want to."

"I'm not leaving here until you agree to accompany me to Tucson."

She rose abruptly, glaring down at him. "I wish you a pleasant night, Ryan, or what's left of it. I'm going to bed. You can let yourself out."

Ryan grasped her arm, pulling her down onto his lap. She felt the determination in every sinew, muscle, and bone in his hard body. Frustrated with him and herself, and above all with her weakness where this man was concerned, Kitty opened her mouth to give him the sharp edge of her tongue.

Obviously it was all the invitation Ryan needed, for he seized her half-parted lips in a hard, demanding kiss, his tongue gliding inside, teasing the soft inner surfaces until dizziness claimed her and her breath came in short little gasps.

The kiss was everything Kitty remembered, had dreamed of, had longed for. She melted against him, overwhelmed by sensations, drowning in a maelstrom of desire. Before Ryan entered her life she'd known nothing of passion or wanting. She'd existed in a sexless limbo, fearing to think or look like a woman. She'd suppressed all female tendencies, forsaken all womanly trappings.

Until Ryan.

His mouth was driving her mad. She felt his lips against her jaw, felt the moistness of his rough tongue dart along the rim of her ear. She didn't realize he had unbuttoned her nightgown until she felt his lips nipping a burning path down her neck to her bare shoulder. Then she felt his mouth settle over her breast and suckle her nipple. She gave a startled cry as a wave of unexpected pleasure shot through her.

"Ryan . . . no . . ."

"Kitty, don't stop me."

He lowered his head and sought her other breast, his tongue encircling her nipple, making it pucker and throb. A soft sigh escaped her lips as the erotic sensations he created seemed to settle low in her belly. She felt his hand beneath the hem of her nightgown, raising it upward along her calf, her knee, resting briefly on the high curve of her thigh. A burning beneath his hand created a fire within her that blazed out of control.

She shuddered and sighed. He caught her sigh in his mouth and gave it back to her. She moaned, assailed by disturbing feelings that dissolved the hard knot of anger she'd felt upon finding Ryan inside her house. She kissed him back with innocent enthusiasm, savoring his unique scent, blissfully unaware where this was leading.

"Oh, woman, what in hell am I going to do with you?" Ryan said on a sigh. "I want you so damn bad I ache." He dragged her closer, one callused hand settling between her legs. He felt her stiffen but gentled her with another kiss as his fingers tangled in the moist curls protecting her womanhood. He found her slick entrance and eased a finger inside her.

She was hot and tight and wet. Too tight. He eased another finger beside the first, stretching gently. He felt her shift as if in discomfort and realized with dismaying certainty that Kitty couldn't have been anyone's doxy. She was too damn small and untried to have been sexually active. Ignoring her murmur of protest, he slid his fingers deeper, until they butted up against the barrier of her maidenhead. He removed his hand, broke off the kiss, and searched her face.

"You're a damn virgin." He made it sound like an insult.

"What made you think I wasn't?" Kitty challenged.

"The kind of life you led, for one thing.

As I said before, you and Lex weren't blood relatives."

"You have a dirty mind, Ryan Delaney."

He gave her a sexually charged grin. "How determined are you to remain a virgin?"

His statement must have left her speechless, for her mouth opened and shut without uttering a word.

"I've made no secret about wanting to make love to you, Kitty. I'm damn near ready to explode. The only thing holding me back now is Bert Lowry. I don't know what he'd say were he to learn I made love to his daughter."

"The subject is moot, Bert Lowry and I will never meet."

"You're wrong. I'm taking you to Tucson, even if I have to hogtie you to get you there."

She flew at him, her weight dragging them both downward to topple onto the bed. Her tiny fists battered his chest, his shoulders, probably hurting her more than it did him. One moment she was on top of him, and the next he had reversed their positions, straddling her.

Blood surged through Ryan like liquid fire. Hot. Dark. Hungry. Her nightgown offered little protection to her modesty. He felt the firmness of her unfettered breasts against his chest, felt her quiver, as if she were suddenly aware of her helplessness and his superior strength. Her hands suddenly stilled, and he heard the catch of her breath in her throat.

When she moaned, Ryan realized she was as aroused as he was. He gave an exultant shout when her arms wound around his neck and she pulled his head down to meet her lips.

"Ryan."

He stayed her words with a kiss as he hastily removed his gunbelt and dropped it on the floor beside the bed. Then he dragged her thighs apart and settled between them, his throbbing sex nestled against her heat. It took all of his willpower to keep from tearing open his trousers, shoving himself into her and thrusting to completion. But Ryan was not a selfish man when it came to loving. He'd never to his knowledge left a woman wanting. He'd not had a virgin before, but he knew that a woman's first experience was important to her future approach to sex.

"Do you want me, Kitty?" he whispered against his mouth.

"I don't know," Kitty said truthfully. "I've never felt like this before."

"Tell me how you feel."

She closed her eyes and dragged in a

shuddering sigh. "I feel all shivery inside. Moments ago I was so angry at you I wanted to kill you. Now I can't think beyond the way you make my body feel."

He dragged down her nightgown and kissed her breast, his hand closing over the other sweet, tempting mound as his nimble fingers kneaded the taut nipple. Her gasping moan made something warm unfurl inside his chest.

"Purr for me, Kitten. Tell me what you want. What do you feel?"

Kitty blushed but didn't hesitate to reveal her innermost feelings. "When you touch me like that, I feel swollen and wet in . . . certain places, not just where you're touching me."

Her innocent words made him feel as if he'd just been given a gift. His hand moved downward over her taut stomach to the juncture of her thighs. He cupped her there. "Do you feel swollen and wet here?"

"And hot. Oh, God. I knew men enjoyed rutting with whores but I never realized a woman could feel like this."

"What you and I are going to do, if you agree, is to make love," Ryan said. "Rutting is what unfeeling men do with women they care nothing about. Men like the Bartons rut, I don't."

He sensed Kitty's indecision, combined with a certain degree of curiosity. "Will you let me love you, Kitten?"

"It's not right."

"It is if we say it is. But if you truly don't want this I won't force you. It's your decision, love."

While she was making up her mind he stripped the nightgown from her, baring her body to his rapt gaze. "What a damn shame to hide all this glorious womanhood beneath baggy trousers and coat. Well, love, what shall it be? Are you going to make me suffer? Or will you put me out of my misery and let me love you?"

"I ain't a whore," Kitty said, lapsing into rough language.

"No, you're certainly not that," Ryan agreed. With a pang of regret he started to rise. "You're right. This is wrong. Bert would kill me if I despoiled his daughter."

Ryan had no idea his words would make up Kitty's mind as nothing else could. "I don't give a damn what Bert thinks," she spat. "I'll never acknowledge him as my father. I've always done exactly as I pleased. I . . ." She gulped nervously. "I want you to make love to me."

"To spite Bert?" Ryan asked. She wanted him for all the wrong reasons, he thought, disgruntled. He should have followed his first instinct and found his pleasure elsewhere. He could go back to The Bird Cage and try out Bev, Lee, Angie or Pat. But with Kitty lying naked beneath him, his judgment was flawed.

"To please myself," Kitty said defiantly. "I'm nearly twenty years old. I've seen more of men's bodies than an unmarried girl had aught to, but I have never been curious about lovemaking until you came along. I simply accepted it as something all men did to satisfy their lust. I've seen that . . . piece of flesh men have between their legs and wanted nothing to do with it. But you make loving seem like something I should want, perhaps even enjoy. Will I enjoy it, Ryan?"

"I can make it enjoyable for you," Ryan promised. "But only if you truly want it. Will you trust me, Kitten?"

Kitty stared at him. Trust Ryan? Never. Want him? Definitely. "Make love to me, Ryan. Show me the difference between making love and rutting."

CHAPTER 6

He stood beside the bed and removed his clothing. His boots hit the floor with a thud. She wanted to look away but couldn't. It was true she'd seen men's bodies before, but none as magnificent as Ryan's. So long, so lean and powerful. His chest was corded with rippling muscles, and lightly furred, the dark hair narrowing down his taut stomach in a vee to his groin. Her gaze did not stop there but continued downward. Standing proudly erect in the thick black bush between his legs, his sex seemed to grow even larger beneath her intense perusal.

"I hope you like what you see."

She felt heat staining her cheeks and raised her eyes to his face. "You're . . . I mean, I didn't know men grew so big when aroused."

His green eyes glittered with what Kitty interpreted as anticipation as he stretched out beside her. "I suspect there are a lot of things you don't know. I intend to end your curiosity very soon. Give me your mouth, love."

She closed her eyes and raised her lips for his kiss. She felt the extraordinary heat emanating from him as he pressed hot kisses on her mouth, felt the rough texture of his tongue as he licked the seam of her lips, coaxing them to open for him. He cupped her face, fitting their lips together perfectly. She sighed as the hot thrust of his tongue sent excitement spilling through her.

She was on fire. She gasped her delight when his mouth slid down her throat to her breasts, thoroughly exploring the tender mounds and their rosy crests with sweeping strokes of his tongue. Then he added a new dimension to their loving when his hand sought the slick inner folds between her legs. She nearly jumped out of her skin when he located a place so profoundly sensitive that his slightest touch brought a jolt of intense pleasure. But he did more than touch her there.

With thumb and forefinger he slowly rubbed the hardening bud, until her loins began to move and arch into his caress. She didn't know exactly what she wanted, she only knew she had to have it or die from its lack.

"Ryan. I feel . . . I want . . . Oh God, what are you doing to me?"

"Don't fight it, love," Ryan whispered against her lips. "You're almost there. Go with the feeling."

Fierce desire throbbed through her. Though his words made little sense, she wanted to obey. She felt her flesh swell, felt moisture weeping onto his fingers. She knew she should be embarrassed, but there were too many other sensations to savor. Her body felt light and bouyant; her heart pounded and blood sang through her veins.

"Come to me now, Kitten, I know you're ready," Ryan urged raggedly. His voice sounded strained, as if he were fighting a losing battle.

"I . . . don't know . . . what . . ."

"Perhaps this will help."

He returned his attention to her nipples, licking them into tautly pebbled peaks as his hand continued to tease her from below. Warmth radiated from her breasts to her stomach to her loins, spinning her into a vortex of whirling pleasure. Indescribable sensations overwhelmed her, dampness gathered in her core as something shattered inside her. She screamed out her pleasure and went limp.

She was still trembling from the force of her climax when Ryan eased himself up and over her. She felt his hot, hard flesh probing her softness, and she caught her breath. Before she had time to absorb those new feelings she felt his fingers opening her, stretching her, preparing her for his entry.

"You're tight, love. I'll try to do this as painlessly as possible."

Kitty was beyond rational thought; her body was still quivering with the force and wonder of her very first climax. She stiffened when he nudged her legs apart with his knees and felt his erection probe her.

"Don't freeze," he advised. "Try to relax. I'm told the pain doesn't last very long. I promise you the pleasure will be well worth it."

"Pretty sure of yourself, aren't you?" Kitty said in a strained voice. "Are all men as conceited as you?"

"Not all men are as good as I am," he replied with blunt arrogance. "Kiss me, Kitten."

She found his mouth hovering over hers and met his lips with a ragged sigh. While she was pleasantly absorbed in his kiss, he eased his hardness inside her and began a slow slide forward, hissing out his delight.

Kitty arched her back, a soft moan escaping her. Her heart began to pound erratically as pleasure suddenly gave way to pain. He pressed inexorably deeper, and the pain intensified.

She cried out a protest, trying to shove him away. "Stop! It hurts."

"Easy, love, it will be over soon." He spread her legs even wider, then he flexed his hips and tore through her maidenhead.

She blinked up at him, her face pale, her mouth open in a silent scream. She felt as if she'd been ripped apart. White-hot pain shot through her body, and she couldn't stop the tears that sprang into her eyes.

"Are you all right?" Ryan asked anxiously.

"I didn't know it would hurt so much," she said, swallowing a sob.

"I won't move until you tell me to. Pray God it's not too long else I'll die before this is finished."

His strained voice told Kitty exactly how much the effort to control himself was costing him. She wanted to tell him that she appreciated his effort, but the strangeness and novelty of having him inside her body robbed her of coherent speech. He filled her so completely she thought she would surely burst. But to his credit he held himself still, allowing time for her to recover.

She felt him trembling, heard him groan, and looked up at him, shocked by what she saw. Beads of perspiration dotted his forehead, corded tendons strained against his neck, and his lips were flattened into a grimace. His expression was one of studied concentration and Kitty wondered how something that was supposed to bring pleasure could be so painful, not just to her but apparently to Ryan.

"Can I move now?" Ryan asked from between clenched teeth. Without waiting for an answer, he pressed in and then out. Kitty caught her breath as pleasurable sensations brought her body to new awareness.

She moved her hips experimentally. Tentatively she met his thrust and returned it. "It doesn't hurt so much now," Kitty said shyly. "I think I'd like you to move."

"Thank God," she heard him say.

He began to move his hips, thrusting slowly and steadily until she began to relax, then he picked up the pace, setting a rhythm that sent heat shimmering through her. The pain had receded, replaced by delicious sensations that quickly turned into blinding pleasure. She was aware of nothing now but his pounding loins, his penetrating strokes, and the nearly unbearable excitement building inside her.

Her hands came up to his brawny shoulders, her fingers curled into his flesh as he quickened his thrusts, driving into her harder, faster, deeper. Kitty had heard coarse remarks about sex from the Bartons, but she had never realized a woman could attain the same pleasure granted to men. Ryan was proving how wrong she had been. If this didn't end soon Kitty feared she would die from the pleasure.

Moved by instinct, her legs went around his hips, and she could feel the tension in his body increase. Still he drove on, until she felt the hard knot inside her begin to uncoil and expand. Then suddenly it burst. She cried out his name as she scaled the peak and soared.

Ryan continued pumping, his breath hissing from his throat in ragged bursts as he grasped the cheeks of her buttocks and lifted her higher for his deeper penetration. After several more thrusts his body went rigid, and she felt him shudder with pleasure. He dropped his head on her breasts and groaned, then he collapsed against her.

The sound of their heavy breathing was the only sound in the room. They lay motionless for several minutes, arms and legs entwined, their bodies silvered with sweat, hearts pumping furiously.

Ryan was the first to move. He placed a kiss upon her sweet lips and drank in her sigh of pleasure before shifting his weight off of her.

His expression was anxious as he searched her face. Had Ryan been asked to explain how it felt to be inside Kitty, he couldn't have done so. He'd had more women than he could count, but none could compare with the little wildcat curled next to him in bed. She'd fit him like a tight glove. When he broke through her barrier he would have been hard pressed to explain how he felt. Empowered, perhaps. Strong and virile, certainly. One thing was clear. He'd never felt like that before.

"Did I hurt you badly?"

"It hurt more than I thought it would," Kitty complained.

"But you did enjoy it," he said with sure knowledge. "A man can tell when he pleases a woman."

She flushed and looked away. "I didn't know . . . I never thought . . . after the pain went away I felt . . . incredible pleasure. Is it possible to feel those same sensations more than once?"

He gave her a roguish grin. "Not only possible but extremely desirable."

"Will I feel that way with another man?"

The smile slid from his face. The vision of Kitty making love with another man made him decidedly uncomfortable. "I can't answer that. Not all men are considerate of a woman's feelings. I happen to enjoy giving my partner pleasure before taking my own."

Kitty looked thoughtful, as if mulling over his answer. "I did enjoy making love with you, Ryan, but if you thought it would change my mind about going to Tucson, you're wrong. I still ain't going with you."

Ryan felt a knot of anger building inside him. Making love was serious business. He'd never use it as leverage, or to hurt anyone. "I made love to you because I wanted you. It had nothing to do with Bert Lowry or Tucson. You wanted it as much as I did."

He heard her sigh and knew she had no rebuttal for his logic.

"As for Tucson, you're going and that's final."

"It's my life, Ryan, why can't you let me live it like I want to? I was doing fine before I met you."

"Oh, yeah, fine," Ryan mocked. "Look, I'll make a deal with you. Agree to accompany me to Tucson to meet Bert and I promise you can leave whenever you please. The next day, if you wish."

"You mean it?"

"Of course. I don't lie."

"I'll think about it."

"Kitty . . ."

"No! Dammit, Ryan! Don't you see? They ain't gonna like me. I ain't a lady. I don't act or think like one. Listen to the way I talk. My speech is rough, my English terrible. I don't always remember to watch my words. I can cuss like a trooper, shoot like a man, and ride like an Indian. I won't fit in. Bert Lowry is gonna expect me to be something I'm not. I can't change overnight. What if I slip and use language no lady would use?"

"I'll explain to Bert. He'll understand."

"What about his stepdaughter? She's probably a gently bred young woman far superior to someone like me."

"Teresa is . . ."

How could he explain Teresa? She was a beautiful, spoiled young woman who worked her wiles on any male unlucky enough to come into contact with her. She was a hot little piece, in many ways more experienced than Kitty, who had lived with rough outlaws during the formative years of her life. He had initiated a mild flirtation with Teresa during his stay at the Lowry ranch and was relieved when the time came for him to leave. Teresa had become too aggressive in her pursuit of him for his comfort.

It wasn't as if he intended to marry the girl. His flirtation had been no more or less than Rogue Ryan would have engaged in with any other beautiful woman who captured his fancy. Ryan's flirtations were usually intense but brief affairs. His flirtation with Teresa had been different in that he'd been smart enough to avoid a sexual relationship. He had a distinct feeling that had he bedded Teresa he would have found himself hogtied and standing before a preacher before he knew what had hit him.

"Teresa is . . . well, I don't think her opinion will influence Bert. He's anxious to meet you. You are his daughter, after all."

"Give me a few days to make up my mind," Kitty said.

Ryan had the uncanny impression that it was going to take more than a few days of consideration for Kitty to agree to go to Tucson. And time was something they didn't have. Kitty was going to go whether she wanted to or not. But he had to be very careful about how he went about it. His first step toward his goal was to appear to give her the time she requested. It would take a few days to prepare for their trip to Tucson anyway.

"Very well, a few days, no longer," Ryan said. Reluctantly he climbed out of bed. "Get some sleep."

"Where are you going? It's nearly dawn."

The corners of his full lips curved into a roguish smile. "Are you asking me to stay?"

He sensed the war being waged inside her but didn't press her. It had to be her choice.

The ponderous burden of indecision weighed heavily upon Kitty. She knew the difference between right and wrong and knew what she and Ryan had done together was frowned upon by society. Unless one was a whore, of course. Kitty didn't think letting Ryan love her made her a bad person. She didn't feel like a whore. The thought of another man doing to her what Ryan had done made her physically ill. On the other hand, she knew better than to expect Ryan to marry her; he'd already stated his opinion on that subject. Besides, she wasn't lady enough for a man like Ryan.

Somehow, making love with Ryan had seemed right. When she was with him nothing existed but the moment. No past, no future, no consequences. Only the man and the insatiable hunger fed by his hands and mouth upon her flesh. She'd already allowed him liberties that went far beyond anything she'd ever imagined and had decided that this night would be the only one she'd ever spend in Ryan's arms.

She was becoming far too fond of the handsome rancher for her own peace of mind. She knew that when he walked out of her life he'd never look back, but could she say the same? The answer was painfully obvious. Ryan would always be someone special in her life. Someone she could easily love were he the kind of man who appreciated or wanted a woman's love, but she wasn't the kind of woman with whom Ryan would associate socially.

"I reckon your silence means you want me to leave," Ryan said when she remained thoughtful.

"Stay," Kitty whispered, knowing she'd regret it later but unable to deny the need to be with him one last time. "I . . . I don't want you to leave." *If tonight is the only time I can allow this to happen I don't want to waste a moment of it,* she thought. Ryan was conceited enough — she didn't need to add to his arrogance by letting him know how deeply he affected her, how very much she wanted him.

She heard Ryan groan and felt her body grow taut in anticipation as his green eyes slid over her with undisguised heat. "I don't know if I could have left even if you had ordered me away," Ryan whispered as he slid into bed beside her and cuddled her against him. "I thought that having you once would be enough, but it wasn't. I still want you, love. But if you're too sore to make love again, I'll understand."

His kiss was more gentle than she'd expected or wanted. Just a tasting of lips, the slow slide of his tongue into her mouth. If she was too sore, his kisses sent the thought fleeing. She wanted him. Oh, God, yes. The fires of hell licked at her, and she knew without a doubt that her fate had been sealed. Her hell on earth would be to live the rest of her life without Ryan.

"I'm not too sore," she said when he broke off the kiss. "Show me again what it means to be a woman. I never knew it could be like this."

He loved her again, taking his time to arouse her, his mouth and hands moving with tenderness and expertise over her flushed skin, until Kitty pleaded with him to take her. She was more than ready when he raised her over him and slowly slid her onto his erection. He began to move. She felt his body tense, and her own responded in rhythm to his, until the world exploded around her and she fell exhausted upon his chest.

Kitty awakened to brilliant sunlight streaming through the bedroom window. From the position of the sun in the sky, she assumed it was well past noon. She shifted and felt a strange soreness between her legs. A groan slipped past her lips when she recalled everything she and Ryan had done last night. It had been the most glorious experience of her life, and one she knew she'd come to regret in time.

Raising herself up on one elbow, Kitty realized she was alone. Apparently Ryan had left as mysteriously as he had appeared. She knew he wouldn't quietly leave Tombstone without completing his mission, so she reckoned she'd see him again. But not in her bed. That episode was over and done with. Ryan Delaney wasn't the kind of man to settle down with one woman. He needed variety, and she wasn't the kind of woman to let a man take without giving something of himself in return.

Later that night Ryan walked through the swinging doors of the Lucky Wheel saloon, his gaze scanning the crowded public room for Kitty. He didn't see her immediately and found an unoccupied table amidst the chaos. He motioned for a waitress, ordered a plate of chicken and dumplings with biscuits, and surveyed the evening crowd.

The saloon was busier and rowdier than ever tonight, it being a Saturday when cowhands crowded into town to drink and carouse. Ryan had spent the day making provisions for the trip to Tucson and hadn't seen Kitty since he'd left her sleeping soundly in her bed. She'd looked like an angel with her riot of short tousled curls framing her beautiful face. The sheet had slipped down to her waist, and he had watched with avid interest as her breasts rose and fell with each breath she took. Firm and rosy-tipped, he recalled how their weight overflowed his hands, and it had taken considerable willpower to turn and walk away from all that glorious woman-hood.

As if thinking about Kitty had conjured up her image, he saw her carrying a pitcher of beer to customers seated at a nearby table. She hadn't seen him yet, and he preferred it that way. For the time being he just wanted to sit and observe her.

She was dressed in sunny yellow satin

tonight, and her short mop of curls was tied back from her face with a matching ribbon. She looked harried and tired, and he felt a twinge of remorse for keeping her up so late the night before. His gaze settled on her partially exposed bosom, and rage seethed through him. Seeing her exposed like that made him want to punch out the men ogling her.

He leaped to his feet when he saw one of the drunken cowhands reach down the front of Kitty's dress and pinch her breast as she bent over the table. Ryan was halfway across the room when he saw Kitty, her eyes shooting blue fire, slap the man's face. He silently applauded her courage and returned to his table. But he hadn't reckoned with the cowhand's reaction. The man pulled Kitty onto his lap and held her down as he ruthlessly plundered her tender breasts, while his drunken friends laughed and urged him on.

Ryan leaped forward again, but he couldn't reach Kitty in time to prevent the cowhand from lifting her skirts and pinching her bottom. Nor could he stop curious onlookers from viewing a pair of curvaceous legs and thighs. Ryan pushed through the crowd in a blind rage. When he reached Kitty he tore her from the cowhand's lap.

"What the hell?" the cowhand said, staggering to his feet. "Go find yer own woman, mister, this one's mine." He made a grab for Kitty, but she successfully scooted out of his reach.

"The lady doesn't like being pawed," Ryan said, shoving Kitty behind him.

"Says who?" the cowhand challenged. "Besides, any woman who works in a saloon ain't no lady." He fixed Kitty with a bleary-eyed gaze. "Name yer price, honey. I'm hankerin' fer more than a feel."

"The lady isn't for sale," Ryan said, answering for Kitty.

"I say she is," the cowhand said belligerently. "And I got friends to back me up." His companions moved closer as his hand slid toward his weapon.

"Get out of here, Kitty," Ryan hissed. "Meet me back at the house."

"No, there are too many of them. Leave. I can handle this."

"Sure, like you were doing so well before I intervened," Ryan said sarcastically. "Do as I say."

"Don't listen to him, honey," the cowhand said. "You can leave with me if ya want. I'll make it right with yer boss. I got me a pocketful of money and can afford to pay fer yer time."

Kitty's mind worked furiously. She'd do anything to stop gunplay, if it came to that. She'd seen the cowhand in the saloon before. He always came with a bunch of rowdy friends ready and willing to come to his aid. Unfortunately Chet Marlow had business elsewhere tonight and wasn't around to stop the fight. And the bartender was outnumbered. If she wanted to save Ryan, she had to act fast.

"Very well, I'll go with you," she said, refusing to look at Ryan. Had she done so, she would have seen the look of utter disbelief on his handsome features. "We can go to my place, it's just down the street."

The cowhand gave her a lopsided grin. "I knew you'd see it my way, honey. Let's go."

"Like hell!" Ryan shouted. "Are you mad, Kitty?"

"Let me handle this, Ryan," Kitty pleaded, finally looking at him. She wished she hadn't, for his face was as dark and turbulent as a thundercloud.

"Yeah, let the little lady alone," the cowhand warned. "She knows what she's doin'."

"I doubt that," Ryan said harshly. He grasped Kitty's arm, as if preparing to drag her away.

Suddenly his arms were pinned behind him by two of the cowhand's rowdy companions. "You heard what the lady said, mister," one of the men said. "She wants to go with Sparky."

"Shall we go?" Sparky said, grabbing her arm and staggering toward the swinging doors.

"Damn you, Kitty," Ryan yelled, straining against his captors.

Kitty knew he was confused and angry, but that was better than being dead. Where was Marshal Earp when she needed him? Not that the law on the Western outposts was very effective.

"Just a minute," Kitty said. "I want to get my wrap."

"Don't be long," Sparky said, burping loudly. "I got a rock in my pants that's gettin' bigger and harder by the minute."

"Don't let him go," Kitty said, gesturing toward Ryan. "He thinks I belong to him."

"He ain't goin' nowhere, lady," Sparky's friends assured her.

Kitty hurried away, Ryan's curses ringing in her ears.

"Are you sure you know what you're doing?" Nellie asked as she followed Kitty into the kitchen.

"I'm afraid Ryan will get hurt," Kitty said. "I can take care of Sparky."

She found her wrap and threw it over her

shoulders, patting her pocket to make sure the gun she carried was still there. It was. Squaring her shoulders, she left the kitchen and joined Sparky. Ryan looked as if he wanted to kill her as they left the saloon.

Kitty was making plans as she walked down the dark street with Sparky. She didn't really want to shoot the man and considered her options. As he staggered along beside her, she realized he was even more drunk than she had originally thought. Heartened, she decided she could easily handle one drunk without using her gun. Before making her move, she waited until they were too far from the saloon to be heard. She stopped abruptly when they came abreast of a dark alley.

"Huh? Whatsa matter, honey?" Sparky asked, slurring his words. "You ain't changed yer mind, have ya? I might be drunk but I can still handle one small woman." He clutched his crotch. "I got somethin' here yer gonna like."

"I'm sure I will," Kitty cooed. "But I don't think I can wait. How about a little kiss now?" She backed him up against a dark building, pressing herself against him.

"Yer a hot little piece, ain't ya? Pucker up, honey, I don't mind handin' out a few kisses."

"You're gonna get more than a few kisses, bastard!" Kitty rasped as she drew back her knee and rammed it into his crotch.

Sparky made a gagging sound deep in his throat and doubled over. "Ya bitch!" he screamed, clutching his balls as he fell, writhing, to the ground.

Kitty felt little remorse as she watched him hit the dirt with a loud thud. But when he went suddenly still, she feared she'd killed him. A quick examination of the stricken cowboy revealed a huge lump on his head, and Kitty assumed that he had hit his head on a protruding corner of the building when he'd fallen. He was out cold but far from dead. In a few hours he would wake up with a gigantic headache. And hopefully he wouldn't remember what had happened tonight. But first she had to get rid of him. Grasping his arms, she pulled him into the alley where he couldn't be seen by passersby.

Ryan strained against his captors, listening to their coarse jokes about Kitty and Sparky and what they were doing now. Sparky's friends held a gun on him while they drank and remarked upon Kitty's attributes. Ryan saw red when they wagered on who would be next to win her favors.

Ryan found it difficult to believe that Kitty had agreed to go with Sparky. Kitty wasn't a whore. No one knew it better than he. She'd been a virgin until last night. No other man had ever touched her. Blind, unmitigated rage sent adrenaline coursing through his veins. Kitty was too damn naive for her own good. Did she think her sacrifice was going to save him? If she thought she could outwit Sparky, or use her strength to hold him off, she was sadly mistaken. No, he had to do something to save the little fool from her folly.

"Drinks for everyone," Ryan shouted above the din. "I'm paying."

"Huh? Why would you do that?" one of Sparky's companions asked.

"Because I've changed my mind about you fellas. I don't own Kitty, she can bed the whole damn lot of you for all I care. There are plenty of other women around, so who needs her? How about it? Let's all belly up to the bar, it's on me."

Men began crowding up to the bar. When Sparky's companions saw the others being served free drinks, they dragged Ryan to the bar with them, demanding their share. Ryan reached into his vest pocket, removed several gold coins, and tossed them on the bar.

"Keep the drinks coming," he told the bartender, pretending to join in the revelry.

Before long the reason for keeping Ryan in the saloon was forgotten as men fought to find a place at the bar where free drinks were flowing like water. Amidst the disorder, Ryan was able to slip away. He was out the door and away before anyone realized he was gone.

Ryan didn't take the time to retrieve his horse from the livery as he raced down the street toward Kitty's small house. His fists were clenched, his face a mask of fear. He would kill Sparky if he had hurt Kitty. As for Kitty, he couldn't decide whether he would kiss her or strangle her once he got his hands on her. He was rushing past a dark alley when he thought he saw a movement. A flash of color. Yellow silk. He came to a screeching halt just as Kitty sauntered out of the alley, looking extremely satisfied with herself.

She saw Ryan and gave him a saucy grin. "What took you so long?"

CHAPTER 7

Ryan regarded Kitty with no little amount of concern. All he could think to say was, "Are you all right?"

She dusted off her skirts. "I'm fine."

Relief, sharp and poignant, shuddered through Ryan. And something else. Anger. Rich, ripe anger. He grasped her shoulders and gave her a hard shake.

"Little fool! What did you hope to accomplish by your dangerous game back there?"

"I was expecting a thank you for saving your life," she said tartly.

"At what cost?" Ryan retorted. "You could have been raped, or hurt, or worse. You should have trusted me. I would have thought of something." He looked around and frowned, suddenly aware that someone was missing. "What did you do with Sparky?"

"He'll be nursing a headache in the morning," Kitty said, obviously pleased with herself. "Not to mention aching balls."

Ryan groaned. "Ladies don't mention men's private parts. Especially not in vulgar language."

Kitty frowned. "What are they if they're not ba—"

"Kitty, for God's sake, leave off. Let's get the hell out of here."

"I just proved a point, didn't I, Ryan?" Kitty asked sweetly as he grasped her hand and dragged her off down the street. "I ain't a lady. I'll never be a lady. I don't know the right words, and having to monitor my speech every minute ain't worth it."

Ryan grit his teeth in frustration. "For your information, Kitty, you kicked Sparky in his testicles."

"That sounds ridiculous," Kitty said. "I know where I kicked Sparky and it was his ba—"

"Dammit, Kitty," Ryan interrupted, trying to keep the laughter from his voice. "Just forget it for now. We can concentrate on refining your speech during the trip to Tucson. You aren't ignorant. I've heard you speak better than that. Try to remember what your mother taught you before Lex took you away to live with outlaws."

"I already told you I *ain't* goin' with you,"

Kitty proclaimed defiantly.

When they reached her house, Ryan held his hand out for the key. With marked reluctance she handed it to him and glowered sullenly as he unlocked the door and held it open for her. She marched inside and started to close the door in his face. He pushed it open and followed her inside. He slammed the door shut and turned to confront her. Muted lamplight cast her face in shadows, but Ryan could tell she wasn't as composed as she wanted him to believe. That little episode with Sparky had to have been stressful despite her outward calm.

"Consider this, Kitty," Ryan said in a reasonable tone of voice. "What do you suppose Sparky is going to do when he wakes up in the alley with a splitting head and aching ba . . . testicles? He's going to be mad as hell and hot for revenge. Neither you nor I are going to be safe in this town after today. And you're sadly mistaken if you think your boss will take you back. Not after he hears about the ruckus you caused."

It was clear to Ryan that his logic had gotten through to Kitty, for her brow furrowed.

"I suppose you're right," she allowed.

Ryan knew her answer was grudgingly given and felt an unaccustomed twinge of pity. But he was giving her no choice.

Tombstone was too damn dangerous for both of them. The sooner Kitty was safely with Bert, the sooner he could return to Montana. After this little escapade, a rancher's life no longer seemed dull and boring.

"I know you're frightened at the prospect of being thrust into a new and strange environment," he cajoled. "Meeting your father for the first time will probably be a traumatic experience. But I'll be there, Kitty, at least for a time."

"I don't know what my reaction will be when I meet my father," Kitty admitted. "I don't want to be deliberately cruel to a dying man but I can't pretend something I don't feel. I hate my real father, though I've never met him. And we both know he's going to be ashamed of me."

Ryan felt something inside him begin to crumble. He'd felt compassion so seldom in the past that he scarcely recognized it now. Without volition his arms reached for her, bringing her against the hard wall of his chest. "We know nothing of the sort. Besides, I won't let anyone hurt you, love."

She clutched his shoulders, her blue eyes intent upon his face. "Do you swear, Ryan?"

Ryan swallowed a groan. Kitty might act tough, but she was faced with more fears and problems than a woman her age should have to bear. Her fragile vulnerability spoke to him in the most elemental way. It brought out a protectiveness in him that was utterly foreign to his nature. He'd do anything for his brothers, of course, but Kitty was a whole new canvas on which to paint these unfamiliar emotions.

Ryan's first reaction to his feelings was to run. As far and as fast as he could. This whole situation was becoming too personal. He didn't want to be drawn into Kitty's complicated life, but that's exactly what was happening. Involvement meant caring. Caring could lead to commitment, something he'd resisted all his life. He didn't want to be controlled by any one woman. He liked variety. He enjoyed flitting from woman to woman, sampling their charms, then moving on to new conquests.

Ryan's second reaction was to hold Kitty securely in his arms and promise her whatever she wanted if it would ease her fright. However much he wanted to follow his first reaction, his second won out.

"I swear it, love. Now give me a kiss and go to bed. I've already purchased the supplies we'll need for our journey, so we can get an early start tomorrow. I'll bring along a packhorse to carry our supplies and your belongings. I have few personal belongings of my own; I've been traveling light."

Kitty nodded jerkily. "I'll be ready." She lifted her face for his kiss and seemed almost disappointed when he gave her a light peck on the lips.

"I don't dare give you the kind of kiss we both want," he said regretfully. "We both know where that would lead. And right now you need to rest. Lock the door after I leave."

Kitty locked the door behind Ryan and went directly to the bedroom. She was glad Ryan hadn't asked to stay the night. No matter how difficult, she would have refused him. She had meant it when she'd vowed not to let Ryan make love to her again. She knew instinctively that she would lose a little more of her heart to the charming rogue each time she allowed him to love her. When he walked out of her life, and she knew he would, she would have to go on without him.

As she packed her saddlebags and prepared for bed, she spared a few moments' thought on the dying man who waited for her in Tucson. Intuition told her the meeting wasn't going to go as smoothly as Ryan predicted. Besides her own reluctance to be someone she wasn't, there was the stepsister Ryan had mentioned. Were she in Teresa's place, Kitty was sure she wouldn't welcome an interloper into her comfortable life. Time would tell, she sighed as she climbed into bed.

Ryan arrived promptly at eight the following morning. He was pleased to find Kitty dressed in a split riding skirt and waiting. While she packed some last-minute items she'd forgotten, he saddled her mare. She was locking the front door when he led her mount around to the front to join his gelding and the packhorse he'd purchased early this morning and loaded with supplies.

"I hope the windows are still intact when I return," Kitty remarked.

"*If* you return," Ryan countered as he helped her to mount. He led the way out of town, waiting for her to catch up so he could continue their conversation. "I heard through the grapevine that Sparky was pretty upset when he woke up in the alley and realized what had happened."

"Upset is mild compared to what he's probably feeling right now," Kitty said dryly.

"Needless to say, it's a good thing you're leaving. He and his friends could make life pretty miserable for you."

Without waiting for an answer, he spurred his horse forward, leaving that uncomfortable thought for Kitty to ponder.

They camped that night beneath a bluff rising above a desert of cactus. They were fortunate to find a trickle of water in a narrow stream running past their campsite, and Ryan led the horses to drink while Kitty gathered the supplies and pots she would need to prepare an evening meal.

They dined that night on beans, biscuits, and thick slices of ham Ryan had purchased in Tombstone. The sky was clear, no sign of rain in sight. They spread out their bedrolls beneath a rocky ledge and turned in for the night.

Kitty pulled the blanket over her eyes to shield them from the brilliant moonlight spilling down upon her. But even that did not help. As tired as she was, sleep eluded her. She turned and tossed, trying to seek a comfortable position on the hard ground. The problem, she decided, was that she'd become accustomed to the comforts of a bed. Even the cot on which she'd slept during the years she'd ridden with the Bartons beat the hard ground beneath her tonight.

She turned toward Ryan, envying his ability to find sleep with such ease. In sleep his face was as smooth and flawless as a boy's, marred only by the stubbly dark growth on his chin and jaw. She watched his chest rise and fall with each breath and felt a tingling sensation deep within her core. Ryan had made no move to renew their intimate relationship, and she tried to convince herself that she was glad. Sharing intimacies with Ryan would complicate her life, and it was already complicated enough. She told herself she'd be better off accepting nothing from Ryan but his friendship. Unfortunately her heart refused to listen, and her body was even more insistent.

She watched Ryan for several minutes. Then she heaved a sigh and closed her eyes, ignoring the thumping of her heart and clamoring of her body. She let out a startled gasp when Ryan's voice came to her through the moonlit night.

"Are you having as much difficulty sleeping as I am?"

"I . . . how did you know? I thought you were asleep."

"How do you expect me to sleep with you near enough to reach out and touch? I want you, Kitty. Every time I look at you, I get so hard I ache," he said thickly. "I can't sleep for recalling how it felt to be inside you, how delicious you taste. Only my conscience is keeping me from making love to you."

"Your conscience?" Kitty asked, incredulous. "I wasn't aware you had one."

His lips curved up into a smile. "Occasionally my conscience asserts itself. Mostly when I wish it wouldn't. I would be making love to you right now if I wasn't worrying about Bert's reaction when he learns I've bedded his daughter without offering marriage. Which of course I'm unlikely to do. There isn't a woman alive for whom I'd give up my freedom."

"What makes you think I'd let you make love to me again?" Kitty asked huffily. "I may be naive in the ways of men and women but I'm smart enough to recognize lust. I made a mistake once, Ryan, but never again. I'm not going to become your whore, then pretend I'm Bert Lowry's innocent daughter. Besides, there isn't a man I'd trust enough to marry."

"Go to sleep," Ryan said grumpily as he flopped on his side away from her. "I don't know what we're going to do about this unholy attraction we have for one another," he muttered in a voice barely above a whisper.

Kitty heard, and wondered the same thing. She'd been attracted to Ryan from the first, even when posing as a scruffy lad. She'd die before she'd tell him that what she felt for him now went far beyond mere attraction. He had engaged her heart and made her body want his. And now she had to suffer the rest of her life for the single night of bliss she had shared with him.

Sleep finally came, and with it dreams that placed her squarely in Ryan's arms, exactly where she wanted to be.

Ryan estimated that the trip to Tucson, barring any kind of mishaps, would take three or four days of steady riding. Kitty dreaded the journey for many reasons. Each day would bring her closer to the man who had left her mother with a babe in her belly and never looked back. Her distrust of men began when her father abandoned her mother, and it had not wavered during her years as Deke Johnson's stepdaughter. Kitty and her mother had learned to live in fear of his nasty moods and heavy hand.

They stopped early the next night beside the Santa Cruz River. The site was peaceful, with plenty of water nearby in which to bathe. Kitty's body felt saturated with sand; even her clothing held copious amounts of gritty dust. She couldn't wait to scrub her whole body and wash her hair, which had grown to nearly shoulder length since she no longer had to hack it off with her knife. She wondered if Ryan had noticed.

"Can I bathe first?" Kitty asked after they had dismounted and taken care of the horses.

Kitty could have sworn she heard Ryan groan. "You can bathe while I hunt for our supper. Don't stray too far from the campsite."

Kitty gathered soap, towel, and a change of clothing while Ryan walked off toward a forest of mesquite and tall cactus. "Watch out for snakes," he called over his shoulder.

Kitty shuddered. She'd camped out often enough in her life to respect all manner of slithery creatures. And that included lizards and scorpions.

She walked down to the river and wandered a short distance along the shore until she found the perfect spot to bathe. She sat down on a rock, removed her boots and dirty clothing, and waded out into the water, clutching a bar of soap. The river wasn't deep this time of year, and she was able to wade nearly to the middle, where the water lapped at her hips. Then she knelt on the sandy bottom and dipped her head back to wet it. As she applied soap to her sopping head, she heard two gunshots and smiled, her mouth already watering for the roasted game.

She was blissfully rinsing soap from her

hair after the first scrubbing when she heard a noise. She dashed the soap from her eyes and glanced behind her, seeing nothing but cactus and mesquite. Feeling foolish, she continued her bath. Moments later she heard the noise again. Whipping around, she nearly fainted when she saw a group of Indians standing several yards away on the riverbank.

While Kitty might have been knowledgeable about snakes and crawling creatures, she knew nothing good about, and thus feared, Indians. The Bartons had come across Indians a few times and had successfully chased them off. But she and Lex had almost lost their lives to Indians once, and she'd never forgotten it. This time she was alone and helpless to defend herself against armed warriors.

Kitty followed her first inclination, which was to scream.

Ryan returned to camp with two fat rabbits. Since Kitty hadn't returned yet, he skinned and cleaned them, started a fire, and threaded them on green limbs to roast. Then he walked down to the river to wash. He didn't see Kitty and assumed she had walked out of sight of camp to bathe. He smiled to himself, thinking she was smart to remove herself from his sight. He felt himself harden just thinking about a nude Kitty frolicking in the water.

Tugging off his soiled shirt, he used it to wipe his hands and face. Then he headed back to camp, intending to bathe later. Suddenly a scream rent the air. Ryan felt the hair rise on the back of his neck as he recognized Kitty's voice. He dropped his shirt and willed his legs into motion, his heart thumping wildly. The fear he felt was indescribable. Should something happen to Kitty he'd never forgive himself.

He ran along the riverbank in the direction from which the scream had come, calling her name. She didn't answer. He was beyond frantic when he saw her standing in the middle of the river, her arms crossed protectively over her breasts. He couldn't determine whether she was hurt or merely frightened as he unbuckled his gunbelt, flung it to the ground, and splashed into the water.

She was shaking uncontrollably when he reached her. He pulled her into his arms, trying to make sense out of her words.

"In . . . In . . . Indians," she stammered. She was nearly hysterical with fear, and Ryan tightened his hold on her.

"Indians?" Ryan asked, finally understanding. "Where?"

She pointed to where the Indians stood among the mesquite. "There."

He saw them and grimaced. "Damn! I left my guns on the riverbank. Can you walk?"

Kitty nodded, and Ryan hurried her through the water toward shore. Suddenly Ryan heard one of the Indians shout something at them, and he stopped. "Look," he cried, relief shuddering through him. "They're giving us the peace sign. They're friendly Indians. My brother Chad learned something about Indians when they held his wife Sarah and her son Abner hostage. They're probably out hunting and couldn't resist watching a beautiful woman bathe."

He remained watchful as they turned and disappeared as silently as they had appeared. He felt Kitty tremble, and his arms tightened around her. There had been at least a dozen warriors; he and Kitty would have had virtually no chance of escaping had they decided to attack. But he didn't tell Kitty that. She was still shaking, still pale and frightened when they reached the riverbank.

Ryan placed the towel around her bare shoulders, then bent to retrieve his guns. "I'll gather your clothing," Ryan said as he buckled on his gunbelt.

"No!" she cried, clinging to him. "I don't trust them. Take me back to camp, please. You can get my clothes later."

"They're gone, love, they're not coming back," Ryan comforted. "Had they meant us harm we would both be dead by now."

He felt her shuddering against him, felt the stiffness in her limbs, and he swept her up into his arms. "I didn't think anything could frighten you," he teased. "You single-handedly laid low a drunken cowboy, what makes you think you can't defeat a few Indians?"

"This is no joking matter, Ryan," Kitty scolded. "Lex and I had a close call once and I've never forgotten it. We barely escaped with our lives."

Her arms tightened around his neck, and Ryan savored the arousing sensation of her bare breasts plastered against his naked chest. If she knew how *much* he enjoyed it she'd probably jump out of his arms.

"They won't come back," he vowed. "You can relax now."

They reached the campsite, and he let her slide down his body to the ground. The sensation was pure torture. The towel hid little of her naked beauty, and Ryan felt his staff harden and push upward against his belly. He groaned, wishing she'd either put on some clothes or let him love her. But to his surprise she didn't move. Her eyes were locked with his. He read blatant desire in them and felt his control slipping. If she didn't move *now,* he wouldn't be responsible for his actions.

"Kitty, if you don't stop looking at me like that I'm going to give you what we obviously both want."

Kitty couldn't look away, couldn't move, didn't even want to. She was drawn into his heated gaze like a moth to flame. His eyes glowed with desire, and she felt the hard ridge of his sex pushing against the material of his denims. Knowing he desired her made her own need spiral out of control. She strained toward him, feeling dampness gathering in her core as her body prepared itself for love. Her breasts felt heavy; her nipples were pebbled and swollen into taut nubs.

Embarrassed by her need, she turned away from him. It wouldn't do to let him see how very much she wanted him. She had promised herself this wouldn't happen again, but here she was, all but begging Ryan to make love to her. Did he know? Did he have any idea how much she desired him?

Then she felt his hands on her shoulders,

turning her roughly. "I seriously doubt either of us have the strength to fight this, Kitten," he whispered against her ear. "This attraction is bigger than both of us. I want you. You want me. In a couple of days we'll reach our destination. Strange surroundings and new experiences will leave us both with little time or inclination to indulge our mutual attraction. As you embark upon a new life with your father you'll doubtlessly look back on this as a pleasant memory. What I'm saying, love, is that we shouldn't deny ourselves now. Let's take what we can, while we can, and savor the pleasure."

A pleasant memory? Kitty thought bleakly. Is that all she'd ever be to Ryan? A brief interlude of shared passion and lust? Could she live with that? Did she have the strength to deny him, when she wanted him as desperately as he wanted her?

She was still pondering the answer when Ryan lifted her into his arms and carried her to the bedroll he had laid out earlier. He placed her on the blanket and covered her with his body. She felt the pressure of his hard sex against her softness and couldn't stop the tiny moan that worked its way past her throat.

His mouth covered hers, stealing her breath and replacing it with his own. Her mouth opened to his probing tongue, cherishing the masculine taste and scent of him. She kissed him back, slid her fingers in his dark, silky hair. Were she to kiss a thousand men she would always know Ryan by his unique taste. He sucked her tongue into his mouth, and she shivered in response. She moaned out a protest when his mouth left hers, trailing warm, moist kisses along her jaw, down her throat, pausing to lick the rapid pulse beating out her pleasure.

He shifted his body, his mouth sliding down to her chest, lavishing careful attention to her throbbing breasts and swollen nipples, making them ache and distend. But he did not linger however much Kitty writhed against him and gasped out her pleasure. She caught her breath as the liquid fire of his mouth continued its downward path over her stomach. She felt her muscles jump as his tongue traced patterns on her belly, ringed her navel, then claimed the hot, quivering center of her core.

She screamed. "Ryan, what are you doing? I want you inside me."

"Not yet," he murmured, raising his head and smiling at her. "There are many ways to make love. I want to show you all of them in the short time we have together. Don't stop me, Kitten. I won't hurt you. Trust me."

Dimly Kitty wondered how many women Ryan had asked to trust him. More than she could count, she'd wager. But she hadn't the strength or the will to stop him. She wanted . . . everything.

Ryan must have sensed her acquiescence, for he lowered his head and continued his erotic torment. When his tongue parted the golden curls protecting her mound, Kitty arched sharply upward, shocked by what he intended and thinking she must be wrong to even think that he'd consider such a sinful thing. Then he shoved her legs wide, parted her tender folds with his fingers, and placed his mouth on a place so intensely sensitive that she jerked violently and cried out.

"Ryan! No! You can't!"

He showed her by action rather than words that he could do precisely what he intended as he held her thighs firmly apart and plundered her slick flesh with his mouth and tongue. Her breathing grew erratic, her heart pounded, and those places he was tonguing with sweet dexterity throbbed. Fire leaped through her veins, pooling in her tender parts. When Ryan thrust a finger inside her, the tension burst in wave after wave of undulating pleasure.

Still immersed in her climax, she didn't realize he'd stripped off his denims until she felt his hair-roughened skin glide upward along her own smooth flesh. Strong contractions were still vibrating through her when she felt the blunt point of his sex probe her entrance. She opened her trembling legs, and he slid forward, hissing a sigh into her ear as he pierced her deeply. He began to move, and all rational thought vanished. Kitty had no idea her body could quicken again so swiftly. Her first climax had been so satisfying she would never have believed it possible to reach another. But Ryan was proving how wrong she had been.

Having him inside her was pure bliss. With his mouth and hands arousing her and his sex bringing her closer and closer to an explosive ending, Kitty knew she would never love another. She reached down to clutch his buttocks, felt him tauten as he thrust into her, again and again. Her second climax hit her, scattering her senses as she grew brittle and shattered into a million brilliant shards. She heard Ryan's harsh breathing, felt him go rigid, felt the wet splash of his hot seed inside her as he called out her name.

Kitty welcomed his weight as he collapsed

against her. She wished they could lie like this forever, but she knew better than to wish for impossible things. Ryan wasn't a forever kind of man. She would have to look elsewhere for a man to love. Unfortunately Ryan was the only man she wanted. She had given her heart to a man who would trample it beneath his feet if she failed to protect it properly.

Ryan shifted to Kitty's side and pulled a blanket over them. "I wouldn't be surprised if the rabbits are too tough to eat," he remarked. "Don't move, I'll see to them," he said when she started to rise. "I've pushed you pretty hard the last two days. You must be exhausted."

"I've ridden harder," Kitty said, reminding him of her life outside the law.

He gave her a wry smile. "Have you made love after a hard day's ride?"

"You know I haven't."

"Then rest. I'll start the coffee, open a can of beans and call you when everything is ready."

Ryan pulled on his denims and went to see about the rabbits. He needed a few minutes alone to think. He was bothered by the speed with which Kitty was becoming important to him and relieved that the mission he had undertaken was drawing to a close. Quite successfully, he reflected, proud of his accomplishment. Intuition told him that remaining in Kitty's company longer than absolutely necessary would be unwise. In fact, it would be downright dangerous. Kitty had a way of getting to him on a personal level. The more times he made love to her, the more he wanted her. His response to her was unusual and completely out of character for him.

Despite the warning bells ringing in his head, Ryan knew he'd throw caution to the wind and make love to Kitty as often as she allowed it. "Consequences be damned," he muttered to himself. He'd had plenty of experience distancing himself from relationships grown stale. Why should Kitty be any different? Why shouldn't he tire of her like he did the others? When the time came, he would simply walk away and not look back. It was what Rogue Ryan did best. But right now all he could think about was Kitty's sweet body and the pleasure she'd given him. There was plenty of time left before he had to walk away.

CHAPTER 8

They had found a perfect place beneath a ledge to camp that night. There was water nearby, but when Kitty went to bathe she found that it went no deeper than her ankles, forcing her to sit in the narrow stream and splash water on herself. But it felt refreshing nonetheless. Much to Kitty's relief, the Indians did not reappear.

Ryan shot a pheasant and they dined on roasted meat, potatoes cooked in the fire, and canned peaches. It didn't matter if they used up their store of supplies, for Ryan told her they would reach her father's ranch tomorrow.

Father. The word tasted like ashes in her mouth. She would be perfectly happy to spend the rest of her life without meeting the man who claimed to be her father.

"What are you thinking?" Ryan asked as he gathered up the leftovers and stomped out the fire. Apparently he had noticed her contemplative mood.

Kitty sighed. "About tomorrow. Meeting Bert Lowry isn't going to be easy."

"Why can't you think of him as your father?" Ryan asked. "It would help, you know."

"Don't ask that of me, Ryan. I'll always think of him as the bastard who left Mama and me to fend for ourselves."

"He didn't know about you, Kitty." He frowned at her. "I thought you were working on cleaning up your coarse language. Your lapses are becoming less frequent, but the cuss words seem to reappear whenever you're upset."

Kitty's chin rose pugnaciously. "I can't help how I talk. I just open my mouth and out it comes. I told you this was a mistake."

"I am sure Bert won't care how you talk," Ryan said, as if trying to reassure himself as well as Kitty. But Kitty didn't believe it.

"We'll see," she said cryptically.

Kitty stretched and yawned, glad in a way that this journey was ending. Ryan was becoming too important to her. She didn't know what she was going to do when he returned to his ranch in Montana. She glanced up at him when she felt the searing heat of his gaze resting upon her and knew precisely what he was thinking. But he needn't worry. She had neither the strength nor the will to deny them one last night together. Her thoughts must have conveyed themselves to him, for he reached for her, bringing her roughly into his arms.

"If this is to be our last night together, we shouldn't waste it. I hope you're not too tired."

His breathtaking smile nearly stopped her heart. She would have to be dead not to want the same thing he did. Making love with Ryan was the only thing in her miserable life she had to look forward to, and even that would end soon.

"I'm not too tired," she said, finding her mouth gone suddenly dry with anticipation.

He gave her another of his devastating smiles and slowly began to undress her. Needing to touch him, she unbuttoned his shirt and splayed her hands on his bare shoulders. She heard him drag in a shuddering breath as her hands moved over his chest, down his taut belly, to his belt.

She rested her hands on his waist as he removed her remaining clothing. When she was naked, she tugged at his belt, and he eagerly complied to her unspoken command. She shuddered with need as he ripped off his breeches and boots and tossed them aside. He stood before her as naked as she, a magnificent, virile animal. They moved as one to the bedroll, mouths clinging, hands seeking pleasure points, both fully aroused even before reaching their destination.

She lay beneath him, trembling with need as he caressed her body, his fingers probing, stroking, working their skillful magic as his mouth found the throbbing pulse at the base of her throat. Then he parted her legs and thrust into her, so deep she felt him touch her soul. Her tenuous hold on reality fled, and she climaxed violently, the pleasure so incredible she nearly swooned. He needed only a few forceful strokes before she felt him go rigid as his own climax came upon him. She stroked his back, his shoulders, whispering that she loved him, achingly aware that he couldn't hear her and fearing to say the words aloud.

They fell asleep in each other's arms, awakening later to make love again. Just before dawn she felt his mouth upon her breasts, suckling her, and for the third time that night she gave herself up to passion.

Morning came too soon. They got a later start than usual, and after a breakfast of leftovers they broke camp and rode off.

After a few hours of hard riding they

stopped to rest the horses. "The Lowry spread is dead ahead," Ryan said. He searched her face, then asked, "Are you all right?"

No! she wanted to scream, *I'm not all right. I'm scared, and I'm afraid I'll lose you. You're the only thing I have to cling to in this strange new world gone suddenly awry.*

She gave a mirthless chuckle. "Don't even ask."

"Everything is going to be fine, you'll see," Ryan assured her. "You'll be home soon."

"Home," she said dryly. "I can hardly wait."

Ryan gave her a hard look but did not belabor the subject.

After a short rest they remounted and resumed their journey. Two hours later they crossed the outer boundaries of Lowry land. A short time after that the ranch house came into view. The land, the grand house, the fat cows grazing on the hillsides, everything Kitty saw indicated prosperity. Bert Lowry must be a rich man, she reflected, vowing to take nothing from him, not that she expected anything. She'd never had a father before, and she didn't need one now. She had suffered deprivation and faced dangerous situations while Bert Lowry was living an affluent life with his wife and stepdaughter. They had nothing in common.

Chickens and geese scattered as they rode through the gate into the yard. Kitty eyed the numerous outbuildings — the barn, the stables, the corral. She was impressed by the large number of cowhands engaged in activity, and felt completely out of her element. She couldn't deal with prosperity. During her early years she had eaten when her mother earned money to provide a decent meal. Deke had been of no help at all. He'd drunk up his money and then tried to wrest money from her mother's meager income when his ran out. During her later years she'd subsisted on standard camp fare of beans, wild game, and jerky. She'd felt fortunate when flour or cornmeal was available.

A cowboy ambled up to take their horses as they reined in before the rambling two-story ranch house. The cowboy gave Kitty a hard stare, then led the horses off after greeting Ryan by name.

"I became acquainted with the hands during my stay here," he explained when Kitty looked at him askance. "Shall we go inside?"

Kitty swallowed past the lump in her throat and nodded. Sand crunched under her feet as she walked up the stairs and onto the front porch, and she concentrated on the sound to take her mind off her anxiety. The wide front porch looked exactly like the one in a recurring dream she had about living in a real house with a front porch just like this one. But in her dreams the house and porch belonged to her, not to a stranger she had to pretend to like.

Kitty stared at the petite raven-haired beauty who opened the front door to them. She was fashionably dressed in a pale green dimity gown that hugged her curvaceous figure and revealed a rather large portion of creamy white breasts. Her skin was so pale that Kitty seriously doubted whether the woman ever stepped foot outside without first swathing herself from head to toe. Her face lit up when she saw Ryan.

"You're back!" the woman cried, launching herself at Ryan.

To Kitty's dismay, Ryan appeared more than eager to see the curvy beauty as he opened his arms to receive her. She watched the young woman give Ryan an exuberant hug, but she was puzzled by the smug smile the girl sent her over Ryan's shoulder.

"I didn't know I'd be missed," Ryan said jokingly as he carefully removed the girl's arms from around his neck and stepped back. He turned to Kitty with a smile she thought looked a tad strained and said, "Teresa, I'd like you to meet your stepsister, Kathryn. She likes to be called Kitty. Kitty, this is Teresa. I know you two are going to be good friends, since you are nearly the same age."

Kitty gave Teresa a tentative smile, hoping to forge a friendship. But Teresa's cold stare soon disabused her of that notion. Nonetheless, Kitty offered a polite greeting, which Teresa all but ignored.

"I'm three years older," Teresa said, sniffing disdainfully as she raked Kitty with a look that spoke of her disdain. "Where did Ryan find you?"

"It doesn't matter where I found Kitty," Ryan answered. "Aren't you going to invite us inside?" he asked, dragging a reluctant Kitty with him as she stepped around Teresa and entered the house. "I'd like to see your stepfather immediately, if possible."

"Papa Bert is resting. Are you sure you have the right woman? I would hate to see Papa Bert disappointed. I don't know how much more his poor heart can take."

"I have the right woman," Ryan assured her.

Kitty couldn't blame Teresa for being suspicious and resentful. Until Kitty's arrival she had been Bert's only daughter.

193

Now suddenly she was being demoted to the position of stepdaughter, pushed aside by Bert's biological daughter. Kitty would have told Teresa she had nothing to worry about on that score, for she had no intention of sticking around long enough for Teresa to get her nose out of joint.

"Why don't you show Kitty to her room while I speak with Bert," Ryan suggested. "Kitty can probably use a bath and a rest before meeting her father."

Kitty blessed Ryan for his thoughtfulness but thought that Teresa didn't look any too pleased with Ryan's dismissal.

"Very well," Teresa agreed with less than good grace. "I'll see you later, Ryan. We need to talk," she added, giving Kitty a look that spoke of her animosity.

On the other hand, the silky purr and inviting smile Teresa bestowed upon Ryan left little doubt in Kitty's mind that Ryan and Teresa had been more than mere acquaintances. She'd realized long ago that Ryan was a womanizer but it hurt to see another woman fawning over him.

Granted Ryan was a handsome devil who could charm the drawers off a statue, but Kitty wondered if Teresa knew she'd never get Ryan to the altar. Her thoughts skid to a halt when Teresa started up the staircase, motioning for Kitty to follow.

"We're short on rooms," Teresa contended. "You'll have to take an unoccupied room in the attic. It was used as a maid's room until Papa Bert built small cottages for the help and their families. Only Rosita, the cook, resides in the house. Her room is off the kitchen."

"It makes no difference where you put me, since I won't be staying long."

Teresa whirled, her elegant eyebrows raised. "What do you mean, you're not staying long?"

Kitty gave her a defiant glare. "I never had a father growing up, why should I want one now? I came to meet a dying man, one who says he's my father. I have no proof that he really is who he claims. Besides," she added with a shrug, "Ryan said I need only stay long enough to meet . . . Bert."

Teresa led the way up a second staircase to the attic. Halfway up she turned to confront Kitty. "I don't believe you. You're just a scheming little hussy after Papa Bert's worldly goods, which, as you may have guessed, are considerable."

Kitty's temper, never very stable, exploded. "You bitch! I ain't no hussy and I don't give a crap about Mr. Lowry's worldly goods. You're welcome to them. Show me

195

which room is mine and get the hell away from me."

Teresa retreated a step, her hand splayed over her chest in obvious shock. "My word! I've never heard such filth coming from a woman's mouth. Where did you grow up, in the gutter? Papa Bert isn't going to like that at all."

"I don't give a damn what Bert Lowry likes or dislikes. He's never been a father to me. He abandoned my mother for yours, why should I care what he thinks? Now if you'll show me to my room, I intend to have a bath and rest. Would you see that hot water is carried up for me?"

Kitty could tell by the way Teresa bristled that she didn't take kindly to being ordered around. Teresa opened the door to the room she'd assigned to Kitty, stepped out of the way so Kitty could enter, and said, "I'm not a servant. We have a bathing room with hot and cold running water."

Kitty knew she had blundered badly, but Teresa had made her angry enough to spit nails. Sighing, she entered the room and came to an abrupt halt. The roof slanted so steeply on one side that Kitty doubted she'd be able to stand upright. A narrow cot was pushed up against the slanted roof. Should she rise suddenly from sleep she'd bash her head on the slanting wall. The rest of the furnishings consisted of a single ladder-back chair, a washstand, cracked bowl and pitcher, and nails pounded into the wall to hold her clothing. She immediately opened the one small uncurtained window and breathed deeply of the fresh air wafting into the musty room.

Kitty ran a finger over the nightstand and snorted in disgust. A thick layer of dust covered her finger. She'd slept in some pretty dismal places before, including the hard ground, but this was one of the worst. Before she could lay her head on the pillow she would have to take all the bedclothes outside and give them a thorough shaking. If this was how Bert Lowry meant to treat his daughter, she wanted nothing to do with the man.

Bert was sleeping when Ryan tiptoed into his room. He looked so peaceful that Ryan decided to wait until Bert awakened to give him the good news. Meanwhile, he'd carry Kitty's belongings up to her room so she could settle in.

With Kitty's saddlebags flung over one broad shoulder, Ryan started up the stairs. At the top landing he paused to get his bearings. He recalled that there were three bedrooms and a bathing room on the second floor. One bedroom was Teresa's, one he'd occupied during his stay, and the other was empty. Bert slept downstairs in a converted den where his needs could be attended to more easily. Ryan strode to the room he knew to be empty and knocked on the door. When no one answered, he barged in.

The room was empty. A puzzled frown marred his wide brow. No sign existed that either Kitty or Teresa had been there. He dropped the saddlebags on the floor and returned to the hallway just as Teresa was descending the attic stairs. Now he really was baffled. To his knowledge there was just a small room under the eaves that no one had occupied in years.

Teresa stopped abruptly when she saw Ryan, obviously not expecting to see him there. Ignoring her apparent confusion, he asked, "Where is Kitty?"

"In her room, of course," Teresa said, sending him a dazzling smile. Instead of placating him, the smile made him edgy and set off warning bells in his head. Something wasn't right.

"I've just been to Kitty's room and she's not there."

Teresa's smile turned brittle. "I thought

she would prefer privacy, so I gave her the attic room. She'll be quite comfortable there."

"You what?" Ryan shouted, afraid his hearing had gone bad.

Teresa repeated her previous words.

Ryan's temper flared. "You know damn good and well that room isn't fit for human occupancy. What made you do such a damn fool thing?"

"Don't you dare use that kind of language with me, Ryan Delaney," Teresa said in a wounded voice. "It's bad enough hearing it from that vulgar little hussy you brought here. I was shocked. I don't know where you found Kitty, but in my opinion she's a coarse, foulmouthed tramp."

"Your opinion doesn't count, Teresa," Ryan said with remarkable patience, when what he'd really like to do was wring Teresa's spoiled little neck. She had no business ridiculing Kitty or her language when she knew nothing about the life Kitty had been forced to live.

"I don't want to see Papa Bert hurt," Teresa explained with mock innocence.

Ryan searched her face, then nodded grudgingly. "Very well, I'll overlook your rudeness since we can right this wrong with little effort." He started up the narrow staircase.

"Where are you going?"

"To take Kitty to the room that should rightfully be hers," Ryan threw over his shoulder. "I'll try to convince her this was all a mistake."

"Yes, yes, a mistake," Teresa agreed with alacrity. "Shall I come with you and explain?"

"No need. I can find my own way."

Fortunately he didn't see the look of fury Teresa delivered to his back as he continued up the stairs. He reached the tiny alcove and rapped lightly on the door. When no one answered, he opened the door and stepped inside. He saw Kitty leaning out the window, shaking something that created a flurry of dust.

"What are you doing?"

Kitty yelped and spun around. "You frightened me. Don't you believe in knocking first?"

"I did knock but apparently you didn't hear me. What are you doing?" he repeated.

"Shaking out the sheets and blanket." She sneezed twice and gave him a sheepish look. "Truth to tell, I'd rather bed down outside than sleep in this room."

"Come away from the window. You're not going to sleep outside, nor are you going to remain in this room."

She gave him a skeptical look. "Why not? I hope you're not suggesting that I share *your* room. I don't think Teresa would like that."

"I don't care what Teresa likes or doesn't like. This isn't the room you were supposed to occupy. Although, come to think of it, sharing my bed isn't a bad idea," he added, grinning wolfishly. "Your room is on the second floor, next to mine and across from Teresa's. The bathing room is down the hall a few steps."

"Teresa said the bedrooms on the second floor were occupied."

"Teresa made a mistake. I'm afraid she's a tad jealous, but hopefully she'll reconsider and you two can become real sisters."

"That's not going to happen. We had a short conversation before you arrived, and it wasn't pleasant."

"So I heard. What did you say to her? I told you to curb your tongue. I thought you had that problem under control."

"I couldn't help it. I'm not used to being insulted without retaliating. I told you I don't belong here."

"You've been here less than two hours," Ryan said. "Give yourself a chance to adjust. You haven't even met Bert yet."

To Ryan's dismay, he saw tears forming in the corner of Kitty's eyes. He realized she was near the breaking point, and he felt another unaccustomed jolt of compassion. That seemed to happen a lot around Kitty. Without really knowing how it happened, she was in his arms.

"Dry your eyes, Kitten, there's nothing to cry about."

"I'm not crying," Kitty sniffed. "I never cry. It's all this damn dust."

He lifted her chin and brushed away the tears with his fingertips. He felt her tremble beneath his touch and couldn't resist the urge to kiss her sweet lips. He was going to miss Kitty's responsive little body beside him in his bedroll tonight. But it was more than her body that set Kitty apart from other women. Kitty brought out a fierce protectiveness he'd rarely, if ever, felt before. He wanted to shield her from anyone who would take advantage of her, and that included himself. The feeling made him un-comfortable.

Despite his discomfort, Ryan made a silent vow to protect Kitty from those who would harm her, no matter what happened between Kitty and her father. He didn't stop to think that he wouldn't be around forever, that he would be returning to Montana soon. He couldn't think beyond Kitty's immediate welfare.

Kitty's fierce resentment of Bert gave Ryan another cause to worry. Had he done the right thing by bringing father and daughter together? he wondered. Was Teresa going to be more of a problem than he had anticipated? All these questions and more ran through Ryan's head as he held Kitty's face between his hands and wiped away her tears. He sensed her anxiety, felt the tension coiling inside her, and his body responded to her unspoken need.

Compelled by a feeling older than time, he pulled her against him, lost in a sensual fog of need. His lips came down hard on hers, tasting, savoring, his tongue probing her lips until she opened her mouth. He groaned as his tongue slipped inside, stabbing deeply, unable to get enough of her. He heard her moan and would have forgotten where they were and taken her on the dusty bed if Kitty hadn't shoved him away.

"We can't do this. Not now. Not here. Damnation, Ryan, Teresa would have me for breakfast if she suspected we were intimate. It would be best for all concerned if we simply forgot what went on before and pretended casual friendship."

Ryan frowned. "I don't give a damn what Teresa thinks, but I reckon you're right. We don't want to upset Bert. For all his illness, Bert is a perceptive man. I'd hate for him to learn I was the one who stole his daughter's innocence."

"You didn't steal anything, I gave it to you."

Ryan gave her a cheeky grin. "That's what you think. I charmed you out of it. Come on, I'll take you to your room. Then you can enjoy a long bath before you meet Bert. Are you hungry? I'm sure Rosita can fix something to hold you over until dinner."

"I can wait. I'm more interested in that bath right now."

Suddenly Teresa popped her head into the room. "Oh, there you are. I couldn't imagine what was keeping you two." She gave Kitty a hard look. "Bert should be waking up soon."

Teresa's dark brown eyes were fixed on Kitty with almost malevolent intent. Ryan noticed it and wondered if he was the cause of Teresa's animosity. Instinctively he sensed it went far deeper than simple jealousy. He saw Kitty flinch and knew she was fully aware of the undercurrent of hostility swirling around her.

While Kitty bathed, Ryan returned to Bert's room, pleased to find him awake this time. As far as Ryan could tell, Bert's condition had not changed during his absence. He was no better, no worse. He was still pale, still frail. According to a description provided by Ryan's father years ago, Bert had once been a robust man.

Bert's eyes lit up when he saw Ryan. "Ryan, thank God you're back." He glanced toward the door. "Do you have my daughter? For God's sake, man, did you find her? Where is she? You can't believe how long I've waited for this day. Finding Kathryn is all that has kept me alive these last few years."

Ryan searched Bert's drawn features and wondered how long the man would have lived had he failed to find Kitty. Not long, he'd wager.

"I found your daughter, Bert. But I wanted you to know her history before I introduce you to her. You need to be aware of the circumstances in which I found her."

"Can I come in?" Teresa asked as she entered the room carrying a bottle and glass of water. "It's time for Papa Bert's medicine.

I try to take care of the dear man, don't I, Papa Bert?"

Bert gave her a weak smile. "You've been a tremendous help during my illness, my dear," he allowed. "Ryan was about to tell me about Kathryn. Why don't you pull up a chair. This concerns you, too."

"I would like that," Teresa said sweetly, sending Ryan a coquettish smile. "I'm quite anxious to learn about Kathryn's life before Ryan found her."

Ryan would have preferred to speak in private to Bert but accepted Bert's decision to include Teresa. "Very well, I'll start from the beginning. First, Kathryn prefers to be called Kitty. I think it would make her feel more at ease and please her if you both addressed her by that name."

"Then Kitty it is," Bert eagerly agreed. "Is she beautiful and blond like her mother? Are her eyes brown?"

"Kitty is . . . well, one of the loveliest women I've ever known. There is a special quality about her I can't explain. She's more vulnerable than she lets on. And she's blond and has magnificent blue eyes. You'll see for yourself soon enough. But there is something you should know before meeting her." He took a deep breath. "Kitty bears you no love. She blames you for abandoning her mother and forcing her into a demeaning life with Deke Johnson."

"That's ridiculous!" Teresa blasted. "Papa Bert didn't even know Kathryn . . . Kitty existed."

"No, Teresa, Kitty has every right to dislike me," Bert said sadly. "After all, I did abandon her mother for yours, even though Rena was the love of my life. You see, I was young at the time, and needed money to save my ranch. Teresa's mother had an abundance of cash and was willing to invest in my ranch. I abandoned the woman I loved because I wasn't strong enough to face poverty. I had little backbone as a youth. The army did wonders for me, but by then I was trapped in marriage to another."

"Papa Bert! Are you saying you never loved my mother?" Teresa asked, scandalized.

"I grew quite fond of your mother, my dear, but to be perfectly honest, what I felt for her was nothing compared to the love I bore Rena. Nevertheless, your mother never suffered neglect or lacked my regard. Go on, Ryan. Tell me what happened to Kitty after Rena and Deke died. My private investigators turned up little to indicate what had become of her."

"What follows is likely to disturb you, but you have a right to know the truth," Ryan said, "and I hope you'll keep an open mind about what I am about to reveal."

"Kitty is my daughter, how can I think badly of her? I want to know everything, Ryan. You've done me a great service, the least I can do is listen and not judge harshly."

"Perhaps this should wait," Teresa said. "Papa Bert is tiring."

"Nonsense," Bert said with surprising vigor. "Time enough to rest when I'm dead. Go on, Ryan."

"Kitty was thirteen when Rena died. From what I gathered from Kitty, Deke made no bones about wanting her to take her mother's place in his bed."

"Oh, my," Teresa said. "Poor Papa Bert. It must be heartbreaking to know that his daughter became a whore."

"Your pity is misplaced," Ryan said, sending Teresa a censuring scowl. "Before Deke could force her to his bed, he was caught cheating at poker and shot dead."

"You have only Kitty's word on that," Teresa said with sly innuendo.

"I believe Kitty even if I don't know her," Bert said weakly. He was beginning to tire, and he was showing it. Ryan hurried on with his story.

"Kitty had a stepbrother she saw only infrequently. He heard about his father's death, knew Kitty was too young to be left on her own, and he took her away."

"Took her where?" Bert asked.

"For the first couple of years they traveled a lot. Lex was an outlaw, and they lived on his illegal earnings during that time. Then he met up with the Barton gang."

"I've heard about them," Bert said slowly. "They hit banks and disappear over the border into Mexico."

"Lex joined up with the Bartons. He and Kitty rode with the gang until just recently, when I crossed paths with the Bartons in Tombstone. Lex was shot and killed during a bank robbery, and I met Kitty through an unusual set of circumstances, which I won't go into now. It took me awhile, but I finally convinced Kitty to accompany me back here to meet you."

"My poor, poor child," lamented Bert.

"Poor child, indeed!" spouted Teresa. "Have you thought about the implications of a young girl living with outlaws?"

"Kitty posed as a lad. No one but Lex ever knew she was female. Lex may not have been the best of brothers, but apparently he protected her to the best of his ability."

"Of course you saw through her disguise immediately," Teresa said with derision.

"Actually, I did," Ryan allowed. "Fortunately none of the Bartons were as observant."

"Papa Bert can think what he wants but the whole thing sounds rather far-fetched to me," Teresa sniffed. "I've heard the foul language Kitty uses. I don't believe she is as innocent as you would like us to believe, Ryan."

"The Bartons did not corrupt Kitty," Ryan insisted. He experienced a twinge of unaccustomed guilt. The Bartons didn't corrupt Kitty, he did.

"How do you know?" Teresa charged.

"Teresa, don't badger Ryan," Bert chided. "I believe him. Now, bring my daughter to me, I can't wait to meet her. I pray God grants me sufficient time on earth to get to know her."

"I think you're making a big mistake," Teresa warned. "We would be better advised to lock up the good silver and valuables."

CHAPTER 9

Kitty finished her bath and decided to find Ryan. She wanted to get the meeting between herself and Bert over and done with. Then she could concentrate on where she was going to settle and what she was going to do when she left here. For obvious reasons she couldn't return to Tombstone. She still had some money left and gave serious thought to settling further north, perhaps in another state.

She couldn't depend on Ryan forever, however much she might want him in her life. She had no false expectations where Ryan was concerned. He had completed his mission for Bert and was probably itching to leave. If he could tear himself away from the delectable Teresa, that is. She tried to convince herself that Ryan wasn't important to her, but her heart told her otherwise. She didn't want to love him, it had just happened. Life would never be the same without Ryan, but she was strong, and somehow she'd manage.

All these concerns and more ran through Kitty's head as she descended the stairs in search of Ryan. She heard voices coming from a room just beyond the parlor and headed in that direction. The door was open, and she stepped inside. She froze on the threshold as she heard Teresa say, "We would be better advised to lock up the good silver and valuables."

Kitty stepped into the room. "You needn't be concerned about the silver or valuables. You have nothing here I'd want," she said, holding her head high despite the pain lancing through her. Rejection hurt. But it was precisely the kind of greeting she'd expected.

Ryan leaped to his feet. "Kitty! Don't take Teresa's words to heart. She doesn't speak for everyone. Come and meet your father."

Kitty looked at the wizened man in the bed, saw the expectant look in his watery eyes, and felt the overwhelming urge to turn and flee. The pressure to like this man, to accept him unconditionally was overwhelming. How could she like, much less love, the man who had been the cause of all her mother's misery? The answer was clear and concise. She couldn't.

"Hello, Mr. Lowry," Kitty said coolly.

"Kitty . . ." Ryan began.

"No, let the child be," Bert interjected. "Come closer, Kitty. My eyes aren't as good as they used to be."

Kitty's legs wobbled as she walked to the bed and stared down at Bert Lowry. His skin was ashen, his lips nearly blue, but his eyes were bright and inquisitive as they settled on her with a mixture of excitement and curiosity. Kitty was surprised to see that he still retained his hair, which was thick and gray, and that his hands were surprisingly strong as they grasped hers. She wanted to pull them away but didn't have the heart to be deliberately cruel to a dying man however much she disliked him.

"Perhaps we should leave Kitty and her father alone," Ryan suggested. When Teresa made no move to leave, he grasped her arm and all but pulled her from the room, closing the door softly behind him.

"Sit down, Kitty," Bert said. When Kitty made no move to obey, he said, "Please hear me out. For your mother's sake."

Put like that, Kitty had no choice. She sat in the chair just recently occupied by Teresa, her shoulders stiff and uncompromising. "What is it you wish to say to me, Mr. Lowry?"

She saw Bert wince and tried not to let it bother her. "If you can't find it in your heart to call me Father, I'd prefer to be called Bert. Mr. Lowry sounds so . . . cold."

"It's . . . strange suddenly finding I have a father after all these years, and difficult to love where none exists. If that hurts you, I'm sorry."

"Did your mother tell you nothing about me? She was the love of my life. The only woman I *ever* loved."

Kitty gave a snort of derision. "You had a funny way of showing it. Did you ever try to contact my mother in all these years? And no, Mama never told me about you. She said she was going to, but she died suddenly, before revealing that information to me. Not that it would have mattered. You were the last person I'd turn to for help."

"Apparently Rena was concerned enough about you to write me. Her letter arrived shortly before her death. She told me about you and asked me to take care of you after she was gone. I'm sorry she died before telling you about me or mentioning the letter."

"Then why didn't you come for me?" Kitty asked, raising her chin aggressively.

"I . . . it was impossible at the time. My own wife was ill and dying. I didn't want to hurt her by bringing forth a daughter she never knew existed. I waited until after her death to act upon Rena's letter. Unfortunately I waited too long. By then Deke was dead and you had disappeared.

"I was devastated when my private investigator failed to locate you. I retained the man on a permanent basis but he had no success during the following years. When I fell ill, I became despondent and more determined than ever to see my only child before I left this earth. Out of desperation I wrote to my old friend, unaware that he had died some years earlier. I knew he had three sons and asked if he could spare one to help find my daughter, since I had no sons of my own. Ryan volunteered."

"What made you think Ryan could find me if your investigator couldn't?" Kitty asked.

"I don't know. A hunch maybe. I told you I was desperate and willing to try anything. I felt that new blood, new ideas would be helpful."

"It was only a coincidence that Ryan and I crossed paths," Kitty contended.

"But he *did* succeed where others failed," Bert argued. "Maybe it *was* coincidence. Maybe it was God's intervention. Whatever it was, I'm grateful."

He gazed at her, his eyes wet with tears.

"You're beautiful, just like your mother. The sorriest thing I ever did was to place wealth and prosperity above love, and I suffered my whole life for it."

A curl of pity worked its way to Kitty's heart. "I'm sorry for both you and Mama, but it changes nothing. You're a stranger to me. What exactly do you want from me, Mister . . . er, Bert? My time here is limited."

Bert closed his eyes. His face was drawn and gray, and Kitty could tell their conversation had exhausted him. "Can we speak of this later?" he asked weakly. "I'm at my best in the morning. Come back then. There's so much more I want to say to you."

Kitty nodded jerkily. She really didn't want to remain at the ranch, but she'd come this far and owed it to her mother to hear Bert out. "Very well. We'll talk further in the morning." She rose to leave.

"Kitty." Kitty turned, one brow raised askance. "Don't let Teresa scare you off. She's never had to share my affections before. She came here many years after I married her mother. She'd been living with an aunt and preferred to remain in San Francisco. She didn't arrive at the ranch until shortly before her mother died. I treated her like a daughter, but unlike you she has none of my blood flowing through her veins."

Kitty remained thoughtful as she left Bert's room. She had arrived at the ranch prepared to hate the man who claimed to be her father, and so far nothing Bert said had changed her mind. But seeing him lying weak and ill in his bed had moved her more than she cared to admit. Moved not to love, but to pity. She'd known the initial meeting with her father wasn't going to be easy, but she'd had no idea it would be traumatic, as well as painful. Something had stirred inside her when she finally came face to face with her father, something deep and disturbing and utterly devastating.

While Kitty and Bert spoke privately in Bert's room, Ryan and Teresa wandered into the parlor. Ryan paced the room nervously while Teresa seated herself on the sofa and watched him.

"Ryan, come and sit down," Teresa invited, patting the cushion beside her.

"What do you suppose Bert and Kitty are talking about?" Ryan wondered as he flopped down on the sofa.

"She's probably pulling the wool over poor Papa Bert's eyes," Teresa maintained. "How could either of you believe a woman of Kitty's ilk could be Papa Bert's daughter?"

"Do you think I would bring an imposter here?" Ryan asked, hanging on to his temper with difficulty.

Teresa shook her head in mock dismay. "You're as gullible as my stepfather. What did Kitty do to convince you she's Kathryn? She's a sly baggage. It wouldn't surprise me if you've already bedded her."

Ryan flushed, refusing to look at her. It was none of Teresa's damn business what went on between him and Kitty. Teresa was too perceptive by half. Though he and Kitty had indeed made love, it was not for the reasons Teresa thought.

"So I *am* right!" Teresa exulted, her eyes gleaming with malice. "Forget Kitty, she's a slut. No decent woman would chop off her hair. I'm going to tell Papa Bert that Kitty is an imposter, that she hoodwinked you into believing she was his daughter."

"You'll do no such thing!" Ryan shouted, losing what temper he had left. "There's been no mistake. Kitty is Bert's daughter."

Teresa scooted over until she was seated so close to Ryan that he could feel the heat of her body pressing against him. He tried to move, but she wound her arms around his waist and held him fast.

"I'm better than Kitty," she whispered into his ear. "We never completed what we started when you were here before. I want you, Ryan, surely you know that. If you were honest you'd admit that you want me." She preened for his benefit. "I'm prettier than Kitty, and better in bed. Give me a chance, Ryan. I'll come to your room tonight and show you how happy I can make you."

Ryan had suspected that Teresa was no innocent, and her words just now proved it. He wondered if Bert knew his stepdaughter was sexually active. He was sorry now that he'd begun that mild flirtation with Teresa. He'd had no idea Teresa would pursue him with such tenacity, or demand an intimate relationship when he returned.

He was still pondering the precarious situation he had gotten himself into with Teresa when she surprised him by pulling his head down and lifting her lips to his. There was no way to avoid Teresa's kiss. Her full red lips were attached to his like glue as she pressed herself against him. Their mouths were still locked together when he happened to glance over Teresa's shoulder and saw Kitty standing on the threshold. Her eyes were wide and filled with pain as she stared at them with a look Ryan could only describe as horror.

■ ■ ■ ■

Kitty hadn't expected to be greeted by an intimate display between Ryan and Teresa when she left Bert's room. She gasped and stopped dead in her tracks when she saw the two entwined on the sofa, their lips locked in a passionate kiss. She'd wanted to turn away, to run, but something perverse inside her had made her stay after hearing Teresa tell Ryan to expect her in his room tonight. She'd been somewhat heartened when Ryan hadn't verbally encouraged her, but then they had kissed, and she knew Ryan wasn't averse to having Teresa in his bed.

Kitty knew Ryan had seen her, and she turned abruptly toward the stairs, wanting the privacy of her room to nurse her heartache. She didn't see Ryan disentangle himself from Teresa and sprint after her. He caught her at the foot of the stairs.

"It's not what it seems, Kitty."

Kitty put her hands on her hips and said combatively, "I'm not blind. I knew immediately that you and Teresa had been . . . were still . . . intimate. I have no right to interfere in whatever you two have together. I've never had delusions about our relationship. You made me no promises and I asked for none. I'm just wondering if Teresa knows you'll never marry her."

"What's this about marriage?" Teresa asked as she sidled up beside Ryan and pressed herself against him.

"I said you're whistling in the dark if you think Ryan will marry you," Kitty repeated.

"Surely you're not stupid enough to think he'll marry *you*," Teresa hissed.

"Enough!" Ryan blasted. "You both know how I feel about marriage, and that's all I'm going to say on the subject."

Kitty gave Teresa an I-told-you-so smile. "If you'll excuse me, I'm going to my room to rest."

"Supper is at seven," Teresa called after her. "You do know how to eat with a knife and fork, don't you?"

Kitty didn't bother answering as she gave them her back and marched up the stairs.

Teresa put her arm through Ryan's and all but pulled him away from the staircase. "Why do you concern yourself with Kitty? A woman who consorts with outlaws has to be a wh—"

"Don't say it, Teresa," Ryan warned. "Kitty is Bert's daughter, that's all you need to know about her." He removed her arm and roughly flung it away. "I'm going out to

221

the bunkhouse to visit the hands. I'll see you at supper."

"You're going to see a lot more of me," Teresa muttered as she stared after him.

Kitty wore one of her two good dresses down to supper that night. It was light blue linen and quite fetching, with puffed sleeves and a square neckline that showed just a hint of pale breasts and the shadowy cleft in between. She wasn't looking forward to sharing a meal with Teresa and Ryan, but she didn't want to impose upon the cook by asking to have her meal sent up to her. Since she planned to leave fairly soon, she figured she could put up with Teresa's insults for the time being. As for Ryan, it was going to be a long time before she learned to live without him. Love wasn't so easily disposed of.

Teresa had arrived in the dining room before Kitty and was seated at the head of the table. Kitty couldn't help being impressed with Teresa's vibrant beauty. Her lustrous hair floated around her shoulders like a dark cloud, and the violet dress she wore enhanced the satiny texture of her pale skin. Her dark eyes kept shifting to the doorway, and Kitty knew she was waiting for Ryan to appear. Ignoring

Teresa, Kitty slid into one of the two places where silver and china had been laid out.

"I'm sorry you had to witness that intimate scene between me and Ryan this afternoon," Teresa said, sounding not at all sorry. "Ryan and I became . . . close during his previous stay at the ranch." She batted her long eyelashes. "I'm expecting a proposal. I know Ryan is against marriage, but I have so much to offer him he can't possibly refuse."

"Like what?" Kitty asked dryly, amazed at Teresa's audacity.

"Until you arrived I was Papa Bert's only heir. This ranch and all his worldly goods would have been mine after he passes on."

Kitty grit her teeth. "Aren't you merely Bert's stepdaughter?" she asked sweetly.

"I am all he had until you came around," Teresa bit out. "You can't fool me. I will never believe you're the real Kathryn. You're an imposter, and I intend to make Papa Bert accept it. It should be obvious to everyone that the real Kathryn is dead. No outlaw's whore is going to steal what is mine."

Kitty started to rise, determined to leave this horrible place before she did something she'd be sorry for. She was halfway out of her chair when she felt a hand on her shoulder.

"I'm sorry to have kept you waiting. Were you going someplace, Kitty? I hope not, for I'm starving, and I'm sure you are too."

"Kitty and I were just discussing . . ."

"We were discussing the fact that Teresa thinks I'm a whore," Kitty said, cutting off Teresa's words. "For your information, I don't give a damn what that uppity bitch thinks. She can go to hell and take you with her. Only a mule-headed jackass would stay here, and I ain't no jackass." She glared at Ryan. "As for you, Mr. Delaney, Teresa thinks you're gonna marry her, but I say you ain't got the balls to marry anyone."

Ryan made a gurgling noise in his throat that could have been either a suppressed laugh or an angry growl. "Kitty, for the love of God, watch your mouth!"

"How dare you!" Teresa sputtered. "I've never . . ."

"Yes you have and we both know it," Kitty charged. "I ain't gonna apologize. I was prepared to be friends with Teresa, but I can see now how wrong I was. I'll make my peace with Bert and move on. Teresa is welcome to Bert's money and property, I never wanted anything from him." She picked up her fork. "Can we eat now? I'm

224

famished."

As if on cue, Rosita bustled in from the kitchen and began setting dishes on the table. Kitty dug in with gusto. The food was delicious, and she wasn't about to let Teresa spoil her enjoyment of it.

"Your table manners are atrocious," Teresa chided as she daintily picked at her food. "But what could one expect from someone raised in the gutter?"

"Will you two stop bickering?" Ryan gritted out from between clenched teeth. "For Bert's sake you should try to get along. Although Kitty is Bert's natural daughter, he's not going to abandon Teresa. I brought Kitty here so Bert could see his daughter before meeting his maker. I'd advise you both to settle your differences and let the old man die in peace."

"Of course you're right, Ryan," Teresa said sweetly. "I'll try not to be judgmental of Kitty. But I do wish she'd watch her language."

"Kitty can speak as well as you or I," Ryan claimed. "The rough language doesn't surface unless she's angry."

"Don't apologize for me, Ryan," Kitty said testily. "I'm not looking for trouble. I've had enough of that in my lifetime. I can behave if Teresa can. It's not like I'm going to be here forever."

A tense silence ensued as the meal continued. Kitty chewed the last morsel of pie on her plate and sat back, replete. "Rosita is a wonderful cook," she said. "Beans and biscuits cooked over a campfire become monotonous after a while. Especially when I'm doing the cooking." She scraped her chair back. "It's been a long day." Head held high, she made a hasty exit.

"I think I'll turn in, too," Ryan said, "after I look in on Bert."

"I'll see you later, Ryan," Teresa said in a tone ripe with promise.

Utterly exhausted, Kitty prepared for bed. The day had been long and eventful. She'd met her father, discovered that her stepsister hated her, and learned that Teresa and Ryan had been, and probably still were, lovers. Tonight Teresa was going to join Ryan in his room so they could take up where they had left off. God, it hurt. But she could expect no less from a man who claimed marriage was for fools and had promised her nothing but passion.

Even if Ryan did change his mind and marry, she wasn't the kind of woman he would want for a wife, Kitty reflected. She had too many shortcomings and wasn't polished enough for polite society. She was sure her father would feel the same way once he knew how she'd lived the last six years of her life. She'd always known that having a home and real family was out of her reach. She wasn't good enough. Her former life would always be there to haunt her, marring her happiness.

Kitty pulled back the covers and sank down into the feather mattress, sighing in pleasure. This kind of comfort had only been available to her in her dreams. She closed her eyes and drifted off to sleep. She didn't know how long she'd been asleep when she heard the distinct click of a door latch and the whisper of footsteps across the floor. She jerked upright and reached for the gun she kept under her pillow, a trick she'd learned from her lawless past. She aimed it at the shadowy figure moving stealthily toward the bed.

"Stop! There's a gun aimed at your gut."

A rumbling chuckle reached her from across the room. "I believe you *would* shoot," Ryan said. "But I hope you won't find it necessary."

He moved into the beam of moonlight streaming through the window, and Kitty's trigger finger relaxed. "What are you doing here? I almost shot you," she said, shaken by the close call. She could have killed Ryan.

"I didn't expect you to sleep with a gun beneath your pillow." He chuckled again. "I should have known a wildcat like you would be prepared for any eventuality."

"What do you want, Ryan? It's late. Shouldn't you be with Teresa?"

"The hell with Teresa. I just came from Bert's room and decided to see if you were all right. It didn't occur to me that Teresa would turn vicious. I saw no signs of it when I was here before."

"I can't blame Teresa for disliking me. She thinks I'm going to usurp her place in Bert's affections and fears I'm a rival for yours. She wants me gone."

"That's hogwash! I don't have any feelings for Teresa. We had a mild flirtation but it went no further. I don't care what she said, I never bedded her."

"You don't have feelings for any woman," Kitty said with conviction. "You don't have to lie to me, Ryan. I don't care who you take to your bed." *Lies! All lies.*

"Kitty . . ." He perched on the edge of the bed and curled his fingers around her narrow shoulders. "I don't want to see you hurt. I'm concerned about you and care what happens to you. I think you can be happy here, but not if I'm going to cause

228

trouble between you and Teresa. Perhaps I should leave. I've completed my mission, there's nothing to keep me from returning home."

"Nothing," Kitty said, choking on the word. Did Ryan expect her to beg him to stay? "I won't be staying long myself."

"Dammit, Kitty, don't let my leaving influence you. You belong here. I don't."

"I can't help the way I feel," Kitty whispered. The scorching heat of his hands on her shoulders and his drugging scent made it difficult to forget anything about Ryan Delaney. Not his kisses, not the way his hands and lips felt on her body, not the pleasure that male part of him brought her when he thrust inside her. "Go away, Ryan."

"I'm here because I thought you might need me. It's tough being among strangers. I just wanted you to know that you can always depend on me for as long as I'm here."

"How long is that?" she asked softly. "A day? A week? Two weeks? What exactly are you offering?"

"I . . . damn, I'm bungling this badly. I don't know exactly . . . that is, damn, I care about your future. I admire you. Few women would have survived the kind of life you were forced to live. Your fortitude, your courage; you not only endured but prospered. And . . . dammit, I still want you. I thought once we reached the ranch the attraction would die of natural causes." He shook his head. "Nothing has changed. I still want you."

Kitty's mouth fell open. She had no idea Ryan admired her, and his words left her speechless. She'd always known he wanted her, but wanting and loving weren't the same.

"You'd better leave, Ryan, before we both make fools of ourselves. We're in Bert's house now. The rules are different here."

His hands slid down her arms, brushing the sensitive sides of her breasts. She exhaled sharply, her body responding automatically to his touch, remembering the pleasure of their loving.

"You're right, of course," he replied, but he seemed in no hurry to remove his hands or to leave.

Her mind rebelled, but her heart soared when he lowered his head and kissed her. She knew this shouldn't be happening. Kissing Ryan always made her want things she had no right to. When he deepened the kiss, using his tongue to pry open her lips, she moaned and succumbed to the temptation of his mouth. Then she felt his hands beneath her nightgown, shoving it up as he skimmed her thighs, higher still, until he found that warm, moist place between her legs.

Somehow Kitty found the strength to push Ryan's hands away. "We can't do this, Ryan. I know how babies are made. We've been lucky so far, why push fate?"

Ryan backed away and shook his head as if to clear it. "I'm sorry. I don't know what I was thinking. I didn't come here for this. I just wanted to be sure you're all right. Something seems to happen to me whenever I'm with you. I reckon it's time for me to move on. Good night, Kitty."

Kitty said nothing. When she heard the door latch firmly behind him, she whispered into the darkness, "You're a damn coward, Ryan Delaney."

Ryan returned to his own room in a daze. He didn't know what had gotten into him. He'd always prided himself on his restraint when the situation called for such measures, but with Kitty he behaved like a callow youth. He couldn't imagine what Kitty had that made her irresistible to him.

Ryan's room was dark when he entered. He didn't bother lighting the lamp as he undressed in the dark and crawled into bed.

"What took you so long?" Teresa whispered into his ear as she pressed her silken body against his.

Ryan let out a curse and leaped out of bed. "Dammit, Teresa, are you mad? What are you doing in my bed?"

"I told you to expect me," she purred seductively. "Come back to bed. You won't be disappointed."

He fumbled in the dark for his denims, then struck a match to the lamp. He glowered at her from beneath slitted eyes. She was stretched out naked on the bed, all pink and white and flushed with excitement. Ryan reined in his lust and looked away. "I don't think Bert would appreciate me ruining his daughter."

"Obviously you had no such qualms with Kitty," Teresa charged. "You won't be ruining me, Ryan. I lost my innocence long ago. I know how to pleasure a man. I had many beaus in San Francisco. One in particular taught me to enjoy sex, and I've found I can't live without it. I've been searching for the right man for a long time, and at last I've found him. With you I could be faithful."

"Marriage isn't for me, Teresa. I'm perfectly content with my life as it is. I have no intention of taking a wife . . . ever."

"It's Kitty, isn't it?" Teresa charged. "You want her because you think Papa Bert will leave her his fortune. I'm not stupid. I know you've bedded her. A woman can tell these things."

"I told you, I'm not the marrying kind. Turn your sights to someone more inclined to make an honest woman of you than I am. I suggest you leave so I can get some sleep."

"We're not finished yet, Ryan Delaney," Teresa contended as she rose from the bed and flounced out of the room as naked as the day she was born.

"As far as I'm concerned we are," Ryan muttered beneath his breath as he closed and locked the door.

He removed his denims and fell into bed, wondering what in the hell Kitty had done to him. A few weeks ago he wouldn't have hesitated to give Teresa what she wanted. He would have bedded her and felt no guilt when it came time to leave. It was how Rogue Ryan operated. But after Kitty, Teresa no longer appealed to him. He had this terrifying thought that no woman would ever satisfy him like Kitty O'Shay Lowry.

He groaned in frustration as he recalled everything about Kitty he lusted after. Her delicious taste. Her responsive body. Her unique scent he found so alluring.

Everything about her spelled danger.

Ryan had faced danger before, but Kitty topped them all. She had turned his life upside down.

CHAPTER 10

Kitty dressed with little care the following morning, for she knew she'd look like hell no matter what she wore. There were dark smudges under her eyes, and her face was gray with fatigue. After Ryan's unexpected visit the night before she hadn't slept at all well. The longer she thought about it, the clearer it became that one woman wasn't enough for Ryan. He was an unrepentant womanizer. Regrettably she had allowed her heart to rule her head and had fallen head over heels for him. She congratulated herself for having had the fortitude to send him away last night, even if it had hurt her more than it had him.

Afterward she had tossed and turned, imagining Teresa in Ryan's bed, the recipient of his special brand of loving. Her body still ached from frustration. Denying herself what she craved, what she needed to be fulfilled again, had been costly to her peace of mind.

Kitty gave her unruly curls one last pat before descending the stairs to the dining room. It was still early, but she'd heard others up and about so she knew the household was stirring. When she found the dining room empty, she poked her head into the kitchen.

Rosita saw her and motioned her inside, her dark face alight with pleasure. "You are *Senor* Lowry's daughter. I am pleased to meet you. You have made your father very happy. I am Rosita. I didn't get a chance to meet you properly yesterday. I was just fixing your papa's breakfast. There is fresh coffee in the pot."

"Thank you," Kitty said, delighted by the cook's warm welcome. "Coffee would be great. Please call me Kitty."

"I'll fix your breakfast after I take your papa's tray to him. Teresa doesn't usually rise this early and rarely wants more than a slice of toast and tea," Rosita rambled on. "*Senor* Delaney has already eaten and gone out to give the workers a hand with the chores. He said he needed the exercise."

"I'm hungry enough to eat a horse," Kitty said. She wasn't shy when it came to her appetite. She'd gone hungry too often in the past not to respect food. Thankfully she didn't run to fat and could enjoy Rosita's delicious cooking without guilt.

Rosita laughed and patted her plump hips. "A woman after my own heart."

When Rosita had put the finishing touches on Bert's tray, Kitty said, "Why don't I carry it in to Bert myself?. He wanted to talk to me this morning and this would be a good time."

"*Si,*" Rosita agreed, handing her the tray. "Tell me what you'd like to eat and I'll bring it to you in *Senor* Lowry's room."

"That's very kind of you. Bacon, eggs, and biscuits would be wonderful. And black coffee."

Kitty carried the tray to Bert's room, knocked once, and pushed open the door at Bert's command. She found her father seated in a chair by the window. He was freshly shaved and looked better than he had yesterday. His eyes lit up when he saw her.

"Kitty, come in, my dear. I hope you're up to a nice long chat this morning. Onc of the hands came in earlier to shave me and help me with personal chores. I'm eager now to continue where we left off yesterday. In fact, having you here has invigorated me."

Kitty set the tray on his lap and whisked the covers from a dish containing oatmeal and another holding two thick biscuits slathered with butter and jam. Steam rose up from the cup of strong black coffee.

"Have you eaten?" Bert asked as he took a bite of biscuit and chewed without apparent appetite.

"Rosita offered to bring my breakfast in here to me."

He looked so genuinely pleased that Kitty couldn't help answering his smile with one of her own. Her presence seemed to spur his appetite, for he ate his oatmeal as if he truly enjoyed it. Kitty's breakfast arrived a few minutes later, and she dug into her plate of bacon and eggs. She saved her biscuit for last, sighing contentedly a short time later as she set her tray aside.

"Can I take your tray?" Kitty asked when she saw that Bert had finished all his oatmeal and most of his biscuits. He nodded, and she set his empty tray on the floor beside hers.

"You can't begin to know how happy I am to see you," Bert said in a voice thick with emotion. "My own child. Until Rena wrote me about you, I never expected to have a child of my own. I've always regretted being childless, but now I have you. It's a dream come true."

Kitty knew she had to stop this emotional

outpouring before it went any further. "I . . . I'm sorry, Bert, but I'm not comfortable with your feelings for me. I don't even know you. As I told you yesterday, I'll be riding on soon. This isn't my home. It belongs to Teresa, and she doesn't want me here. I promised nothing except that I'd come here and meet you."

The happiness Bert displayed earlier slowly dissipated, replaced by distress. "I thought . . . that is . . . I hoped you'd make the ranch your home. Give me a chance to make up for the wrong I did to you and your mother. I've dreamed of this moment since receiving Rena's letter. As the years passed I feared that fate had conspired against us, that we would never meet. With you here my life is finally complete. If you leave now, you take my life with you."

Kitty couldn't deny that Bert's speech touched her. She wondered if he knew where and under what circumstances Ryan had found her, and if that knowledge would change his mind about her.

"I don't know how much Ryan told you about me," Kitty began somewhat hesitantly. "You might change your mind about wanting me in your home when I tell you about myself."

Bert gave her a puzzled frown. "Why

would I change my mind? You are my daughter. This is your home. Nothing you can tell me will change that."

"I lived with outlaws," Kitty blurted out. "Lex Johnson disguised me as a boy and I rode with him and the Barton gang for several years. None of the Bartons ever suspected. But I always knew I would have to leave one day or risk discovery. Then Lex was killed during a bank robbery, and I realized how precarious my situation was without Lex's protection.

"Ryan joined the gang about that time," she explained. "I thought at first that Ryan was an outlaw, but it was all a pretense. He asked a lot of questions about Lex and his family, especially about a woman named Kathryn. I didn't know he'd seen through my disguise, and I think he had a good time with it at my expense." Her chin lifted fractionally. "Ryan thought I was Lex's . . . doxy."

Bert's face turned red with anger. "How could he? He never mentioned that to me. Did he . . . was he disrespectful toward you? When Pierce, Ryan's older brother, wrote and said Ryan was coming to aid me, he hinted that Ryan had earned quite a reputation with women. If he hurt you . . ."

"Oh, no," Kitty quickly contradicted.

"Ryan may be a womanizer, but he is kind and compassionate. I reckon he'd deny it, but it's true. He'd never hurt me or any other woman, no matter how distrustful he is of them. He figured out that I was Kathryn through simple deduction." It was not exactly the truth, but close enough. "Once he realized I was Kathryn, he knew I wasn't Lex's doxy."

Bert let out a sigh, apparently satisfied with her answer. "None of that matters to me. Whatever happened to you was not your fault. You were a child when Lex took you away."

"He did his best to protect me. I don't know what would have become of me after Deke died if Lex hadn't arrived when he did. I was left on my own with no means of support."

"I blame myself for that," Bert said regretfully. "I let too many months go by after Rena's death. I should have acted immediately upon receiving her letter."

"I agree," Kitty said with asperity. They both fell silent, lost in their private recollections. After an uncomfortable silence, Kitty said, "I'm going to speak bluntly, Bert, 'cause that's my way. Teresa resents me. She fears I'm supplanting her in your affections. She thinks I'm a whore and a thief. I can't remain where I'm not wanted.

"My language and manners are unacceptable," she continued. "I'm rough around the edges and have little education. I can ride and shoot but don't know which fork to use. Sometimes I slip and say shocking things. In truth, do you want a daughter like that? I'm not good enough to live the kind of life you want for me."

Bert patted Kitty's hand, as if to reassure her. "Ryan already told me most of what you've just said and none of it matters. Nobody needs to know about your life prior to coming here. There are many fine bachelors in the area, I'm sure you can find a good husband from among them, if that is your wish. If not, just having you here with me will make me happy."

"Bert, I . . ."

"No, don't say anything just yet. Promise you'll stay a while longer. If you find you can't adjust, or bring yourself to like me, then you must do as your heart directs. But know this, when I pass on, the bulk of my estate will be yours."

Kitty stared at him, appalled. "No! That's not what I want. I didn't come here for material gain. I came to meet the father I'd never known so I could tell him how much I resent him for abandoning me and my mother. I don't mean to be cruel, but that's how I felt."

"How do you feel now?" Bert asked in a raspy voice.

"I . . . I reckon I can understand how it happened. Mama was a proud woman. She wouldn't have told you about me knowing you were another woman's husband. You are both to blame, but I was the one who suffered for it. I don't hate you anymore, Bert, but don't ask me to love you."

Bert seemed to collapse inwardly. "I won't ask you to love me, Kitty. Just knowing you don't hate me anymore is enough for now. I can accept that. Just don't leave. Give us more time." He gave her a wry grin. "I'm sure your wait won't be a lengthy one."

"I'll stay on a while, Bert," Kitty agreed. Bert was dying, and he was her father, though she felt none of the warm feelings one would for a father. Her mother must have seen something in Bert to love.

"Thank you, my dear," Bert said gratefully. "Why don't you explore the ranch? There are numerous horses in the corral to choose from. Ask Ryan to go with you, he's familiar with the layout here. Teresa can show you around the house and introduce you to the help."

"I've already met Rosita. She's a treasure."

243

"Am I intruding?" Ryan asked as he poked his head in the door.

"No, come in," Bert invited. "I wanted to talk to you, anyway."

Kitty rose abruptly. "I'll leave you two alone. I feel in need of some air. Perhaps I'll explore the corral. I've always loved horses."

She spared Ryan a quick glance on her way out the door and wished she hadn't. He was staring at her with those sensual green eyes as if he wanted to devour her, and her body responded with its usual lack of control. Her breasts felt heavy, and a melting sensation began low in her belly.

"You don't have to go on my account," Ryan said.

Did he know how he affected her? Kitty wondered. "I've finished my visit with Bert. He's all yours." She hurried out the door before her reddened cheeks and wayward body embarrassed her.

Ryan reluctantly withdrew his gaze from Kitty and turned his attention to Bert. "You look chipper this morning."

"Because of Kitty," Bert beamed. "I owe you more than I can ever repay. Name your price, Ryan. It's yours if it's within my means. I'm a wealthy man, I can afford to be generous."

"I don't want your money, Bert. Finding

Kitty for you is all the payment I need. I did it for Pa. He would be pleased to know I've helped his old friend. Besides, it's been a great adventure. I needed to get away from the ranch for awhile and this was the perfect opportunity. Chad and Sarah are newly married and needed time alone. All that mooning and lovey-dovey stuff got a little boring."

"I'm glad to hear you say that, Ryan, for I have another favor to ask of you. How anxious are you to return to Montana?"

Ryan thought of Kitty and the temptation she presented. To remain in the same house with her and not be able to love her would certainly stretch the limits of his control. He'd hoped that leaving Kitty and returning to Montana would diminish his need for the little wildcat. It wasn't like him to want a woman so desperately. His damn lust for Kitty was going to get him into trouble, he speculated. It wasn't like him to remain attracted to one woman this long. He knew it was time to move on, yet something deep and unsettled within him urged him to stay and see this to the end . . . wherever it led. That thought frightened him excessively. Involvement meant commitment, and commitment meant . . . God, he couldn't even say the word, much less think it.

Marriage definitely wasn't for him. He liked variety. He trusted women about as far as he could toss them. So far nothing he'd seen disproved his theory about women. In his opinion, self-centered, jealous women like Teresa were more common than loving, unselfish women like his sisters-in-law Zoey and Sarah. And he knew first-hand that it had been no easy task for Pierce and Chad's wives to prove themselves.

Ryan realized Bert was waiting for an answer. How badly *did* he want to return to Montana? Not too badly, obviously, for the thought of leaving Kitty gave him a twinge of discomfort.

"Why do you ask? I reckon Chad can get along without me for a while longer if you have need of me."

"What I'm about to ask is for Kitty's sake," Bert explained. "Kitty seems comfortable with you. You know her better than anyone. I don't want to impose upon your time, but I would appreciate it if you would stay on here until Kitty settles in."

Ryan gave him a hard look. "What makes you think Kitty will settle in? She's determined to leave."

"We had a long talk this morning. She agreed to stay on for a time. I'm hoping it will be forever. Did you know she feared I wouldn't welcome her once I knew the kind of life she led? She thinks she isn't good enough to fit in here."

Ryan heaved an angry sigh. "I know. She tried to tell me the same thing. Nothing I said convinced her otherwise. She's a stubborn woman. She thinks her colorful past will be held against her. She even worried that *you* wouldn't accept her for what she was."

"I told her that was hogwash," Bert replied. "Kitty is my daughter. I'd accept her any way she came to me." He gave Ryan a speculative glance. "Kitty said you thought she was Lex's doxy when you first met."

"I'm not sure I really believed that, but it did enter my mind. After I got to know Kitty I realized I was wrong. You'll have to trust me when I say Kitty was no doxy."

Bert looked as if he wanted to say more but let the subject drop. Ryan knew Bert was an astute man and wondered what he was thinking. Did Bert suspect that Ryan and Kitty were lovers? If he did, he wasn't voicing his opinion.

"Back to my original question, Ryan," Bert said. "Would you consider staying on for awhile? You'd be doing me a great service. My greatest fear is that Teresa will frighten Kitty off. I may be confined to this room, but I know what's going on in my own house. Teresa is jealous of Kitty. She has a mean streak I wasn't aware of until Kitty arrived.

"Teresa lived many years with an aunt after her mother and I were married. Louise didn't want to disrupt her daughter's life by bringing her to a strange place. She didn't come to the ranch until her mother became ill. She has only been with me for a little over six years and I thought I knew her, but now I'm not so sure."

Ryan could tell him things about Teresa that would curl the old man's hair, but he decided they were better left unsaid. "I reckon I can stay on for awhile," he allowed. "I'll ride into town tomorrow and wire Chad so he and Pierce won't worry about my continued absence. Those two are like mother hens when it comes to family."

Bert's relief was apparent as his face lifted in a genuine smile. "Thank you. You don't know what this means to me. I advised Kitty to explore the ranch, get the lay of the land, so to speak. I hoped you'd show her around. I want Kitty to feel comfortable here."

"You're both making a dangerous mistake," Teresa said as she flounced into the room. "Kitty is an imposter. She fooled Ryan and now she's got Papa Bert hoodwinked. You'd be doing yourself a favor if you turned her out, Papa Bert. You have only the word of a dead woman that Kitty is *your* daughter. If Rena slept with you she probably slept with a dozen other men. You can't possibly know that Kitty is your daughter."

Bert glowered at her. "I feel it here," he said, placing his hand over his heart. "Rena would never lie about something like that. Rena's eyes were brown, mine are blue, just like Kitty's. Kitty is the image of Rena, yet I can see something of myself in her. Kitty is my daughter, Teresa. It would please me if you accepted her and welcomed her into our household."

"I don't think so," Teresa said testily. "Her language is coarse, she has no education or manners, and she looks like a slut with her indecently shorn hair."

"I think Kitty speaks just fine. As for her manners, they seemed good enough to me when she ate breakfast in my room this morning," Bert said. "You can't judge a woman by the length of her hair."

"Papa Bert," Teresa ventured slyly, "did you ask Ryan just how . . . close he and Kitty became before he brought her to the ranch? He was alone with her a long time."

Bert gave her a censuring scowl. "I trust

Ryan. He'd do nothing to hurt Kitty."

"But they . . ."

"Enough, Teresa. Ryan and Kitty know what they're doing. I don't want to hear another word against my daughter. Ryan has just agreed to stay on here until Kitty settles in. She seems to trust him, and she needs all the friends she can get now."

Ryan listened to the conversation with more than a little guilt. Bert's trust was an awesome burden, but he couldn't just blurt out that he and Kitty were lovers. Had he been smart he would have refused Bert's request and gone home. Nothing good could come of this, he reflected, not with the kind of temptation Kitty presented.

"I think I'd like to rest now," Bert said. "Go find Kitty, Ryan. She's probably with the horses."

Ryan took his leave, but Teresa lingered behind. "I'll help you into bed, Papa Bert," she said sweetly. "I hope you don't think I'm being deliberately cruel to Kitty. I just can't bear to see you hurt by a woman who may or may not be your daughter."

"Teresa, honey, your jealousy is unwarranted. When I pass on you'll be well provided for."

"Forgive me, Papa Bert," Teresa purred. "The last thing I want is to upset you." She kissed his forehead. "I'll leave you now to rest."

Before searching for Kitty, Ryan made a detour to the kitchen and another to the stables. He'd promised Bert to help Kitty settle in, and he intended to make sure the old man died in peace, with his daughter by his side. He'd grown quite fond of Bert in the short time he'd known him.

Ryan found Kitty leaning on the corral railing, watching a cowboy breaking a wild mustang. "What a beautiful animal," Ryan said as he walked up behind her.

As if she had sensed his arrival beforehand, she accepted his presence without being startled by it. "It seems a shame to break something so wild and free."

Ryan wondered if she were referring to herself. "Being wild and free is fine for an animal, but people have obligations that sometimes make those things impossible."

Kitty raised a finely arched eyebrow, finally turning to face him. "What exactly are you trying to say?"

"Make anything you want of it, I wouldn't presume to tell you anything."

"You think I should stay here, don't you?"

"I think you owe it to your father."

"Damnation, Ryan, but you're infuriating.

Have you come to tell me good-bye, then? Are you leaving?"

"No, I'm not leaving. Not soon, anyway."

She searched his face. "Did Teresa talk you into staying?"

"No, she has no influence over me." God, she was lovely, he thought, searching Kitty's features. A man could get lost in the mystery of those big blue eyes of hers and forget all about vows and resolutions that had once been important to him.

She returned her attention to the bucking horse and the man trying to stay on his back. Ryan thought her next words took a lot of courage. "I'm glad you're not leaving. I feel . . . alone here. I'll never belong. Bert might think he wants me now, but in time he'd come to realize I'm not the kind of woman he wants for a daughter."

"Sometimes you make me so angry I could . . ." He was going to say strangle, but kissing her would more aptly describe what he wanted to do to Kitty. He grasped her arm and led her away from the corral. "Come on, let's get the hell out of here. Bert suggested we take a ride and I'm in full agreement. I took the liberty of asking Rosita to pack us a lunch. Our horses are saddled and waiting. What about it? Will you join me?"

"Why not?" Kitty said. "I think I'd enjoy a ride and picnic lunch. Is Teresa joining us?"

Ryan gave an exasperated snort. "Not if I can help it."

They rode through pasture land, then into the desert beyond. Kitty was surprised at the stark beauty of the land. The weather had been hot and dry, and the vegetation looked withered, brown, and windblown. Only the stately saguaro cactus, embracing the sky with open arms, seemed undisturbed by the passage of time and seasons. Ryan led Kitty along a trail that cut through cactus and sagebrush, toward a range of mountains dead ahead of them. Off in the distance she could see cattle grazing on the hillsides, scavenging for food.

"This is really . . . awesome," Kitty said of the magnificent forest of cactus.

"You should see the desert in bloom," Ryan replied. "It was carpeted with wildflowers when I arrived. And the blooming cacti were a sight I'll long remember. You'll see what I mean next spring."

"Perhaps," Kitty said doubtfully. Truth to tell, she had no idea where she'd be next spring. That was a long time. "Where are we going?"

"I rode out with the hands one day to round up strays and found this perfect place for a picnic. There's even a stream, though I'm not sure there's water in it this time of year. It's in the mountains. You'll find it cooler up there than it is down here on the desert floor."

"That looks like a storm brewing over the mountains," Kitty said with misgiving.

"It's still a long way off," Ryan said after studying the fluffy clouds hanging over the lofty peaks. "No need to worry, though, there's shelter where we're going. The cowboys built a line cabin beside a mountain stream. They use it when one of those sudden Arizona gullywashers catches them out this way."

"I think I know Arizona better than you do," Kitty said, "and that storm looks close to me. Perhaps we should turn back."

"Not on your life," Ryan replied, giving her one of his ravishing smiles. "I planned a picnic and we're going to have one."

The weather held, much to Kitty's surprise. The stream even contained a trickle of water running through it — enough to water their thirsty horses. She noticed the small, windowless shack sitting back from the stream but otherwise gave it little thought as Ryan untied the basket of food

254

he'd attached to his saddle and set it on the ground beside the stream.

"There's a blanket inside the basket," Ryan said. "Rosita thought it would come in handy. Spread it out and I'll set out the food."

In no time at all they were seated on the blanket enjoying fried chicken, fluffy biscuits, baked beans, and thick wedges of chocolate cake. Rosita had even included a jug of cool lemonade.

"I'd steal Rosita away from Bert if I didn't think Cookie would raise a ruckus," Ryan said, licking a bit of chocolate frosting from his thumb.

"Who is Cookie?" Kitty asked.

"He's our cook at home. Been with us forever." He stretched out lazily, resting his head on his folded arms, and crossing his legs.

Kitty's gaze traveled appreciatively over his long length. She'd never seen a man as handsome or as well made physically as Ryan Delaney. Her mouth watered just thinking about his naked body and how it felt pressed against hers. She blinked, trying to dislodge Ryan's unclothed image from her brain. Thoughts like that could get her in a heap of trouble.

When she looked over at him again his

eyes were closed, and he appeared to be sleeping. Kitty lay down beside him and watched him sleep, until her own eyes floated shut.

The first raindrops hit her with a resounding splat, awakening her with a start. She'd been dreaming. A pleasant dream she could only vaguely recall. Rain was falling harder now, and she shook Ryan awake.

"It's raining, Ryan, wake up. We should have started back hours ago."

Ryan sat up groggily, dashing raindrops from his eyes. "I guess I fell asleep." He raised his eyes to the angry sky and frowned. "This is going to be a real gullywasher."

He'd no sooner spoken than the sky opened up. The rain came in torrents, driven by a howling wind.

"Run for the shack!" Ryan shouted over the wailing wind as he picked up the blanket and handed it to her along with the basket holding the remains of their repast. "I'll get the saddles."

Kitty made a mad dash for the shack. It wasn't far, but by the time she reached it she was soaked to the skin. Ryan joined her with their saddles a few minutes later. He was even wetter than she was.

"There should be a lantern and matches on the shelf," Ryan said. "I'll have a light in here in no time. Are you cold?"

"Fre . . . freezing," Kitty said through chattering teeth.

"If we're lucky, the hands will have left firewood beside the hearth." A light flared as Ryan struck a match to the lantern.

"Ah, we're in luck," Ryan crowed. "There's both wood and kindling. Once I get the fire going good, we can dry our clothes. You'd better strip before you catch your death. Wrap yourself in a blanket. There should be one folded up at the end of each bunk."

There were four bunks in the shed, each with a blanket folded at the foot. Kitty was grateful that the last people to use this shack had left it well provisioned. After a quick glance to make sure Ryan was busy with the fire, she stripped off her clothing and wrapped herself in the blanket. Then she sat on the edge of the bunk, listening to the rain pounding on the tin roof and watching the play of muscles beneath Ryan's wet clothing as he bent over the fireplace.

The dry wood burst into flames. "There," Ryan said. "That should warm us up." He turned around and saw Kitty sitting on the bunk, wrapped in a woolen blanket. Ryan thought she'd never looked so fetching. Just the thought that she wore nothing beneath that blanket made him go hard as stone.

"There are more blankets. You should get out of your wet clothes," Kitty advised.

Blood pounded through his loins, and his denims had become so tight in the crotch that he feared he would burst the seams. Getting out of them would be a huge relief.

He was aware of her warm gaze on him as he walked to the bunk, picked up a folded blanket, and turned away from her to undress. Just knowing that she watched him sent heat racing up his spine. He didn't need the fire to warm him. His fingers were all thumbs, but he finally managed to remove his wet clothing and wrap himself in the blanket.

"We should spread our clothes on chairs before the fire to dry." He saw two straight-backed chairs pushed up against the scarred table, and he pulled them over to the hearth.

Kitty joined him with her wet dress and underthings after he'd set the chairs in place. As she spread her clothing out to dry, the blanket shielding her nudity slipped and fell to the floor. She glanced at Ryan, a helpless look on her face.

Ryan's heated gaze slid down the length of her flushed body with avid appreciation. He opened his mouth to speak, but he could think of no words to convey what he was feeling. When she reached for her fallen blanket he stepped on it, holding it in place on the floor.

"Ryan . . ."

He saw her shudder and knew she was thinking the same thing he was. Without a thought to the right or wrong of it, he released his hold on his own blanket. It pooled in a dark puddle around his feet. He saw Kitty's eyes drop to his arousal, already full and hard and pressing upward against his belly. He groaned and pulled her hard against him, letting her feel how very much he wanted her.

"Tell me you want me, Kitten."

Kitty's silence was driving him insane. If she didn't say yes he didn't know what . . .

"Yes. Please, yes." The words were the sweetest music he'd ever heard. "I want you . . . inside me. I'd be a liar if I said I didn't."

CHAPTER 11

He swept her into his arms, tender and forceful at the same time. Green eyes beneath heavy-lashed lids glittered like shards of splintered glass as he smiled down at her.

"Sweet Kitten," he murmured beneath his breath.

Kitty couldn't breathe, couldn't speak as Ryan kissed her parted mouth. She sensed his desperation and opened her mouth to his probing tongue with a wanting that matched his in intensity. She shuddered with need, drowning in the mindless whirlwind of desire consuming her.

With a gentleness that nearly brought Kitty to tears, he placed her on the bunk and stretched out beside her, his body partially covering hers. She felt the thick proof of his need pressing against her thigh as his fingers kneaded her breasts and toyed with her aching nipples. She writhed against him, savoring the contact of bare flesh against bare flesh. She felt his body slowly sliding down hers and inhaled sharply as his lips blazed a trail across her flesh. She moaned encouragement as he kissed his way to the nest of golden curls between her legs.

She arched sharply upward when his mouth closed over a place so sensitive she feared she would shatter. Then she felt his tongue sliding over that swollen place, and she screamed out his name. Never had anything given her so much pleasure. It was wonderfully erotic. Sinfully delicious. She didn't hear the rain beating against the shack, or the wind howling around the corners. All she heard were the furious pounding of her heart and the rush of blood throbbing through her veins. Her hands tangled in the thick, dark strands of his hair, and she urged him on with guttural sounds.

She was coming too quickly. Her body writhed, sobs mixed with moans. Frenzied, reckless, desperate, she clung to him, feeling the splendor take her. She tried to stop it, but when Ryan thrust a finger inside her she went wild, arching up into his mouth and letting him carry her over the edge. She came explosively, sobbing and shuddering as ecstasy burst inside her.

God, he loved the sounds she made; those

little sighs and moans and sobbing pleas. He waited until she quieted, then he moved his body upward over hers, shoved her legs apart, and thrust into her hot, wet passage in a deep slide that produced a new round of shuddering. Her eyes widened, conveying without words her pleasure, and he smiled.

"Oh, God, Ryan, yes, I want you inside me." She ground her hips into his loins and he nearly exploded, hanging on by sheer will.

"This is where I belong," Ryan moaned thickly as the hot, clenching friction brought him close to the edge. He closed his eyes, grit his teeth, and pushed himself so deeply inside her he felt as if he'd found heaven. Then he began thrusting in earnest, stroking, withdrawing, deep, shallow, intensifying the already unbearable pressure building inside him. He wanted to bring Kitty to climax again and prayed for the staying power.

Just when he feared he was going to leave her behind, she stiffened and cried out his name. "Ryan . . . oh please . . ." Her soft, plaintive cries spurred him to greater effort, and then he felt her contract around him, felt her heave and tremble, and heard her scream. Then he knew nothing more, for his own volatile climax carried him beyond the bounds of mental comprehension. Pleasure such as he'd never known before shattered inside him, bathing him in wave after wave of unbearable brilliance.

Ryan rolled to his side and lay beside Kitty, his breath spewing through his lips in harsh, uneven puffs of air. He had no idea what made loving Kitty so special. A frown settled between his brows. He had made love countless times. It was always enjoyable but never like this. Loving Kitty was unlike any of his previous encounters. Instead of growing bored and eager to go on to the next conquest, he wanted to hang around until he learned what made Kitty different. It was almost as if she had uncovered a side of him he didn't know existed.

"Ryan, what are you thinking?" Kitty asked, snuggling against him to share his warmth.

Ryan was silent for a long time, then he said, "About my brothers and home, I reckon."

"Are you anxious to go home? Your brothers must be extraordinary men. Tell me about them."

"They can be bossy, but I reckon they're better than most brothers. They've had their share of troubles, but that's what made them strong men."

"You said your father is dead. What about your mother? Is she still living?"

Though nothing compelled Ryan to reveal family secrets to Kitty, somehow telling her seemed right.

"I believe I already mentioned that my mother ran away with another man when my brothers and I were young boys. My father raised us. He was a good father, but he instilled in us his distrust of women. We were hell-raisers, my brothers and I. We were known in Dry Gulch for our wild ways," he reminisced. "I can still recall many of those rousing fights we had at the saloon. We always stood together and nearly always won. Bad times came when we least expected them."

"What happened?"

"A woman named Cora Lee Doolittle tore our lives apart. I won't go into details, but her lies almost got Pierce hanged. Chad married Cora Lee in order to stop the hanging, but it wasn't enough to prevent four senseless deaths. Chad held himself responsible, though none of it was his fault.

"Chad's conscience drove him away. He was gone two years. When he returned, he brought a woman named Sarah and her son with him. It all worked out. Chad married Sarah and Pierce married Zoey, but the experience left me with a healthy distrust of women."

He heard Kitty sigh and wondered what she was thinking.

"I'm sorry my curiosity brought back unpleasant memories," she said. "Thank you for telling me. Pierce and Chad must have married exceptional women."

Ryan gave her a genuine grin. "They were lucky."

"Don't you have any desire to have a wife and family of your own?" Kitty asked hopefully.

"I have a niece and two nephews. Probably more are on the way by now. I don't need children of my own."

Silence reigned. Even the rain and wind had ceased. Ryan wanted to make love to Kitty again, but he knew they should return to the ranch. Bert would worry if they didn't check in soon. "We should leave," Kitty said, giving voice to Ryan's thoughts. "The rain has stopped."

"I want to make love to you again," Ryan said, "but I reckon you're right. Bert's health is fragile, we shouldn't worry him." He raised up on his elbow and kissed her breasts, then her mouth. Heaving a reluctant sigh, he rose and walked over to the hearth to retrieve their clothing. "Our clothes are still damp but they'll have to do," he said, handing hers to her.

Ryan pulled on his soggy denims and shirt. His boots squished when he stepped into them. "Are your boots as wet as mine?" he asked as he buckled his gunbelt over his slim hips.

"Mine aren't too bad," Kitty said. "I can still get them on."

"The fire has nearly burnt itself out, we can safely leave it. I'll saddle the horses while you fold the blankets and set the room to rights. Meet me outside when you're finished."

Ryan left the cabin, wondering why he had divulged so much of his personal history to Kitty. He'd never felt the need or inclination to confide in a woman before. Though the residents of Dry Gulch were familiar with the tragedies that had plagued his family, few knew the personal, intimate details, and that's the way he and his brothers wanted to keep it.

Kitty joined Ryan a few minutes later. She handed him the picnic basket, and he tied it onto his saddle. She looked so delightfully disheveled that he couldn't resist the urge to kiss her. When his hands settled around her waist to boost her into the saddle, he turned her instead into his arms and covered her mouth with his. His kiss was not a gentle one. It was hard and proprietary, a searing flame meant to brand his property.

Kitty spoke little on the ride back to the ranch. The newly soaked ground needed all her attention as she guided her horse around gullies and ditches recently formed by the downpour. But she had plenty of time to think. Her lips still stung from the fierce kiss Ryan had given her before they'd left. She felt branded by it, marked for life. Why had he given her such an inspiring kiss when he had no intention of making a commitment to her? She'd be a fool to believe Ryan wanted more from her than a few hours, days, or weeks of passion. Ryan was a prominent rancher, a man of means. If he ever found the need to marry, she knew she would never fit Ryan's vision of a perfect wife. She couldn't possibly become the kind of person everyone wanted her to be.

At one time Kitty had thought Ryan was the answer to a woman's dreams, to her dreams, but that was before she knew how unattainable he was. It wasn't just his vow to remain single that made her dream of being with Ryan forever impossible. It was the sure knowledge that she would never be accepted by Ryan's extraordinary brothers and the two perfect women they had married.

Kitty felt a strange sense of homecoming when the ranch came into view. She'd never had that feeling before, and she held it to her heart, knowing that her time here was limited.

"Thought you got lost," a cowboy hollered as they rode into the yard. "The boss was worried but I told him you knew your way around, that you and Miss Kitty were probably holed up somewhere, waiting out the storm."

"We took shelter in that line cabin up in the mountains. Sure was a gullywasher," Ryan yelled back.

"Go on inside and get out of those damp clothes," Ryan said as he dismounted and lifted Kitty from the saddle.

Kitty nodded and walked toward the house. She frowned in consternation when she saw Teresa holding the door open for her. She'd hoped to slip unnoticed to her room to change her clothes and fix her hair before facing anyone. She knew she looked a mess. What she didn't know was how tellingly disheveled she was. Her lips were swollen, her cheeks were abraded from the stubble on Ryan's chin, and her eyes still had that dreamy look of a woman well loved.

"Where have you been?" Teresa asked harshly.

"Ryan and I went riding. We got caught in the storm."

Teresa eyed her disdainfully. "Why aren't you wet?"

"We found shelter. If you'll excuse me, I need to change." She headed for the stairs. Teresa followed close on her heels.

"You look like a whore," Teresa charged. "One look at you and everyone will know what you and Ryan have been up to."

Kitty whirled at the top of the staircase, her eyes glinting dangerously. "Speculate all you want, Teresa, only Ryan and I know what happened."

"You can't have him," Teresa hissed. "I claimed him first. I set my sights on him the moment I saw him."

Seething with fury, Kitty entered her room and tried to slam the door, but Teresa slipped inside.

"What the hell do you want?" Kitty lashed out. "I suggest you leave before I kick your dainty little ass out the door."

"Listen to yourself talk," Teresa goaded. "You don't belong in polite company. Go back to your outlaw friends. I'm sure they'll welcome you back with open arms. I'm warning you to stay away from Ryan or you won't like the consequences. Ryan is mine, you're not good enough for him. And don't think seducing him into your bed means anything to him, 'cause it doesn't."

"I feel sorry for you, Teresa," Kitty contended. "Ryan will never marry you. He's not the marrying kind."

"I can change his mind," Teresa said with conviction. "Don't interfere. You'll never inherit Bert's fortune if I have anything to say about it. I already have Papa Bert half convinced that you're an imposter. It's just a matter of time before he tells you to leave."

"Get the hell out of here!" Kitty shouted. "You've got balls, I'll give you that. You should have been born a man."

"I'm going," Teresa said, spinning on her heel and marching toward the door. "Oh, by the way," she said, pausing with her hand on the doorknob. "Papa Bert has company. He wants you to meet our neighbor. You're to join them when you're ready. The man's name is Norm Tucker. He's a widower with two children. Lives a few miles down the road from us. At one time he wanted to marry me, but I turned him down. I'll remain a spinster before wasting my youth raising two motherless children."

Teresa's little discourse left Kitty speechless. The more she knew about her stepsister, the less she liked her. Had she known her appearance at the ranch would have caused such an outpouring of malice, she would not have come.

Kitty changed into dry clothes quickly, then sat before the mirror to fix her hair. She picked up the comb and let out a gasp of dismay when she gazed at her image in the mirror. Teresa was right. She looked like a satisfied whore. Her lips were swollen and bruised, and her cheeks were red and raw.

Trying not to look too closely at the love bites on her neck, she spread powder over her cheeks and neck and ran the comb through her curls, patting them into some semblance of order. When she had done all she could to repair her image, she went to join Bert and his guest.

"Come in," Bert called when she knocked discreetly on the door. She pasted a smile on her face and walked into the room.

"Ah, Kitty," Bert greeted warmly. "Teresa told me you and Ryan had returned. You two gave me quite a scare. I hope you found a place to shelter from the storm."

"We did," Kitty said, unconsciously returning his smile. "I'm sorry you were worried."

"I should have known Ryan would take good care of you. Pull up a chair, daughter.

There's someone I'd like you to meet."

Kitty gazed at the man who had leaped to his feet the moment she had entered the room. He was older than Ryan by a few years, and somewhat shorter. But there was nothing weak about his appearance. His sturdy build implied strength, and his brown eyes glinted with quick intelligence. Kitty flushed beneath his openly admiring glance.

"Kitty, this is Norm Tucker, a neighbor and good friend," Bert said. "Norm, this is Kitty, my long lost daughter. Now that she's here, I can die happily."

Kitty was somewhat rattled when Norm took one of her hands in both of his and squeezed. "Welcome, Kitty. I know how long Bert has waited for this day. And may I say I can't blame him?"

Bert chuckled. "She's a beauty, isn't she, Norm? I can't wait for all the neighbors to meet her."

"We can take care of that right away if Kitty will accompany me to the barn dance next Saturday at the Stuarts'. That is if you don't mind, Bert," Norm was quick to add.

"It's not my permission you need," Bert said cagily.

"What do you say, Kitty?" Norm asked. "I know this is sudden, but Bert can vouch for me. It would be an honor to escort you to the barn dance and introduce you to all your neighbors."

Now Kitty was really flustered. Was Norm courting her? She hardly knew the man. Besides, there was only one man for her despite the fact that Ryan didn't want her on a permanent basis.

"Go on, Kitty," Bert urged. "It will do you good to get out in public."

"Well," Kitty said after a long pause, "I suppose it wouldn't hurt, although I'm not sure I have anything appropriate to wear."

"Calico would be fine. Folks around here don't dress fancy," Norm assured her. "No matter what you wear you'll be the prettiest girl there. I'll pick you up at six o'clock. Most of the women will be bringing a box supper. I could have my housekeeper fix us something."

"No, I'll take care of it," Kitty said, wishing she'd refused Norm's invitation. What if she did or said something to embarrass Norm? She wondered what Ryan would say when he learned Norm was courting her. He had no right to complain or consider her his private property. He'd made no commitment, had no hold on her. She belonged to no man. She almost smiled as she imagined Ryan's expression when she told him she was being courted.

That moment came sooner than Kitty would have liked. Ryan strolled into Bert's room a few minutes later.

"Ryan, come in," Bert invited. "Meet Norm Tucker, my neighbor and good friend." Bert chuckled, showing amazing animation for a man so ill. "I think Norm and Kitty hit it off right well. She's agreed to accompany Norm to a barn dance next Saturday night. Norm, this is Ryan Delaney, the man who found my Kitty for me."

Kitty flinched as Ryan's gaze cut over to her, sharp and reproving, before offering Norm his hand. She listened to their exchange of pleasantries, blotting out all but the note of disapproval she felt certain only she could hear in Ryan's voice. It was almost as if he were . . . jealous. But of course he wasn't. How could Ryan be jealous when his feelings for her didn't go beyond simple lust?

Norm took his leave shortly after that. Kitty walked him to the door, then went up to her room to rest till dinner. She'd had quite a day and a whole lot to think about. It surprised her that Norm found her attractive. She thought everyone would notice her lack of poise and ridicule her for it. But obviously Norm had no complaints.

Kitty lay down on the neatly made bed and closed her eyes, letting her imagination carry her away to the barn dance. She saw herself standing at the edge of the crowd, a lone figure amid a sea of staring people, all of whom were pointing their fingers at her as if she had committed some terrible crime. Even Norm had turned away from her, shamed by something she'd either done or said.

Oh, God, how could she have let herself be coerced into accepting Norm's invitation? She couldn't even dance. She'd be ridiculed and shunned. Someone to be pitied.

Immersed in her disturbing thoughts, Kitty didn't hear the door open or see Ryan step inside and close the door behind him. She didn't know he was there until he said, "What in the hell do you think you're doing?"

Kitty's eyes shot open as she squinted into the dark. "Don't you believe in knocking?"

"I was in a hurry. Whatever possessed you to accept Tucker's invitation? He only wants one thing from you."

Kitty's temper blew. "Go to hell, Ryan Delaney! Not all men think like you do. Some men are looking for a wife. They don't live by your standards."

"What standards are you referring to?" Ryan asked, his eyes slitted in cold fury.

"The only standards that mean anything to you. The ones upon which you've built your life. You make love to women but can't bring yourself to trust them. You take them for the pleasure they give you, not for the richness they can bring into your life. You shun commitment and marriage, yet you expect me to be at your beck and call whenever you want me.

"I want commitment, Ryan Delaney, all those things you've avoided most of your life. I want a man to love me, a home, children. Norm Tucker might not be the man for me, but how will I know if I don't let him prove his worth? If I thought you wanted me for more than sex, I'd tell Norm Tucker to go to hell."

She watched his expression change from anger to incredulity, wondering if she had gone too far. His mouth worked wordlessly before the words finally came out.

"You want a commitment? You know how I feel about marriage. I freely admit I've never felt for any woman what I feel for you, Kitten. This is difficult for me to say, but if I were a marrying man I would consider you for my wife."

"Liar!" Kitty cried. "You'd find someone

who knows all the rules of etiquette, someone with manners and refinement. Someone more like the women who married your brothers. I can't be anyone but myself, Ryan. I'll always be the woman who ate, rode, and shared a camp with outlaws. I held their horses while they robbed banks and took a share of the loot. I was an outlaw, Ryan. That's something not even you can easily forgive."

Ryan's face was like a thundercloud on a stormy day, dark and forbidding. "What in the hell has gotten into you? You know that's not the way I feel. Your past means nothing to me. My God, we made love scant hours ago! I hardly expected you to fall into another man's arms so quickly."

Why don't you tell me you love me, Ryan? her heart cried in silent supplication. "I didn't fall into Norm Tucker's arms. Far from it. I simply agreed to go to the barn dance because Bert seemed to think I should."

"Since when did you care what Bert thought?"

That stopped her cold. Ryan was right. If she disliked Bert as much as she thought, why did she suddenly want to please him?

"I don't want to discuss this, Ryan. I'm going to the barn dance with Norm and that's final. Why don't you take Teresa?"

He let out a furious oath and turned away. "Maybe I will."

Norm's frequent visits to the ranch during the following week did nothing to improve Ryan's mood. It was obvious to him that Norm's visits had nothing to do with Bert and everything to do with Kitty. The damn fool was head over heels for Kitty. He followed her like a puppy and had even taken her to his ranch to meet his two children.

To make an infuriating situation even worse, Kitty had gushed on for hours about Norm's darling little girls. Ryan had had no idea she was so damn fond of children, and Norm Tucker seemed only too willing to give them to her. All Ryan could do was fume in impotent rage whenever Tucker took Kitty out to ride, or on a picnic, or to visit his children. Didn't Kitty know what her behavior with Tucker was doing to him? Ryan wondered. His imagination worked overtime each time Kitty was alone with Tucker. He envisioned them in all kinds of intimate situations and couldn't bear the thought of Kitty and Tucker together like that.

The day of the barn dance arrived. Desperate to keep an eye on Kitty, Ryan had asked Teresa to accompany him. The night promised to be fair and warm, unlike the cold fury Ryan was feeling when Tucker arrived all spiffed up for Kitty's benefit.

Kitty appeared at the top of the stairs, looking like a vision in her new dress. Bert had encouraged Kitty to go to town to buy something fetching to wear, and Ryan had accompanied both her and Teresa. He hadn't seen what Kitty purchased, but as she floated down the stairs, Ryan thought she couldn't have chosen anything more provocative than the deep rose dimity gown whose wide sweeping skirts emphasized her tiny waist and full breasts. Small puffed sleeves clung to her bare shoulders, exposing far too much flesh for Ryan's liking.

Ryan's darkening gaze lingered on the creamy slope of her firm breasts visible above the low neckline, and he had the unaccountable urge to toss his jacket over her shoulders. He swallowed the bitter taste in his mouth and started forward. Tucker beat him to it.

"You look lovely, Kitty," Tucker said, drawing her hand beneath his arm. "You'll be the prettiest woman at the barn dance."

"What about me?"

Ryan's gaze drifted upward, to where Teresa stood at the top of the stairs, waiting to be noticed. With Ryan's attention focused on her, Teresa slowly descended. Ryan had to admit that Teresa had outdone herself. She was gloriously arrayed in red silk, her neckline even lower than Kitty's. She was a vision, but not the vision Ryan wanted. He knew Teresa was expecting him to say something, so he moved forward and offered her his arm. "You look lovely, Teresa. Shall we go?"

"I brought my buggy," Tucker said. "We can all go together, if you like."

"I don't think . . ."

"Oh, Ryan, let's," Teresa gushed. "It will be great fun."

Ryan shrugged. "I suppose. Is that all right with you, Kitty?" he inquired with a polite smile and a slight edge of wariness.

"I don't mind," Kitty replied. He could tell nothing from her expression.

The ladies collected the box suppers Rosita had prepared for them, and they all climbed into Tucker's buggy. It was a tight fit. Kitty's enticing scent played havoc with Ryan's senses as Tucker took up the reins. Strange, he thought, Teresa was sitting as close to him as Kitty was but he wasn't even aware of her as a woman.

The ride wasn't overly long, but to Ryan it was the longest one he'd ever taken. The

Stuart ranch lay a scant five miles to the north, and as they drew near they could hear the fiddles. Tucker eased the buggy into place beside several others and leaped to the ground to help Kitty alight. Ryan followed, swinging Teresa to the ground. Greetings and introductions were made all around, and they joined a group sitting at a long table eating and enjoying the music.

Ryan was munching on a chicken leg when he heard a dark-eyed brunette sitting next to Kitty ask, "So you're Bert's daughter. You must be thrilled to finally meet your father after being separated all these years."

Ryan saw Kitty's fork pause midway to her mouth and sensed her apprehension. He was about to step into the void, but Teresa beat him to it.

"Can you imagine?" Teresa gushed in a loud voice. "Papa Bert had never seen Kitty before she arrived at the ranch. She claims to be his daughter, but how can one be certain she's really Papa Bert's daughter when she has no proof?"

"You're the only one with doubts, Teresa," Ryan said from between clenched teeth. He wanted to muzzle her before she said something really hurtful. Women like Teresa did little to alter his low opinion of their gender.

Kitty couldn't believe Teresa could be so

crass. She knew her stepsister disliked her but never thought Teresa would humiliate her in public. She sent Ryan a grateful look and continued eating. But the woman, whose name was Sally, was unwilling to let the subject drop.

"It's strange that you and your father never met before," Sally remarked.

Kitty shot a quick glance at Ryan and shook her head when she saw him open his mouth to reply. She couldn't spend her life letting others speak for her.

"My mother and father weren't married," she explained. "Mama never told Bert he had a daughter. When he finally tracked me down, I agreed to come here to meet him. I probably won't stay."

"Where were you living?" a young man named Steve asked. Apparently everyone was more interested in her history than the food or music, Kitty lamented. She'd always known she wouldn't fit in, and having to field embarrassing questions proved it.

"Strange that you should ask that," Teresa said, gloating. "You'll never guess where Ryan found Kitty. She was living with . . . ow! Why did you do that, Ryan?"

"I found Kitty living with her stepbrother and his . . . family," Ryan informed those listening. "I convinced her to come to

Tucson to meet her father. Bert is thrilled to finally have his daughter with him."

Kitty stifled a smile at the way Teresa was rubbing her ankle.

"I for one am glad Kitty came to Tucson," Norm proclaimed loudly. "I don't care where she came from. It's enough to have her here."

Kitty could have kissed Norm for defending her. Ryan, too. Of the two, she'd rather kiss Ryan.

Further questions died of natural causes, and everyone drifted off to dance. Kitty listened to the music, tapping her toes to the rhythm and humming along.

"Would you like to dance?" Norm asked. "I do a credible two-step."

Kitty flushed, embarrassed to admit another of her shortcomings. "I don't dance."

"No time like the present to learn." Norm grasped her hand, pulled her to her feet, and dragged her into the barn, where the dancers were engaged in a lively reel. "Just follow me," he yelled over the din.

Kitty learned something that night. Dancing came easily to her. She loved the music, the beat, the laughter . . . the fun. Fate had robbed her of the joy and companionship of her peers during her childhood when she should have been happy and carefree. Her unconventional upbringing made her feel like a misfit, but having a good time was definitely exhilarating.

Kitty danced with Norm and several other young men, but the one man she wanted to dance with hadn't asked her. Ryan had danced with Teresa a time or two, and with others, spreading his charm around indiscriminately. Rogue Ryan seemed to be at his best tonight, and she wondered why she even cared. Tonight seemed to reinforce her conviction that Rogue Ryan wasn't the kind to confine his attentions to one woman.

CHAPTER 12

It was nearly midnight. Norm had gone off to get Kitty something to drink before their long ride home. Kitty stood on the sidelines, watching the thinning crowd of dancers whirling about the dance floor. She sensed Ryan's presence before she saw him, ever aware of where he was at any given time. She supposed it was because she loved him so much.

Then he was standing before her, tempting her with his smile. "Would you like to dance? They're playing a waltz. I know you can waltz because I saw you with Tucker."

"Norm makes dancing easy," Kitty replied. "I've never danced before tonight."

"I've been told I'm a good dancer," Ryan boasted.

His words struck a responsive chord in her, and she couldn't help returning his smile. Surely the devil made her say, "You're good at many things, Ryan Delaney."

He grinned, then burst into laughter. Kitty thought he had the sexiest laugh she'd ever heard. "If we weren't in public I'd kiss you, Kitten," he murmured into her ear. "Come on, let's dance. I need to feel you in my arms."

Ryan hadn't been lying, Kitty thought as they whirled around the floor. He *was* a good dancer. Better than Norm. He even made *her* look good on the dance floor.

"Are you having a good time?" he asked.

"Hmmm, wonderful. I never knew people lived like this. Why aren't you dancing with Teresa? She's standing on the sidelines, glaring daggers at us."

"I'd rather dance with you." He swung her around and dipped her. Kitty caught her breath and clutched his broad shoulders. Without his firm grip on her waist she would have fallen.

"Is Tucker treating you right?" Ryan asked bluntly.

"Norm is a gentleman."

Ryan gave her an amused look. "All men want the same thing from a woman. Eventually he'll get around to telling you what he really wants from you."

"Don't judge all men by your standards," Kitty countered. "I already know what Norm wants; a wife and mother for his children."

Kitty could have sworn Ryan turned slightly green around the gills. "Has he proposed already?"

"No, of course not. We've just met."

The look he gave her made his green eyes glow with intoxicating brightness. The dance ended, and she disengaged herself from Ryan's arms just as Teresa flounced up to them and announced that Norm was looking for them. It was time to leave.

Feeling Ryan's piercing gaze resting on her as they rode home through the moonlit night, Kitty tried to ignore it. Teresa chattered away, apparently unaware of the mounting tension between Kitty and Ryan. Finally Teresa stopped talking and fell asleep against Ryan's shoulder.

Ryan awakened Teresa when they arrived home, and they all climbed down from the buggy. Kitty started to follow Ryan and Teresa into the house, but Norm held her back. "Would you sit in the buggy with me a few minutes?" he asked. "We've hardly had a minute alone all night."

"Sure, but not too long. It's getting late."

He swung her up into the buggy and climbed up beside her. Norm appeared nervous as he cleared his throat and said,

"You're a special woman, Kitty. I feel comfortable with you and hope you feel the same."

"I do, Norm. I had a good time tonight."

He placed his arm around her. Kitty stiffened, then relaxed. It was the first time he had attempted any kind of intimacy, and she'd been curious to know if another man could produce the same intense feelings Ryan aroused in her. When she didn't object, Norm turned her toward him and slowly covered her mouth with his.

Kitty thought the kiss pleasant but not particularly uplifting or exciting. It certainly had none of the earthshaking impact of Ryan's kisses. Analyzing her response further, Kitty decided that Norm's arms held none of the heat or urgency she'd come to expect from Ryan. In conclusion, while Norm was a nice man, he ignited no spark, produced no burning desire. To be perfectly truthful, compared to Ryan, Norm was boring.

Norm broke off the kiss, and Kitty assumed from the pleased look on his face that what he was feeling was completely opposite from her own interpretation of the kiss. His face was glowing, his eyes were luminous with pleasure.

"Kitty," he began breathlessly. "I know we've just met but I feel as if I've known you forever. I want you for my wife, Kitty. I've fallen in love with you. Say you'll marry me. The children will be so pleased. They think the world of you."

"Oh, no," Kitty protested. "It's too soon. We've just met. I can't . . . I don't know . . ."

"Kitty, sweetheart, look at me." She raised her head, and what she saw in his eyes made her groan in despair. She'd never wanted this to happen. She'd never meant to hurt Norm.

"Kitty, what is it? Is . . . is there someone else? Are you promised to another?"

"I . . ." How could she tell him Ryan was the only man she'd ever love? How could she explain that she'd given to Ryan what she should have saved for her husband? Even worse, how could she tell Norm that she'd made love with Ryan even though she knew he would never make her his wife?

"Don't be upset, Kitty. I'm sorry. Take your time. I'm willing to wait for your answer. Talk it over with Bert. He can vouch for my character."

"I don't need Bert to vouch for your character, Norm, I already know the kind of man you are. It's me. You know nothing about me."

"I know all I need to know. You'll make a

wonderful mother for my children. I'll give you children of your own, too. Would you like that?"

Kitty nodded. Having children of her own would be a dream come true. But she could only think of Ryan as their father. "Teresa thinks I'm an imposter, that I'm not really Bert's daughter. She'd say a lot more if you asked."

"I'm not asking. I don't care. Bert believes you're his daughter and that's good enough for me. I've known Teresa a long time. She tends to be somewhat uppity."

"That's not the half of it," Kitty muttered.

"Will you at least think about my proposal, sweetheart? I have to go out of town for a few days. I hope you'll have an answer for me when I return."

"I'll think about it," Kitty promised. In view of Ryan's opposition to marriage, she would be stupid to turn down a good man like Norm.

He kissed her again, then walked her to the door.

Seething with impotent rage, Ryan peered through the front window. He had seen Tucker kiss Kitty, and he'd had the unaccountable urge to tear her out of Tucker's arms but knew he had no right. Conflicting emotions about Kitty warred within him, leaving him confused and doubting his own narrow view of love and commitment.

Hell, he knew he was right about marriage, he tried to convince himself. He didn't believe in it, didn't want it, and wasn't about to change his mind. His attraction to Kitty puzzled him, but he explained it by telling himself that she was different from other women of his acquaintance, and she had overwhelmed his senses. He reckoned it couldn't last. Their passion was so spontaneous, so hot, so consuming, it was bound to burn itself out soon. But what was he supposed to do in the meantime? His hunger for the little wildcat showed no signs of waning any time soon, and now another man was courting her, and he didn't like it one damn bit.

The longer Ryan thought about Tucker kissing Kitty, the angrier he became. Jealousy was a new sensation, one he rarely experienced, and he felt at odds with the conflicting emotions warring within him. Incredibly, Ryan was too angry to recognize the emotion for what it was. All he saw was the danger Kitty presented to him and his inability to prevent it from continuing.

Ryan remained hidden in the shadows as Kitty let herself into the house, picked up the lantern on the hall table, and ascended the stairs to her room. She appeared preoccupied, and he wondered what Tucker had said to her to cause such intense introspection. He heard her bedroom door click shut and without a thought to propriety, he followed.

Kitty remained in deep thought as she entered the house and trudged up the staircase to her room. She realized that men like Norm Tucker were few and far between. He was sweet, kind, gentle . . . and not Ryan. Still, he might be her only chance at obtaining the home and family she'd always craved. His two children were adorable and would present no problem to the marriage. If she were smart she would accept Norm's proposal and the hell with Ryan Delaney.

She had just donned her nightgown and reached out to douse the lamp when the door opened and Ryan slipped inside. Her hand froze in midair. "This is getting to be a habit," she said tartly. "I reckon I'm going to have to start locking my door."

Time stood suspended as Ryan stared at her. His eyes glittered like cold green emeralds in the lamplight. She'd seen that look on his face before, and a thrill of anticipation shot through her.

"I saw you kiss him," Ryan accused in a voice taut with fury. "What else did he do? Did he touch your breasts? Did he put his hand beneath your skirts? Did you like it?"

"Damn you, Ryan," Kitty hissed. "What Norm and I do is none of your business."

"I'm making it my business. I brought you here. I'm responsible for . . . for . . ." He appeared to have lost his train of thought. "I don't want to see you hurt," he added lamely.

"Norm asked me to marry him," Kitty blurted out.

That seemed to take the wind out of his sails. "Did you agree?"

"I'm thinking it over. It wouldn't be such a bad thing," she said unconvincingly. "Norm is a good man. I . . . I think I can be happy with him."

A muscle twitched in Ryan's jaw. "You've made up your mind, then?"

She stared at him, willing him to say the words she longed to hear. When they did not come, she said, "Perhaps I have, unless you can give me a good reason why I shouldn't."

Three steps brought him so close that she felt suffocated by his heat. She tried to retreat but had nowhere to go. The backs of her knees were pressed against the edge of the bed.

"You need a reason? I'll give you one," he growled as his hands curled around her narrow shoulders and pulled her against the hard wall of his chest. Then he dipped his head and took her lips.

The fierceness of his kiss stunned her. There seemed to be a whole new depth of emotion in his kiss as his mouth moved over hers. The heat, the intensity, the raw sexuality of his kiss sent her senses reeling. Forgetting everything but the man she loved and his kisses, she opened her mouth to his probing tongue and kissed him back.

He broke off the kiss with an abruptness that stunned her, and he gave her a knowing grin. "Does Tucker kiss you like that? Do his kisses make you burn for more? Can you marry a man knowing he'll never make you feel the way I do?"

"I can marry a man knowing he loves me. Damn it!" Kitty retorted. "I don't understand you, Ryan Delaney. You don't want another man to have me even though you don't want me yourself. Make up your mind."

"That's not true," Ryan murmured as he brought her back into his arms. "I want you, love. I want you now. Here. On this bed." He pushed her backward onto the bed and followed her down. "You want me, too, don't deny it."

"You can make a statue want you," Kitty gasped as Ryan made a shambles of her defenses. "That doesn't mean a damn thing except you're doing what Ryan does best."

He caressed her breasts. "Tell me you don't want Tucker," he said raggedly.

She felt his manhood stirring against her leg as he lifted her nightgown above her waist and cupped her between her legs. A shudder passed through her, scattering her thoughts.

"Kitty, tell me," he urged as he massaged the tiny nub at the entrance to her sex.

"Tell you what? That you're incredibly arrogant? That you like having sex with me? You're the man I want, Ryan," Kitty exhaled on a puff of air. "You're just too damn set in your ways to realize what it is *you* want."

"You talk too much, love," Ryan groaned as he released himself from his denims, spread her legs with his knees, flexed his hips, and thrust upward and in. Kitty arched her back and took him deeply, knowing in her heart she would never love anyone like she loved Ryan, even if she did marry Norm.

Kitty convulsed almost immediately,

vaguely aware that Ryan's climax came so close upon hers that she couldn't distinguish his cries from hers.

Later, Ryan undressed and loved her again, taking his time to arouse her as his lips mapped a fiery trail across her flesh and his hands found new, intensely intimate ways to pleasure her. But when he tried to enter her, Kitty shook her head and pushed him away.

Ryan sat back on his heels. "You don't want this?" he asked in a puzzled voice.

"Yes, eventually," Kitty said shyly. "What I really want to do is love you in the same ways you love me." She shoved him backward on the bed.

Her hands spread across his chest, touching his flat male nipples. She lowered her head and touched each with her tongue and was gratified when he let out a hoarse groan. She loved touching him and was thrilled to know he enjoyed having her touch him as much as she enjoyed being touched. Her fingertips followed the dark, silky path that led downward to his groin, then lower, until she encountered the thick proof of his arousal. She took him between her palms, caressing and stroking, savoring the look of blissful agony on his contorted features.

"You're killing me, Kitten," he growled as he tried to pull her up and over him.

"No, not yet," Kitty said, purring like her namesake.

Then she dipped her head and touched the tip of his sex with her tongue. Ryan nearly leaped off the bed, making a grab for her, which she deftly dodged. She felt him heave and shudder when she ran her tongue down his length, but she wasn't ready to end the torture just yet. Then she took him into her mouth.

"Kitten!" He shouted her name and lifted her away. "I can't stand any more." Dragging her upward along his body, he spread her legs with his knees and thrust upward into her heated center.

They came together in a fiery burst that threatened to incinerate them. Kitty arched, taking him deeper and riding him ruthlessly. They climaxed simultaneously, roaring toward Paradise on the tail of a shooting star. As Kitty floated back to earth on a wave of pleasure she realized it wouldn't be fair to marry Norm when her love belonged to Ryan. She'd rather spend her life alone than accept second best.

"Do you still intend to marry Tucker?" Ryan murmured as he stroked her back and bottom.

Realizing she was still sprawled atop Ryan, Kitty shifted off of him as she pondered her answer. At length she said, "I would be doing Norm a disservice by marrying him, but Norm doesn't seem to care. He wants me just as I am."

Ryan frowned. "What kind of an answer is that?"

"The only kind you're going to get. I haven't made up my mind yet."

Ryan felt a crushing blow of disappointment but couldn't come up with the words that would stop Kitty from marrying Tucker. He knew what she wanted to hear, but it went against everything he believed in, the standard upon which he'd based his life. Yet what he felt for Kitty could not be described in words he was willing to give voice to. He needed time to think, to review his life and decide if he'd been wrong to judge all women by the actions of a few. Perhaps there was room in his life for a special woman like Kitty. Perhaps there was room for . . .

. . . Love.

"I'd better leave," Ryan said as he pushed himself out of bed. "We'll talk more about this later," he added as he gathered his hastily discarded clothing.

Kitty saw her opening and bore down

ruthlessly. "There's nothing more to discuss, Ryan."

He walked back to the bed, rested his knee on the edge, and kissed her. There was a raw aching need in his kiss that brought tears to her eyes. Why did he have to be so stubborn? Kitty wondered with blank despair. Couldn't he sense how much she loved him? Did his freedom mean more to him than her love?

Kitty lay awake long after Ryan left. Her body still tingled and burned from his loving, and she knew she'd never be able to marry Norm after tonight. Her life was more difficult now than it had been when she rode with outlaws. All she'd had to worry about then was maintaining her disguise and staying alive. Now she had Bert and Teresa complicating her life, and Ryan Delaney taunting her with his kisses.

Kitty thought long and hard about Bert. She felt sorry for him, had even grown fond of him, but she still couldn't bring herself to love him unconditionally. As for Teresa, her stepsister was bound and determined to make her life a living hell. Kitty didn't want to be Bert's heir. Teresa deserved that honor more than she did.

Kitty considered Bert's grave condition and decided his health had improved somewhat over the past few weeks. If she was going to leave, now was the time. Rather than making sad farewells, Kitty decided it would be best for everyone if she just wrote a note of explanation to Bert and another to Norm and quietly disappeared. If she remained she knew Norm would continue to pressure her for marriage and Bert would doubtlessly approve the match.

Had Kitty held the slightest hope of becoming more to Ryan than a lover, she would stay, but she knew that that would never happen. She drifted off to sleep composing notes of farewell in her head.

Kitty awakened late the next morning. Her eyes were barely open when Teresa burst into her room. She strode purposely to the bed, her nose wrinkled in disgust.

"What happened last night? This room reeks of sex. And don't tell me you invited Norm Tucker up to your room, for I won't believe you."

Kitty sat up, pulling the sheet up to her chin. "Don't you believe in knocking?"

"Why should I? This is my house."

Kitty's eyes widened when Teresa reached down, picked up Kitty's discarded nightgown, and dangled it as if it were something offensive. "Were you too warm last night?"

she taunted, her eyes glittering with malice.

"You could say that," Kitty said, admitting nothing.

"Ryan was here, wasn't he? How do you think Papa Bert will react when I tell him you and Ryan are lovers?"

"I don't know," Kitty said. "Do you want to risk telling him something that might or might not be true? You could damage your own standing with him."

Apparently Teresa decided to give the matter further thought, for she spun on her heel and marched out the door. Kitty heaved a sigh of relief. The situation between her and Teresa was becoming intolerable. If she'd been torn about her decision to leave the ranch, this clash with Teresa made up her mind. She began to plan her departure as she gathered her clean clothing and went to bathe.

"You want me to what?" Ryan asked, clearly disconcerted by what Bert had just asked him. He had paid an early morning visit to Bert's sickroom and had been floored by Bert's request.

"I may be sick, but I'm neither blind nor stupid," Bert contended. "I know there are strong feelings between you and Kitty. No one can be in the same room with you two without sensing the attraction. In view of my observations I don't think I'm asking too much, or being unreasonable."

"You want me to marry Kitty," Ryan repeated slowly.

"I'm growing weaker," Bert said. "I can feel my life slipping away, and I want my own flesh and blood to inherit the ranch. Unfortunately Kitty has no experience. She needs a strong man to help her and you're the man I want my daughter to marry.

"You're my best friend's son. You and your family can protect her. I know Kitty is rough around the edges and lacks polish, but I feel strongly that she will make you a loving wife. Right now she's vulnerable to outside influence and doesn't know her own mind. You can help her through the ordeal after my death."

"You're asking a lot of me, Bert," Ryan said, frowning. "My home is in Montana. I have a responsibility to my brothers."

"From what you've told me, Chad and his wife are capable of running the Montana ranch without your help. And Pierce has Zoey's ranch to take care of. Why shouldn't you have a place of your own?"

Stunned, Ryan gaped at Bert, a thousand reasons why he shouldn't take a wife running through his mind. "I know for a fact that Norm Tucker proposed to Kitty."

"Tucker is a good man," Bert acknowledged. "But he isn't the man for my daughter. Kitty would never be happy with a mildmannered, uninteresting man like Tucker. She needs someone to curb her wild nature without damaging her spirit. I'm damn proud of that girl, Ryan, and I think you're perfect for her."

"What about Teresa?" Ryan asked, forestalling his answer. "I understand she expects to inherit."

"Don't worry about Teresa. She will be well provided for. Teresa is a good girl at heart but lately she has displayed flaws in her character I can't admire. My lawyer was here the day before yesterday with a new will for me to sign. Teresa will have a home here for life and a nice little nest egg to live on should she decide to leave. But Kitty is to inherit the ranch and the bulk of my estate."

"I don't know what to say," Ryan said. "I'm not the marrying kind. You know about Pa and what happened between him and my mother. I vowed long ago not to let myself get romantically involved with any woman. I *like* women, don't get me wrong. It's permanent relationships I fear."

Bert blinked, his stamina all but depleted.

"Are you refusing me?" he asked weakly.

"How do you know Kitty will have me?" Ryan asked. The pressure was getting to him. Until Bert, no one had ever asked him to compromise his ideals. He asked himself if the sacrifice was worth it and didn't like the answer.

"How do you feel about Kitty?" Bert shot back. "How much do you care for her?"

"Papa Bert! You have no right to ask Ryan such a personal question," Teresa exclaimed as she rushed to Bert's bedside. "I just happened to be passing your room and decided to look in on you. I heard what you said." She grasped Ryan's arm and smiled up at him. "Ryan and I had such a good time last night. I don't think he cares anything about Kitty."

"Teresa, honey, this is a private conversation."

"That's all right, Bert," Ryan said. "I was ready to leave anyway. I'll think about your request and let you know in a day or two."

Ryan, his thoughts in turmoil, made a hasty exit. He knew he should get on his horse and ride hell for leather back to Montana and not look back. He had accomplished what he set out to do and owed Bert nothing. It had been a grand adventure, but all good things have a beginning and an end. And clearly Kitty had been one of the good things about this venture.

Kitty . . .

He loved the way she responded to him, adored the way she looked; her soft mouth, her slim body, everything about Kitty pleased him. But marriage . . .

That was asking a bit much. He didn't know if he had it in him to be faithful to one woman for the rest of his life. He was Rogue Ryan, a man who took love where he found it and left for greener pastures when he became bored. But to be truthful, nothing about Kitty bored him. If anything, she intrigued him more with each passing day. And if he wanted to be brutally honest, he'd admit to the possibility that Kitty would never bore him. Then there was the jealousy issue. He couldn't recall a time when he'd been jealous of another man's attention to his woman of the moment. Yet when he'd seen Tucker romancing Kitty, he'd flown into a rage.

What in the hell had gotten into him?

He needed space, Ryan decided as he left the house and walked to the corral to saddle his horse. He always thought better on horseback, with nothing but blue skies and mountains to influence him. He was so confused. Bert's startling request had caught him off guard, and he needed time to come to grips with his feelings for Kitty. Both Pierce and Chad had conquered their aversion to marriage and taken wives, why couldn't he? Each of his brothers had fallen in love, but Ryan wasn't certain he would recognize love were it to bite him.

Kitty watched from the window as Ryan rode away from the ranch. He wasn't carrying saddlebags, so she knew he'd be returning. Turning abruptly, she hurried back upstairs to write farewell notes to her father and Norm in the privacy of her room, and to pack her few belongings. How could she marry Norm when she loved Ryan? She couldn't. How could she remain in Bert's house, despised by Teresa and taunted by Ryan's daunting presence? The answer was the same. She couldn't. Her only alternative was to leave.

She had a horse and enough money to live on, if she were frugal, until she settled and found a job. Tucson was too close to the ranch and Tombstone was too dangerous, so she had to look elsewhere to settle. Perhaps north, she decided as she sat down to compose her notes. When she finished, she folded each sheet of paper in half and wrote Bert's name on one and Norm's on the other. Then she pulled her saddlebags from beneath the bed and packed her meager belongings.

The hallway was deserted as Kitty, clad in baggy shirt, trousers, and coat, crept down the stairs. She paused just long enough to prop the notes on the hall table before slipping out the door. The hands were in the north pasture today, so no one saw her enter the corral and saddle her horse. Tears were streaming down her cheeks as she rode toward Tucson, where she intended to purchase supplies for her journey north.

Kitty didn't dare look back. The ranch and everything it stood form — stability, a permanent home, a family — weren't for her. Teresa was more of a daughter to Bert than she was. Had Ryan made a commitment to her, things would have ended differently, but he hadn't, and the time had come for her to leave. She'd never wanted to come here in the first place.

Something was bothering Ryan. It nagged at him relentlessly. He had ridden to the foot of the mountains, when a gut feeling told him he should return to the ranch. Not one to ignore his hunches, he turned his mount and rode back to the ranch. He dismounted quickly and strode into the house. He found Teresa standing in the entrance hall, holding a folded sheet of paper and smiling. The knot in his stomach tightened.

"What's wrong?"

"Ryan, I thought you'd ridden out." She tried to hide the paper in the folds of her skirt. "Nothing is wrong. Why do you ask?"

"What are you hiding?"

"N-nothing," she stammered.

Ryan didn't believe her. His hand closed around her wrist and dragged forth the fist clutching the note. He plucked it away and scanned the contents.

"She's gone! Dammit, Teresa, what were you going to do with the note? Tear it up? Burn it?"

"N-no, I was going to give it to Papa Bert. There's another on the table for Norm."

Ryan saw the other note, read it, and tossed it aside. "I hope you're pleased," Ryan hissed as he reread the note to Bert. "You never did want Kitty here."

"She doesn't belong here," Teresa said pugnaciously. "I'm convinced she's an imposter. She's crude and unprincipled and not good enough to inherit. You found her living with outlaws! That alone should give you a clue to her character. Have you any idea as to the number of men she's slept with?"

"I know precisely how many men Kitty has slept with," Ryan said through clenched teeth. He spun on his heel.

"Where are you going?"

"To give Bert his note. Then I'm going after Kitty."

"Don't go! She's not worth it."

"Neither are you," Ryan shot back as he strode purposefully toward Bert's room.

CHAPTER 13

Ryan rode hard toward Tucson. He had decided, and Bert had agreed, that Kitty would probably head to town to buy supplies for her journey to God only knew where. If Ryan failed to find her in Tucson, he held virtually no hope of finding her at all.

Ryan recalled Bert's pallor when he'd read Kitty's brief farewell note, and he was still furious with her for abandoning her father, and him, if he wanted to be truthful. Her short, callous note of explanation contained little information beyond the fact that she felt she could never fit in or live up to Bert's expectations. The note to Tucker was basically identical in wording, except for a terse refusal of his proposal. Kitty had left nothing, no note, not a word, for Ryan, and her neglect left a bitter taste in his mouth.

After searching his heart, Ryan had an inkling of why his brothers had taken wives when they had been as adamantly opposed to marriage as he was. They had found women worthy of their love. Had the same thing happened to him? He never considered *not* going after Kitty. It was just something he had to do, not only for Bert's sake but also for his own peace of mind. He had to find out for himself if the hold Kitty had upon his heart was fleeting or something more substantial.

Even more distressing was visualizing Kitty on her own in a world she knew virtually nothing about. He had to find her before trouble did.

Ryan was so lost in thought that he didn't notice a group of riders approaching from the west. Nor did he realize their paths would cross very soon. They were nearly upon him before he saw them. When he recognized them a moment later, it was too late to change the course of fate.

Muttering a string of oaths, Ryan identified Billy Barton and his gang of outlaws at the same time they recognized him. Moments later they had surrounded him. Billy Barton reined to a halt in front of Ryan, cutting off his escape.

"Well, lookee here!" Billy crowed. "Damned if it ain't Ryan. It weren't bad enough that Kit lit out, leaving us shorthanded, but I never thought Ryan was the kind to abandon his friends. Why did you sneak away in the middle of the night?"

Cursing his rotten luck, Ryan pasted on a false smile and said, "I remembered I had business elsewhere."

"Where are ya headed?" Clank asked.

"Nowhere in particular," Ryan hedged.

Durango grunted, sliding Ryan a skeptical look. But it was Billy who voiced his suspicion about Ryan's destination. "I'll be damned. You're going to rob the bank in Tucson, ain't ya? Well, well, ain't that a coincidence."

Ryan groaned in frustration. Each moment he spent in pointless conversation with the Bartons meant less time he had to catch Kitty. "I don't know what you're talking about."

"We've been casing the Tucson bank for a week. The payroll for the railroad arrived yesterday. We've got a contact at the bank who told us the best time to strike is late afternoon, just before closing. Coming upon you like this is a stroke of luck. We're shorthanded and need your gun."

"Sorry, boys," Ryan said. "I've got other business to take care of. Another time."

He tried to ride away but was cut off by Billy's horse. "Not so fast, Ryan. You owe us. Help us pull this job and you can go your own way afterward. There's a lot of money involved here."

Ryan shook his head. "I don't have time for this."

"Make the time," Billy growled, tossing the reins back to Ryan. "Durango, Clank, don't take your eyes off the bastard. We need him and he ain't gonna split like he did before." Spurring his horse, he set the pace.

Cursing roundly beneath his breath, Ryan had no choice but to follow. His mind worked furiously. Until they reached Tucson there was virtually no chance of escaping. But once they hit town Ryan vowed to find a way to rid himself of the Bartons. Robbing banks wasn't exactly his line of work. With a bit of luck he'd find a way to extricate himself before they entered the bank. He thanked his lucky stars that his brothers would never learn about his stint as an outlaw. It wasn't as if Pierce or Chad had never gotten into scrapes with the law, but he'd damn well better get himself out of this one.

The sun was disappearing behind a mountain when they rode into Tucson. The streets were emptying fast. Women were already home preparing the evening meal, and their men were either leaving their jobs to return home or on their way. Store owners were pulling down their shades, and one of the last customers had just left the bank as the Bartons rode into town.

They dismounted in front of the bank and cast furtive glances down the nearly deserted street before approaching the entrance. Ryan saw his chance and lingered behind, intending to turn back for his horse and ride away while the Bartons were entering the bank. Suddenly all hell broke loose. Men sprang at them from out of nowhere, ambushing the Bartons before they could enter the bank. Gunshots were exchanged. Ryan saw Clank fall, a blossom of red spreading across his chest. Billy went down next.

At first Ryan was too stunned to react. It sure looked as if the law had known the Bartons were coming. He finally regained his wits when he saw Billy fall. But by then it was too late. He was quickly surrounded, disarmed, and held at gunpoint by two lawmen. He glanced over at Durango and saw that the half-breed was still alive but was also disarmed and being held at gunpoint.

Ryan identified the marshal by his badge and made as if to approach him. He hadn't taken two steps before he was roughly seized and thrown to the ground.

"You're not going anyplace, mister," the marshal growled, "unless it's to jail." Someone produced a rope and bound Ryan's hands behind him. Then the marshal hauled him to his feet. "This is one bank you're not going to rob. Thanks to an informant, we knew you were coming."

Durango bared his teeth and asked, "Who told you?"

The marshal laughed. "Why, your contact at the bank. Seems he wasn't as good a friend as Billy Barton thought. Or else the reward money looked too good to him. Either way, you boys are going to hang. I'm Marshal Jeb Pringle and I'm going to make damn certain the Bartons will never ride again."

"Now wait a damn minute," Ryan protested. "I'm not one of the Bartons. I'm innocent."

Someone snickered. "Sure you are," Pringle said. "If you're so innocent, what were you doing riding with the Bartons?"

"They forced me to accompany them. My name is Ryan Delaney. I'm a rancher from Montana."

"I don't give a hoot who you are. You were with the Bartons when they rode in to rob the bank. That's all the proof I need." He gave Ryan a shove. "Get moving, Delaney. There are two empty cells waiting for you and your friend." He glanced down at Barton and Clank, who lay bleeding in the dusty street. "Too bad they can't join you but I reckon they're the lucky ones. They won't have to face a hangman's noose."

At a loss for words, Ryan stumbled forward, wondering how in the hell he was going to get out of this one. For the first time in his life he wished his brothers were here to help him out of this mess.

Kitty was just leaving the general store when she heard gunshots. She froze, forgetting for a moment that she was no longer an outlaw and had no reason to fear gunplay. Feeling more confident, she packed her purchases in her saddlebags and mounted up, intending to ride north like she originally planned.

Her curiosity was piqued when she saw people running down the street to investigate the ruckus. She heard someone shout, "Bank robbery," and thought nothing of it until she heard someone else call out the name of the bank robbers. The Bartons! That alone should have convinced Kitty to hightail it out of town, but something held her back. A sense of foreboding made her dismount and follow the crowd to the bank.

Fearing to get too close to where the law had the Bartons pinned down, Kitty hung back, peering over heads in order to see what was taking place.

Her cry of dismay was lost amid a jumble of voices when she saw Ryan being led off by the marshal. Her head spun dizzily, and she leaned against a hitching post until the world stopped whirling. What was Ryan doing in Tucson? More importantly, what was he doing with the Bartons? Ryan was no bank robber, yet the proof of his intent was indisputable. According to rumors flying around her, Ryan had been caught approaching the bank with the Bartons.

Nothing made sense. She wanted to rush to Ryan's defense but feared she might be identified as a member of the gang dressed as she was as a boy. There had to be a way to save Ryan from the hangman, and it was up to her to find it. The crowd was starting to disperse, and Kitty got her first look at the two bodies sprawled in the dirt. She gagged and looked away. At least she'd never have to worry about Billy and Clank again. She was grateful that Ryan's life had been spared and immediately began making plans to save him.

Leaving Tucson was out of the question now. Ryan needed her. She had to keep a level head if Ryan was to survive. But first things first. Getting permission to see Ryan might pose a problem, but Kitty had determination in abundance.

Kitty waited until the crowd began to drift away before heading over to the jailhouse. She paused briefly to shove stray bits of russet hair beneath her hat before pushing the door open and stepping inside. Marshal Pringle was sitting behind his desk. He looked up and frowned at Kitty.

"What do you want, kid? Can't you see I'm busy?"

Kitty looked down at her boots, pretending shyness. "Sorry, Marshal. I don't mean to bother you but I need permission to see the prisoner."

Pringle cocked back his hat and stared at Kitty. "Which prisoner is that, sonny?"

"Ryan Delaney. He's accused of attempted robbery but Ryan would never rob a bank, or ride with the Bartons."

"What makes you such an expert?"

"Ryan is my . . . cousin," she lied. "We were riding through town minding our own business when the law opened fire."

"Is that so?" Pringle asked, apparently unconvinced. "I checked out Delaney's story with Durango and he said Delaney rode with them a while back and joined up with them again today to help rob the bank. Durango said Delaney was alone. That's all the proof I need, sonny. But don't worry, if Delaney is really your cousin, which I seriously doubt, he's going to get a fair trial before we hang him."

Kitty grasped the edge of the desk to keep herself upright. The marshal's words offered scant hope of saving Ryan. There must be something she could do. Swallowing past the lump growing in her throat, she turned her potent blue gaze on the marshal. "Can I just speak to my cousin, Marshal? It would mean a great deal to me."

The marshal peered at Kitty through narrowed lids. "Who are you? I've never seen you in town before."

"I'm Kit. Ryan Delaney is my cousin. We're from Montana."

"And I'm Jesse James. Listen, kid, if it's hero worship, Delaney is an outlaw, not a man to look up to."

"Ryan really is my cousin," Kitty persisted.

"Very well, you look harmless enough. I reckon it can't hurt. You got any weapons on you?"

"No," Kitty said truthfully as she held her coat open for inspection. She'd deliberately left her gun in her saddlebags, knowing she'd be unable to sneak it in to Ryan.

"Okay, kid, I'm in a generous mood today. I'll give you a few minutes alone with your 'cousin.' "

"Thank you," Kitty said, jubilant. "I appreciate it, Marshal. Ryan's Ma is gonna want to know how Ryan got into this mess."

"You'll find Delaney's cell at the end of the corridor," Pringle said as he pointed the way to the passage. "He's in cell number four." He watched her stride down the hall, then turned away.

Kitty crept past Durango's cell, taking extra care not to awaken him when she saw him sleeping on a shelf in the first cell. At last she reached Ryan's cell. She wasn't surprised to see him pacing back and forth, his hands clenched into fists at his sides. She clutched the bars and sobbed his name.

Ryan was at his wit's end. Not only was Kitty probably out of his reach by now, but he had gotten himself into one helluva mess. Somehow he needed to contact Bert. He knew Bert couldn't possibly leave his sickbed, but perhaps he could send Teresa to vouch for him. Damn, what rotten luck to run into the Bartons outside Tucson. He was confused, angry, and still hurt over Kitty's defection.

Suddenly he heard a cry and whirled

toward the sound. He blinked, convinced his eyes were deceiving him and the apparition would disappear. Gingerly he approached the bars, but Kitty did not disappear. She clung to the bars, her face raised to him, tears streaming down her cheeks.

"Kitty . . . what the hell . . ."

"Oh, Ryan, I'm so sorry. I heard the gunplay and followed the crowd to the bank. I saw the marshal take you away. What happened? How did you get mixed up with the Bartons again?"

Ryan grasped her hands, afraid to let go lest she evaporate in a wisp of smoke. "I took off after you when I learned you had left the ranch. I wanted to catch up with you in town. Unfortunately I crossed paths with the Bartons outside Tucson. They said they were shorthanded and forced me to ride with them to rob the bank. Their contact at the bank ratted on them and the marshal set up an ambush. I had intended to sneak away when the Bartons entered the bank but there wasn't time. You know the rest."

"Oh God, what are we going to do?" Kitty lamented on a rising note of panic. "The marshal says you'll be brought to trial and hanged. The trial will be a farce, we both know that."

"Calm down, love," Ryan said in an effort to reassure her. "First, how long do we have together before the marshal makes you leave?"

"Not long. Tell me what I should do. I can't let you hang, Ryan. It would kill me."

Ryan squeezed her hands, wishing he could kiss her sweet lips. "Do you care so much, love?"

"How can you even ask that?" she cried, trying to pull her hands free. "Of course I care for you. Why do you think I left the ranch?"

"You tell me why you left. Was it because Tucker was pressuring you to marry him?"

"That's part of it," Kitty admitted. "We both know I didn't fit in. Bert was kind to accept me as his daughter but I couldn't summon the love he deserved from a daughter."

"Why didn't you accept Tucker's proposal?"

Kitty averted her face.

"Kitten, look at me." She did. "I have feelings for you, too. I was devastated when you left without a word to me. You left notes for Bert and Tucker, but nothing for me."

"I-I couldn't. You say you care for me but obviously not enough to marry me. You'll never change, Ryan, I know that. Your opposition to marriage is too deeply ingrained. You're too stubborn to admit there might be a woman you can commit to. I saw no future for us so I chose to leave. As for Bert, he still has Teresa and doesn't need me."

I need you, Ryan thought. Unfortunately he'd waited too long to give Kitty the words she wanted to hear. In view of his precarious position, telling Kitty he loved her now would only complicate her life.

"You're so wrong, Kitten," Ryan murmured. "But it's senseless to go into what might have been when I'm so close to losing my life." His gaze traveled the length of her and back. "Why are you dressed like that? Someone might recognize you as a member of the Bartons."

"I thought it safer to travel as a male." She paused for breath. "What can I do, Ryan? There must be someone who can help you."

As much as he hated to call on his brothers for help, Ryan knew he had no choice. They had always pulled together in adversity, and he knew they wouldn't let him down. But time was against him. His trial could be history and so could he by the time they arrived in Tucson.

"Wire my brothers," Ryan said. "Tell them

I'm in Tucson and in desperate need of help. Send telegrams to Chad in Dry Gulch and to Pierce in Rolling Prairie. Then pray they'll arrive in time to testify for me."

"I'll ride back to the ranch and tell Bert," Kitty suggested. "Maybe there is something he can do. He's sure to know influential people in town."

"Bert is a sick man, Kitten. Don't expect too much from him."

"Ryan, I'm so sorry," Kitty said shakily. "This is all my fault. You wouldn't have been with the Bartons in the first place if you hadn't been searching for me. And you wouldn't have been involved today if I hadn't left the ranch. You shouldn't have come after me."

Ryan released Kitty's hands and cupped her face, bringing it close to the bars. Then he kissed her. He tasted salt on her lips and felt something inside him break loose. Something he'd held sacred for more years than he cared to count. He felt his own tears mingle with hers and abruptly broke off the kiss, turning away before she saw how deeply he was moved.

"I'll wire your brothers immediately," Kitty promised. "And I'll change into a dress. Not even Durango will be able to identify me as Kit when I become Kathryn

Lowry."

"I have one more request, love," Ryan said, feeling as if his heart were being torn out. "Don't come back here. There's no guarantee you won't be recognized. It's too dangerous. I couldn't bear to have you identified as a member of the Barton gang."

"I told the marshal I was your cousin but I'm not sure he believed me," Kitty explained. "I'll come up with something else when I return."

"Don't come back. It's probably for the best, anyway. If you were smart, you'd marry Tucker and forget about me."

Kitty opened her mouth to reply but shut it quickly when she saw the marshal's bulky form outlined in a shaft of sunlight at the end of the corridor.

"Time's up, kid," Pringle said as he ambled down the passage to Ryan's cell. "I stopped by to see Judge McFee and he's agreed to set the trial for two weeks from Saturday. Thought you'd both like to know."

Ryan cursed softly beneath his breath. He seriously doubted his brothers could get here that fast.

Kitty must have concurred, for she gave voice to her fears. "That's too soon. Ryan has to find a lawyer and witnesses to testify in his behalf."

"I'll try to find a lawyer willing to defend a guilty man," Pringle said.

"Don't bother," Ryan said dryly. "I'll defend myself."

"Suit yourself, Delaney. Come on, kid, time to go."

"One more moment," Kitty pleaded.

"Sorry," Pringle said as he grasped her arm and escorted her down the corridor. When they passed Durango's cell, she averted her face. Durango was no longer sleeping. He stood at the bars, eyeing Kitty with suspicion as she passed. Fortunately for Kitty, he didn't get a good look at her face.

Kitty dashed the tears from her eyes as she stepped out into the sunlight. She had no time to waste on tears. With Ryan's trial two weeks away she had to act fast. She quickly located the telegraph office and sent off the telegrams to Ryan's brothers. By the time she returned for her horse, darkness covered the land and she knew it would be difficult to find her way to the ranch.

Deciding to stay in Tucson overnight, Kitty took her horse to the livery and rented a room at a second-rate hotel. She was still disguised as a lad when she checked in with the clerk. The color of her money seemed to allay the clerk's suspicious nature, and she was soon ensconced in a small room with a sagging bed and dingy furnishings.

Kitty removed a nightgown from the saddlebags she'd brought to the room with her, and she quickly undressed. She was afraid to inspect the sheets for cleanliness as she crawled into bed, but at this point clean bed linen was the least of her worries. She didn't know what she would do if Ryan's brothers didn't get here in time. Sleep finally came, but so did terrifying dreams in which she was forced to watch Ryan swinging from the end of a rope.

Kitty awoke just as dawn was breaking. She rose, washed, and donned one of the dresses she had stuffed in her saddlebags. It was in desperate need of an iron, but Kitty couldn't afford to worry over small things at a time like this. Ryan's best chance for freedom lay with Bert, and it was imperative that she return to the ranch as soon as possible. Kitty had no idea what Bert could do for Ryan, but anything was better than nothing.

The clerk did a double take when Kitty, transformed, strode up to the desk and handed him her room key. He stared at her, then at the saddlebags slung over her arm, and his brows shot upward. She was out the door before he found his voice to ask questions of her. A half hour later she had left the town behind in her dust.

Kitty frowned at the horse and buggy parked close to the front door as she dismounted and strode up the steps. She grabbed the door handle, but it was jerked out of her hand when the door opened suddenly.

"So you've come back," Teresa said with a sneer. "Did Ryan come with you?"

"I'm alone. I need to speak to Bert." She stepped around Teresa and was brought up short when Teresa grasped her elbow in a surprisingly strong grip.

"You can't see Bert now. You've already done enough harm as it is."

Waves of dread washed over Kitty. "Something is wrong. What is it?"

"It's Papa Bert. He's had another attack. It's bad this time, and you're to blame. Your leaving hit him hard. I hope you're satisfied."

Kitty twisted her arm free. "I'm going in there. You can't stop me."

"The doctor is with him," Teresa said. "He's been here all night."

"Oh God," Kitty said, sagging with despair. "Bert can't die now. Ryan needs him."

"Ryan? What are you talking about? Ryan

took off after you yesterday like the devil was on his tail."

"Ryan is in jail. He was caught attempting to rob the Tucson bank with the Bartons. Only he isn't guilty. The marshal refuses to believe Ryan's story. There's going to be a trial and Ryan is sure to hang if Bert doesn't speak up for him."

"Ryan is in jail? That's rich," Teresa gloated. "Serves him right. He chased after you like a dog after a bitch in heat. He should have stayed here with me. I offered him everything but all he wanted was you."

"I can't stand here bickering with you, Teresa. I'm going in to see Bert. He must know someone in town who can help Ryan."

"Did I hear you say you wanted to see Bert, young lady?"

Kitty whirled toward the voice. "Are you the doctor?"

"Doctor Sheedy. And you are?"

"Kitty . . . Lowry," Kitty said, using her father's last name for the first time. Somehow it seemed right. "How is my . . . father?"

"Ah, so you're the long lost daughter. I'm glad Bert found you before he . . . well, you know what I mean. Bert is a very sick man."

"Can I see him?"

"I told her Papa Bert couldn't have visitors," Teresa snapped.

"Teresa is right, my dear. But I see no harm in you looking in on him. Keep in mind that Bert isn't to be disturbed or excited in any way. His heart is very weak, and the slightest distress could be fatal."

Kitty felt as if the earth had opened up and swallowed her. Bert's fragile condition prevented her from asking him for help. Now Ryan had no one but his brothers to depend upon, and they lived hundreds of miles away.

"I'll just go in for a minute," Kitty said. "It might ease his mind to know I am here."

"Very well," Doctor Sheedy said. "I was hoping Rosita could rustle up some breakfast for me before I return to town."

"You're leaving?" Kitty asked.

"There's nothing more I can do here. It's all in God's hands now." He turned to Teresa. "About that breakfast . . ."

Kitty watched Teresa and the doctor walk toward the kitchen, girding herself for her visit to Bert's room. Guilt rode her. If not for her Bert wouldn't be in this shape.

Kitty opened the door to Bert's room and stepped inside. The drapes were open, filling the room with sunshine, just the way Bert liked it, she thought as she tiptoed to his bedside. His eyes were closed, and she perched on the edge of the bed, watching the shallow rise and fall of his chest. His color was ashen and his lips blue. Tears sprang to Kitty's eyes. Until that moment she had had no idea her feelings for her father had developed into something stronger than fondness.

Kitty groped for Bert's hand and squeezed, trying to convey her presence to him. It must have worked, for Bert opened his eyes, turned his head toward her, and smiled. "You've come back," he whispered weakly. "You won't go away again, will you?" It was a desperate plea, one Kitty felt dutybound to honor.

"I'll not go away again, Bert . . . Father," she said, holding back her tears. "You mustn't die when we've just found one another."

"I'll . . . try not to." His lids fluttered downward, and Kitty knew it was time to leave.

"Try to get some rest, Father. I'll return later." Bert was already asleep when Kitty quietly let herself out of the room.

There was no way now she could ask Bert to help save Ryan. In all likelihood Bert would never leave his bed again. With a heavy heart, Kitty went to the kitchen in search of Teresa. If Bert couldn't testify on Ryan's behalf, perhaps Teresa would be willing to aid Ryan.

The doctor had already left when Kitty arrived in the kitchen. But Teresa was still there, conferring with the cook. Rosita went to Kitty immediately and gave her a hug. "It's so sad, Kitty," Rosita sobbed. "*Senor* Bert is such a good man. I'm glad you're here to comfort him in his last days."

"So am I, Rosita," Kitty replied, giving the woman a quick hug.

"How was Bert?" Teresa asked. "Did he recognize you?"

"He's not good," Kitty replied. "And yes, he did recognize me. If you have a spare moment I'd like to speak to you in private, Teresa."

"Will the parlor do?"

Kitty followed Teresa into the parlor, waited until she settled into a chair, then said, "I need your help, Teresa. Will you go into town and tell the marshal that Ryan is no outlaw? I had intended to ask Bert for help but that's impossible now."

"Of course," Teresa said with alacrity. Had Kitty not been so distraught she would have known Teresa was too accommodating to be believed. "I'll ride into town tomorrow and speak with the marshal. You'll stay with Papa Bert while I'm gone, won't you? I can't leave him alone."

"Yes. Anything. Just convince the marshal that Ryan is innocent."

"I'll do my best," Teresa promised.

Kitty didn't know why, but Teresa's words gave her little comfort.

CHAPTER 14

Marshal Pringle offered Teresa a chair and resumed his seat behind his desk. "What can I do for you, Miss Cowling?"

Teresa smoothed her skirts over her knees and gave the marshal a brilliant smile. "I understand you have Ryan Delaney in your jail."

"Not another one," Pringle groaned. "Don't tell me you're Delaney's cousin, too."

"Oh, no, Marshal, Ryan and I are definitely not related. I thought you should know that he's been staying out at the ranch with Papa Bert and me."

"Is that so, Miss Cowling. Bert is a good man. Did he know he was harboring an outlaw?"

"Well," Teresa began coyly, "I *did* hear Ryan tell Papa Bert that he rode with the Barton gang at one time." She batted her eyelashes at the marshal. "And Ryan *did* ride out alone the day of the attempted bank robbery. There is something else that might interest you. My stepsister also rode with the Bartons. She dressed as a boy and called herself Kit."

Pringle shot to his feet. "That lad who came to see Delaney! He said he was Delaney's cousin. Was that your stepsister?"

"I'd be willing to bet on it, Marshal," Teresa said with conviction.

"This is my lucky day. You're going to be our star witness, Miss Cowling! Are you willing to testify in court? All you need do is to repeat what you just told me."

"Of course," Teresa said complacently. "Everything I just told you is the truth. You can depend on me."

She rose to leave, then, almost as an afterthought, asked, "May I see the prisoner, Marshal? I'd like to ask him how he could abuse our trust like he did. Papa Bert thought he had reformed."

"I see no harm in that," Pringle said. "Fifteen minutes is all I can allow."

"That's all the time I need, Marshal."

Pringle escorted Teresa to the corridor. "Delaney's cell is at the end of the corridor. Do you want me to accompany you?"

"That won't be necessary, Marshal,"

Teresa said as she started down the dim passage.

Ryan heard footsteps padding down the corridor, and he pressed his face against the bars. The rustle of skirts told him it was a woman, and he feared it was Kitty. He couldn't bear seeing her again, knowing that he might be dead in less than two weeks. The steps came closer. He squinted into the murky passageway and was more than a little dismayed to see Teresa.

"Hello, Ryan," she said in a tone that raised hackles on the back of his neck.

"Teresa, what in the devil are you doing here? Have you come to speak to the marshal in my defense? Did Kitty tell you what happened?"

"You mean did Kitty tell me you attempted to rob the bank with the Bartons, don't you?"

Ryan spit out a curse. "You know better than that. What did Kitty tell you and Bert?"

"Papa Bert doesn't know. He had another attack, and the doctor said that any kind of excitement or stress would kill him."

"I appreciate you coming here to speak on my behalf," Ryan said. "Did the marshal believe you? Did you tell him who I am, and that I have never been an outlaw?"

Teresa's smile did not reach her eyes. "I told Marshal Pringle the truth, Ryan. How could I lie when I knew you had ridden with the Bartons? I have no idea what happened after you left the ranch the day of the attempted robbery. You could have joined the Bartons."

Ryan paled. He didn't even know this woman standing before him. She embodied everything he despised in a woman. Deceit, jealousy, lack of morals. She was vindictive and a liar to boot, no better than Cora Lee Doolittle, who had caused Pierce and Chad such anguish.

"Why are you doing this, Teresa? Will seeing me hang make you happy?"

Teresa tossed her head. "You spurned me. We would have been good together had you not lusted after Kitty. You deserve everything you get. I'm not going to lie on the witness stand, Ryan. Everything I say will be the truth as I know it."

"You know I'm not an outlaw," Ryan spat, wishing he could get his hands on the lying witch, but she stood just out of his reach. "How do you think Bert will react when he learns what you've done? He cares about you, Teresa, but he won't be able to forgive you for what you're doing to me."

"Papa Bert will never know," Teresa contended. "The doctor says it will take a miracle to bring him out of this latest attack. His heart is too weak to recover."

"Gloat all you want," Ryan said from between clenched teeth. "The fact remains that Kitty will inherit the bulk of Bert's estate."

"I've already engaged a lawyer to contest the will," Teresa claimed. "It won't be difficult to prove that Kitty is an imposter."

"I'm glad Bert never glimpsed your true character," Ryan said sadly. "He'll die thinking only the best about you."

"Your fifteen minutes are up, Miss Cowling," the marshal called from the end of the hallway.

"Thank you, Marshal," Teresa answered. "I'm ready to leave. Good-bye, Ryan. I'm sorry it had to end like this." She turned on her heel and walked away without a backward glance.

Ryan sagged against the bars. He wondered if Kitty knew about Teresa's duplicity and quickly decided she didn't. Teresa had done him irreparable damage, and he doubted his brothers could get him out of this one. Teresa's damning testimony was likely to hang him. Barring a miracle, he was doomed.

■ ■ ■ ■

Kitty waited anxiously at the ranch for Teresa to return. She might not like Teresa, but she appreciated her effort to defend Ryan. Kitty thought Bert's condition seemed somewhat improved today, but she was no expert. Only the doctor could determine that. Still, Bert recognized her and even let her feed him some broth. When he'd asked about Ryan, Kitty told him Ryan had gone with the hands to mend fences. Bert seemed to accept that and had soon fallen asleep.

Kitty walked to the window and peered out through the gloomy dusk. Teresa should have returned by now, and Kitty paced back and forth before the front door, filled with nervous energy. She uttered a cry of gladness when she finally saw a cloud of dust approaching the house. She stepped out onto the porch and waited for the wagon to grind to a halt before the house.

One of the hands had driven Teresa into town, and the wagon bed was loaded with supplies. Kitty fidgeted impatiently while Teresa waited for the cowboy to hand her down and then for him to remove her purchases from the wagon bed.

"Where have you been? It's getting late," Kitty chided. "Did you see Ryan?"

"Oh, yes, I saw him," Teresa said as she carried her packages into the house. "I did some shopping. Wait till you see. I picked up the prettiest bonnet, and some silk stockings, and . . ."

"Dammit, Teresa! Stop jabbering and tell me what happened. Did you inform the marshal that Ryan couldn't possibly be an outlaw?"

"I'm to testify at the trial," Teresa said, deftly skirting the subject.

"What did you tell Marshal Pringle?" Kitty persisted.

"I told the truth as I know it," Teresa said smugly.

A prickle of suspicion slid down Kitty's spine. Teresa's words did not offer the comfort she expected. "What about the trial? Is it still on? Weren't you able to convince the marshal to drop the case against Ryan?"

"There is still going to be a trial," Teresa said, giving a fatalistic shrug. "Ryan *was* caught red-handed."

"But your testimony will clear him, I know it will," Kitty said in an effort to convince herself. "Thank you, Teresa. You don't know what this means to me."

Teresa's eyes darkened with an emotion Kitty found difficult to interpret. "You sound like a woman in love. *Have* you fallen in love with the rogue, Kitty?"

Kitty saw no reason to deny what she knew to be the truth. "I fell in love with Ryan a very long time ago, for all the good it did me. Ryan is adamantly opposed to marriage and commitment. He'll never love me like I love him."

"I'm glad you realize that," Teresa returned. "You once warned me about Ryan's aversion to marriage and I'm happy to see you're taking your own words to heart. If you'll excuse me, I want to try on my new clothes."

Kitty had a terrifying premonition that Teresa was keeping something from her. There was only one way to find out for sure. She had to return to Tucson and speak to the marshal. Perhaps he'd let her see Ryan and allow her to testify in his defense.

Unfortunately, three days went by before Kitty was able to return to Tucson. Bert appeared to approach some kind of crisis, and he clung to Kitty as if she were his lifeline. Doctor Sheedy returned and seemed surprised that Bert still clung tenaciously to life. He told Kitty that her presence seemed

341

to comfort Bert, and Kitty hadn't the heart to leave Bert's side. Torn between her father's need and Ryan's desperate situation, Kitty felt as if her heart were being split in two directions.

When Bert's condition continued to improve, Kitty told him she had an errand to perform in town. At first Bert looked fearful, as if he expected Kitty to run off again. But when she assured him she'd be back long before dark, he let her go.

Kitty was almost out the door when Bert asked, "Where is Ryan? I haven't seen him in days. Or is my memory failing?"

Kitty had no idea how to explain Ryan's prolonged absence so as not to alarm Bert. The doctor was pleased with Bert's progress thus far and voiced cautious hope. But he continued to warn against upsetting Bert, insisting that any small upset could end Bert's tenuous hold on life.

"Ryan received a wire from his brother Pierce a few days ago," Kitty lied. "Pierce asked Ryan to check on a prize horse he heard about up near Phoenix. I don't expect him back for awhile."

"Tell him I want to speak to him as soon as he returns," Bert said. "We have some unfinished business. He was to give me an answer to a question I asked him."

"Of course," Kitty said, relieved that Bert didn't question her rather lame explanation.

Kitty dressed carefully for her visit to the marshal. She wanted nothing about her appearance to remind him of the lad who had claimed to be Ryan's cousin. She didn't bother with the wagon, nor did she ask one of the hands to accompany her. She saddled her own horse and rode off alone.

Kitty arrived in Tucson at noon and looped her horse's reins over the hitching post in front of the jailhouse. Dragging in a shaky breath, she opened the door to the marshal's office and stepped inside.

The marshal was seated at his desk, perusing wanted posters. He looked up and smiled at Kitty. "Can I help you, miss?"

"I hope so, Marshal. I'm Kathryn Lowry and . . ."

"Teresa Cowling's stepsister? Bert's long lost daughter?"

"Yes. Teresa told me she spoke with you."

"She did indeed. I learned a great deal from your stepsister."

Kitty nearly collapsed with relief, but it was short-lived. The marshal's next words sent her reeling.

"Perhaps you'd like to explain how you happened to become a member of the

Barton gang. I understand you disguised yourself as a boy during the time you rode with them."

Color drained from Kitty's face. Had Ryan divulged her secret in order to save himself? No, she decided. Ryan would never destroy her life. That left only Teresa, unless someone else had recognized her as Kit while she was in town the day of the attempted robbery.

Unnerved, she gathered her wits and gave a shaky laugh. "You must be mistaken, Marshal. Do I look like an outlaw? Mercy sakes," she tittered, "I can't imagine how you came to that conclusion."

Pringle searched her face, as if weighing her innocence against Teresa's claim. At length, he said, "I can't name my informant but there is a way to settle this once and for all."

"I hope you're not thinking of questioning my father. He's very ill. The doctor wouldn't let you get anywhere near him."

"I heard your father was critical, but what I propose has nothing to do with Bert Lowry."

"I don't know what you're talking about," Kitty claimed.

"Maybe not, but someone who could positively identify the outlaw Kit is right here. Durango has nothing to gain by lying."

Durango! Had he recognized her that day she'd visited Ryan in his cell? Kitty swallowed convulsively and prayed that Durango hadn't seen her face. "I don't know anyone named Durango, but go ahead and ask him. I'm sure he'll verify that I have never ridden with the Bartons. I am a woman, Marshal, only a fool would question my femininity."

"Sit down, Miss Lowry," Pringle invited. "I'll bring Durango out so he can look at you in the light." Kitty paid close attention as he removed a key from one of the hooks and disappeared down the passage. She was still sitting stiffly in the chair when the marshal returned with Durango in tow.

The half-breed was unshaven and disheveled, his expression as surly as always. "What is this all about, Marshal?" he asked, curling his lip in derision. "Ain't it enough that you're gonna hang me?"

"You'll get a fair trial first, *then* you'll hang. Take a good look at the lady, Durango, and tell me if you've ever seen her before."

Durango scrutinized Kitty through half-closed lids while Kitty forced down her panic. She stared boldly back at the half-breed, chin raised, defying him to identify her.

"Is this some kind of joke, Marshal?" Durango asked. "I ain't never seen this lady before. The only ladies I know are whores, and they ain't real ladies."

"Are you sure? Look closely, Durango. Imagine her dressed as a lad, wearing baggy clothing and calling herself Kit."

Durango studied Kitty closely. Kitty could feel sweat gathering at her temples and between her breasts. Suddenly Durango gave a shout of laughter.

"Kit was an ornery brat who swore like a trooper and rode like the wind. His hair was brown, not that purty shade of blond, and he stank like hell 'cause he never took a bath. If that lady is Kit, I'm a cross-eyed polecat. Can I go back to my cell now?"

Pringle nodded, apparently satisfied that Kitty had never been a member of the Barton gang. "Wait here, Miss Lowry, I'll be right back," he said.

Kitty collapsed against the chair, shaken to the core. Had Durango identified her, she didn't know what would have happened to her. She'd probably have hanged alongside Ryan and Durango. Her thoughts skid to a halt when Pringle returned.

"Are you satisfied, Marshal?" Kitty asked

tartly. "That was quite embarrassing."

"Sorry," Pringle muttered. "My informant must have been mistaken. You don't look like a boy, or someone who could be mistaken for a boy, but I had to follow through."

"Apology accepted," Kitty said haughtily. "But what about Ryan Delaney? Didn't Teresa tell you that he couldn't possibly be an outlaw? I can vouch for him. He's been our guest at the ranch and has never shown any tendencies toward lawlessness."

"Miss Cowling gave some valuable information," Pringle hedged cryptically. "Apparently Delaney fooled you all. Durango positively identified him as a member of the gang. I know Bert Lowry is gravely ill, and has been for some time, but he should have notified the law when Delaney showed up at his ranch."

"You don't understand, Marshal," Kitty protested. Her next words died before they were born. There was no way she could prove Ryan's innocence without revealing her identity as Kit. It was Kit who rode with the Bartons, not Ryan. "Ryan Delaney is no outlaw," she said lamely. If my father were able, he'd tell you himself. Unfortunately his health is too delicate to explain about Ryan. Why can't you take my word for it?"

"Your word can't nullify the fact that I

personally saw Delaney ride into town with the Bartons and dismount in front of the bank. All the men I deputized that day can confirm what I saw. Delaney is a handsome man," he said slyly. "I can understand how he fooled you."

"I'd like to see Ryan, if I may," Kitty said.

"Sorry, Miss Cowling, he's not allowed visitors."

"Why . . . why, that's illegal," Kitty sputtered.

"I'm perfectly within my rights. With the trial so close, I can't afford to take chances. There is already talk circulating about an illegal lynching. The Bartons have terrorized the territory too long, and people are clamoring for their heads. I've had to deputize five extra men to keep order and make certain both Durango and Delaney have their day in court."

Kitty bit her tongue to keep from lashing out against the marshal. The case against Ryan seemed ironclad. In a few short days he'd be brought to trial, found guilty and sentenced to hang, and there was nothing she could do about it. Life had never looked so bleak.

"Are you sure you won't change your mind, Marshal?" Kitty asked, swallowing a sob. Dear God, she couldn't cry now. Ryan's life was at stake, and she had to keep a clear head.

"Very sure. Why don't you go on home and forget about Delaney. He's as good as dead anyway. Concentrate on getting your father well. Good day, Miss Lowry."

Kitty recognized dismissal and rose unsteadily from her chair. "I understand my sister is going to testify at the trial," she said in parting.

"Indeed she is."

"Will you tell me what she told you about Ryan?"

Pringle stared at her. "You'll have to wait for the trial, Miss Lowry. I can't divulge that information at this time."

"I'd like to testify for Ryan," Kitty said.

"I suppose it won't hurt anything."

"Does Ryan have a lawyer?"

"No, he's going to defend himself. A lawyer wouldn't do him any good anyway."

"Is that legal?"

"Perfectly legal. Don't much matter anyway, Delaney is guilty as sin."

Kitty left then, praying her doubts about Teresa's testimony were unfounded. Teresa had implied that she was going to testify on Ryan's behalf, but now Kitty wasn't so sure. If her suspicions were correct, it was Teresa who had told the marshal that Kitty had been a member of the Barton gang. Surely Teresa couldn't be so vindictive as to seek Ryan's death simply because Ryan had spurned her, could she? Kitty didn't like the answer.

Kitty arrived back at the ranch in time to check on Bert before supper. She was pleased to see that he had regained a bit of color. Rosita brought his tray, and Kitty fed him bits of bread soaked in broth.

"You're looking better, Father," Kitty said, pleased with his progress.

"I can't die yet," Bert said, lifting his hand to caress her cheek. "There is unfinished business between me and Ryan that needs settling. I hope he returns soon."

Kitty gulped back her tears. "What kind of business? Can you tell me?"

"Not yet, Kitty, but soon, I hope. Now go eat your own supper. You're looking peaked lately. Are you unwell?"

"I'm fine," she said, giving him a bright smile. "I'll come back and say good night later."

The smile disappeared from Kitty's face as she closed the door behind her. She needed to speak to Teresa and hastened off to find her. She located her stepsister in the dining room.

"How did your visit to town go?" Teresa

greeted Kitty as she ladled soup from a tureen into her bowl. "Did you see Ryan?"

"Ryan isn't allowed visitors. Nothing I said would change the marshal's mind."

"Too bad," Teresa said with exaggerated concern. "What did you and the marshal talk about?"

"First, tell me what you said to the marshal when you saw him," Kitty demanded.

"Didn't he tell you?"

"He said you were going to testify, but I already knew that. I'm going to testify, too. What I want to know is are you going to testify for or against Ryan?"

"What makes you ask that?"

"Many things. First, did you tell Marshal Pringle that I rode with the Bartons disguised as a boy?"

Teresa blinked, sending Kitty a wide-eyed look of innocence. "Whyever would I do that?"

"You tell me."

"Kitty, for heaven's sake, you're imagining things. If the marshal thought you rode with the Bartons then someone besides myself knows about you. Perhaps Ryan . . ."

Teresa's implied suggestion hung in the air like autumn smoke. Kitty had considered that Ryan might have revealed her identity as Kit in order to clear himself, but she couldn't bring herself to believe it. If neither Ryan nor Teresa had told, then obviously someone else had seen and identified her to the law. But who?

Kitty had little appetite. What she did manage to swallow sat like a lump in her stomach. Ryan was going to die. Even if his brothers did arrive in time, she doubted they could do anything to save him.

When Teresa scraped her chair back, Kitty came out of her stupor and rose with her. "I just want to say one thing, Teresa. If you say anything in court to hurt Ryan, I'll take my knife and peel the skin from your stinking hide strip by strip and feed it to the pigs."

Kitty's threat must have frightened Teresa, for her face turned ashen and she ran from the room as if the devil were nipping at her heels.

"And don't think I won't!" Kitty called after her.

Norm Tucker returned from his business trip. He called on Kitty immediately after checking on his children and finding the note Kitty had written him. Kitty had all but forgotten about the note and realized that Teresa must have found it and had it delivered to Norm. Kitty was alone in the parlor when Norm arrived.

"What is this all about, Kitty?" Norm asked, waving the note under Kitty's nose. "What do you mean you're not good enough for me?"

Kitty heaved a sigh. She didn't need this now but realized she owed Norm an explanation. "There's a lot you don't know about me, Norm. My background is rather . . . er . . . colorful. Sit down and I'll tell you about my past, and why I can't marry you."

Tucker perched on the edge of a chair, waiting for her to begin.

"I rode with the Barton gang," she blurted out. "I was thirteen when my mother and stepfather died a few months apart. My stepbrother was an outlaw at the time and I rarely saw him. When he heard that I was left alone, he took custody of me. We traveled a lot for the first couple of years, then he joined up with the Barton gang."

"What! You're a woman, for God's sake!"

"Lex changed me into a boy when he took me under his wing. He bought me oversized clothing and cropped my hair short. I rode with the Bartons for five years without them suspecting. Then Lex was killed in a bank robbery and Ryan found me."

"I can't believe . . . it doesn't seem possible . . ."

"Haven't you ever wondered about my lack of social graces?"

"Well, yes, but it never bothered me. It's part of your charm."

Kitty could have kissed him for that. "I'm not good enough for you, Norm."

"Hogwash! There's more to it than that, isn't there, Kitty?"

"I'm afraid so. You see, I'm in love with another man."

Norm frowned. "Not some outlaw, I refuse to believe that. Who could . . ." Suddenly his face cleared. "Delaney! I should have suspected. Does he feel the same about you? I thought he was sweet on Teresa."

A streak of red crawled up Kitty's cheeks. "That's what Teresa would like to believe, but I know differently."

"So that's how it is," Tucker said with perfect understanding.

"A lot has happened since you left, Norm," Kitty explained. "Did you stop in town on your way home?"

"No, I got off the train and rode straight home. Why?"

"Ryan is in jail. There was an attempted bank robbery and Ryan was mistakenly identified as a member of the Barton gang."

"Was he? A member, I mean."

"No. But I have to explain something

first." Kitty went on to tell him how Ryan had joined the Bartons while searching for her on Bert's behalf, and how he'd met them again on the outskirts of Tucson on the day of the attempted robbery. "Ryan is in jail now, awaiting trial. It doesn't look good."

"I'm sorry, Kitty, truly I am. Is there anything I can do?"

Kitty shook her head. "No, nothing that I'm aware of. I just wish . . ."

"What do you wish?"

". . . that I could have loved you instead of Ryan. You're a good man, Norm, but so is Ryan."

"Kitty, if Ryan . . . isn't found innocent, know that I'll be here for you. What you and Ryan had doesn't matter. I still want you."

Kitty blinked back her tears. "That means a great deal to me, Norm, but I refuse to give up. Ryan *has* to be found innocent. I've wired his brothers, but I fear they won't arrive in time to help him. I don't know what else to do."

"Pray," Norm said, holding her as she dampened his chest with her tears.

"My, my, isn't this cozy," Teresa sneered, barging into the parlor. "The man you claim to love isn't dead yet and already you're picking his replacement. Does Norm know about your background?"

Kitty and Norm sprang apart. "I was just comforting Kitty," Norm said. "And yes, Kitty told me everything."

"Did she tell you that Bert had a severe attack after she left? She abandoned her own father, not caring that her absence might hurt him physically and emotionally."

"Uh, I think I'll pay my respects to Bert," Norm said, obviously unequipped or unwilling to handle the conflict between Teresa and Kitty. He beat a hasty retreat, leaving Kitty and Teresa alone to play out the drama.

Kitty turned her attention to Teresa, her blue eyes dark with anger. "Jealous bitch! A jackass has more brains than you do. Your hurtful words mean nothing to me. If Ryan is found guilty neither of us can have him. You can save him by telling the truth. That's what I'm going to do on the witness stand. It all depends on who the jury believes. But if we both tell the same story, it could make a difference."

"I intend to tell the truth as I know it," Teresa said. "I told you that before."

"And I told you you'd better not testify against Ryan," Kitty warned, her eyes dark with menace. "You already know I'm no lady. I don't think like a lady, and I don't act like a lady. So be forewarned, my revenge won't be pretty."

Teresa backed away, her eyes round as saucers. "Hurt me and I'll see you rot in jail."

"It would be worth it," Kitty said through clenched teeth. Head held high, she stalked from the room, praying that her threats made an impression upon Teresa.

As the day of Ryan's trial came closer, Bert continued to improve, but not enough to be told the truth about Ryan. The doctor was still cautious about his recovery and continued to warn against agitating Bert in any way.

Kitty had gone into town twice to find out if Ryan's brothers had arrived and was told by the marshal that they hadn't. Nor was she allowed to visit Ryan. Kitty knew Bert was concerned about Ryan's absence, and she didn't know how much longer she could keep the truth from him. She also learned that Durango had already had his trial and would be hung along with Ryan on a date set by the judge after Ryan's trial. Kitty feared the trial would be a farce, held only to appease the law, and that the verdict had already been determined.

Ryan was going to die, and she couldn't do a damn thing about it.

CHAPTER 15

The day of Ryan's trial arrived on a shimmering wave of heat that radiated across the arid plains. Norm Tucker arrived early to escort Kitty and Teresa to what Kitty knew was going to be the worst day of her life.

Though Bert's condition had improved, the doctor still forbid the family to tell him about Ryan's trial. Kitty could tell that Bert suspected something was afoot, but she tried to soothe his apprehension as best she could by telling him that Norm was driving her and Teresa to town to shop. Rosita promised to take good care of Bert in their absence, and Kitty cautioned her about saying anything to upset him.

Their horses had been saddled and were waiting. Both women wore split skirts so they could ride astride. The ranch hands were gathered at the gate as they rode through, offering words of encouragement and expressing hope that Ryan would be found innocent and freed. Ryan had become a favorite with the hired hands during the time he had spent on the ranch, and no one wanted to see him hang.

Lacking a courthouse, the trial was to be held in the Silver Nugget Saloon at eleven o'clock, presided over by Judge Roy McFee. The jury of twelve men had been haphazardly selected the day before by lottery. Norm told Kitty that normal procedure for a raw frontier town like Tucson was for the marshal to present his charges, call forth witnesses, and then allow the defendant to have his say. At that time the defendant could call his own witnesses. If Ryan didn't call her to testify, Kitty intended to volunteer, even if clearing Ryan meant revealing her own involvement with the Bartons.

A crowd had already formed outside the saloon by the time they arrived. It was still early, and the doors hadn't been opened to the public yet. They dismounted and pushed their way through the throng to the saloon door.

"How long do you think we'll have to wait?" Kitty asked anxiously.

"Not too long," Norm said. "The trial is set for eleven o'clock, and it's almost time. Try to relax."

"How can I?" Kitty cried, "when Ryan's

life is at stake."

"It's rather late for regrets, isn't it?" Teresa observed. "You're the one who involved Ryan with the Bartons in the first place."

"For godsake, Teresa, must you taunt Kitty?" Norm chided. "Can't you see how distraught she is?"

"Why is everyone so concerned about Kitty?" Teresa asked sullenly. "She's capable of taking care of herself. It's disgusting how she has both you and Ryan panting after her."

Neither Kitty nor Norm had time to answer, for just then a roar erupted from the crowd. Kitty looked over her shoulder and saw Marshal Pringle prodding Ryan through the crush of people. Though she had expected it, Kitty was startled to see Ryan looking so drawn and haggard.

A path was cleared for the marshal and his prisoner, and when they came abreast of her, Kitty cried out. "Ryan!"

His hands shackled, Ryan walked stoically through the surly crowd toward the make-shift courtroom. Loud jeers followed in his wake, dashing Ryan's hopes for a fair trial. The jury consisted of twelve men who probably held the same views as the people jeering at him. He didn't have a snowball's chance in hell of being acquitted, and he knew it.

As he approached the saloon the crowd parted. Chin held high, he looked neither right nor left, ignoring those who would probably cheer at his hanging. Then he heard Kitty call his name, and in the next moment she had dashed to his side and clutched his arm. The stoic facade he'd been trying to maintain deserted him.

Her beautiful face was creased with worry, and her expressive blue eyes spoke eloquently of her anguish. He'd give anything in the world to spare her.

"What are you doing here?" Ryan hissed.

"I couldn't stay home," Kitty replied. "I want to testify for you, Ryan. I want to tell the truth about your involvement with the Bartons."

"Are you crazy? It's too dangerous. I'll not allow it!"

"Get moving, Delaney," Pringle said, poking him with the butt of his pistol. "Your days of smooth-talking beautiful women are over."

Ryan sent Kitty one last desperate look then pushed through the saloon doors. The crowd elbowed its way in behind him, carrying Kitty, Norm, and Teresa along with it. Ryan was ushered to a table set up in front of the judge's podium and pressed down into a chair. He darted a glance over his shoulder at Kitty and saw that she and the rest of her party had found seats in the front row, close enough to touch.

After much shuffling and jostling by people trying to find seats, the bailiff called the court to order. Seconds later the rear door opened, and Judge McFee entered. He seated himself on the chair behind a table that served as a podium and pounded his gavel. When the room quieted, he intoned grumpily, "Let's get on with it, Marshal." He pulled out his pocket watch and perused the time. "It's exactly eleven o'clock. I have a prisoner to try down in Nogales and hope to be on my way before noon."

Ryan heard someone behind him groan, and he knew it was Kitty. He turned to give her a reassuring smile, but the best he could manage was a pained grimace. Before he turned back to face the judge, he scanned the crowd for his brothers' faces, but as he suspected, they hadn't arrived yet. Sighing in resignation, he focused his attention on Marshal Pringle, who had risen to present the charges.

"Ryan Delaney was caught trying to rob the bank with the Barton gang," Pringle began. "Billy Barton and Clank Porter were shot dead during gunplay, and Delaney and

Durango were taken prisoner. You heard Durango's testimony during his trial, Judge. He swore under oath that Delaney was a member of the gang."

"Any other witnesses?" Judge McFee asked gruffly.

"All the men I deputized saw Delaney ride into town with the Bartons. But there is another witness I think you should hear," Pringle said. "Miss Teresa Cowling has agreed to testify."

"Bring her on, Marshal," Judge McFee said, glancing again at his watch.

"You're going to testify against Ryan!" Kitty gasped as Teresa rose and walked to the witness chair, hips swaying provocatively.

Ryan groaned in dismay. Teresa had vowed to see him in hell, and he reckoned she was going to make sure he got there.

A Bible was brought forth, and Teresa was sworn in. She turned to the judge and smiled. "What do you want to know, Judge?"

"Tell the jury what you know about the defendant's involvement with the Barton gang, Miss Cowling."

Teresa turned her smile on the jury. "Ryan Delaney was a member of the Barton gang," she said convincingly. "I heard him admit as much to Papa Bert. Unfortunately my stepfather is too ill to appear in court."

Ryan heard a ruckus behind him and swiveled his head, shocked when he saw Kitty leap to her feet. "Liar! You're only telling part of the story," Kitty cried.

The judge pounded his gavel, calling for order. "I will have you evicted if you don't sit down, miss," he said sternly. "You may continue, Miss Cowling."

"The woman who just made a scene is my stepsister and Ryan Delaney's lover," Teresa said smugly. "She belonged to the gang, same as Ryan. She posed as a boy and called herself Kit."

A collective gasp could be heard throughout the courtroom as Marshal Pringle approached the judge and whispered something to him. The judge listened intently, then nodded.

"The jury is to disregard Miss Cowling's last statement. Miss Kathryn Lowry has already been cleared by a member of the Barton gang," the judge directed. "You are dismissed, Miss Cowling."

"Wait a minute!" Teresa exploded. "I saw Ryan leave the ranch early on the day of the attempted robbery. I think he rode out to join the Bartons. He probably met up with them outside town."

Ryan shot to his feet. "I strongly protest Miss Cowling's testimony, Judge. She knows damn well why I rode out that morning. She has already lied once and can't be believed."

"Sit down, Delaney," Pringle said. "You'll get your turn in a few minutes."

"You may return to your seat, Miss Cowling," the judge said.

She left in a huff, casting a spiteful glance at Kitty on her way back to her seat.

Next, the men the marshal had deputized the day of the attempted robbery testified individually as to Ryan's involvement. Each man swore he saw Ryan ride into town with the Bartons. As the last man finished his testimony, the judge took out his pocket watch again and scowled at the advancing hour.

"What does the defendant have to say?" he asked abruptly. "Do you have witnesses willing to testify on your behalf?"

Ryan knew he could say nothing about his reasons for being with the Bartons without implicating Kitty. Though Kitty had been cleared by Durango, that didn't mean the judge wouldn't examine her past more fully were he given cause to do so.

"The only witness I wish to call is myself, Your Honor," Ryan said. "I had hoped my brothers would arrive in time to testify on my behalf, but they had a long way to go and travel is precarious in this part of the country."

Ryan's heart nearly stopped when he heard Kitty say, "I want to testify, Your Honor." He swung around to face her, his expression bleak. Didn't she realize he wouldn't let her get up and tell the world about her involvement with outlaws?

"What about it, Mr. Delaney?" the judge asked. "Are we going to hear the lady's testimony or not?"

"No, sir, I wish to disallow Miss Lowry's testimony."

"Are you sure?" the judge repeated.

"Very sure."

"No! You can't do that!" Kitty cried.

"Sit down, Miss Lowry, or I'll have the bailiff escort you from the courtroom," Judge McFee warned.

"Kitty, please," Ryan pleaded. "I know what I'm doing."

"Sit down, Kitty," Norm urged. "Do you want to be ushered outside?"

"But why won't Ryan let me testify?" Kitty said with a sob.

"You know why, Kitty," Ryan said softly. "Just let it go." He turned to Tucker. "Keep her safe, will you, Tucker?"

Tucker nodded his compliance. "It's for your own good, Kitty. I believe Ryan loves you as much as you love him."

His words offered Kitty little comfort as she took her seat.

"Well, what have you got to say for yourself, Delaney?" Judge McFee asked impatiently. "Say it now or I'll send the jury out for a verdict."

"I'd like to be sworn in, Judge," Ryan said, stepping toward the witness chair.

"Very well, not that it's going to make a smidgeon of difference."

The bailiff stepped forward and swore Ryan in.

"I want the jury to know that I never actually rode with the Bartons," Ryan testified. "I knew them but did not join them in any of their robberies. I met them outside town the morning of the attempted robbery and was forced at gunpoint to join them. They said they were shorthanded and needed another gun.

"I'm not an outlaw, I'm a rancher from Montana. I had no intention of robbing the bank that morning. I was attempting to sneak away when the marshal's posse ambushed the gang and wrongly assumed I was one of them."

"Can anyone verify what you've just told me?" the judge asked.

"My brothers, but they haven't arrived

yet." Ryan did not mention Bert Lowry. The man was too ill to be dragged into court. A trip to town would probably kill him, and Ryan had enough on his conscience without adding Bert's death to the list.

"Very well, you're dismissed. The jury will leave the room until they reach a verdict. I'd appreciate a short deliberation," he instructed.

Ryan glanced at the twelve surly men who made up the jury and knew his fate was sealed when he saw them put their heads together and nod in unison.

The foreman of the jury stood. "Hell, there ain't no need for us to leave the room, Judge. The man is guilty and that's our verdict."

The judge smiled. "Once again justice prevails. A guilty verdict demands but one punishment," he intoned solemnly. "Two weeks from today, Ryan Delaney will be taken from his cell at high noon and hung from the neck until dead. May God have mercy on his soul." Then he banged the gavel on the table, bringing the proceedings to an end.

Ryan was seized and hustled through the cheering crowd before he could speak to Kitty. He saw her stricken face in passing and wished he'd had time to tell her how much he loved her. Then he saw Tucker place his arms around her and knew she would be in good hands after he was gone.

Kitty's world spun upon hearing the guilty verdict. She wanted to scream, to rant, to make someone pay for the injustice done to Ryan. She looked at Teresa, her eyes dark with fury. If it was the last thing she did she'd make damn sure Teresa paid for her damaging testimony. When Ryan was dragged past her she tried to follow, but Tucker's arms held her firmly in place.

"Let me go!" Kitty cried. "I have to go to him."

"Later," Norm said, ushering her out the door and away from the crowd that was milling outside the saloon to hash over the trial. "You're in no shape to talk to Ryan right now. Let me take you home. You can come back tomorrow."

Kitty started to protest but knew Norm was right. She was too upset to see Ryan right now. She allowed Norm to guide her to where their horses were tethered and to help her mount.

"Teresa's horse is gone," Kitty said, suddenly realizing there were only two horses where there should have been three.

"She lit out right after the verdict. She's

probably halfway home by now."

Kitty's face hardened. "There's nowhere she can go to escape me."

"Kitty, don't do anything you'll regret later," Norm pleaded. "Think of Bert. Let him die in peace."

"Ryan is going to die," Kitty cried, "and you expect me to do nothing? Teresa lied on the witness stand."

"Truthfully, I doubt Teresa's testimony hurt Ryan. The evidence against him was overwhelming. There isn't a jury in the country that wouldn't convict him on the evidence presented, with or without Teresa's testimony. Come on, let's go home."

Kitty felt dead inside. How could justice be so blind? Any fool could see that Ryan wasn't an outlaw. Kitty couldn't imagine a world without Ryan in it. Even if he never made a commitment to her, at least she'd have the satisfaction of knowing he was alive and well.

Norm rode to the ranch with Kitty and left immediately to return to his children. Kitty entered the house and went to find Rosita. She found the cook in the kitchen, rolling out pie dough.

"Oh, Kitty, I'm so glad you're home," Rosita cried, her round face filled with compassion.

"How is Bert?" Kitty asked with little enthusiasm. She felt nothing beyond the pain of knowing that Ryan was going to die in two weeks.

"As well as can be expected. Maybe a little better than yesterday. I heard what happened in town, Kitty. Teresa told me."

Kitty dissolved into tears as something inside her broke loose, allowing her grief to burst forth. "Ryan is going to hang, Rosita. The jury didn't even pretend to deliberate, they had him tried and judged guilty before his trial began. Ryan's brothers failed to arrive in time, and even if they had I doubt their testimony would have changed anything."

"Teresa said the evidence against *Senor* Ryan was overwhelming," Rosita lamented.

"Teresa!" Kitty spat. "She helped convict Ryan. She couldn't stand it that Ryan preferred me to her and exacted revenge by skirting the truth on the witness stand. She even tried to connect me to the Barton gang. By the way, where is my conniving stepsister?"

"Here I am," Teresa said from the doorway.

Her voice fueled a rage in Kitty that burned out of control. With a cry of fury, she flung herself at Teresa, knocking her to the floor. Kitty got in a couple of good punches before Rosita pulled her off.

"Kitty, *Dios,* don't," Rosita cried. "Think of *Senor* Bert. He's in his bedroom right now, wondering what's going on. Do you want to kill him?"

With difficulty, Kitty pulled herself together and backed away from Teresa.

"Don't touch me again," Teresa said, taking a shaky step backward. "I'll tell Papa Bert everything and you know what that will do to him."

It was almost as if Teresa knew exactly what to say to cool Kitty's rage. "You're not off the hook yet, Teresa," Kitty vowed. "One day you'll pay for lying about Ryan."

"That day will never come," Teresa sniffed. "When Papa Bert dies I intend to contest his will. My lawyer is already working to prove you're an imposter."

"Get out of my sight," Kitty snarled. "I have half a notion to tell Bert myself what you've done."

"Go ahead," Teresa smirked. "I dare you." Having had the last word, she turned on her heel and flounced off.

Rosita handed Kitty a cup of coffee and urged her to sit down until her temper cooled. Kitty took her advice, sipping the coffee and imagining the various kinds of torture she'd like to inflict on Teresa. When she'd calmed enough to face Bert, she left the kitchen and entered his room. To her surprise she found him sitting by the window.

"Father, what are you doing up? Does the doctor know?"

"Aw, Kitty, don't scold. That sawbones don't know everything. I'm not ready to check out yet. I need to talk to Ryan. Has he returned yet?"

Kitty desperately wanted to tell Bert about Ryan's difficulty but didn't dare until she cleared it with the doctor. She intended to make a special effort to visit the doctor tomorrow when she returned to town to see Ryan.

Kitty left the house the following morning before either Bert or Teresa awoke. She hated fielding Bert's questions with lies and left early to avoid them. She arrived at the jailhouse just as the marshal was strolling back to his office from a local restaurant. He tipped his hat.

"What can I do for you, Miss Lowry?"

"You can let me see Ryan Delaney," Kitty said, grimly determined to have her way this time.

"Come inside," Pringle invited, opening

the door to his office and ushering her inside.

"I won't take no for an answer," Kitty persisted.

"You're a mighty determined young woman," Pringle observed. "Very well, you can visit the prisoner. No harm can come from it now. Wouldn't be Christian to deny a condemned man visitation rights."

Kitty's heart soared. She was so happy that she could have kissed the marshal. "Thank you. Can I see him now?"

"Just as soon as I unlock the door," Pringle said. He gave her a shrewd look. "You don't have any weapons on you, do you?"

"No, sir," Kitty said. Actually, she *had* thought about smuggling in a gun but feared Ryan would be killed during an attempted jail break. "There are no firearms concealed on my person."

"Very well," Pringle said, moving aside so she could proceed to the cell area. "I'll let you know when your time is up."

Kitty hurried down the passage, past Durango's small cell, to Ryan's. Her heart went out to Ryan when she saw him sitting on the bunk, his shoulders slumped dejectedly.

"Ryan."

He leaped to his feet. "Kitty! You

shouldn't be here."

"I have to be here. Have your brothers arrived?"

He approached the bars, and Kitty was appalled when she saw his face. He had appeared drawn and pale at his trial, but he looked even worse today.

"Are they feeding you?" Kitty asked, alarmed at his apparent loss of weight.

"Three times a day. The food can't compare with Rosita's cooking, but it's adequate." He fell silent, then blurted out, "Kitty, I've thought a lot about this and I want you to accept Tucker's proposal. He'll take good care of you and the ranch after Bert is gone."

Hands on hips, Kitty faced him squarely, her chin raised pugnaciously. "Damn you, Ryan Delaney! I know you ain't a lily-livered coward. I won't let you give up without a fight. You've got too much to live for. Your brothers would be appalled at your attitude. Where are your balls?"

Ryan grinned despite himself. "Exactly where they belong, love. I'd show you if I could." The low rumble Kitty heard in his chest could only be laughter. "You'd better not let the marshal hear you talk like that or he'll suspect you really are Kit," Ryan went on, still chuckling. "I kind of miss that feisty little wildcat."

Kitty reached for him through the bars, bringing his face close to hers until she could reach his lips. "I haven't changed all that much, Ryan. Kiss me."

She groaned when their mouths touched, and his moved hungrily over hers, as if he couldn't get enough of her . . . as if he was bidding her good-bye. Kitty was determined not to let him lose heart.

"Do you have a plan for your brothers when they arrive?" she asked, trying to instill hope in the man she loved.

"Nothing has come to mind," Ryan admitted. "I'm not even sure they'll arrive before . . ." His sentence trailed off.

"They'll be here, I know they will," Kitty said fiercely. "I love you, Ryan, you're not going to die."

"Forget my brothers for a moment, there's something I want to say to you. Maybe next time you come the marshal will refuse to let you see me and this has to be said."

"If you're going to tell me again to accept Norm's proposal, forget it. I don't love him."

Ryan clasped her hands through the bars and brought them against his heart. "I never thought I'd see the day when I was ready to make a commitment to a woman. Now that it has arrived I can do nothing about it. For what it's worth, Kitty, I love you. I reckon I fell in love with you the day I realized you were a woman and not a foulmouthed lad with a chip on his shoulder. I couldn't believe no one saw through your disguise. I've been lying to myself all these months, denying my heart's desire because I was too stubborn to admit I could fall in love."

Kitty's smile lit up her face. "You love me?"

"Didn't I just say so?"

"I knew it all along," Kitty said smugly. "I'm sorry you didn't realize it sooner. Do you love me enough to marry me?"

"I love you enough to spend the rest of my life with you," Ryan said solemnly.

Stunned into silence, Kitty stared at him, painfully aware that Ryan's life could end in less than two weeks, depriving them of a lifetime of happiness. Ryan fell silent too, apparently having come to the same conclusion. Tears of remorse trailed down her cheeks and she dashed them away, determined to remain cheerful despite her aching heart.

"What can I do for you?" Kitty asked in a shaky voice. "Against all odds Bert appears to be improving. Perhaps I should tell him the truth. Maybe he knows someone who can help you. He's an influential man in the territory."

"What does the doctor say?"

"He says Bert's condition is critical. Another upset could kill him. God, Ryan, I'm so torn! I don't want to kill Bert but I don't want you to die, either."

"The choice is mine to make, Kitty," Ryan said slowly. "Don't tell Bert. Let him enjoy the time he has left in this world."

"I don't know how much longer I can lie to him about your absence. He's no fool. He's beginning to suspect something is amiss."

"Tell him I returned to Montana," Ryan advised. "And tell him . . . tell him I decided not to take him up on his offer. He'll understand what I'm talking about. That should stop his questions. What about Teresa? Can you trust her to keep silent about all this?"

Kitty's mouth flattened. "One word from that lying bitch and I swear I'll skin her alive."

"Still the fierce little wildcat," Ryan said fondly. "That's one of the things I love about you. As far as I'm concerned Teresa deserves to be skinned alive, but we have to think of Bert. Threaten her all you like but I strongly advise against skinning her. She's already proven how vindictive she can be. I fear you're going to have a battle on your hands after Bert dies. Teresa is determined to keep you from inheriting."

"I know, she already has a lawyer working to disprove my relationship to Bert."

"Honey, when my brothers get here, tell them about Teresa and let them take care of her. They won't let you down."

"That won't be necessary," Kitty said with more confidence than she felt. "You're going to be around to help me fight Teresa's claim."

"I wish I had your conviction," Ryan said, pulling her close so he could kiss her again. "This isn't exactly how I want to kiss you but it will have to do until these bars dissolve," he quipped.

He kissed her then, moving his mouth over hers with such tenderness that Kitty felt as if her heart were weeping. She clung to him as he deepened the kiss, cursing the bars that separated her from the man she loved. She wanted to feel his heart beating against hers, bare flesh against bare flesh. She wanted to run her hands over his hard body, feel him moving inside her, hear his cries of completion when his seed left his body.

She clung to him long after he broke off

the kiss, fearing to release him lest this be the last time she would hold him. She didn't let go until she heard the marshal clear his throat.

"Time to leave, Miss Lowry," Pringle said. "I have business elsewhere and you can't stay here while I'm gone."

"Go," Ryan whispered. "I'll understand if you don't come back. This can't be easy for you."

"One more moment, Marshal," Kitty called back. To Ryan, she whispered, "What can I bring you? Would a gun help? I thought about it before but . . ."

"Wait for my brothers and talk it over with them," Ryan whispered back. "They'll know what to do. I'm willing to try whatever they suggest. I'm not going to die, Kitty. I decided to live when I realized how much I love you. I've never been a quitter and I'm not going to become one now."

He gave her a quick kiss, then pushed her away from the bars. "The marshal is waiting."

Kitty's steps dragged as she walked toward the marshal. Her mind whirled with everything Ryan had told her. He loved her. Had always loved her. He'd just been too stubborn and settled in his ways to open his heart to her.

Before Kitty left town she made a quick detour to the doctor's office and was told he was out on a call. She didn't wait, but rode home in a daze, her mind consumed with Ryan. Where were Ryan's brothers? she wondered. They were long overdue. All her hopes were pinned on two men she didn't even know. Yet Ryan seemed confident that they could help him. It must be wonderful to trust someone so completely, she mused. Until Ryan had come along she'd distrusted all males, except perhaps for Lex, who had done his best for her. But her experience with the Bartons had taught her to rely on no one but herself.

That notion got her to thinking. Less than two weeks remained before Ryan's hanging. Should Ryan's brothers fail to arrive in time, she was the only one he could rely upon for help. Her spirits lifted as she contemplated the difficulties she would encounter breaking Ryan out of jail and how she could overcome them.

Kitty reached the ranch before a viable plan made itself known. But she wasn't about to give up. She rode her horse into the barn and dismounted, handing the reins to a stable hand who was mucking out the stalls.

"Two men came calling, Miss Kitty," the

man said as Kitty started toward the house.

"Two men? Do you know them?"

"No, ma'am. They arrived about an hour ago asking for Ryan Delaney. I told them Ryan was in jail, and they skedaddled up to the house to talk to Bert."

"Ryan's brothers!" Kitty cried, feeling as if a great weight had been lifted from her. Suddenly a terrifying thought occurred to her. "Bert! Oh, no! He doesn't know about Ryan. I have to hurry before they tell him. The shock could kill him."

She didn't hear the man's reply as she raced to the house.

CHAPTER 16

By the time Kitty burst into Bert's room she was out of breath and her heart was beating like a trip-hammer. When she saw two men standing beside Bert's bed she feared the worst. Both men turned toward her at her abrupt entrance.

"Is Bert all right?" Kitty asked anxiously. "He's not . . . you didn't . . ."

"I'm sorry. We didn't know Bert was so ill. We came here first to find out from Bert the kind of trouble Ryan was in," the older of the two men said. Kitty thought his resemblance to Ryan was remarkable. They both possessed the same dark hair and extraordinary green eyes.

"I'm Pierce Delaney, and this is my brother Chad," Pierce said. "You must be Bert's daughter."

Kitty turned her gaze on Chad and thought him every bit as handsome as his two brothers. In contrast to Pierce's and

Ryan's darker coloring, Chad's hair was brown and his eyes hazel. Both men exuded the same power and strength she admired in Ryan.

"Call me Kitty," Kitty said. Her gaze turned anxiously toward Bert. She thought he looked paler than he had been looking, except for his eyes, which blazed like two burning coals in his wan face.

"What did you tell Bert?" Kitty asked, fearful of the damage that might have been caused. "The doctor said he's not to be upset."

Chad sent Kitty a sheepish look. "Sorry, Kitty, we had no idea. Your stepsister said it would be all right to talk to Bert. We hoped he could tell us about the trouble our little brother has gotten himself into, but Bert doesn't seem to know."

"Teresa had no business allowing you into Bert's room," Kitty said with asperity. "I told you, Bert's not supposed to . . ."

"It's all right, Kitty," Bert interrupted. "You should have told me about Ryan's arrest. I think it's time for explanations. If you won't tell me, I'm sure Teresa will. Shall I call her?"

Kitty shook her head. "I wanted to spare you. I had no idea Ryan's brothers would come here first."

"Perhaps we should talk about this in private," Pierce suggested, apparently concerned about Bert's grave condition.

"I won't hear of it," Bert said, becoming agitated. "It would hurt me more not to know. I've grown fond of Ryan in the short time I've known him. I had hoped . . . well, that's not important now. If Ryan is in serious trouble we have to band together to help him."

"That's why we're here," Pierce said, his expression solemn. "Go ahead, Kitty, tell us everything, don't leave anything out."

"Ryan is going to die in less than two weeks!" Kitty exclaimed on a rising note of panic. "He hoped you would arrive before his trial."

"Ryan's going to die?" Chad asked in a hushed voice. "Why? What trial?"

"It's a long story."

"We have time," Pierce said. "But if what you just told us is true, time is running out for Ryan."

"That's why he's counting on your help. It all started when Ryan agreed to find Bert's missing daughter," Kitty began. She then launched into the details, save for intimate ones, about her involvement with the Barton gang and how Ryan had found her and briefly joined the gang in order to question her about Kathryn Lowry. Pierce stared at her in disbelief. "You posed as a boy all those years without anyone seeing through your disguise?" Kitty gave him a wobbly smile. "Except for Ryan. He knew I was a woman almost immediately."

"That's our brother," Chad chuckled. "Rogue Ryan could smell a woman at fifty yards. Go on with the story, Kitty."

"I won't go into all the details, but when Ryan realized I was the missing Kathryn Lowry he convinced me to come to the ranch to meet Bert. At first I wasn't happy here. There was a great deal of antagonism between me and Teresa. One day I decided to leave the ranch and live my own life."

"Why would you do that?" Pierce asked, pinning her to the wall with his probing green gaze.

"The reasons are no longer important. What matters is that Ryan came after me and ran into the Barton gang outside Tucson. They were on their way to rob the bank. They recognized Ryan and forced him to ride with them. Ryan intended to escape before the robbery took place but it didn't work out that way," she said on a sob. "Billy Barton's contact at the bank betrayed him for the reward and the marshal was waiting with a posse. Two members of the gang were killed outright. Ryan and Durango were captured and taken to jail."

"Good God!" Pierce exclaimed. His dismay was mirrored on Chad's face. "Didn't Ryan explain the circumstances to the marshal?"

"He tried but Marshal Pringle wouldn't listen." Kitty swallowed past the huge lump growing in her throat. "Ryan was brought to trial, found guilty, and will hang in less than two weeks for crimes he didn't commit."

"Damn!" Chad muttered, fracturing the profound silence that Kitty's words had produced.

"Didn't Ryan speak in his own defense at the trial?" Pierce asked.

Kitty flushed. "He was afraid to say too much for fear of revealing my involvement with the Bartons. He wanted to protect me. I rode with the Bartons several years and played a minor role in their robberies. I was perfectly willing to testify, even if it meant revealing my identity, but Ryan wouldn't allow it."

"What about Teresa?" Bert asked after hearing Kitty's story. "I may have been too ill to attend the trial but Teresa knows the truth and should have testified on Ryan's behalf."

Chad and Pierce waited for Kitty's answer, placing her in an awkward position. She had no idea how Bert would react when he learned how Teresa had betrayed Ryan.

"Spit it out, honey," Bert urged. "I already have some idea of what took place at the trial. Teresa changed the day Kitty walked into the house," he explained to the Delaneys. "I would put nothing past her."

"I'm sorry, Father," Kitty said regretfully. "Teresa lied about Ryan on the witness stand. Oh, I don't suppose one could call it lying, exactly. What she did was skirt the truth. She confirmed that Ryan rode with the Bartons and tried to implicate me at the same time. But Durango had already testified that I was not Kit, so the judge disallowed that part. I suppose that's why Ryan chose not to tell the whole truth. Suspicion had already touched me and he didn't want to raise the subject again."

"So Ryan was found guilty and sentenced to hang," Pierce said grimly.

"If only we could have gotten here on time," Chad lamented. "We would have if the train hadn't broken down outside Cheyenne and forced us to make the trip on horseback. Took us two weeks of steady riding. I'm sure my legs will be permanently bowed after this trip."

Kitty glanced at Bert and suddenly feared for his life. His eyes were closed and his breathing erratic. "Father! I knew this would be too much for you. That's why the doctor forbid us to excite you. I'll send someone for the doctor right away."

Bert opened his eyes and stretched his hand out to cover hers. "No, honey, I'll be fine. There is nothing more the sawbones can do for me. I'm not going to die yet. Not until I know Ryan's been cleared and released from jail. Ryan and I have unfinished business."

"What business is that, Father?"

"That's between me and Ryan," he said with a trace of his old sparkle.

"Try not to worry, Bert," Pierce advised. "Chad and I won't let our brother hang. The marshal will have to listen to us. If that fails, we'll locate the judge and tell him our story. And as a last resort, we'll break him out of jail. We'll take a room in town so as to be near Ryan and check back with you when we know something."

"I'll walk you to the door," Kitty said. "Bert needs to get some rest. He's had enough excitement for one day."

"Kitty . . ." Bert's voice was weak, but his

tone was resolute.

"Yes, Father."

"Tell Teresa I'll speak with her as soon as I'm up to it."

"Very well, Father," Kitty said, wondering what Bert would say to Teresa. But she couldn't worry about that now. She wanted to speak privately with Ryan's brothers before they left.

"I'm sorry we arrived too late," Pierce said when he and Chad stood alone with Kitty in the parlor. "We had no idea the trouble you mentioned in your telegram would be so devastating. We thought Ryan had gotten into one of his usual scrapes."

"We brought enough money to pay off the unhappy papa of the woman Rogue Ryan had compromised," Chad added, "but we never suspected anything like this." He ran his fingers through his brown hair and spit out a curse. "How could anyone mistake Ryan for an outlaw?"

"It wasn't much of a trial," Kitty admitted. "The jury tried and found Ryan guilty before the trial began. Is there nothing you can do? I'd die if Ryan were to lose his life because of me. He doesn't deserve to die. Ryan is good and kind and . . . and, well, you both know that Ryan is a special man."

Chad and Pierce exchanged startled looks.

"You think Ryan is special?" Chad asked, trying to hide his amusement. "Has he added you to his stable of women?"

"That's enough, Chad," Pierce reprimanded. "Kitty is too distraught to appreciate your teasing. We need to speak to Ryan pronto, if we're to help him. Take care of Bert, Kitty, he looks mighty peaked."

Kitty nodded. "I'm really worded about Bert. I didn't want to love my father when I first heard about him because I hated what he did to my mother and me. But in time I came to realize that what happened wasn't entirely Bert's fault. He didn't even know I existed until a few years ago. I reckon we both have a lot to be grateful for. During the weeks I've been here I've grown quite fond of Bert, and I have Ryan to thank for bringing us together."

"I'm glad Ryan found you before Bert . . . well, in time for Bert to get to know you," Pierce replied. "We'll be on our way now. There is much to be accomplished in a short time."

"Are you leaving already?" Teresa asked as she ambled into the parlor. "I told Rosita to put two more plates on the table for dinner."

Hotheaded Chad took one look at Teresa and lit into her. "Kitty told us that your testimony helped convict Ryan," he charged. "What in the hell were you thinking of? You know damn good and well that Ryan is no outlaw."

"Easy, Chad," Pierce warned.

Teresa sent Kitty a venomous look and backed away from Chad. "I told the truth," she claimed. "Ryan *did* ride with the Bartons."

"That's not the truth and you know it," Kitty berated. "You were green with jealousy because Ryan showed me too much attention. Testifying against Ryan was your way of punishing him."

Pierce stifled a groan. "I told Ryan a woman was going to be his ruination one day. Are you saying that Teresa's jealousy is behind all this? Sounds all too familiar to me."

"Not exactly," Kitty admitted. "Ryan *was* caught riding into town with the Bartons, and the evidence against him was overwhelming. I will say in Teresa's defense that her testimony was only the icing on the cake. As I said before, the jury had reached a verdict before the trial began. Ryan didn't have a chance."

Teresa's eyes widened, apparently stunned by Kitty's words.

"We haven't time to debate the issue,"

Pierce, ever the practical brother, said. "Our first priority is Ryan, and getting him out of jail."

Kitty's hopes soared for the first time since Ryan's trial as she watched the Delaney brothers ride off. She knew now why Ryan believed them special, and she thought their women were lucky to have them. They were fiercely loyal, handsome, strong, and determined. She prayed their determination would work in Ryan's favor.

Ryan stared at a square place on the floor where sunlight pierced through the tiny barred window and puddled in the dirt. He couldn't even recall what day it was. How many days remained until he left this earth in a horrible manner? he wondered distractedly. No matter when it came, it would be too soon.

Ryan's thoughts returned time and again to Kitty, recalling her luminous beauty, unmatched by any other woman. For her sake Ryan hoped she'd change her mind and marry Tucker after he was gone. Kitty needed someone to comfort her after his death. He reminisced about their last time together, recalling her passionate response to his loving. No woman, and there had been plenty, had ever pleased him like Kitty.

He closed his eyes and imagined the sweetness of her kisses, the erotic scent of her arousal, the heat of her when she opened to him and took him inside her. The feeling was so vivid that he dropped his head into his hands, surprised when he felt tears upon his fingers.

He was brought back to reality when he heard footsteps echoing down the corridor. Expectantly, he peered through the bars, hoping yet fearing that Kitty had returned. He didn't know if he could handle another visit from her, given his state of mind. He heard the jingle of spurs and decided the footsteps were too firm and heavy to be those of a woman. His spirits rose considerably when he recognized his brothers advancing toward him.

"Well, brother, you've gotten yourself into one helluva mess," Chad greeted as he clasped Ryan's hand through the bars.

Ryan offered his other hand to Pierce. They stood united, staring at one another in perfect understanding. After a long pause, Ryan asked, "What in the hell took you so long?"

"Blame it on the railroad," Pierce explained. "We rode our butts off getting here. The locomotive broke down, and when we learned a replacement wouldn't arrive for days, we continued on horseback." He rubbed his backside. "Talk about rough country."

"I reckon you know why I'm here," Ryan said.

"Yep," Chad answered. "We stopped off at the ranch first."

"You didn't talk to Bert, did you?" Ryan asked worriedly.

"Yeah, we did," Pierce answered. "Kitty wasn't home and Teresa told us it would be all right to talk to Bert. We found out he knew nothing about your arrest and trial."

"God! Did your information upset him? Is he all right?"

"He was fine when we left. A bit weak but still breathing. We didn't learn the full truth until Kitty arrived home. She told us the whole incredible story. Whatever possessed you to join the Bartons? If you weren't behind bars I'd beat the shit out of you," Pierce said.

"Not until I finished with him," Chad echoed.

"It was the only way I could get to Kitty," Ryan explained. "Didn't Kitty tell you how we met?"

"Kitty told us everything. Almost everything," Chad clarified. "Knowing you as I do, I imagine there are things she didn't want to divulge. What exactly are your feelings for Kitty? She gave the impression that she is in love with you. Is Kitty just another feather in your cap?"

"I never thought I'd say this, but I love Kitty," Ryan admitted somewhat sheepishly. "Kitty is every bit as perfect for me as Sarah and Zoey are for you and Pierce. I'll admit I was skeptical at first, doubting my own feelings. But I know now I could be happy with Kitty as my wife. She's not like most women. She's loyal and trustworthy and . . ." He shrugged. "Oh, well, what's the use?"

"Rogue Ryan in love?" Pierce chortled. "Aren't you the one who laughed at us for falling in love?"

"I didn't know then . . . I mean, who would have thought I'd meet someone who has come to mean the world to me? But it's too late to worry about what might have been. I'm going to die in a few days."

"Not if we can help it," Pierce retorted. "We spoke to the marshal last night, but he wouldn't let us see you until this morning. Pringle is convinced you were involved with the Bartons. He says there is no solid proof that you never joined the gang in any of their robberies."

"And he says," Chad added, "that you've

already been tried and convicted. Nothing short of a governor's pardon will help you."

Ryan gave a bitter laugh. "So where does that leave me?"

"I wired the mayor of Dry Gulch this morning and asked him to wire the marshal a testimonial to your good character," Pierce confided.

"We're also going to look into the possibility of breaking you out of here if all else fails. Take heart, brother, we're not going to let you die," Chad said, sending him a cocky grin.

"We're going to try to find the judge first," Pierce said. "We need to get you a new trial, and only the judge can decide that. It might take us a couple of days, but we'll be back in plenty of time to concoct another plan should the judge deny you a new trial."

Ryan hated to see them leave, but he knew that if they didn't find the judge he had virtually no hope of living beyond the ten days left till his hanging.

"Good luck!" Ryan called as they strode away.

God, it was good to see them, Ryan thought as he clung to the bars and listened to the sound of their retreating footsteps. For the first time since this mess began, he felt something besides total dejection. He felt hope. Hope that he might live, hope that he could make Kitty his wife, and that he would have the same loving relationship his brothers enjoyed with their wives.

Ryan's attention sharpened when he heard the marshal's distinctive footsteps approaching. "Here's your lunch," Pringle said, balancing a tray in one hand. "Step back, Delaney. I'm going to open the door and hand the tray through to you."

Ryan backed up a step, hands clenched at his sides, aching to jump the marshal and hightail it away from here as fast as he could. But the pair of six-shooters riding low on the marshal's hips were powerful deterrents. Perhaps, he mused, he would contemplate escape if his brothers failed to free him through legal means.

Pringle set the tray on the floor, opened the door, and slid the tray to Ryan. Then he backed away, never taking his eyes off Ryan. Once the cell door was slammed shut and locked, Pringle seemed in the mood for conversation.

"I had a long talk with your brothers, Delaney," he began. "They seem like decent men. You must be the bad apple in the crate. Too bad they had to come all this way to see you hang."

"I'm not an outlaw," Ryan said through

clenched teeth.

"Yeah, that's what they all say. Thought you'd like to know a gallows is being erected in the town square. Should be done in plenty of time for the hangings. By the way," he added in parting, "those brothers of yours seem determined to set you free, so I'm deputizing four extra men. Two to take turns guarding the jailhouse and two to follow your brothers just in case they get ideas."

What else could go wrong? Ryan wondered as he sank down onto the bunk. If he didn't have bad luck he wouldn't have any luck at all. Now his brothers were going to be put under surveillance, making escape, if it came to that, virtually impossible. God, why had he ever come to Arizona? he silently lamented. But that thought ended as quickly as it was born. If he hadn't come to Arizona he would never have met Kitty.

If he hadn't met Kitty, he would have never known love.

The excitement must have been too much for Bert, for he slept through the night and into the following day. When he finally awoke and ate a meager breakfast, he asked Rosita to fetch Kitty and Teresa.

Kitty entered Bert's room, her heart in

her mouth, afraid to see his condition. To her relief, Bert was sitting up in bed and seemed no worse after the shock he'd received. Teresa arrived moments later.

Bert motioned for Teresa to move closer. "I waited to confront you until after my temper cooled," Bert said to Teresa. "What have you got to say for yourself? And don't tell me you told the truth in court, for I know differently. Have you no conscience? No honor? Your testimony condemned an innocent man to death."

"I doubt if my testimony made a difference one way or the other," Teresa contended. "Ask Kitty if you don't believe me."

"That's besides the point," Bert charged. "What you did was morally wrong. Were you driven by jealousy? I knew you'd set your cap for Ryan but I also know Ryan wasn't interested in you. It's Kitty he wants. It's always been Kitty."

"I'm sorry, Papa Bert," Teresa said. "I . . . I was wrong. I know that now. What are you going to do to me?"

"I've sent one of the hands for my lawyer. I'd already made arrangements to settle a generous sum on you after I'm gone, but I want you to have it now, before I die. You'll be able to live quite comfortably with your mother's sister in San Francisco until you find a husband."

"You're sending me away?" Teresa gasped. "I was like a daughter to you. More of a daughter than Kitty."

"I'm aware of that," Bert acknowledged. "That's why I'm being generous with you. It's not as if I've raised you from a child, for I didn't even know you until shortly before your mother's death six years ago. It was your decision to stay on at the ranch to look after me. It makes me wonder," he mused, "if you only came because you thought you might inherit after my death."

He paused to catch his breath and take a sip of water. "I know you've hired a lawyer to prove that Kitty is an imposter," Bert continued. "I may be tied to this bed but I'm aware of what's going on. My lawyer learned of your intentions and informed me. I've taken precautions to make sure you get no more than what I've set aside for you."

"Papa Bert! You know how fond I am of you. Don't send me away."

"Don't send Teresa away on my account," Kitty injected, feeling as if she'd just broken up a family. That had not been her intention at all. Still and all, Teresa deserved some sort of punishment for her deceitful machinations.

"Teresa will be much happier in San

Francisco," Bert insisted. "She has always preferred the excitement of city life to the isolation out here, haven't you, Teresa?"

"Well, yes, but I would have been happy living here with Ryan."

"For how long?" Bert queried.

"Forever," Teresa claimed.

"I don't buy it, Teresa," Bert said sadly. "Pack your things. My lawyer will be here soon with your money. You can leave with him. He'll take you and your belongings to town and purchase a train ticket for you. Leave me now, I'm in need of rest."

"Papa Bert . . ."

"Please, Teresa, just go," Kitty urged, frightened by Bert's sudden pallor. "Bert is being more than generous with you. I wouldn't have been so lenient had your punishment been left to me. You know what *I* intended for you."

"You've won," Teresa hissed. "You have Ryan and you'll have everything that should have been mine. From the moment you walked into this house I knew you were trouble. I'm going, but you'll always have my hatred." Having had the last word, she flounced off.

"Are you sure you want Teresa to leave?" Kitty asked once Teresa had left the room. "Don't do it on my account."

"Very sure, honey. Teresa would have been welcome here for as long as she wished to stay had she not destroyed my trust in her. Don't worry, she'll be just fine. Her aunt in San Francisco dotes on her. That's why she never cared to move to the ranch after her mother and I married. Save your concern for Ryan. You *do* love him, don't you?"

"With all my heart," Kitty said.

"I thought as much. Go on into town to visit him. Tell Ryan I'm counting on him to make an honest woman of you."

Bright red stained Kitty's cheeks. "Father!"

"I'm not as incapacitated as you think," he said with a chuckle.

Too embarrassed to speak, Kitty kissed his forehead and let herself out of the room. A half hour later she left the house without having encountered Teresa, which she counted as a blessing, and she aimed her horse toward town. When she reached the outskirts of town she noticed a little mission church she hadn't paid much attention to before. The squat adobe building sat on a sandy plot of ground supporting a meager growth of sagebrush and cactus. The cracked walls and crumbling steeple looked in desperate need of repair, and Kitty passed by without giving it a second thought.

Kitty reined in at the jailhouse and found the marshal sitting on the porch, gazing idly down the dusty street. He rose to greet her as she dismounted and approached the jailhouse. "I reckon you want to see the prisoner. Delaney is mighty popular these days. Those two brothers of his were here to see him earlier. I hope they're not hatching some plan because I've hired extra men to watch them and to patrol the jail just in case they have ideas of breaking him out."

"Ryan's brothers wouldn't break the law," Kitty contended. "They'll use legal methods to free him."

"Too late for that, little lady," Pringle said. "We did everything by the book. Delaney had a fair trial. It's going to take a governor's pardon to free him, and that's not likely to happen."

Kitty followed the marshal inside, received permission to enter the cell area and hurried down the corridor.

Ryan must have heard her coming, for he was clutching the bars, waiting for her. "I know your footsteps," he said, reaching for her and bringing her close so he could kiss her. "Ummm," he said, licking her lips, "you taste good."

"Are you all right?" Kitty asked, searching

his face.

"Just fine, now that my brothers are here."

"What are they going to do?"

"I don't know yet, maybe nothing. Marshal Pringle said he deputized extra men to watch my brothers and to patrol the jailhouse. I think he suspects a jailbreak."

"I know, he told me the same thing. Bert knows what's going on. Your brothers arrived at the ranch while I was gone and questioned Bert about the trouble you were in. I had to tell Bert everything."

"I know. My brothers told me. How is he taking it?"

"He's still weak, that hasn't changed. But there is something else you should know. Bert wasn't pleased to learn that Teresa testified against you. He settled a sum on her and asked her to leave. He's sending her to San Francisco to live with her aunt."

"It's probably best for everyone," Ryan said.

Kitty clutched his shoulders through the bars, wanting to hold him forever and never let him go. Things had never looked so bleak. With men watching their every move, Pierce and Chad's hands were literally tied. There was little they could do to free Ryan. That thought served only to firm Kitty's resolve to do something on her own. Since

Ryan's brothers were powerless to help him, it fell to her to see that Ryan didn't die.

"What are you thinking?" Ryan asked. "I've seen that look before. I hope you're not thinking of placing your own life in jeopardy because I won't allow it. Let my brothers handle this, they're better equipped than you are."

"Is that so?" Kitty retorted. "If you recall, Kit was a capable lad. I haven't changed that much in a few short months. I've got to go now, Ryan. I'll come back tomorrow."

"Kitty! Wait!" Ryan cried on a note of panic. "What are you planning? Come back! Don't you dare leave without telling me what is in that cunning little mind of yours."

Kitty didn't turn back. She didn't want to listen to Ryan's logic, or let him talk her out of anything. She had no idea what she was going to do, but she knew beyond a doubt that she wasn't going to sit back and let Ryan hang.

"Hey, lady, how come you don't visit me?" Durango called as she whizzed past his cell. "I could use a little comforting."

"Go to hell," Kitty threw over her shoulder. Moments later she walked past the marshal and out of the office into the sunshine.

Kitty had one foot in the stirrups when

she saw Ryan's brothers crossing the street from the hotel. She waved to them and waited for them to approach.

"You been to see Ryan?" Pierce asked. Kitty nodded. "How is he doing?"

"Despair is his worst enemy," Kitty revealed. "I think he's lost all hope of being set free."

"Dammit, this is so frustrating," Chad ground out. "The marshal says he can't free a prisoner already tried and found guilty no matter how many letters of reference he receives. And only the judge can declare a new trial."

"Then you have to find the judge," Kitty said firmly.

"He's in Nogales," Pierce explained. "We're going to leave within the hour. We should be back in a couple of days. If that doesn't work, we'll still have time to figure out something else."

"Look behind you," Kitty warned in a hushed voice. "Those two men watching you are deputies. They're not to let you out of their sight. They'll probably follow you to Nogales."

"Shit!" Chad spit out. "Don't worry, Kitty, they can follow us to hell and back if they want to."

Kitty's eyes narrowed. Perhaps the absence of the deputies would work in her favor. She tucked the knowledge in the back of her mind.

"You must love Ryan a great deal," Pierce probed. His intent perusal sent a flush of red to Kitty's cheeks.

"With all my heart," Kitty admitted. "I'll do anything to keep him from hanging."

"Chad and I want to thank you for proving to Ryan that love can be a grand experience. We despaired of our little brother ever finding a special woman and we're glad you're the one who finally conquered his stubborn heart."

Though Pierce's words made Kitty's heart soar, they still didn't solve Ryan's problems.

CHAPTER 17

After the Delaney brothers left, Kitty turned back to contemplate the jailhouse, her expression thoughtful. It was growing dark and she should be getting on back to the ranch, but something prevented her from leaving. Her patience was rewarded when she saw Marshal Pringle leave the jailhouse and walk across the street to the restaurant to have his supper. A deputy met him in the street, and she heard Pringle tell him to sit in the office until he returned in a couple of hours. Kitty didn't know why, but she tucked the information away for future consideration as she mounted and rode away.

When Kitty passed the small mission chapel on the outskirts of town, something made her turn her horse into the dusty churchyard. Indulging the unaccountable urge to go inside the chapel and present her problems to God, Kitty dismounted and looped her horse's reins through the hitching post. Praying didn't come easy for Kitty. She'd been raised without religion and knew few formal prayers. But she hoped God wouldn't think it amiss if she just sat quietly in the chapel and spoke from the heart.

The church and small adobe building next to it looked deserted, but Kitty was not deterred as she pulled open the heavy chapel door and peered inside. Dust motes danced upon the dying rays of daylight, instilling in Kitty a sense of peace and tranquility. The altar stood stark and abandoned against a backdrop of lifelike statues, lending the small chapel an air of quiet reverence.

Kitty walked down the aisle and slid into the front pew. She ran her hand over the wood, strangely comforted by the well-worn patina that had been lovingly polished. She knelt on the wooden kneeler and concentrated on the face of Jesus looking so compassionately down on her from the cross. Then she started to pray, uttering informal words beneath her breath that poured forth from her heart. She knelt there for a very long time, her eyes closed, seeking answers to questions she feared had no solution.

"You seem troubled, daughter. How can I help you?"

Kitty gave a yelp of surprise when a stout, brown-robed priest appeared beside her. Of medium height and bald as an egg, the priest had the kindest eyes Kitty had ever seen. "I . . . I didn't hear you," Kitty said, willing her heart to settle down. The priest had frightened her nearly out of her wits.

"You were lost in prayer," the priest said. "I am Padre Enrico. This is my mission."

"I didn't mean to intrude," Kitty apologized.

"One can never intrude upon God, daughter. You seem troubled. Would it make you feel better to tell me about it?"

Kitty thought about it and decided that the padre was probably the only person she could confide in. "I . . . yes, I'd like to tell you, Padre, if you have time to listen. I'm not of your faith, but God is my last hope."

"No, child, God is your first hope." He slid into the pew beside her. "Tell me what is troubling you. Perhaps it is not as bad as it seems."

"It's worse, Padre," Kitty said with a sob. "An innocent man is going to die very soon, and no one can help him."

"So you've turned to God," Padre Enrico said, nodding his approval. "It is a beginning, child. Who is going to die and why?"

Feeling that she could trust this man of God, Kitty launched into her tale of woe. The further she got into the story, the rounder the good padre's eyes became. Her throat was parched and raw by the time she finished.

"Ah, so you are *Senor* Lowry's missing daughter. It is good that he has found you. Are you certain Ryan Delaney is innocent, *Senorita* Kitty?" Padre Enrico asked when Kitty fell silent.

"As sure as I am that I love him with all my heart," Kitty answered honestly. "I told you why Ryan became involved with outlaws. He was doing a dying man a favor and look how God rewarded him," Kitty said bitterly. "What am I to do, Padre? Ryan's brothers are worried sick about him, and so am I."

"Where are his brothers now?"

"They've gone off to look for Judge Mc-Fee. Even if they find him I doubt they can get him to grant another trial."

"I came to this lawless territory hoping my presence would make a difference," Padre Enrico mused, "but justice has been lax despite my best efforts to preach reform. Outlaws still rob and kill and juries still convict innocent men." He heaved a weary sigh. "I wish I could be of some help to you."

Suddenly Kitty had an inspiration she knew must have come from a higher authority. It was dangerous, and it would take the good padre's cooperation, but it could work.

She sucked in a steadying breath and asked, "Will you help me, Padre?"

The priest gave her a startled look. "Help you? What can I do, child? I am a man of God."

"Are you allowed to visit condemned prisoners in jail?"

"*Si.* Especially those of my faith. But religious persuasion means little if I can help a man find peace in his final hours. What are you asking of me?"

"Only your cooperation."

He gave her a shrewd look. "Why do I get the impression that you are asking more of me than merely offering comfort to a condemned man?"

"You may not believe me, Padre, but I heard God speaking to me just now. He revealed a way I might save Ryan from the hangman, until his brothers can legally clear his name. Time is so short, I fear they won't succeed before Ryan is led to his death."

"God works in mysterious ways," Padre Enrico praised. "What did God say to you?"

"He revealed a simple plan to me. But I can't do it without your help."

"In good conscience, I cannot break the law."

"What law?" Kitty exclaimed. "Ryan was tried and found guilty before his trial began! I'm not asking you to break the law, all I'm asking for is your cooperation. I'll do the rest."

Kitty watched Padre Enrico closely, thrilled by the gleam of excitement she saw in his soft brown eyes.

"What would you have me do, child?"

Kitty spent the next half hour outlining her plan to the good padre. The longer she talked the more incredulous his expression became. When she finished, he sat back and stared for so long at the large cross hanging over the altar that Kitty feared he would refuse.

"As I said before," he began, "God works in mysterious ways. He wouldn't have sent you here if He hadn't wanted me to help you. A love such as you have for Ryan Delaney cannot go unrewarded. Love between a man and woman is more precious than gold, and you deserve a chance to find happiness with the man you love. But your plan has many flaws. If *Senor* Delaney loves you he will not let you sacrifice yourself."

"The flaws can be worked out," Kitty vowed. "What can the law do to me? Certainly not hang me. God won't let me fail!" she said with conviction. "You're right, Padre, I should have come to Him first. Now, this is what I intend to do . . ."

It was very late when Kitty arrived home. The house seemed eerily quiet as she entered Bert's room to check on his condition.

"I'm awake, Kitty, you don't have to tiptoe," Bert said from the bed. "I told you, I'm not ready yet to kick the bucket. Did you see Ryan?"

"Yes, he sends his regards." Kitty debated whether or not to tell Bert about her plan to free Ryan and decided to wait until tomorrow to make a decision. She knew Bert would forbid it and she hated to disobey him, but she had no choice.

"Did you see Ryan's brothers in town?"

"I spoke with them before they left for Nogales to find Judge McFee. They're hoping to get him to set a new trial. If that fails, I don't know what they'll do. The marshal says it will take a governor's pardon to free Ryan."

Bert's attention sharpened despite his weariness. "Governor's pardon, you say? Hmmm. Go have your supper, honey, I

416

need to think."

"Good night, Father," Kitty said, kissing his wrinkled brow. "Sleep well."

"Teresa is gone," Bert said moments before Kitty reached the door. Kitty thought he sounded sad.

"I'm sorry, Father. I never wanted to come between you and Teresa."

"I know, daughter, I know. Good night."

Kitty slept late the following morning, ate a leisurely breakfast, and paid a visit to Bert before readying herself for the evening's activity. She still hadn't decided if she would tell Bert her plans, for she knew he would try to stop her. She was stunned to see Bert up and moving around the room with the help of a gnarled cane.

"Father! Should you be up?"

"I've been walking around this room for several days," Bert revealed. "I've even walked to the parlor. I can get around pretty well if I don't overdo."

"But the doctor . . ."

". . . doesn't know everything, honey. I've got too much to live for right now. Besides, I know you're up to something and I want to help."

Kitty sent him a startled look. "I don't know what you're talking about."

"You might as well tell me, Kitty. Whatever it is, I want to be a part of it."

Kitty worried her bottom lip with her teeth as she pondered her options. Telling Bert what she was planning could be detrimental to his health. But letting him sit home and stew could be equally disastrous. Whatever she decided could go either way where Bert's health was concerned.

"Kitty, honey, I insist you tell me," Bert said. "I can handle it."

The decision was made. "Very well, Father, but sit down first, this might take a while."

Bert perched on the edge of the bed, his gaze intent upon her face. "What are you planning?"

Kitty knelt at his feet and grasped his hands. "Do you recall Padre Enrico from the mission outside Tucson?"

"Of course. I haven't seen him in ages, but I remember him. What's he got to do with anything?"

"I was so distraught after visiting Ryan yesterday that I stopped at the chapel to pray. I'm not a regular churchgoer, but I know there is a God and I wanted to ask his help."

She paused to catch her breath. "I met Padre Enrico and the words just poured out. Something about him made me unburden myself when he encouraged me to talk to him. The padre was appalled to learn that an innocent man was going to be hung. Unlike the marshal, he believed me, believed in Ryan's innocence, and he offered assistance."

"What! I'm sure the good padre would do nothing to break the law."

"He's not going to break the law. I am," Kitty confided. "I've devised a plan to break Ryan out of jail."

Bert started violently. "Leave that to Ryan's brothers, honey. They're better equipped to deal with such things."

Kitty rose and glared down at Bert, hands on hips, her face hardened into determined lines. "I've ridden with outlaws, remember? I know how they think, how they react to certain situations, and I think I can pull this off."

Bert gave her a skeptical look. "Perhaps you should tell me exactly how you intend to accomplish this feat on your own."

"It's simple, really," Kitty said as she began to pace. "Here's what I intend to do."

Perched on the edge of the bed, she told him in detail how she planned to break Ryan out of jail. "Padre Enrico told me of a hiding place where Ryan would be safe until his brothers found a way to clear his name," Kitty said after she had outlined the details to Bert.

"Absolutely, positively not!" Bert exclaimed in horror. "What makes you think Ryan would allow you to sacrifice yourself for him?"

"Well," Kitty admitted, "that *is* going to be a problem. But what can the law do to me except keep me in jail for awhile? If I'm willing to make the sacrifice, Ryan should be willing to let me do it."

"There is no way I'm going to let you go into that jail robed like a priest and change places with Ryan."

"You can't stop me," Kitty said truculently. "I knew you'd say that, that's why I didn't want to tell you."

"Basically your idea has merit," Bert mused. "Where does Padre Enrico intend to hide Ryan?"

"There's a cave on the side of the mountain behind the mission. Years ago his parishioners used it to hide from marauding Indians. Padre Enrico agreed to lend me one of his robes and to keep Ryan's hiding place a secret. He says he can do so without lying. I trust him."

"What makes you think you can fool the marshal?"

"I intend to pull this off during the marshal's dinner hour. The deputy doesn't know me, and my face will be covered by a hood. I intend to provide some kind of diversion and steal the key to Ryan's cell when the deputy's attention is diverted. I've been to the jailhouse enough times to know where the keys to the individual cells are kept. It won't be too difficult to steal the key when I create the opportunity."

"How do you propose to do that?" Bert asked.

"I . . . I'll think of something."

"That settles it," Bert said with more strength than he had displayed during the entire time Kitty had known him. "I'm going with you. It's going to take two to pull this off. Ryan's brothers haven't returned yet, and you said yourself they are being watched. It's unlikely they could help even if they were in town.

"It's partly my fault Ryan is in this situation and I'm going to help you free him," Bert added. "I've had some thoughts on how to get him a pardon. But it will take time, and time isn't something Ryan has right now. How many days before his hanging? Three, four?"

"Three, Father, that's why I have to act quickly."

"That's why *we* have to act quickly," Bert clarified.

"I can't let you do this, Father. Your health . . . two weeks ago you were on your deathbed."

"I know I'm dying, honey, let me do this for Ryan while I still can. God knows Ryan gave me something more precious than my own life. Now, stop jawing and let's devise a plan that will work. One that Ryan will agree to. You and I both know he'd never let you take his place in jail while he walked away free."

Kitty flushed. In the back of her mind she *did* know that Ryan would balk at her plan, but her stubbornness was as strong as his. And when push came to shove, he had no other choice.

"The trip to the mission will be easier on me if we take the wagon. I want to preserve my strength for the walk to the jailhouse. Or perhaps we can ride the mission's mule," Bert said, warming to the subject. "I'm sure Padre Enrico will loan us an extra robe. Does the marshal's office have a rear door?"

Kitty thought a moment, then nodded, recalling the door at the back of the office.

"Good. I can divert the deputies' attention while you steal the key to Ryan's cell. When we leave, I can create another diversion while Ryan sneaks out the rear door. He can meet us at the mission and go immediately into hiding. I think you should stay with him. I'll inform Ryan's brothers when they return."

Kitty liked Bert's plan better than her own. But she still wasn't convinced Bert's fragile health would allow his participation. "I don't know . . ."

"Well I do, honey. You can't deny me this chance to thank Ryan for all he's done for me. Having you in my life, if only for a short time, has made my final days worth living. Never forget that. Why don't you go find one of the hands and arrange for a wagon. And don't forget to pack food, blankets, and anything else you and Ryan will need during your stay in the cave. Hopefully your stay won't be too long. I'm going to get Ryan pardoned if it's the last thing I do."

Kitty feared it *would* be the last thing he did. "Are you sure, Father?"

Bert looked her right in the eye and said, "Very sure. Let me know when all is ready. I hope the marshal cooperates and goes out for his supper as usual tonight."

"So do I," Kitty said reverently. "Why don't you rest while I take care of the details. And Father, thank you."

■ ■ ■ ■

Kitty and Bert arrived at the mission late that afternoon. Kitty drove the team while Bert rode in the wagonbed, propped up by quilts and pillows intended for the cave. When they reached the mission, Padre Enrico seemed surprised to see Bert but said nothing as he helped Bert from the wagon and instructed Kitty to drive it around to the back of the chapel where it couldn't be seen by passersby.

Padre Enrico guided Bert to his small adobe house and settled him in a chair. "Don't scold, Padre," Bert advised. "I've made my mind up to help my daughter and that's final. We are both grateful for your help."

The priest rocked back and forth on his heels as he searched Bert's face. "I can see you're determined on this course, *Senor* Lowry," he said, "but perhaps you should wait here for your daughter to return."

"No, Padre, I'm going with Kitty," Bert replied. "She can't possibly carry this off by herself, and we don't expect you to involve yourself in this more than you already have."

"Saving innocent souls is my calling," Padre Enrico intoned. "God never told me how I was to do this. He left it to me to find those souls most in need of my help. Your daughter's story touched me deeply. God would wish for such a grand love to survive and prosper. I hope that one day I can baptize their daughters and sons. I must go now and show *Senorita* Kitty where to take the supplies she brought."

Kitty sighed in relief when she saw Padre Enrico approaching the front of the wagon. He had taken so long she'd feared something had happened to Bert.

"Is my father all right?" Kitty asked as the priest hoisted his considerable bulk onto the wagon seat.

"He is resting," Padre Enrico said. "He is determined to help you, and I must confess I feel better about this with your father beside you. I did not like your idea of taking *Senor* Delaney's place in jail. I feared the marshal would react unfavorably and keep you incarcerated. God has shown you another way, child. Who am I to gainsay God?"

"Which way, Padre?" Kitty said as she took up the reins.

"Follow the narrow path toward the mountains," Padre Enrico said. "I will point out the cave when we reach it. The way will be rough, for few wagons have traveled this trail, but I believe we can make it."

They bounced along the uneven trail, dodging stately cactus and skirting sagebrush. When they came to where the mountain began its upward incline, Padre Enrico said, "Turn left." Kitty obeyed. Several minutes later, the priest said, "Stop! There it is! See that ledge? It is only a short climb from here."

"I don't see a thing," Kitty said, straining her eyes.

"That is what makes it a perfect hiding place. The cave is behind that thick growth of sagebrush growing on the ledge. Come, I'll help you stow the supplies. If I remember correctly, there is a good selection of cooking pots and a stack of firewood inside. There is also an underground river feeding clear, cold water into a pool back a ways from the entrance. That is what makes the cave unique. You can bathe in the pool and still drink the river water before it flows into the pool. My people have hidden here many times in the past."

A half hour later all the supplies Kitty had brought were stored in the surprisingly large and pleasantly dry cave. She had worked up a sweat and hoped she'd have time to wash away the stench before going to the jailhouse. She wished she would have had time to tell Ryan about their plan, but it was too late now to worry about small details.

Bert was waiting for them in the priest's hut. Kitty searched his face and was heartened to see a bit of color staining his cheeks. She prayed this escapade wouldn't be the death of him and knew the doctor would have apoplexy were he to learn of Bert's plans.

"It's growing dark, Kitty," Bert said. "Shouldn't we start for the jailhouse now? I hope the good padre has robes for both of us."

"I have robes," the Padre said. "They are patched and worn thin, but people are accustomed to seeing priests poorly garbed. Come with me, *Senorita* Kitty. I will show you where you can wash up before you don the robe."

"Thank you," Kitty said gratefully. "Can you manage alone, Father?"

"I will help him," the padre said. "I usually ride my mule into town. Old Pepito can carry both of you. He is mild mannered and will give you no trouble. Before you leave, I will give you my blessing."

Dusk was settling when Kitty and Bert rode into town on Pepito's broad back. As luck would have it, they arrived just as Marshal Pringle left the jailhouse and walked across the street to his favorite restaurant.

"Are you all right?" Kitty asked softly as she hopped off Pepito's back and helped Bert dismount.

"Don't worry about me, honey," Bert said. Kitty thought he sounded a bit breathless, but he dismissed her fussing with a wave of his hand.

"You'll not have much time to filch the key after I create a diversion," Bert warned, "so be prepared to act swiftly."

Kitty nodded, pulling the hood of the robe forward to conceal her features and adjusting Bert's hood in the same way. "I'm ready," she said with more confidence than she felt.

"Let me do the talking," Bert cautioned.

The deputy was seated in the marshal's chair with his feet propped on the desk. When he saw the two priests enter, his feet slammed down on the floor.

"Good evening, my son," Bert said. "I am Padre Carmello and this is Brother Ambrose. We have come from the mission to offer last rites to the condemned men."

"That would be Durango and Delaney," the deputy replied. "The marshal is having his supper, but I see no harm in letting you offer your services to the prisoners. Fifteen minutes is all I can allow you. Unless you want to wait an hour for the marshal to return. He's the only one who can grant you more time."

"Fifteen minutes will do," Bert said. "Bless you, my son." He made a crude sign of the cross over the deputy.

Suddenly Bert staggered backward. At first Kitty was alarmed, until she realized Bert was creating the diversion he'd promised. And it seemed to work, as the deputy leaped forward to steady Bert.

"Are you all right, Padre?" the deputy asked.

"Yes, my son. I have been fasting all day in preparation for the holy day tomorrow. Perhaps a little water, if you would be so kind."

The moment the deputy turned his back on her to administer to Bert, Kitty sprang into action. Edging around the two men, she backed against the wall where the keys hung. When the deputy walked across the room to scoop up a dipper of water from a pail, she stealthily removed the key with the number 4 written on a tag and hid it in the folds of her robe. By the time the deputy handed Bert the dipper of water, Kitty had returned to Bert's side.

"Thank you, my son, your kindness will

be rewarded," Bert intoned as he drank from the dipper. "I feel much better. May we see the prisoners now?"

"Sure thing, Padre," the deputy said as he ushered them to the corridor leading to the cell area.

Kitty held her breath, fearing he'd notice that there were only three keys hanging from hooks where there should have been four. She truly believed Padre Enrico's blessing must have helped, for the deputy didn't even glance at the row of keys.

"Fifteen minutes," the deputy called after them as they entered the corridor.

Ryan studied the marks he'd scratched into the wall and realized he had two more days after tonight to live. He'd already eaten his supper and had nothing to look forward to except a long boring night haunted by dreams of Kitty. Once his supper tray had been removed he knew he'd see no one until morning, when either the marshal or a deputy delivered his first meal of the day. There was no light in the cell, only that provided by the sliver of moonlight that had arrived on the heels of dusk.

Stretching out on the shelf that served as his bunk, Ryan stared up at the window and wished he were ten feet tall so he could look out at the world he was about to leave. There was so much he wanted to accomplish before he died. He wanted to help Chad make the Delaney ranch the best spread in Montana. He wanted to bounce his nieces and nephews on his knee. And he wanted something he'd never even considered before. He wanted to look into the faces of his own children. His and Kitty's.

It was strange how contemplating one's death brought forth regrets for what might have been. Ryan thought of all those years he'd wasted earning the name Rogue Ryan and wondered if being a womanizer would be the only thing people would remember about him after he was gone. He chuckled despite his gloomy mood. At one time he would have been pleased to have such an epitaph engraved upon his tombstone.

Before Kitty.

Before he'd found love.

Lost in thought, Ryan didn't immediately hear the footsteps shuffling down the corridor. When he did hear them he leaped to his feet and rushed to the bars. It was so unusual to have visitors after the supper hour that he knew something extraordinary must have happened. His face fell in disappointment when he saw two brown-robed priests stop before his cell.

431

"You've come to the wrong place, Padres," he said, summoning a smile. "I'm afraid I'm beyond redemption. But I appreciate your effort."

Suddenly one of the priests threw back his hood, and Ryan's mouth fell open, shocked to the core. "Kitty!" he hissed. "What in the hell are you doing here dressed like that?" He peered closely at the second priest and nearly lost the ability to speak. When he finally found his voice he blurted out, "Bert! Are you both mad?"

"Shhh," Kitty warned as she produced the key to his cell and fitted it into the lock.

"What are you doing?"

"We're breaking you out," Bert said. "You're to go into hiding until your brothers and I can prove your innocence."

"But . . . but I don't understand. Where did you get the robes?"

"Right from the source," Kitty said cryptically as she turned the key and pulled the door open. "There! Hurry, Ryan. Bert is going to create a diversion while you sneak out the rear door. It's dark enough outside for you to slip into the shadows and make your way to the mission. Padre Enrico will be waiting for you in the chapel. If all goes well here, we'll join you."

"You're both out of your minds," Ryan

whispered. "I can't allow you to put your-selves in danger for me. Look at you, Bert. You can barely stand on your own two feet."

"Worry about yourself, Ryan. This is your last chance to escape the hangman. You and Kitty have your whole lives ahead of you. I know my time is limited and wanted to do this for my daughter. It's the least I can do to atone for all the grief I've caused her. Follow us," he ordered in a tone that brooked no argument. "Stay in the corridor while I create a diversion, then sneak out the rear exit. Understand?"

"Yes, but what about Durango? He might see us and sound the alarm."

"Durango was sleeping when we walked by," Kitty said. "Let's hope he's still sleep-ing. Are you ready, Ryan?"

"I will be in a moment," he said as he pulled Kitty against him and gave her a quick kiss. "Now I'm ready."

Ryan huddled in Bert's shadow as they crept down the corridor. Durango was still sleeping, facing away from the bars on his bunk. Relief shuddered through Ryan when they reached the end of the corridor, but they were far from safe. They still had to get past the deputy.

Bert motioned to Ryan to flatten himself against the wall. Ryan sucked in his breath and blessed his dark clothing that helped him to blend into the deep shadows of the corridor.

"We're finished here, Deputy," Bert said as he and Kitty stepped out from the corridor and into the main office.

"That didn't take long," the deputy said.

"The condemned men were unrepentant," Bert replied. "Thank . . ." Suddenly Bert lurched forward, right into the deputy's arms.

"Padre! Are you all right?"

"Just weak, my son," Bert whispered shakily. Still hidden in the corridor, Ryan feared Bert's weakness was more reality than pretence. "Would you be so kind as to help me outside? I fear I cannot mount my mule without your aid. Brother Ambrose is a good soul but he is lacking in strength. Lend me your arm, my son."

With both arms supporting Bert, the deputy all but carried him outside. Ryan remained watchful as Kitty replaced the key to his cell and scooted out after Bert and the deputy. Once they were out the door, Ryan darted out from the corridor. He already knew where his guns were kept, and he grabbed them from a rack seconds before he made his escape through the rear door.

CHAPTER 18

Ryan reached the chapel without mishap. Padre Enrico was waiting for him inside. The padre's cherubic face crinkled into a wide grin when he turned from his prayers and saw Ryan striding down the aisle toward him.

"*Senor* Delaney! Thank God you have arrived. Did all go well? I have been praying for you."

"Thank you, Padre," Ryan returned. "I'm grateful for your help, though I must admit I thought Bert and Kitty were mad to suggest, much less attempt, such a daring move. I shudder to think what will happen to them if the jailbreak is discovered before they make good their escape. Bert is weaker than he's letting on."

"*Senor* Lowry is seriously ill," the priest said gravely, "but this is something he felt he had to do. He feared for his daughter's safety. She would have attempted your escape alone even though he forbade it."

Ryan glanced anxiously toward the door. "They should be here by now. I'll never forgive myself if anything happens to them. God, I should never have let them talk me into this."

"We will pray together for their safe arrival," Padre Enrico said.

Suddenly Ryan heard a commotion at the door and whirled on his heel, his hand reaching for his gun. His hand fell away and he visibly relaxed when he saw Kitty standing in the doorway, her gaze frantically searching for him in the candlelit chapel. Her face lit up when she saw him.

"Ryan. Thank God."

Ryan opened his arms, and she ran into them, sobbing his name. He held her close, savoring the feel, the scent of her. She felt so right, as if she were made for him. He groaned her name, silently vowing never to let her out of his sight if he emerged from this mess with his life intact. Then his mouth came down on hers, conveying through his kiss how utterly dear she was to him.

"Where is *Senor* Lowry?" Padre Enrico asked, abruptly pulling Ryan back to reality. Ryan broke off the kiss and looked at Kitty.

"Bert is too weak to dismount by himself,"

Kitty said. "He needs your help, Ryan. I knew he shouldn't have attempted this, but he insisted."

"There is a small infirmary behind my house where I treat impoverished Indians and Mexicans," Padre Enrico explained. "Take him there."

Ryan reached Bert first and lifted him off the mule. Bert refused to be carried, so Ryan and the priest supported him while he walked. Kitty fussed around him as he shed the robe and sank onto the narrow bunk in the infirmary.

"Shall I get the doctor?" Kitty asked anxiously.

"No, honey, I'll be fine. I just need to rest. Take Ryan to the cave. I don't think his absence will be discovered until morning, but we've come too far to take chances."

Kitty seemed reluctant to leave, but Padre Enrico promised to take good care of Bert.

"Leave the robes," the priest said. "I will return them to my chest before the law arrives."

"What about Bert?" Ryan wanted to know. "What will they do if he's found here?"

"Padre Enrico and I are old friends," Bert said. "I will say that I came here so he could administer to me in my final hours. No one will suspect me of illegal activities. Go to the cave," he urged. "I can take care of myself."

"Very well," Kitty said with a reluctant sigh. She clasped Ryan's hand as if to lead him away, but Ryan balked.

"Wait. There's something I wish to do before I go into hiding."

"Don't worry about your brothers," Bert said. "I'll explain everything to them. We'll keep you informed as to what is happening in town."

"It's not that," Ryan said, drawing Kitty against him and placing an arm around her shoulders. "I want Padre Enrico to marry Kitty and me first. I don't want to go another minute without making Kitty my wife."

The glowing candles could not match Bert's radiant features. "You don't know how long I've wanted this," he crowed. "You and Kitty were made for one another. I sensed the attraction from the beginning. Knowing that you and Kitty are man and wife will ease my mind considerably."

Ryan turned a stunned Kitty to face him, his green eyes filled with yearning and hope. "What do you say, Kitten, will you have me?"

"Forever," Kitty whispered. He felt her

tremble and knew her emotions were stretched as taut as his.

"We must hurry, children," the priest said. "I will marry you here so *Senor* Lowry can attend the ceremony and act as your witness. Give me a moment to get the Holy Book." He hurried from the room, leaving Kitty and Ryan staring raptly at one another.

"I love you, Kitten," Ryan whispered into her ear. "I don't know what will happen to me, or how I will get out of this mess, but I want you to be my wife for however long we have together."

"We're going to share a lifetime together," Kitty promised. But Ryan wasn't so certain. His lifetime was likely to be shortened by a rope.

Padre Enrico bustled back into the room, interrupting the tender moment. "I am ready. Join hands, children, while I read the words over you."

Ryan listened carefully as the priest read the marriage ceremony from his book. Ryan repeated the words that bound him to Kitty. He couldn't wipe the smile off his face when Kitty spoke her vows. Moments later Padre Enrico pronounced them man and wife. Both the priest and Bert were grinning from ear to ear as Ryan pulled Kitty into his arms and kissed her soundly.

"I will give the marriage paper to *Senor* Lowry for safekeeping after it is signed. Then I will enter your names and the date into the church records so no one will question the legality of your marriage," the padre said. "It will only take a few minutes to prepare the document for your signatures, then you must leave. Can you find the cave in the dark, *Senorita* Kitty?"

"I'm sure I can," Kitty responded.

After all the legalities were completed, Ryan and Kitty bid Bert farewell.

"I have a plan," Bert said in parting. "If it succeeds you will be cleared of all charges."

Ryan wasn't as confident as Bert seemed to be. He entertained no hopes of having his name cleared any time soon, if ever. His best chance for survival was to lay low for awhile and head up to Montana when the furor died down. He could survive anything as long as Kitty was with him.

Kitty picked her way along the uneven trail, guided by moonlight and the lantern she carried. They reached the end of the path, and Kitty paused at the base of the mountain to get her bearings.

"Where to now?" Ryan asked. His glittering gaze settled on her face, making Kitty shudder with anticipation.

She returned his gaze, thinking it magical the way the moonlight transformed his green eyes into gemlike pools of desire. Kitty shivered. She sensed his hunger and knew it matched hers in intensity. She felt the fluid heat of his scalding gaze surge through her body and settle disconcertingly between her legs.

"Kitten, where to now?" Ryan repeated. "Are you lost?"

"No," she said, jarred back to reality by his question. "We turn left here and look for a thick growth of sagebrush growing on a ledge a short distance up from the foot of the mountain."

"Come on," Ryan said, grasping her hand and pulling her along with him.

"There it is!" Kitty cried, pointing upward. "See that tangle of sagebrush? The mouth of the cave lies behind it."

Hand in hand they climbed the incline and found the dark, yawning mouth of the cave. Kitty held the lantern high and led the way inside.

"Just like home," Ryan quipped. "Bedrolls, firewood, cooking pots, lamps, food, everything we need. I reckon I have you to thank for this."

"Me and Padre Enrico. Some things, like

441

the pots, firewood, and lamps were already here. I provided the rest."

Ryan advanced into the cave and lit a second lantern. When he held out his hand to Kitty, her heart beat louder than a hundred drums.

"Shall we find that pool you told me about?" Ryan said. "The stench of jail clings to me, and I don't want to offend you on our wedding night. We can bathe together."

Ryan found a bar of soap and towels Kitty had included with her supplies, then took the lantern from Kitty and led the way down a narrow passageway leading off to the left of the main cavern. They found the pool at the end of the tunnel.

"I hope the water isn't too cold," Ryan said as he set the lantern down on the smooth dirt floor close to the edge of the pool.

"Or too deep," Kitty added.

"Do you need help undressing?" The low timbre of his voice sent shivers of awareness dancing over her skin. He wanted her. Nothing had ever been more apparent to her. And God help her, she wanted him, only this time when he released his seed inside her they would be man and wife.

"I can undress myself," Kitty replied. But her hands shook so badly that she couldn't seem to manage the fastenings on the front of her dress.

"Here, let me," Ryan said, pushing her hands aside. He gave her a cocky grin. "I'm better at this than you are."

"You'd better not play the rogue for anyone but me," Kitty warned him. "I'm a jealous woman, Ryan Delaney."

"And I'm a jealous man," he replied as he shoved her dress over her shoulders and down her arms. Then Kitty took over, pushing her dress past her hips and stepping out of it.

She watched his eyes kindle with desire as she lowered the straps to her chemise and sent it to the ground with her dress. She wore no corset, just drawers and stockings. She hesitated a moment, then quickly stripped them off.

"God, you're beautiful," he whispered with a reverence that touched Kitty's heart. "It's been so long. I feared I'd never be able to touch you again, to feel the softness of your skin, to taste your passion or hear you cry out your pleasure. Sometimes I'd close my eyes and recall the splendor of the moment when we first made love."

His passionate words sent Kitty's senses reeling. Heat suffused her body. At first she feared the water would be too cold, but her skin was so hot that she would welcome the coolness.

"I don't want to touch you, love. Not yet, not until I'm clean."

Kitty watched him undress with avid anticipation, caressing him with her eyes as he bared his flesh. He might have lost some weight but not the rippling muscles lying beneath the taut layer of skin, Kitty thought. His body was still magnificent, if somewhat pale from his enforced imprisonment. Splendidly male and so damn handsome he took her breath away. Her eyes moved over him with slow perusal, starting with his face and moving down to his . . . she gasped aloud when she reached his groin. His staff was already hard and swollen, rising boldly against his stomach.

"Keep on looking at me like that and I'll forget my filth and take you right here," he said in a strangled voice.

Kitty's gaze shot upward to his face. His eyes were narrowed into glittering green slits as his hungry gaze devoured her. At that precise moment she didn't give a hoot about dirt. She reached for him, but Ryan must have read her mind, for he turned abruptly and dove into the pool. He came up in the middle, sputtering and pushing his hair out of his eyes.

"It's not deep at all," he said. "I can touch bottom here. It is cool, but refreshing. Bring the soap when you come in."

Kitty picked up the soap, dipped her toe into the water, and shivered. "It's chilly," she moaned. "Maybe I should get wet a little at a time."

She started into the pool, advancing slowly, until the water lapped at her knees. She paused and looked for Ryan, alarmed when she failed to locate him in the dimly lit cavern. She squealed in surprise when he shot up in front of her, dripping water all over her. Then he dragged her beneath the water. She came up gasping and sputtering.

"Damn you! I've a good mind to whip your sorry ass!"

"Still the foulmouthed little wildcat, I see," Ryan laughed.

"Did you expect me to change overnight?" she retorted.

He handed her the soap. "I don't ever want you to change. I love you just the way you are. Wash my back, love. After I'm clean I'll build a fire to warm you while you have your bath."

He presented his back to her, and Kitty spread lather over it, relishing the feel of smooth skin over sleek muscles.

"Turn around," Kitty said breathlessly.

Just touching him set her afire. He turned to face her, and she soaped his chest, spreading her fingers through the soft, curly mat of hair growing there. He felt like heaven. She wondered if he tasted as good as he looked.

Her hands plunged beneath the water, searching for him, needing to feel him, all of him. She glanced up at his face and saw a look of blissful agony pass over his features as her fingers curled around him. She felt him shudder as he pulled her hand away from him. Then he drew her into his embrace; his lips teased her mouth and brushed her cheek. He nipped her ear and whispered, "This is our wedding night, love. I want to make it last as long as possible. If you touch me there it will end too soon."

His hands slid down to cup her buttocks, pressing her against him. She wrapped her legs around his hips; that aching place between her legs embraced him as she pushed her loins against his. A jolt of pleasure shot through her, so intense that she cried out and clutched at him.

"Oh, God, Kitten, I don't think I can wait," Ryan gasped as his fingers found her heat and began a gentle stroking. Then he bent his head and drew a swollen nipple into his mouth, sucking hard. Kitty arched against him, the burning ache inside her too urgent to be denied.

"Now, Ryan, oh, please, now."

"Kitten, sweet, passionate Kitten," Ryan groaned. "I don't know what I did to deserve you."

He lifted her, then lowered her onto his erection. She felt herself stretching, filled to bursting, the tension nearly unbearable as he plunged and withdrew, then plunged again. Kitty gasped with pleasure. She bucked wildly against him, finding his rhythm and matching it. Their mouths met in brutal combat, tongues probing, fencing, in a battle as old as time.

Faster and faster. Deeper and deeper. The heat within her kindled into a roaring blaze, and then her shrill, wrenching cries of pleasure bounced off the stone walls surrounding them.

Kitty's heart beat so loud and so fast that she barely heard Ryan's shout of ecstasy. But she knew he had found his own fulfillment, for she heard the rapid cadence of his heartbeat drumming within his chest and felt the great shudders racking his body.

"What an incredible beginning to our wedding night," Ryan said when his breathing returned to normal. "Let's finish washing and get out of here."

Ryan washed first and left the water to build a fire. The small blaze was burning brightly by the time Kitty returned to the main cavern.

"Are you hungry?" Ryan asked.

"Not really. What about you?"

"I've already eaten."

Ryan searched her face, waiting for a sign from her. When she nodded, he swept her into his arms and lay her down on the bedroll he had spread out close to the fire. He whipped off the towel and stared at her, worshipping her with his eyes. Then he spread her legs, exposing her heated center to his hungry gaze. She glistened wetly in the firelight. He parted the pink folds of flesh to expose the tiny bud nestled there. He leaned forward to inhale her exotic scent. He felt her fingers tighten in his hair as his tongue flicked out to taste her.

"I love you, Kitten," Ryan whispered. "What a fool I've been."

Kitty blew out a ragged breath. "None of that matters now. We're married, and nothing will ever part us again. Kiss me, Ryan."

He kissed her, only not where she expected. She arched violently against him as his mouth closed over her core and his tongue aroused the small pebble of flesh at her entrance until it grew taut and full.

"Ryan! Please. I can't stand it," she screamed softly.

He rose quickly and settled on top of her. She opened eagerly for him. He placed his hand between them and cupped her. His fingers were covered with the dewy evidence of her passion when he drew them away. "You're weeping for me," he whispered tenderly.

"Only for you, Ryan."

He kissed her roughly, letting her taste herself on his lips, then he drew back and thrust forward into her tight, hot core. She convulsed around him, holding him so snugly inside her that he felt he had somehow become a part of her. That thought made him swell larger, grow longer and heavier. He felt her contract around him, and then all thought ceased as his stroking brought her to a shattering climax. He waited until she stopped trembling before giving in to the wrenching need to release his seed inside her. Everything inside him went rigid. He raised his head and shouted as wave after wave of earthshaking turbulence roared through him.

They rested, then made love again. This time Kitty played the aggressor, loving every inch of Ryan in the same way he had loved her. When she finally took him inside her, they strove for the top and found it together, touched the splendor and clung to it, fearing that everything might change once they floated back to reality. Then they slept.

Padre Enrico waited for the law in the chapel the morning after the jailbreak. They found him kneeling before the altar, his head bowed in prayer. Marshal Pringle invited him outside to answer some questions. Padre Enrico cast one last pleading gaze at Christ on the cross and padded outside behind the marshal.

"What can I do for you, Marshal?" Padre Enrico asked. "Has one of the Indian lads been causing trouble? I try to keep my flock under control, but I don't always succeed."

"This is far more serious than troublesome Indian boys. I've come to arrest Padre Carmello and Brother Ambrose. They're suspected of masterminding a jailbreak. I understand the two priests in question are assigned to the mission."

Father Enrico's brow creased, marring the smooth lines of his round face. "I know no priests bearing those names." It wasn't a lie, Father Enrico reflected. He did not know the names Bert and Kitty had used to gain entrance to the jail. "I am the only priest at the mission. I have asked for help with my flock but have been unsuccessful in obtaining it."

Pringle sent him a skeptical look. "So you tend your flock alone."

"I am a man of God, Marshal, I do not lie. You are free to search if you'd like, but you will find that I am the only priest in residence." Again the truth. Padre Enrico knew himself to be the only priest at the mission.

Pringle stroked his chin as he considered the priest's words. The priest was known to be an honest man of God who performed only good works. "Searching the mission won't be necessary, Padre. I believe you. Obviously the men who broke Delaney out of jail were imposters," he concluded. "Deputy Desmond couldn't even say with conviction that the bogus priests had a hand in the breakout because he didn't see or hear anything suspicious while they were visiting the prisoner. Delaney's absence wasn't noted until this morning, when I carried breakfast in to him. Nothing seemed amiss when I returned from supper last night. All the keys were in place on their hooks. It's as if he disappeared into thin air. It just doesn't make sense."

"What about Delaney's brothers?" Deputy Desmond ventured. "They could have

451

returned to town and visited Delaney dressed as priests."

"We'll soon find out if they were involved," Pringle replied. "Two of my deputies have been trailing them. They can tell us if the Delaney brothers were in town last night about the time the jailbreak took place."

"Sorry I couldn't be of more help, Marshal," Padre Enrico said. "If you'll excuse me, I must prepare for morning Mass. I say Mass every morning whether anyone attends or not. Would you care to stay for the services?"

"Sorry, Padre, I've got an escaped prisoner to catch. The town pays me to keep the law. Allowing a condemned prisoner to escape could be the end of my career in this town. Good day, Padre."

He tipped his hat and rode away with his deputies. Padre Enrico waited until they had ridden from sight before hurrying to the infirmary to report the encounter to Bert.

Bert was awake but obviously much weaker than he had been the day before. His part in Ryan's jailbreak had cost him dearly, but he had known the risks and accepted them. His gaze was anxious as the priest hurried to his bedside.

"What is it, Padre? Are Kitty and Ryan all right?"

"The marshal and his deputies just left. They questioned me about Father Carmello and Brother Ambrose. I told them I knew no one by those names. I did not have to lie, for I had no idea those were the names you and *Senorita* Kitty used to gain entrance to the jail."

"That's the way I wanted it, Padre," Bert said. "Did they believe you?"

"I'm sure they did. I gave them permission to search the mission but they said it wasn't necessary. Thank God they worded their questions so that I did not have to lie." He searched Bert's face. "How do you feel, *senor?*"

Bert gave him a bleak smile. "Not as well as I'd like. There is still something I must do before I leave this earth. But I have one more favor to ask of you, Padre."

"Name it. If it is within my power, it is yours."

"Your help will not go unrewarded," Bert promised. "The favor has nothing to do with the law. I need to speak to Ryan's brothers when they return. They might seek me out at the ranch but I do not feel strong enough yet to return home. There is one more thing I must do before time runs out for Ryan and Kitty, and I need the Delaney brothers' help. They are due back in town today. I need someone I can trust to summon them here."

"Since I have business in town, I will do as you ask, *Senor* Lowry. How will I recognize them?"

Bert gave accurate descriptions of both brothers. "They are staying at the hotel," he concluded.

"I will go after morning Mass," Padre Enrico promised.

Exhausted, disheartened, and carrying a yard of trail dust on their clothing and skin, Chad and Pierce rode into Tucson the day after the jailbreak. Their grim expressions spoke volumes about their unsuccessful efforts on Ryan's behalf. The judge had refused to grant their request for a new trial.

"What in the hell are we going to do now?" Chad asked, giving voice to his brother's fears.

"We'd best be doing it fast. Ryan's hanging is in two days," Pierce muttered grimly. "You got any bright ideas on how to break our little brother out of jail?"

"I'm thinking as fast as I can," Chad complained. "Except for sticking a gun in the marshal's ribs and taking off for parts unknown, nothing comes to mind."

"Reckon we can outrun the posse?" Pierce

wondered.

"The only problem with that is the marshal knows we'll head for Montana, and he'll alert the law there. We break Ryan out of jail and the law will have all three of us under lock and key."

"This is so damn frustrating," Pierce growled as they dismounted at the livery and headed over to the hotel. "Let's wash this trail dust from our hides before we tell Ryan the bad news."

"Are our shadows still trailing us?" Chad asked, glancing behind him.

"Still there," Pierce replied. "Been trailing us for two days. I hope they're as tired as we are."

They walked toward the hotel, saddlebags slung over their shoulders, their steps dragging. They saw the marshal hail them from across the street and waited for him to join them.

"What in the hell do you suppose he wants?" Pierce growled.

"Whatever it is can't be agreeing with him," Chad ventured. "Look at his face. He looks like he ate something rotten."

"Good morning, Marshal," Pierce greeted. "What can we do for you?"

"Did you two just ride into town?" Pringle barked without preamble.

"Why?" Chad asked. "Is something wrong? It's not Ryan, is it?"

"There's been a jailbreak," Pringle said as he searched their faces for their reactions. "Your brother escaped."

"You're kidding!" Pierce crowed. "Who broke him out?"

"That's what I'd like to know. Where were you boys last night around suppertime? We think two men disguised as priests masterminded the escape."

"My butt was planted on an anthill about ten miles outside of town," Chad said, rubbing his behind. "I sat down to eat my supper and found out too late I had chosen an anthill to sit on. I'm surprised you didn't hear me yelling all the way to Tucson. I can drop my pants and show you, if you don't believe me."

"Never mind," Pringle said, grimacing. "I took the precaution of having you followed. Here come my deputies now. They can verify whether or not you were in town last night."

Chad and Pierce exchanged amused glances as they waited for the two deputies to join them. Pierce was heartened by the fact that they looked as tired as he and Chad felt.

"Morning, Marshal," the deputies said in

unison as they joined the group.

"Deputy Asher, Deputy Tuttle," Pringle greeted. "You're just in time to settle something for us. Have either of these men been out of your sight since they left town?"

Asher and Tuttle looked at one another, then shook their heads. "No, sir," Asher said. "Me and Tuttle took turns watching them each night so they were never out of our sights. A real funny thing happened last night. Chad Delaney sat on an anthill and screamed loud enough to wake up the dead."

"Are you certain of this, Asher?"

"Certain as I am of standing here, Marshal. Ask Tuttle."

"That's right, Marshal," Tuttle verified. "Happened around suppertime, about ten miles outside of town, where they bedded down for the night."

"Satisfied, Marshal?" Pierce asked. "Whoever broke Ryan out of jail has our undying gratitude, but it wasn't us."

"We'll find him," Pringle growled. "And we'll find the two men masquerading as priests." He tipped his hat. "Good day, gentlemen."

Pierce felt like jumping for joy, and he could tell by the look on Chad's face that his brother felt the same. "Who do you suppose broke Ryan out of jail?" he asked, thoroughly puzzled.

"I don't know, but we owe him a debt of gratitude," Chad replied. "I can't believe someone found a way to free Ryan when our own plans failed. Who do you suppose . . ."

They exchanged knowing glances, then mouthed in unison, "Kitty!"

"I reckon we should hightail it out to the ranch and find out what's going on."

Chad groaned. "I was hoping I could give my arse a rest after those ants gnawed on me. A bath sure would feel good."

"Later," Pierce said tersely. "First we have to . . ."

"Are you the Delaney brothers?"

The brothers turned on their heels, both registering surprise when a rotund priest with warm brown eyes joined them. "I'm Pierce Delaney and this is my brother Chad, Padre," Pierce said, brimming with curiosity. "What can we do for you?"

"I am Padre Enrico. Do you know where to find the Mission of San Pietro? It is located on the western outskirts of town. I have a message for you from *Senor* Lowry. He is staying on at the mission as my guest. He wants to speak with the both of you as soon as possible."

"I didn't think Bert was capable of leaving his bed," Pierce said somewhat skeptically.

"You can trust me, my son," Padre Enrico assured him. "I can say no more without rousing suspicion."

"Is this about Ryan?" Chad barked.

Padre Enrico gave him a blissful smile. "God is good. Your brother and his wife are safe for the moment. That is all I can say. Come to the mission tonight, *Senor* Lowry will tell you the details."

Without offering another word of explanation, the priest walked away, his brown robe swishing about his ample form.

"Ryan and his *wife?*" Chad repeated dumbly.

"Ryan is *married?*" Pierce gasped, echoing Chad's surprise. "Either I'm crazy or in the short time we were gone Ryan managed to get himself out of jail and acquire a wife."

"Then we're both crazy," Chad contended, "for it appears our little brother has accomplished the impossible."

CHAPTER 19

Chad and Pierce rode to the mission that evening without fear of being followed. Since they were no longer considered a threat, the marshal had no reason to keep them under surveillance. A single light shone through the window of the small adobe house next to the chapel as they rapped lightly on the door. Padre Enrico answered almost immediately.

"Ah, come in, come in," the priest invited. "*Senor* Lowry is waiting for you. Follow me to the infirmary."

Chad and Pierce followed the priest through the small house to a back room set up to treat the sick. There were three narrow cots in the room, and only one was occupied.

"Thank God you've come," Bert said on a shaky breath.

The brothers exchanged worried glances, shocked by Bert's appearance. His skin seemed withered and gray, more so than when they had last seen him.

"The padre said you wanted to see us. What is this all about, Bert? Are you strong enough to tell us what happened? We know about Ryan's escape but little else. The marshal met us with the news shortly after we hit town. At first he thought we were involved, but his deputies soon put him straight. We were camped ten miles from town last night."

Bert managed a weak smile. "It was Kitty's idea. She loves your brother very much, you know. She hatched the plot to visit Ryan dressed as a priest and exchange places with him."

"Shit!" Chad exploded. "Are you saying that Kitty is sitting in jail now? I can't believe Ryan would allow Kitty to do such a foolish thing. Sounds like a coward's way out to me, and Ryan is no coward."

"You're right about Ryan," Bert agreed. "He'd never let Kitty make the sacrifice. When she told me what she intended, I came up with a better plan."

Bert then launched into a retelling of what had happened at the jailhouse, ending by saying they could never have succeeded without Padre Enrico's help.

"I can't believe you got out of a sickbed

to go to Ryan's aid," Pierce said in a stunned voice. "My God, look at you! You've probably done yourself irreparable harm."

Bert managed a wobbly smile. "I'd risk anything to help my daughter free the man she loves. Just seeing them together did my heart good. Isn't that right, Padre?"

"Si," Padre Enrico said, nodding enthusiastically. "Young love is wondrous, indeed. I married them shortly before *Senor* Delaney and his bride went into hiding. Your brother was quite adamant about making *Senorita* Kitty his bride before they went off together."

"Well, I'll be damned," Chad muttered. "Sorry about the language, Padre, but this is so incredible. Ryan has always been dead set against marriage. We never thought to see the day he'd take a wife."

"They are very much in love," Padre Enrico said, beaming. "Your brother wanted to celebrate their love within the sacred bonds of matrimony."

"Where are they?" Pierce asked. "Are they safe? Do they need anything?"

"I feel confident that Kitty and Ryan have everything they need for the moment," Bert said, tongue-in-cheek. "They are hiding in a cave located some distance up the mountain behind the mission. Everything needed for

462

an extended stay was placed beforehand in the cave. I suspect they are enjoying a private honeymoon right now."

"Seems like you've thought of everything," Pierce said. "Now it's up to us to get Ryan out of the territory alive and to make sure the law doesn't catch up with him."

"How would you like to see Ryan's name cleared of all charges?" Bert asked in a hoarse voice that grew progressively weaker as he spoke.

"Can you do that?" Chad asked with alacrity.

"I . . . can . . . try," Bert said, gasping for breath as he clutched at his chest as if in pain.

"Perhaps you should leave and return tomorrow," Padre Enrico suggested to Pierce and Chad when he noted Bert's distress. "I will give him something to ease the pain in his heart, then he will sleep. He must rest until he gains the strength to pursue his plan for your brother's pardon. Come back tomorrow when he is stronger and I'm sure he will tell you what he wishes you to do."

"Yes," Bert agreed. "Come . . . back tomorrow."

Pierce and Chad made a hasty exit so the priest could administer to Bert in private.

"I hope he lives long enough to restore our brother's name," Chad said, obviously worried about Bert's ability to survive the night, much less rise from bed at some future date.

"What do you suppose he has in mind?"

"I reckon we won't know until tomorrow."

Kitty was happier than she had ever been in her entire life. Ryan loved her, and they were husband and wife. She was also pretty certain now of something she'd suspected for a few weeks: She carried Ryan's child. Kitty hummed a snappy tune as she prepared their breakfast over the fire, reliving in her mind all the wonderful, incredibly erotic ways in which they had made love during the long night. She'd be content to remain in this lowly cave forever as long as Ryan was with her.

"Kitty!" Ryan called from the mouth of the cave. "Come outside in the sunlight. No one can see us unless they ride by the base of the mountain, and then I doubt they'll find the cave unless they climb up here."

"I'll be right out," Kitty called back. She dished the eggs, bacon, and potatoes she had just cooked into two tin plates, placed a fork on each plate, and carried them outside to where Ryan was sitting on a fallen stump.

He took the plate from her and dug in with gusto. "I reckon I was hungrier than I thought," he said around a mouthful of food.

"Making love all night does that to one," Kitty teased.

A wicked twinkle lurked in the depths of his green eyes. "Then you'd better eat up, for you'll need all your energy for tonight. Would you like to go for a walk?" he added as he set aside his empty plate.

"Dare we? The law will be out searching for you."

"If they don't find me soon they'll think I took off for Montana. I sincerely doubt they'll scour the mountains; there are too many hiding places like this one."

They trekked a short distance up the mountain and sat on a rock to rest before starting back down. "I can see the mission from here," Kitty enthused. "It looks so quiet and peaceful."

Ryan pointed toward the town. "Look, Marshal Pringle must be gathering a posse. I can see a dozen or so riders milling around in front of the jailhouse."

"We should be getting back to the cave," Kitty said anxiously.

"I reckon you're right. We can come back out tonight. We'll be safe in the dark.

Perhaps we'll even sleep under the stars tonight. It's been a long time since we've made love by moonlight."

They started back down the mountain. "Do you think your brothers know that you escaped?" Kitty wondered.

"They should have returned to Tucson by now. I'm sure Bert got the word to them somehow." A shudder passed through him. "I'd face the hangman day after tomorrow if not for you and Bert. Do you suppose he's all right? I owe him a great deal."

"Bert knew the risks and refused to let ill health stop him from saving your life," Kitty said, though the thought of Bert's imminent death pained her. "I don't know how I'll ever repay him."

"Your love was all he ever wanted, Kitten. Ah, here's the cave. We have many hours to kill before dark, and I know of a perfect way to while away the time."

He brought her hand to his groin, showing her without words how he intended to spend the empty hours. "I can't seem to get enough of you, love." He removed her hand and led her into the cave. Then he lay her down on the bedroll and undressed her, loving her with his eyes, his hands, and his mouth before finally joining their bodies. They came together explosively, and just as explosively found Paradise.

Chad and Pierce returned to the mission the next morning, anxious to learn how Bert intended to clear Ryan's name. They found Bert still weak but somewhat restored after a good night's rest.

"Are you up to explaining how you intend to obtain a pardon for Ryan?" Pierce asked.

"Take your time, Bert," Chad cautioned. "We don't want you to overexert yourself. Just tell us what needs doing and we'll do it. This mess can't be cleared up fast enough for us. Our wives expected us home long before now. We wired them this morning, explaining the delay, but that's not going to satisfy either Zoey or Sarah. Abner is a handful for Sarah, and I know he misses me," Chad explained. "Little Amanda is at the age now where she recognizes me as her father. I miss them."

"I hated to leave Zoey alone with a newborn son and energetic toddler to care for," Pierce said. "Cully and the hands are capable of looking after them, but I miss them. So you can see how anxious we are to clear this up and go home. We're grateful for anything you can do to help Ryan."

"Something the marshal said got me to thinking," Bert revealed. "He said it would take a governor's pardon to save Ryan from the hangman. Well, I'm going to petition the governor for a pardon in Ryan's behalf."

"What makes you think the governor will listen to you?" Chad, ever the skeptic, asked.

"I know Governor Fremont. So did your father. All three of us served in the war together. He was our captain, and we saved his life once. Did your father never tell you about it?"

"Pa never spoke much about the war," Pierce said. "What can we do to help?"

"I can't make the trip up to Prescott to petition the governor personally so I'm counting on you to carry my letter to him."

"Prescott!" Chad cried. "That's a helluva long way from here."

"The railroad just extended a spur line between Prescott and Phoenix so you can complete the entire journey by rail. I don't know when the next train is due, but I hope you'll be on it. I've already written my letter to the governor and I'm counting on you to convince Governor Fremont that Ryan is innocent. With luck you'll have Ryan's pardon within the week."

"I wish I were as certain as you that Fremont will grant Ryan a pardon," Chad groused. "Maybe we should just try to outrun the posse."

"No," Pierce said decisively. "We'll go for the pardon. I can't bear the thought of Ryan going through life with a price on his head. Give us your letter, Bert. We'll deliver it and present a moving plea in Ryan's behalf."

"That's all I can ask," Bert said with a sigh. "I want Kitty to be happy after I'm gone. She's run from the law most of her young life and that's not the kind of future I want for her."

"Here is the letter," Padre Enrico said, handing Pierce a sealed envelope.

"Shouldn't we look in on Ryan and Kitty first?" Chad asked. "He would want to know what we're doing on his behalf."

"There isn't time," Bert explained. "I reckon Kitty will come down to the mission in a day or two anyway. She's in no danger since she's not a suspect in the jailbreak."

"Very well," Pierce said, placing the letter in his vest pocket. "Let's go, Chad. There might even be a train out today."

"God go with you," Padre Enrico intoned solemnly.

Kitty and Ryan lingered outside the cave, soaking up the sunlight after having made love and bathed in the pool. The silence around them was profound, pierced occasionally by bird calls and the scurrying

469

footsteps of wild animals.

"I've never known such solitude or serenity," Kitty sighed happily.

"I know. Still, I can't help worrying about what's happening in town," Ryan admitted. "We've been here nearly a week without a word from Padre Enrico or my brothers. What do you suppose they're up to?"

"Perhaps I'll go down to the mission tonight and find out," Kitty ventured. "I've been worried about Bert. This has been too much for him. I should never have allowed him to get involved."

"It was his choice, love," Ryan allowed. "But I know what you mean. His trip to town and what happened afterward couldn't have been good for him. I reckon it won't hurt anything if you sneak down to the mission later and find out what's going on. Bert said there might be a way to clear my name, and I'm anxious to learn how he intends to accomplish so daunting a feat."

"I'll wait until . . ." Her sentence ended abruptly when Ryan placed a hand over her mouth.

"Someone is coming. Riders. A lot of them. Quick, inside the cave." He pushed her toward the mouth of the cave, then concealed himself behind the sagebrush shielding the entrance.

"What about you?" Kitty hissed.

"I just want to see who's coming. Could be the law. Don't come out unless I say it's okay."

Ryan peered through the thick brush, craning his neck to see who was passing below them. He wanted it to be his brothers but was disappointed when several riders rode into view. He blew out a curse when he recognized Marshal Pringle and his posse. They were riding the trail at the base of the mountain. He quickly pulled his head back and eavesdropped on their conversation as they reined in directly beneath the ledge he was crouched upon.

"Any sign of the prisoner?" he heard Pringle ask.

"Haven't seen any tracks," one of the deputies answered. "The trail peters out up ahead. Probably just an old Indian trail."

Ryan blessed his lucky stars for the sere dry wind that had blown sand across their trail and the light rain that had fallen last night, which had helped to obscure the footprints and wagon wheel tracks.

"No sense riding into the mountains," Pringle decided. "Even if Delaney is holed up there somewhere we'd never find him."

"We haven't ridden north yet," the deputy ventured. "If someone gave Delaney a horse he could be halfway to Montana by now, and out of our jurisdiction."

"Let's go," Pringle said, reining his mount away from the mountains. "We'll range farther north and see if we turn up anything."

Ryan sagged in relief. He was safe for the time being.

"Are they gone?" Kitty whispered from the mouth of the cave.

"It's safe to come out now," Ryan answered. "The posse rode away. I heard Pringle say they were going to ride north to see if they could pick up my trail. I reckon they'll give up the search when they fail to find tracks. A week is a long time to hunt down a prisoner when the trail is cold."

Kitty joined him outside the cave. "Nevertheless, we should take precautions. Perhaps you shouldn't leave the cave for awhile."

They sat on the ground in contemplative silence while each pondered their own thoughts. Then Ryan said, "I shouldn't have married you."

"What are you saying?"

"Our marriage condemned you to a lifetime of running from the law. It was wrong of me to think only of my own selfish needs. Forgive me, Kitten."

"You're talking nonsense," Kitty scoffed.

"Are you forgetting that you have two brothers working to clear your name? And what about Bert? He may be ill but don't count him out yet."

"You're always there to bolster my confidence, aren't you, love? I don't know how I ever survived without you."

Kitty remained thoughtful, then said, "I don't know if this is the right time to tell you but I don't want to wait any longer."

"Tell me what?" Ryan asked, distracted by dancing sunbeams reflecting off her bright hair.

"I suspected this for the last few weeks but wanted to be sure before saying anything. We're going to have a child," Kitty revealed in a hushed voice. "Are you happy?"

Gripping her arms, Ryan searched her face, his own expression unreadable. "Are you sure?"

"As sure as I can be."

Ryan's hands tightened on her arms. "You little fool!" he said, giving her a gentle shake. "How could you have put your life in danger knowing you carried my child? Oh God, I shudder to think what might have happened if there had been gunplay during my escape. I love you too much to let you sacrifice your life for mine. I never would have agreed to your plan had I known. You should have stayed at the ranch where you'd be safe."

"And let you hang?" Kitty countered, giving him an incredulous look. "Not on your life. Besides, I was in no danger."

He growled a curt reply and dragged her up against him. Then he bent his head and kissed her with all the passion and love in his heart.

"You haven't told me how you feel about becoming a father," Kitty prodded.

Ryan grew thoughtful. "Becoming a father was something I never considered or aspired to." Kitty looked so stricken that he quickly added, "On the other hand, I never thought I'd marry at all. But knowing that the woman I love more than my own life will be the mother of my children makes fatherhood an unexpected joy. I admit it will take some getting used to, but if my brothers adjusted to marriage and fatherhood I reckon I can too." He puffed out his chest. "In fact, I'll wager I'll be better at it than they are."

He gave her a quick kiss and led her back into the cave. "Shouldn't you rest or something?"

Kitty gave him a hard poke in the ribs. "I don't need to rest and we just did the 'something' you're referring to. I'll fix us something to eat first, then head down to the mission."

Rain squalls passed over the area later that day, continuing on into the following day, preventing Kitty from returning to the mission. They had been in the cave ten days and were nearly out of supplies when Kitty finally ventured out. The mission lay a good mile from the base of the mountain, and she covered the ground quickly, keeping her eyes peeled for snakes as she passed. She reached the chapel without mishap and peeked inside, recognizing Padre Enrico's rotund figure immediately. She hurried down the aisle to join him.

"*Senorita* Kitty!" he exclaimed, holding out his hands to her. "Your father said you'd show up soon. Come, I'll take you to him."

"Father is still here?" Kitty asked, fearing the worst as she followed the priest from the little chapel.

"He is very weak," the padre warned. "I don't know what is keeping him alive. I suppose 'tis God's will that he lives to see his daughter settled happily."

They had reached the infirmary now, and Kitty hurried over to Bert's bedside. His face lit up when he saw her. She grasped his hand; it felt cool, dry, and fragile to her touch.

"I've been waiting for you," Bert greeted. "How are things with you and Ryan?"

"Perfect," Kitty said dreamily. "I love him so much, Father. And he loves me, too."

"How could he not love you? I loved you the moment I saw you. I suppose you're wondering about Ryan's brothers."

"We expected to hear from them before now," Kitty said. "It's been over a week. How much longer do you think Ryan will have to remain hidden? A posse came by a few days ago, but they saw nothing and rode on. Ryan thinks they will give up the search soon."

"Padre Enrico went to town this morning and learned that the posse has disbanded. But I understand Marshal Pringle is still looking for Ryan's accomplices."

"Where are Ryan's brothers, Father?" Kitty wanted to know. "They haven't abandoned Ryan, have they?"

"No, Daughter, Ryan's brothers would never abandon him. They're in Prescott, but I expect them to return soon. Padre Enrico said a train was expected late this afternoon. Perhaps they'll be on it."

Kitty was thoroughly confused. "What are they doing in Prescott? Shouldn't they be trying to clear Ryan's name?"

"Prescott is the capital of the Territory of Arizona," Bert explained. "I sent the Delaney brothers there to petition the governor on Ryan's behalf."

She shot him a startled glance. Ryan's brothers were on a wild-goose chase. Surely the governor had more important things to do than listen to a plea for a man's life when all evidence pointed to his guilt. She studied Bert's face with a sinking heart. "Is that the plan you told me about? What makes you think the governor will listen to you?" she railed. "Oh God, what are we going to do now?"

"We're going to wait for Ryan's brothers," Bert said complacently.

"What am I going to tell Ryan?" Kitty asked on a note of panic.

"You're going to tell him he's a free man." The words came from the doorway. Kitty whirled, and her delight at seeing Pierce and Chad striding into the room was clearly evidenced by the smile on her face.

"I hoped you would be on today's train," Bert greeted.

"We had to wait two days for an interview with the governor. He remembered you, Bert," Pierce said. "And he remembered our pa. Then he listened to our story and actually believed it. He said no son of Corporal Delaney's would turn bank robber."

"We explained everything to Governor Fremont, even the part about Kitty being forced by her stepbrother to ride with the Bartons," Chad concluded.

"Oh, no!" Kitty cried, terrified that the law would come after her.

"Don't worry, Kitty," Pierce said. "Nothing I told the governor will ever become public knowledge. He understands that you had no choice. Besides, you were never identified as one of the bank robbers, and there is no price on your head."

Kitty felt as if a great weight had been lifted from her. "Does the marshal know?"

"He does now," Chad said. "We stopped by his office and showed him the pardon. The governor is going to follow it up with a telegram. Show them the pardon, Pierce."

Pierce removed a scroll from his jacket, unrolled it, and held it out for their inspection.

Kitty swallowed the lump in her throat. "It says Ryan Delaney is cleared of all charges and is granted a full pardon. How can I ever thank you?" she cried.

"Don't thank us," Pierce returned. "It was all Bert's doing. Without the letter he wrote to the governor we couldn't have gotten past the front door."

Kitty was so excited that she passed out hugs all around, even to Padre Enrico. "I can't wait to tell Ryan."

"By the way, how is the honeymoon progressing?" Chad teased. "Is Rogue Ryan behaving himself?"

Kitty's cheeks pinkened becomingly. "Everything is perfect . . . now," she whispered, smiling blissfully.

"Shall we go find our little brother and tell him the good news?" Chad suggested.

"If you don't mind, I'd prefer to do it myself," Kitty said after a slight hesitation. "We'll come down from the cave tomorrow, if that's all right with you."

The brothers exchanged knowing glances. "We understand perfectly," Pierce said. "We were both newlyweds once. We'll all gather here at the mission in the morning and decide on our next move. Chad and I have to be getting on home." He sent Bert a concerned look, then said to Kitty, "I reckon you and Ryan will want to stay on in Tucson until your father recovers his health."

"We'll talk about it tomorrow morning," Kitty said, anxious to leave and tell Ryan the good news. She planted a kiss on Bert's forehead and hurried off.

"Don't forget your lantern," Bert called after her. When she had slipped out the door, Bert muttered to no one in particular, "My daughter is happy; I'm ready to go anytime God calls me."

CHAPTER 20

Ryan met Kitty on the path halfway between the mission and the cave. He had grown impatient waiting for her and decided to risk a trip to the mission. He saw the lantern light from a distance and hid behind a cactus until he recognized Kitty. Then he stepped out and pulled her into his arms. "Thank God," he said with a shaky sigh. "I was worried sick about you. I expected you to return long before now. What kept you? Is Bert . . ."

He left his sentence dangling as he searched Kitty's face. "Something *did* happen!" he exclaimed. "I can tell by your expression. You might as well tell me. Is it Bert?"

"Bert is as well as can be expected," Kitty replied. "I'll tell you everything once we get back to the cave."

"Very well," Ryan said, his mind working furiously. He imagined all manner of dire things that could have happened. If it wasn't Bert, then it had to be his brothers. If anything had happened to them he'd never forgive himself. Neither would their wives or children.

"Dammit, Kitty, give me the bad news now," he growled. "Is it my brothers?"

"Your brothers are fine, Ryan," Kitty assured him. "We just have a short climb to the cave, then I'll tell you everything. And it isn't bad news," she hinted as she scrambled over the ledge.

Ryan caught up to her easily. Taking the lantern from her hand, he hauled her up the mountain and dragged her inside the cave. Then he set down the lantern and imprisoned her against his chest.

"Now, little miss tease, you're going to tell me everything. If your news isn't bad then it has to be good, and I'm damn well ready for good news after all I've been through lately."

"Governor Fremont granted you a full pardon!" Kitty blurted gleefully. "Your brothers have been in Prescott, that's why we've heard nothing from them these past ten days."

"But . . ." Ryan was thoroughly confused. "The evidence against me was overwhelming. What did they say to make the governor grant me a full pardon?"

"It appears that Bert is acquainted with the governor. They served in the army together. Fremont knew your father, too. Bert wrote a letter of explanation and your brothers followed it up with facts. You're free, Ryan! Free!"

"Free," Ryan repeated as he picked her up and swung her around and around until she grew dizzy.

"Put me down, Ryan!"

His eyes gleamed wickedly as he bore her down to the bedroll. "This calls for a celebration. I want to make love to my wife as a free man." He was all thumbs as he began to undress her. Countless emotions warred within him. Love, lust, relief, anticipation, eagerness, impatience. But the one emotion that eclipsed all the others was happiness. Kitty had entered his heart and taken up residence there. She had proved to him that love existed, that it wasn't just an illusion indulged in by dreamers. And she had shown him that there were women in this world worthy of trust.

It occurred to him that he had been searching for Kitty all the years he'd wasted earning his reputation as a womanizer. Lust could never replace love, he realized that now, although a healthy dose of lust when love was present added excitement to marriage. And Ryan had an abundance of love and lust for Kitty.

"I can't seem to work my fingers," Ryan said as he fumbled with her buttons.

"Let me help you," Kitty said, pushing his hands away.

In moments they were both naked. Ryan looked his fill, then he kissed her. Hungrily. Searching her mouth with his tongue as his fingers parted the thick, damp curls between her legs. Then he took his mouth on a downward journey, finally settling on the dewy folds of skin he'd just fondled. A prolonged sigh slid past her lips.

"Oh-h-h, Ryan . . . yes."

He explored her thoroughly and deeply, with his tongue, his lips, his teeth. When her hands clasped his head, urging him closer, he felt as if he'd burst if he didn't put something other than his tongue inside her very soon. The musky taste of her drove him wild. She was hot and wet; he could barely contain himself as he felt her hips jerk against his mouth and heard her cry out.

Only then did he rise up and enter her, his muscles taut as he drove himself deep inside her. Again and again, until he felt her first tentative response. He increased the tempo, muscles straining to bring her again to that exalted pinnacle. She tossed back her head and arched against him. He groaned. She was tight and warm and wild beneath him as they fell into a delicious rhythm. With the greatest effort he prolonged his climax until he felt her convulse around him. Then he spilled himself inside her with a cry of contentment that made the walls of the cave sing.

When he could manage it, he slid off to lie beside her. Several long minutes passed before he could speak.

"Each time we make love is better than the last."

She smiled up at him as she traced the whirls of hair around his nipples with her finger. "Good enough to keep Rogue Ryan from straying?" she teased.

"Rogue Ryan is gone," Ryan assured her. "You're going to like the new Ryan better."

"Will I love the *new* Ryan as much as I loved the *old* Ryan?"

He kissed her soundly. "I guarantee it. Do we have to leave the cave tonight? Are Bert and my brothers expecting us at the mission?"

"Tonight is ours," Kitty whispered. Her seductive smile did unspeakable things to Ryan's body. He felt himself swell and harden, and he knew he had to have her again. "We're to meet at the mission in the morning. All of us."

He reached for her. "Let's make good use of our privacy."

"Ryan, wait," Kitty said, placing a restraining hand against his chest. "Perhaps we should talk about the future. What will happen after we leave here?"

Ryan gave her a puzzled look. "I thought our future was settled long ago. You're my wife, love, what else is there to know?"

"For one thing, we need to decide where we will live. I know I once told you I could never love the man who had abandoned my mother, but my feelings have changed. I've come to love Bert dearly. I can't leave Arizona while Bert still lives. And then there's the ranch to consider. It will be mine one day. How do you feel about settling in Arizona?"

Ryan remained silent a long time as he considered his answer. "I'd like to settle permanently in Montana some day," he finally said. "You'd love it there. I've had my eye on a piece of land a couple of miles from the main ranch house. It's Delaney land. I'm sure my brothers won't mind if I build on it. I'm aware that we can't leave Arizona while Bert is still alive so it might

486

be awhile before I can show it to you."

"What about the ranch?"

"That is a problem. How strong are your feelings for it?" Ryan feared Kitty's prolonged silence meant she didn't want to leave Arizona . . . ever.

"I have no strong feelings for the ranch, or for Arizona," Kitty admitted. "Living in Montana rather appeals to me. I've never had women friends, or any friends, for that matter. I'd like to get to know your brothers' wives." She heaved a wistful sigh. "I wonder how I'll measure up to those 'perfect' women?"

"It doesn't matter what anyone thinks as long as you're perfect for me," Ryan contended. "Seriously, though, we could either rent or sell the ranch when . . . the time comes. I don't think Bert would care. All he's ever wanted was to get to know his daughter before he died."

"Thank you for bringing me here," Kitty said solemnly. "I'm sorry for everything you've had to endure because of me, but without you I would have never known my real father."

"If you recall, I literally had to drag you all the way here," Ryan teased.

"I love you, Ryan," she said as she propped herself up on her elbow and planted a kiss on his lips. It was all the encouragement Ryan needed as he tumbled her backward and slid between her legs. Their loving was wild and wonderful and . . .

Forever.

EPILOGUE

Dry Gulch, Montana
Three years later

"I love the view from the window," Kitty said as she gazed at the snowcapped mountains rising majestically in the distance. "It's so different here. Summers are green and lush and winters, though harsh, are more beautiful than any I've ever seen. I don't care how much it snows as long as we're cozy and warm inside this wonderful house you've built for us."

"You don't regret giving up the Arizona ranch?" Ryan asked as he joined her at the front window.

"Not at all," Kitty assured him. "Bert must have known how we felt, for he gave us permission to sell the ranch before he died." She sighed. "I didn't think it possible to miss Bert so much."

"He died happy, love," Ryan said. "He lived long enough to see our son born. And

I'm certain he was relieved to learn that Teresa was marrying well. Though he didn't let on, I think he worried about her."

"I think so too. I'm glad Teresa wrote him about her wedding plans before he died. I think it pleased him to know her future was secure."

"We should be grateful for the time we had with him. The doctor was surprised Bert's heart held out as long as it did," Ryan mused. "You're happy here, aren't you, love?"

"I've never been happier. I have you and our son. And now a home and a family to love. I never expected to have wonderful friends like Zoey and Sarah, and I do so enjoy the time we spend together. I just know our children will be great friends."

"The Delaney family is growing by leaps and bounds," Ryan said, "and I'm doing my share to increase the numbers." He rubbed the barely noticeable bulge beneath Kitty's rib cage. "I can't believe I'm going to be a father twice over."

"Believe it," Kitty said. "I just wish Bert could be here to see his second grandchild enter the world."

"If there's a God, Bert knows," Ryan said, turning her in his arms.

"There is a God," Kitty said with conviction, "because He gave you to me."

Kitty and Ryan's daughter was born seven months later. She came into the world kicking, screaming, and squalling. Ryan took one look at the red-faced, copper-haired little demon and promptly fell in love for the second time in his life. They named her Katie. Ryan called her Kat.

AUTHOR'S NOTE

To Tempt a Rogue concludes the stories about the stubborn, delightfully sexy, and handsome Delaney brothers. I hope you enjoyed following their antics and reading about the heartaches and tender moments they endured along the road to finding true love.

You met Pierce and Zoey in *To Love a Stranger,* and Chad and Sarah in *To Tame a Renegade.* I hope you enjoyed their reunion with their brother Ryan in *To Tempt a Rogue.* This was a fun series to write. I fell a little bit in love with each brother while writing their stories. They were all so darn stubborn and dead set against marriage that I got a little disgusted with them myself. But as you learned, all is well that ends well.

Thank you for following the Delaney brothers through all their adventures. I enjoy hearing from readers. Write to me at:

1954 Juanita Way
Tarpon Springs, FL 34689

For an answer and a bookmark, please enclose a business-sized, self-addressed, stamped envelope.

All my romantic best,
Connie Mason

ABOUT THE AUTHOR

Connie Mason is the author of more than fifty historical romances and novellas that regularly appear on the *USA Today* bestseller list and the *New York Times* extended list. Her tales of passion and adventure are set in exotic as well as American locales. Connie was named Storyteller of the Year in 1990 and was awarded a Career Achievement Award in the Western category by *Romantic Times* in 1994. Connie makes her home in Florida with her husband, Jerry.

Connie travels extensively, sometimes for pleasure but more often to do research for her books. She likes telling anyone who will listen about her three children and nine grandchildren, and sharing memories of her years living abroad in Europe and Asia as the wife of a career serviceman. In her spare time, Connie enjoys reading almost anything.

The employees of Thorndike Press hope you have enjoyed this Large Print book. All our Thorndike and Wheeler Large Print titles are designed for easy reading, and all our books are made to last. Other Thorndike Press Large Print books are available at your library, through selected bookstores, or directly from us.

For information about titles, please call:
 (800) 223-1244

or visit our Web site at:
 www.gale.com/thorndike
 www.gale.com/wheeler

To share your comments, please write:
 Publisher
 Thorndike Press
 295 Kennedy Memorial Drive
 Waterville, ME 04901